HOWARD FAST

MASUTO
INVESTIGATES

Howard Fast is well known for a literary career that spans more than sixty years. He is the author of over seventy novels, including *Spartacus*, *April Morning*, *Citizen Tom Paine*, *Moses*, *The Immigrants*, and *Freedom Road*, which has been published in eighty-two languages. Among his most recent projects are the novels *Redemption* and *An Independent Woman*, and the screenplay for *The Crossing*, a television movie for the A & E Television Network.

After the loss of his wife Bette, he is now living happily in Connecticut with his new wife, Mercedes O'Connor.

AVAILABLE NOW

COMING SOON

MASUTO INVESTIGATES

HOWARD FAST

ibooks
new york
www.ibooksinc.com

DISTRIBUTED BY SIMON & SCHUSTER, INC

For *Samantha*:

To the memory of
Nat Goldstone
good friend

For *The Case of the One-Penny Orange*:

For Dotty—
who loved all
the Cunninghams

MASUTO INVESTIGATES:

AN INTRODUCTION

The series of books I wrote about Masao Masuto, the Zen Buddhist detective on the Beverly Hills police force, were written during the six years I lived on a beautiful hillside above Beverly Hills. Some ten years prior to this time in California, I had taken up the study and practice of Zen Buddhism. It occurred to me that it would be interesting to write some books—entertainments, to use Graham Greene's phrase—about a Nisei detective on the police force of one of the wealthiest towns in America. He would be a Zen Buddhist, a modest man who lived in Culver City and worked in nearby Beverly Hills. He would think as a Buddhist thinks.

At that same time, I was working at the Paramount studio, and it was there that I heard the story of the rape of a young, eager actress. Do not judge either the studio where it happened—not at Paramount—or Hollywood by this incident. It happened; it can happen anywhere. But it gave me the idea for *Samantha*, the first of the Masao Masuto books.

INTRODUCTION

Writing it was a therapeutic release from my more serious work, and I asked my literary agent to choose another name for its author—he chose "E. V. Cunningham." However, throughout Europe, where they became vastly popular, they were usually printed under my own name. It was great fun to write them, and I trust it will be equally amusing for you to read them.

Yet there is something more than mere entertainment in these tales of Masao Masuto. Years before, a Nisei woman had worked for me. She came to us from the World War II concentration camps of America, where people of Japanese ancestry had been interned. She was a delightful person, and from her I learned much of the life of Japanese-Americans. So when you step into the life of Masuto and the small cottage in Culver City, you also taste the life of a Nisei Zen Buddhist detective—a man who neither judges nor condemns the crime, but seeks only for the inner truth.

ibooks plans to continue the publication of the many books about Masuto, and you can look forward to them, and learn something, I hope, about the Japanese-Americans in California.

Howard Fast
March 2000

SAMANTHA

THE MAIN CAST

STOCKHOLDERS IN NORTHEASTERN FILMS

AL GREENBERG, who is married to Phoebe

MURPHY ANDERSON, who is married to Stacy

SIDNEY BURKE, who is married to Trude

JACK COTTER, who is married to Arlene

MIKE TULLEY, who is married to Lenore

POLICEMEN

Beverly Hills: DETECTIVE SERGEANT MASAO MASUTO (Kati, his wife)

DETECTIVE SY BECKMAN

OFFICER FRANK SEATON

MEDICAL EXAMINER DR. SAM BAXTER

Los Angeles: LIEUTENANT PETE BONES

DETECTIVE KELLY

And numerous others who appear in good time and without confusion.

CHAPTER
ONE

AL GREENBERG

In Beverly Hills, as in so many of the cities, towns and villages of the United States, there is a right and a wrong side of the tracks. The tracks in this case belong to the Southern Pacific Railroad, and they bisect the town from west to east, departing, as they say, no more than a whoop and a holler from the Pacific Ocean. North of Santa Monica Boulevard—upon which the railroad runs—is possibly the most compact conglomeration of rich people that exists anywhere in the world. Southward, to Wilshire Boulevard, is a very posh little shopping area, and south from Wilshire Boulevard lies the "poor" section of Beverly Hills, where you can still buy a one-family house for forty-five thousand dollars.

Detective Sergeant Masao Masuto, of the Beverly Hills Police Force, did not live in the "poor" section of Beverly Hills. He lived in a cottage in Culver City and considered himself most fortunate to be possessed of the cottage, a good wife, three children, and a rose garden upon which he lavished both love and toil. He secretly dreamed of himself

5

as a gardener who devoted all of his working hours to his garden.

He was driving home this evening and dreaming this particular and favorite dream, when the radiotelephone in the car flickered. He picked up the telephone and was informed by the sergeant in charge of dispatching that evening that a man named Al Greenberg was dead in a house on North Canon Drive, and that the circumstances under which the death had occurred might be regarded as somewhat suspicious.

Would he go directly there?

He would. He was on Pico Boulevard, and now he swung into Beverly Drive—a matter of minutes from the address on North Canon Drive.

Detective Masuto knew the address, the place, the house, just as he knew almost every address, place and house in Beverly Hills. This was not as much of an achievement as it sounds. Where he entered Beverly Hills from the south, driving from Pico across Olympic and then up to Wilshire, the city was only thirty-five blocks wide, and that was about its greatest width, even though it extended a long finger into the foothills of the Santa Monica range. North of Santa Monica Boulevard there were the great elegant streets with their palms, their perfect lawns and their quarter-of-a-million-dollar houses, and these streets Detective Masuto could visualize and name, from Trenton Drive on the west, to Walden, Linden, Roxbury, Bedford, Camden, Rodeo, Beverly and Canon—and after Canon, moving east, Crescent, Rexford, Alpine, Foothill, Elm, Maple, Palm, Hillcrest, Arden, Alta, Sierra and Oakhurst—and there the city within a city ended and became Los Angeles. In Los Angeles, there were people and poverty and poolrooms and whorehouses and high-rise apartments and various other ordinary, publicly owned urban equipment. In Beverly Hills, there were property, money and some people.

As his chief of police had explained it to him once, "This is like no other place in the world, Masao. The money is God; the property is sacred; and the people are to be handled with kid gloves until you know who they are—and mostly they are the kind of people you handle with kid gloves after you know who they are."

"Kid gloves." He was a California-born Japanese, and therefore he was an Oriental and not a white man by any means, but excellent with kid gloves.

"The hell with that," he said to himself now. "You have a job, my boy—not a bad job."

He knew the house on North Canon, and he knew who lived there and when they had moved in and how much they had paid for the house and what it was worth today, three years later. Naturally. He knew every house. He knew that "Canon" without accent or similar indication was pronounced "Canon" by some natives—if you can speak of dwellers in Beverly Hills as natives— and "Canyon" by others. He used the latter pronounciation, as had Al Greenberg, who now lay dead in the house on North Canon. He remembered a small conversation he had with Greenberg concerning the word "Canon." Greenberg, very rich, had also been very curious, and Masuto could not help liking curious people—he was so hopelessly curious himself.

Now Greenberg was dead, a short, stout wistful man of sixty-two or three, in a great antebellum type of house with outside pillars two stories high, a proper part of a *Gone with the Wind* sound stage dropped between a Spanish Colonial and an eighteen-room Irish cottage. Greenberg had never been greatly at ease in that house, as Masuto remembered. He had sensitivity, and there was always a shred of shame hanging out of his pocket as if he had never answered the question as to what a small Jew, born and brought up in Bensonhurst in Brooklyn, was doing here in this garden of dreams, repose and dolce vita. It was certainly not de rigueur to be seen on your front lawn at any hour of the day if you lived in Beverly Hills and north of Santa Monica, but Detective Masuto could remember many a late afternoon when he saw Al Greenberg standing in front of the misplaced plantation house, puffing a cigar and regarding the green palm and ivy world that surrounded him with wonder and disbelief.

No more wonder and no more disbelief. Al Greenberg was dead, and they had called the cops.

Masuto double-parked in front of the huge Southern-Colonial plantation house on North Canon. In the driveway of the house were three cars, and five more were parked in front and two more already double-parked; among them, as Masuto noticed, two police cars and two medical cars, one of them belonging to Dr. Sam Baxter, the medical examiner. When Masuto got out of his car, he was met by Detective Sy Beckman, who informed him that Officer Frank Seaton was inside the house and another officer stationed at the door.

"What was it? What went on here tonight?"

"Dinner party—black tie, old buddies, but very formal. Four couples and the host and wife. That's Al Greenberg. He's dead."

"I know. I got that in the car. How was he killed?"

"He wasn't killed. Maybe. He died."

"Of what?" Masuto asked as he and Beckman walked up the path to the house. The planting was old and good, and the air was full of the sweet smell of jasmine. Masuto was never unaware of a planting, and he tasted the cool evening air, mingling his pleasure at the smell with his forlorn reaction to death.

"A heart attack. Baxter's inside and so is Dr. Meyer, Greenberg's physician. I think you better talk to both of them."

"Oh?"

"I mean before you talk to the others."

"All there?"

"They want out, but I'm holding them for you. Nothing has leaked yet, unless some smart reporter was listening on the radio band. There was nobody up at headquarters, and the boss is of the opinion that we should keep it absolutely quiet until we know something."

"What?"

"That it's murder or not murder."

"You said he died of a heart attack."

"That's what the doctors say. One of the guests says different.

"Who?"

Detective Beckman peered at his pad in the poor light that seeped from the windows onto the veranda.

"Feller named Jack Cotter."

Masuto nodded, and then the door was opened by a young and very pretty strawberry blonde, who silently and with a funereal air ushered them into the house. Officer Seaton, a tall uniformed patrolman, came up then and apologized for his partner, who was using the bathroom at the back of the house.

"The doctors are in the living room there," he said, pointing over his shoulder. "The rest of them are in the viewing room."

The viewing room was par for this particular course,

Masuto reflected, hardly listening to the blonde's explanation that this was where "poor Al" showed films. He was looking at the stately double staircase and the spread of the living room beyond, and without even glancing at the blonde, he asked her name.

"Trude Burke—Mrs. Sidney Burke."

"Then would you join the others in the viewing room, Mrs. Burke, and tell them that I would like to talk to them in a few minutes."

"You're very official, aren't you, Detective—?"

"Masuto."

"I thought you were Japanese. Good-looking. You know—"

"Please do as I say, Mrs. Burke."

"I just thought I'd be here to greet the big brass and let them know that there's no murder, and it is all a lot of nonsense, and suppose we all go home and leave poor Phoebe with her grief, such as it is."

"Please do as I say, and later you can tell me all about that."

The other officer came back to the front door. Masuto regarded him without pleasure, waited for Trude Burke to disappear, and then followed Beckman into the living room, where two middle-aged physicians were restlessly observing their wrist watches. Dr. Baxter, the medical examiner—tall, skinny, gray, and tired—shook hands with Masuto and introduced him to Dr. Meyer. Masuto had heard about Meyer, successful, reputable, and expensive.

"What happened?"

"Tell him," Dr. Baxter said impatiently. "The facts, not the nonsense. Beckman can feed him the nonsense after you and I go about our business."

"Mr. Greenberg was a patient of mine," Dr. Meyer said.

"He has suffered for many years from angina. Quite bad. Tonight he had an attack and he died. Very quickly."

"What kind of an attack?" Masuto asked him.

"A heart attack, of course. Coronary. There was a myocardial infarction, and he passed away."

"Quickly?"

"Yes. Before he could reach his medicine."

Masuto turned to Baxter. "Do you agree, doctor?"

"Absolutely."

"No other possibility?"

"There is none that I can see, officer," Meyer said. "No other is being offered. Jack Cotter, who is here and who is Mr. Greenberg's business associate, has made a very serious accusation—namely that Mr. Greenberg was threatened and frightened to death. He calls it murder. I have no desire to comment on the legal aspect or even on the social aspect concerning what happened in this house. I came here. My friend and patient was dead. I examined him and did what I could—which was nothing. This is not a house I enjoy being in at this moment, and there is no grief here for me to assuage. So I wish to go."

"Could Mr. Greenberg have died of fright? Or excitement?" Masuto asked.

"Of course. That's the nature of the disease. Or of ten other trigger causes."

"Is there no way to tell?"

"None."

"Even with an autopsy?"

"No way."

"And you agree?" Masuto asked the medical examiner.

"Yes, Masao. Absolutely."

"Just one or two more questions, Dr. Meyer, and then you can leave. Did you expect Mr. Greenberg to die so suddenly?"

"How does one know?"

"But you must have had some idea of how bad the disease was."

"Of course I had some idea. I had a very good picture of his sickness."

"Suppose he was a lucky man—which he was not. How long might he have lived?"

"Ten years—twelve. You simply cannot pinpoint it. Maybe five years—maybe twice that. Would you like to see his body?"

Masuto nodded, and Meyer led him upstairs to the master bedroom, where under a sheet the mortal remains of Al Greenberg reposed. Masuto uncovered Greenberg's face and looked at him for a long moment.

The living room was French, a combination of several Louis', with a huge, pale Aubusson carpet. The viewing room was practical leather—two enormous leather couches and half a dozen leather lounge chairs. At one end, the projection room, at the other the screen—but both now concealed behind beige drapes. A third wall, where the drapes were drawn back, revealed the planting behind the house, a small tropical jungle which separated the house from the swimming pool. A well-equipped bar and an orange rug completed the furnishings.

There were nine people sprawled on the couches and chairs, and they all looked at the door with a more or less common expression of sullen annoyance as the two men entered, Detective Beckman with Masuto behind him. Death muted them, yet they were annoyed and put upon. One of them, a lean, good-looking man in his middle forties, said something about house arrest being a little less than to his liking. "I have had about enough of it," he said tartly.

There were four men and five women in the room. Masuto recognized the man who had spoken. His name was Mike Tulley, for years a small part player in Westerns, who now was a sort of star in television terms. He had a program of his own called "Lonesome Rider," and his rating was high and he earned well over three thousand dollars a week.

Another man, older, tall, with white wavy hair and very certain of his presence, rose and came toward the detectives. "Easy does it," he said, "We're all under a strain, you know. My name is Murphy Anderson. I was Al's—that is, Mr. Greenberg's lawyer. Also his business associate. We've all been shaken by his death—" He had addressed his words to Masuto.

"You are a policeman, aren't you?" he added.

"That's right."

"You're in charge here?"

"With my colleague, Detective Beckman."

Masuto absorbed the room. You listened and absorbed; you were conscious of many things, which was in the manner of his life and way, and you pressed conclusions away from you. He noted the five women in the room. There was the strawberry blonde, whom he had seen at the door. There was a girl with dark hair. The other three were blondes. But all five, in the particular manner of Beverly Hills, could have been cast from the same mould. Two of them rose after he entered and then slipped onto the chair arms. Another went to the bar and mixed a drink. All appeared to be about the same height, each with the same trim, tight-figure. Even their faces were alike, noses tip-tilted, mouths full. They were a part of a social organism that demanded beauty and alikeness, yet each was different, separate, unique. One of them he recognized—Phoebe Greenberg, widow of the dead man. She was neither prostrated nor weeping, but since she could hardly be more than thirty, with a husband who had been sixty-three and ill and very rich, this was not a matter for surprise.

Of the men, he had recognized only the actor, Mike Tulley. Now he added Murphy Anderson, lawyer, to the file. Anderson would be about fifty. He introduced the widow, then his own wife, Mrs. Anderson, the girl with the dark hair. Then Murphy Anderson introduced Trude Burke, the strawberry blonde.

"I am Detective Sergeant Masuto, Beverly Hills police," Masao Masuto said politely. "I understand that this is a strain for everyone concerned."

The youngest man in the room rose and introduced himself as Sidney Burke, the head of a successful PR agency. That made him the husband of the strawberry blonde. He was about thirty-seven, small, tight, competent, with pebble-black eyes. Tough, dangerous, wily—all words that Masuto remembered and discarded. You simply did not know. It took time.

"More than that, it's a stupid imposition," Burke said.

Masuto's eyes deliberately avoided the final couple. The remaining man, fleshy, balding but once quite handsome, with a long, thin nose and excellent chin and mouth, pinged on the detectives's memory. He had been a sort of a star— just after World War II—but briefly. Then a very successful agent—or was it a producer?

He rose and said, "My name is Jack Cotter, officer. This is my wife, Arlene—"

Of course, the agent. And now Al Greenberg's vice-president in Northeastern Films.

"—and I am afraid that I am responsible for the imposition. Entirely responsible. You see, I have made a damn nusiance of myself by insisting that Al was murdered."

"You can say that again!" Tulley snorted.

"A veritable goddamn nuisance," said Burke.

"Suppose you shut up, Sidney. You talk when you're told to talk," Tulley, the TV actor, said.

"Just who the hell do you think you're putting down?" Burke demanded. "I don't work for you, Mister. You're a client of mine, and now that Al's dead, I don't want such clients. So up your ass!"

"Take it easy, Sidney," Murphy Anderson said. "You too, Mike," he told the actor. "Just take it easy. Jack heard something, and not to report what he heard would make him an accessory after the fact."

"What fact?" Sidney Burke demanded.

"The fact of a murder—if a murder took place. I don't like the whole thing any more than any of you, but there it is—"

Masuto held up his hands for silence at this point. Being a policeman in Beverly Hills might not be exactly like being a diplomat to the Benelux countries. It might be better compared to being a UN representative to a small, new country. It required tact, judgement, and above all, good manners—and control.

"Ladies and gentlemen," he said, "the sooner and the more quietly we conclude this, the better. As you know, Mr. Greenberg was quite ill, and it would appear that he died of natural causes. But appearances are frequently deceiving. Now if you heard something, Mr. Cotter, that bears on Mr. Greenberg's death, I think you should state it for me in as few words as possible, while we are all still here."

Cotter nodded. "We finished dinner a few minutes after nine. Ordinarily, we might sit at the table a while, but Al did not feel too good, and he said that he'd go upstairs and have an Alka Seltzer. Everyone got up. Then the girls left with Mike and Sidney and Al. I am told that Al went up to his bedroom on the second floor. The kitchen people said that. Al went through the kitchen to the pantry, where he has a little private elevator. The others went into the living room."

"Sidney and I went into the viewing room—here," Mike Tulley interrupted. "The girls went to freshen up."

"All right," said Cotter. "Murph—Mr. Anderson—and I sat at the table with cigars. We had things to talk about, and then Murph said about something that before we discussed it any further, we should get Al's point of view. It was almost a yes or no matter, so Murph said that he would wait at the table while I went upstairs. I went through the living room and up the stairs. No one in the hallway up there. I knocked at Al's bedroom door. Then I heard Al say, 'For Christ's sake, put that gun away and give me my medicine—please—' He was pleading, crazy, desperate, pleading. He was pleading for his life.' "

Out of the corner of his eye, Masuto saw Dr. Baxter, the medical examiner, come into the viewing room, and he moved his head for Baxter to join him. Cotter waited. The room was very quiet now. Baxter walked over to Masuto, who whispered to him, "Medicine?"

"He was on quinidine according to Meyer, but also armed with nitroglycerin sublingual. He would have that in his pocket. Every angina does. But his jacket was off and across the room from where he lay."

Baxter spoke softly, but not so softly that everyone in the room could not hear him. Phoebe Greenberg began to cry. She must have washed off her makeup and she was pretty without it. It occurred to Masuto that perhaps she had wept earlier. Emotion and the display of emotion by the population of Beverly Hills was not anything that Masuto felt competent to analyze or predict.

"Please continue," he said to Cotter.

"Yes—of course," Cotter said. "Al was pleading, and then this dame's voice says, 'Like you gave me mine, you bastard—remember?' And Al pleads again, 'Please, please—' Then I start banging on the door and I hear a thud. I hear Al fall, I guess, but the door is locked. I know that Al's room and Phoebe's are connected. Each of them has a dressing room that leads into a bathroom, and the two bathrooms connect. So I run to Phoebe's room—I guess I did some shouting. In Phoebe's room, I saw Stacy—Murph's wife—she was lying on the bed, resting. Then I bust through the connecting rooms to Al's room, and there's Al on the floor, dead. I didn't know he was dead then, but that's what Meyer said. So I go to unlock the hall door and get help, but it's already unlocked. And that's it."

Still silence. Most of them were watching Cotter, not the detective, who said, "Whose voice did you hear, Mr. Cotter?"

"Don't you think we asked him that?" Sidney Burke said. "The other cop asked him. But he's playing cute. Real cute. Now he's going to take you into the next room and pin it on his choice."

"Oh, why don't you shut up," Cotter said tiredly. "What I got to say, I say right here. Murph's my lawyer, and he's here. I don't know whose voice it was. Whoever the dame was, she was crazy mad. Her voice was choking and hoarse. I don't know whose voice it was."

"But it was a woman's voice—of that you're certain?"

"I never gave it a second thought."

"A man's voice can sound like a woman's voice."

"No."

"Very well," Masuto said, smiling sympathetically. "Dr. Baxter here—" pointing to him, "—is our local medical examiner. It is his opinion at this moment that no crime has been committed, that Mr. Greenberg died of natural causes—"

"How in hell you can talk like that after what I heard, I don't know!" Cotter burst out.

"Please, Mr. Cotter—what you heard indicates that violence might have threatened Mr. Greenberg. It would appear, from what you tell me, that a woman was in the room with Mr. Greenberg and that she threatened him with a gun. But it would also appear that Mr. Greenberg's heart attack had already started. Possibly this woman or person refused to hand Mr. Greenberg the sublingual tablets upon which his life depended. We don't know, and we also do not know that a crime has been committed. Murder is a very ugly matter, Mr. Cotter, and for the moment I feel it would be best for everyone concerned to refrain from using the word. This does not mean that we will not pursue our investigation. We certainly shall. But for tonight—well, I think Mr. Anderson will agree with me."

"I certainly do!" Anderson said emphatically.

"Then I think that if I may ask a few questions, brief and to the point, you can then leave. No more than ten minutes."

"I think I have had about all I can stand," Phoebe Greenberg said softly.

"Then two questions and you can leave. Firstly, do you own a gun or is there a gun anywhere in this house?"

"No."

"And where were you when Mr. Cotter shouted?"

"Apparently I was in the pantry elevator on my way up to the second floor. When I got out, there was the commotion—and Al was dead."

"I felt bad," Stacy Anderson said. "That's why I went up to Phoebe's room to lie down. Phoebe said she would bring me a cup of tea. But Al was in his room already, and the doors were closed—two doors, so I could not hear anything. Not possibly."

"Then you went into the kitchen?" Masuto asked Phoebe.

"The pantry. We have a hot-cold water cooler there. No one saw me, if that is what you mean."

"Thank you," Masuto said, bowing almost imperceptably, a tribute to the lady of a house where he once had a friend, for even the small warmth of slight aquaintance is a form of friendship. "You may leave us now, and we will trouble your house only a few minutes more."

"Stay as long as you need to, please."

Masuto decided that he liked her. She either mourned the dead in her own way or not at all; it was her affair. He nodded to Baxter's unspoken question, and the doctor said, "I would like to have an autopsy done, Mrs. Greenberg."

"If you wish. If it will help."

"I think it will only help to put away doubts—but that's important."

"Then do as you see best.

And with that, she left the room.

Detective Masuto turned to Trude Burke.

"I was in the John," the strawberry blonde smiled. "I guess supper agreed with none of us."

"Where?"

"Front hall. Came out, heard the commotion, hotfooted it upstairs and almost fell over Arlene."

"You mean Mrs. Cotter?"

"Yes. Jack, her husband, was in the hall then, yelling for a doctor."

"Mrs. Cotter?"

Arlene Cotter rose, glanced quizzically at her husband and then nodded at Masuto. "No alibis—poor Oriental detective.

"I did not know there was a Nisei on our darling little

police force. I was in the guest powder room, upstairs, when I heard the commotion and bounded into the hall. I went in there with Lenore Tulley—didn't I, darling?"

Lenore Tulley stared narrowly without replying. No love between them, Masuto decided. They were too alike: Beverly Hills twins, same height, same figure, same hairdresser.

"But then Lenore disappeared somewhere. Where did you disappear to, darling?"

"The pot, you bitch. You saw me go in there."

"Temper, temper," Arlene Cotter said.

"Then I went into the guest room, which connected with the guest bathroom," Lenore Tulley told Masuto. "To tell the truth, I was prowling. I have never been to this particular castle before. I was curious. Then I heard the commotion and stepped out into the hallway and joined the crowd in Al's bedroom."

Arlene Cotter smiled tolerantly. Mike Tulley watched them both intently, his wife and Cotter's wife.

"You remained at the dining room table?" Masuto asked Murphy Anderson.

"My cigar and I. I heard the commotion and then Sidney joined me. There is a small, spiral staircase in the projection booth, there—" He pointed. "—and first we thought something had happened in the viewing room. But it was empty. We went upstairs by the projection room staircase, which lets one into the far end of the upstairs hall."

"And before that, Mr. Burke?"

"I was with Mike Tulley in the viewing room. We were going to watch some shorts, and Mike was going to run them. He went into the projection booth. I mixed myself a drink and went into the dining room to see what had happened to the girls."

"Mr. Tulley?" Masuto said.

"Like Sidney says, I was in the projection booth, setting up the film. I heard the yelling from upstairs and I went up the staircase."

Beckman had been making notes. Now Masuto said, "I don't think we need trouble you further now. I would appreciate it if you would give pertinent facts, name, place, telephone to Detective Beckman here. Then you can leave. I think it would be wise if you say nothing about what Mr. Cotter heard—for the time being, that is."

"In other words, you are closing this up," Cotter said.

"No, Mr. Cotter, I am closing nothing. You can give your story to the press if you wish. I only feel that it might be better for everyone concerned if we waited a bit."

Detective Beckman was copying out his notes for Masuto, and Dr. Baxter was sipping at a glass of his dead host's excellent brandy, which the Japanese butler had poured for him. The house was staffed by a Japanese couple, not Niseis but recently come from Japan. The guests had departed. Mrs. Greenberg was asleep under the influence of a sedative; the guests had departed; and Al Greenberg's body had been taken to the hospital for the autopsy. The Japanese house man was dutifully waiting for the policemen to depart, and Masao Masuto was explaining to his wife why he would be late. He spoke in Japanese quite deliberately. He wanted the houseman to overhear him, and when he had finished with the phone, he turned to the butler and said in Japanese, "What do you and your wife think of this?"

"Honorable official, we have no thoughts on the matter."

"That is nonsense, countryman of my father, as you well know. It is too late for witless formalities. I am not going to entrap you or arrest you, and not for a moment do I believe that you had anything to do with this. Do you think Mr. Greenberg was murdered?"

"No one hates such a man," the butler answered simply.

"All murders do not signify hate. What of the wife? Did they love each other?"

"They approached each other with respect. He was more than old enough to be her father."

"Would she kill him?"

"No."

"You are very sure."

"I am a man of small purpose—a house servant. I am poor and I must take what work is offered to earn my bowl of food. But I am not a fool."

"And where were you and your wife when this happened?"

"In the kitchen—where she is now. Would you speak with her?"

"No, it is not necessary. Go to her. I will call you when we are ready to leave."

The butler departed for the kitchen, and Baxter, the medical examiner, asked what it was all about.

"I asked him whether Phoebe Greenberg would have scalped her husband. He says no. He's a student of human nature, so I believe him. I don't have your Occidental gift for telling Jews from Gentiles. But Phoebe is not a Jewish name, is it?"

"Anything's a Jewish name today," Beckman said. "All the rules are broken. I'm a Jewish cop. But if you want to know about the girls—none of them is Jewish."

"How do you know?"

"I know. Take my word for it. About the men, I don't know with any confidence. I would guess that Greenberg was the only Jew in the lot. Maybe Murphy Anderson—"

"With a name like that!" Baxter snorted.

"I told you, names don't figure. It's all mixed up. By the way, Masao, this Mike Tulley, he whispers to me that you should give him half an hour to get home and then call him. I got his number here." He handed the number to Masuto, who nodded and said to Baxter, "What do you think, doc?"

"I don't think. The autopsy will show absolutely nothing. Nothing. Greenberg died of a heart attack."

"Could fear have caused it?"

"Are you going to prove that, Masao? Come off it. If this is a murder, it's a perfect murder. File and forget. Even if one of those babes confesses to being in that bedroom and pointing a gun at Greenberg and refusing to get him the sublinguals, and you put me on the stand and read me the confession ten times over, I will still say that there is no evidence of murder or even reasonable doubt that the heart attack came from natural and inevitable causes. And I think any physician you get will agree with me. So if you got a murder, you got a perfect murder."

"A very few people on this earth," Masuto said thoughtfully, "perfect themselves in all of their being and actions. Such people do not murder."

Then he dialed Mike Tulley's number.

Tulley answered and waited. Masuto reminded the TV actor that he had asked him to call, and then Tulley said, "I think we had better talk, Detective Masuto."

"It's past midnight. Can't it wait for tomorrow?"

"Maybe you sleep good. I take pills but that won't help tonight. I agree with Cotter. Greenberg was murdered."

"You're out in Benedict Canyon?"

"That's right. Five minutes from where you are."

"I'll be there," Masuto said. "Ten or fifteen minutes." He

put down the phone and turned to Beckman. "He thinks Greenberg was murdered and he's frightened."

"Oh, balls," said the doctor. "I am going home to bed if you don't mind."

"Want me to come along with you, Masao?" Detective Beckman asked.

"No—no, you knock off, Sy. I'll see what he has to say. By the way, it seems to me that Anderson and Cotter were Greenberg's partners. Is that right?"

"I think so. Greenberg was the president of an outfit called Northeastern Films."

"And if I remember, I read somewhere that they produced the "Lonesome Rider" or whatever that thing Tulley plays in is called."

"That's right—very big, successful. Number two on the Neilsen for seven months now. I read the *Hollywood Reporter*," Beckman explained to Dr. Baxter. "It's a sort of a damn trade journal, when you labor in Beverly Hills. I know where all the stars live. So does Masao. It gives us some kind of status among cops, but the pay remains lousy. Sidney Burke is press agent for Northeastern, according to what I hear tonight."

"Good night," Dr. Baxter said sourly.

Masuto called the Japanese houseman, said his good-bys formally, and then he and Detective Baxter left. Officer Seaton was still outside, but Masuto felt it would be better to call no attention to the house, and he sent Seaton back to duty.

CHAPTER TWO

MIKE TULLEY

Mike Tulley's home was in Benedict Canyon just north of Lexington, or something over half a mile north of Sunset Boulevard. Three months before, the tourist sightseeing buses had taken to making a right turn on Sunset along Benedict—which was a tribute to his rating. The house was one hundred and fifty thousand dollars modern with a bean shaped swimming pool and a carport wide enough to hold five cars.

Tulley was standing in the carport when Masuto drove up, and he was visibly relieved. He led Masuto toward the house, through the entranceway and living room to the library. Statuswise, this had replaced the den. There was a whole wall of fine leather bindings, Heritage Club, Limited Editions Club, and also several shelves of plain, common books purchased at Martindale's and at Mary Hunter's Bookshop. It made a good wall; people like Mike Tulley had little time for reading. There was an enormous antique globe and four Eames chairs. The couch, upholstered in black vinyl, was built in along one wall.

Tulley motioned for Masuto to sit down and asked whether he would have a drink. Masuto shook his head. Coffee? Again Masuto shook his head, and at that point Lenore Tulley stepped into the library and said, "You don't offer an Oriental coffee. Give him some tea."

"Lenore, suppose you go to bed. What I got to say to the detective here is private."

"You mean it stinks."

"You've had too much."

"Drop dead," she said, and swung around and left. Tulley stared hopelessly at Masuto.

Masuto waited. He was tired and unhappy, but he attempted to be patient and objective, without judgement or identification.

"Great! Great!" Tulley said. He poured himself a drink. "It's a great, stinking life. I am going to tell you something quick—because if I don't tell it quick, I can't tell it." He went to the door, opened it and then closed it again. "I wouldn't put it past her to have this place bugged," he said.

"Why don't you simply tell me whatever you wish to tell me."

"All right. Now look—this happened eleven years ago. I had a rotten small part in a TV thing they were doing at World Wide. They brought in some idiot kid who wanted a part—you got to know how these kids want a part. There are maybe ten thousand girls in this town who came here to make it big, and none of them do and they would sell their souls and their mothers for one stinking little part. So this kid is promised a part if she lets herself get banged once or twice—"

"Just spell that out, please," Masuto said.

"This guy makes a deal with her. He brings her into one of those little movable dressing rooms. She promises to have some sex with a couple of buddies. Then he invites me to be his guest. So I am a louse—you know a man who isn't a louse?"

"Go on, please."

"So I go in with this kid. I don't know how many there are before me. All I know is that I am invited to take a free ride, and I do it. In a crumby little dressing room with some kid I can barely see—except that she's a blond with a good figure. And she tells me her name and I kid her about the part and I hate myself a little and that's it."

Again, Masuto waited. Tulley was sprawled in the Eames chair. Masuto sat on the edge of the built-in couch. He was never at ease sprawling or reclining, and now he sat rather primly.

"I even forgot about it," Tulley said. "It was eleven years ago. Who remembers?"

"There are people who remember," Masuto said.

Tulley glanced at him sharply. Then he reached into his pocket, took out a card case and from it a folded piece of pink note paper. He unfolded it and handed it to the policeman. It was strongly scented and typed on it were the following words:

Mike, you've had your time and I have been patient.
Samantha.

Masuto handed it back to him. "I suppose Samantha was the girl?"

"That was her name. Would you believe it, I forgot. But when I got the note, I remembered."

"When did you get it?"

"In the mail, yesterday. I also know what typewriter was used."

"You do?"

He pointed to the wall opposite the couch, where a portable typewriter sat on a built-in teakwood table. "That one. I compared the type. There's a convenient broken 't' to make it easy. Do you want to keep this note?"

"If you wish." Masuto took the note and put it in his pocket. "Do you think your wife wrote it?"

"You saw her. She's not stupid, is she? Wouldn't she pick another typewriter?"

"I don't know. That is why I asked you."

Tulley stared at Masuto for a while, and then he said, "Something like this happens and you begin to think twice. I mean, nobody's stupid enough to do it this way, but she's smart enough to know we wouldn't believe she was stupid enough."

"Why?" Masuto asked softly. "Do you think your wife is Samantha?"

He sat without answering.

"Eleven years ago, how old was this kid? Samantha?"

"Eighteen, nineteen, twenty—how the hell do you know?"

"You just told me it was eleven years ago. When did you meet your wife?"

"Six years ago."

"An actress?"

Tulley nodded.

"When you go to bed with a woman, don't you look at her?" Masuto asked coldly.

"I told you it was dark in that lousy dressing room."

"Was Al Greenberg involved?"

"I think he was. I can't be sure, but I think I remember him on the set that day."

"Cotter? Murphy Anderson? Sidney Burke?"

"I think so. Burke brought the girl onto the set."

"How old is your wife, Mr. Tulley?"

"Thirty-one."

"Do you think that your wife was in the room with Mr. Greenberg?"

"I don't know."

"Do you own a gun?"

"We have a small thirty-two automatic. I keep it in the bedroom."

"Obviously, you looked for it when you came home tonight. Was it there?"

"No."

"And you asked your wife whether she knew where it was?"

"She didn't know. She said she couldn't care less. She hates guns and she has been after me to get rid of it."

"Why don't you, Mr. Tulley? We have an excellent police force here in Beverly Hills."

"Which couldn't do one cotton-picking thing about keeping Al Greenberg alive."

"We are policemen, not physicians. Those men and women you had dinner with tonight—they have all been here at your home?"

"They have."

"Within the past two weeks?"

"That's right. We entertain a lot—dinner parties, cocktails. Sometimes when Al wanted a conference about the show, we would have it here."

"I see. But to get back to what you were inferring—is it your notion that this Samantha waited patiently for eleven years to have her revenge, and that she began by murdering Al Greenberg?"

"It sounds stupid when you put it that way. Maybe she waited for the one opportunity. Maybe she's patient. It still seems stupid."

"Farfetched, let's say. Still, someone wrote a note on your wife's typewriter and signed it 'Samantha.' "

"Don't you want to compare the note with a sample from the typewriter?"

"What will that prove, Mr. Tulley? If Samantha is patient enough to wait eleven years for her revenge, she's patient enough to wait for a chance at your wife's typewriter."

"What am I supposed to do?"

"I can't say, Mr. Tulley. If you believe you are in danger, you can inform my chief and he will no doubt station a policeman in front of your house."

"Just one thing," said Tulley, shooting out a hand at Masuto. "You're a cop—and this is Beverly Hills. So don't throw your weight around with me."

"I am very sorry if I gave that impression," Masuto said, smiling deferentially. "Thank you for your information."

Tulley's apology was contained in the gesture of rising and escorting Masuto to the door.

Masuto's wife was awake and waiting for him when he got home. She was very gentle and full of many fears, and when a case kept him hours past his regular working time, she could not sleep, and hovered over her two children and allowed her mind to fill with awful possibilities. Although she had been born in Los Angeles, her first years had been spent in an old-fashioned and protected environment, and she had many of the mannerisms of a girl brought up in Japan. Without trying, and very tastefully, she had given a Japanese decor to their little house in Culver City. She liked paper screens and low, black enamel tables, and both she and her husband, when they were alone for the evening, would wear kimono and robe; and tonight she had his robe waiting and tea ready, and she sat dutifully staring at him with great affection and waiting to hear whether he proposed to speak of what had happened.

"Al Greenberg died," he said finally, after he had tasted the tea and relaxed somewhat. "You will remember that when we ride with the children in Beverly Hills and I point out houses, his is the house with the great columns, like the big house in front of the old Selznick Studio."

"I am sorry to hear that. He was your friend."

"I think so. As much as anyone is a cop's friend."

"But why did they need the police?"

"One of the guests said that Mr. Greenberg was murdered."

"Was he?" she asked anxiously.

"I don't know. In the guise of being a philosophical Oriental type—which I am not—I would say that these people murder endlessly. Then there could be no death among them without the charge of murder being justified."

"I don't understand you."

"I am not sure that I want you to. Let's go to bed, and perhaps I will stop dreaming, because this is like a nasty and turgid dream, pointless and with neither dignity nor honor."

"Has it ever occured to you," Rabbi Matthew Gitlen asked Masuto the following morning, "to ponder on the curious parable of the camel and the needle's eye, and the rich man and the gates of heaven? A member of my congregation once coined a rather famous line to the effect that he had been rich and he had been poor and rich was better. The poor are too often maligned when they are accused of happiness, and the rich are maligned by the same accusation. As incredible as it may seem, I preach occasionally to my congregation—in my own words of course—that the Kingdom of God is within them. Which can be a dilly, you know. Are you a Christian? I ask in the most perfunctory professional sense, not to pry—simply to find a manner of discussing your inquiry. I trust the question does not embarrass you?"

"Not at all," Masuto replied, smiling. The rabbi was an enormous man, almost six-foot-four, Masuto would guess, very fat and apparently very civilized, but big enough in his frame to wear his weight with great dignity and to give the impression that a very large and hard-muscled man carried around another, a fat man, not out of indulgence but out of compassion. It had a curious effect on Masuto, who was put at his ease and who continued, "But I am not a Christian. I was never baptized. I am a Zen Buddhist—but that is not to be thought of as a religion in your sense."

"I reject the obvious comment, and I am utterly fascinated," the rabbi rumbled, rising from behind his desk and going to one corner of his study, where there was a small refrigerator with a wood finish. He opened it and peered inside. "Will you join me in a yogurt, Detective Masuto? Supposedly, it reduces me, which is nonsense. A Zen Buddhist."

"It would be my pleasure," Masuto said.

"Plain or orange or strawberry?"

"Plain, if I may."

"Of course." He handed Masuto a cup of yogurt and a spoon and sat on a corner of his desk as he opened his own. "Zen," he said. "What do they say? 'Those who know, speak not. Those who speak, know not.' Do you subscribe to that?"

"Oh, no—not at all," Masuto answered. "Everything can be spoken of, poorly perhaps, but English is a rich language. But a detective's time is not his own."

"Naturally. I might even say that a rabbi's time is not his own. This is the curse of a civilization that rushes so desperately. We must talk about Al Greenberg, may his soul rest in peace."

"He was a member of your congregation."

"In the most nominal sense. He was not a religious man—but pleasant and anxious to quiet his guilts with money. His contributions were generous, and when he married Phoebe three years ago, she decided to become Jewish. She was very grateful to him. Perhaps with reason. She was in the hospital, you know, with TB—in a ward, broke, two suicide attempts behind her. She had worked for him in what they call a 'special' some years before, and when he discovered she was in the hospital, he spared nothing to help her. The best doctors, the newest drugs—and then somehow he got up the nerve to ask her to marry him and she agreed. Gratitude. He endeared himself to her. But it was essentially a father-daughter relationship, no more than that. He was a widower. Of course, her becoming Jewish was not as serious as it might have been. I instructed her for two weeks and then her interest waned. But I got to know her a little—only why should this matter to the police?"

Detective Masuto told him why it mattered to the police, and the rabbi ate his yogurt and listened with interest, and then when Masuto finished, said, "I called the house when you telephoned me. Mrs. Greenberg was still asleep. I think I had better go over there now. She'll need someone to lean on."

"You don't appear surprised."

"At murder?" asked Rabbi Gitlin. "But you don't know that it is murder, and nothing should surprise us in this world."

"I am not completely at home with the social relationships and overlaps of your Western religions, but would a man like Mr. Greenberg, under great stress, cry out the name of Jesus Christ?"

The rabbi shrugged. "Who knows what any of us would do under great stress."

"May I ask you an unspeakable question?"

"Of course," the rabbi smiled. "But you must forgive me if I give you an unspeakable answer."

"In your opinion, could Mrs. Greenberg have murdered her husband?"

"Not unspeakable, but interesting. You do not ask whether I think she had reason to, incitement to—but only whether she could have. But how could either of us, Detective Masuto, even know what the human mind and soul is capable of? Murder is a terrible ultimate. It is the ghost, the monster that lurks wherever human beings live. It is not your question that is unspeakable, but murder itself. I cannot accept the proposition that Al Greenberg was murdered, but if he was murdered, then that defines the murderer. You told me that you met Al Greenberg?"

"Several times."

"Then you must understand that if he was murdered, then your murderer is without heart or compunction, someone who will stop at nothing. The very thought of such a murderer is particularly terrifying. I would be relieved if you told me your own thoughts."

"That there was no murder?"

"I would like to think that, Detective Masuto."

"Have you time enough for me to call Dr. Baxter—our medical examiner? He should be at the hospital now, completing the autopsy."

"If you wish." The rabbi pointed to his telephone, and Masuto dialed the hospital and was transferred to the autopsy room. A nurse answered and asked whether he would wait a moment or two, since Dr. Baxter was washing up. The rabbi watched Masuto thoughtfully. Then Baxter got on the phone and told him testily that he had spent three hours on a lot of nonsense.

"What did you find?" Masuto asked.

"That he died of a heart attack."

"Suppose—Doc, suppose that he fell down and someone held a pillow over his face for a minute or two. Would it show up in the autopsy?"

"No."

"Just like that?"

"Just like that. No. What do you want, an autopsy or the kind of nonsense you read in novels?"

"But the pillow would cause his death?"

"Well, of course it would. You don't breathe, you die."

"That would be murder."

"Not with me on the witness stand, it wouldn't. I told you he died of a myocardial infarction. That still goes."

"But the pillow?"

"I could invent a lot of other ways to kill him, and it would still be a heart attack. So you're on your own, my lad."

Masuto replaced the telephone and turned to the rabbi, who smiled sadly. "I'm afraid I prefer to agree with your doctor," he said. "If you want a murder, Mr. Masuto, you must find it."

"Perhaps whether I want it or not, it'll find me."

"Perhaps."

In school, on being asked his mother's name—that is, her maiden name—Masuto's son had once replied, "Katherine Asuki." Masuto was distressed when he heard about it, as he always was when he noticed any sense or action of inferiority on the part of his children. Her name was Kati or Katy, depending on how far the Anglicization went, and now Masuto pulled up at the loading walk of the Food Giant Supermarket, leaned out of the car and shouted, "Hey, Kati— I'm here!"

It was one of the very few aggressive, extroverted actions he indulged in, and he only did it because he detested supermarkets. Now Kati came rushing out with her cart, exclaiming as always, "Why do you embarrass me so? They will think we are people of no manners whatsoever."

"Let them," he said, stowing the bags into the car. "Come—in with you and off." She would not drive. He drove to his house and she apologized for interrupting his work so often.

"Today I have nothing to do," he said. "The chief gave it to me. Today, tomorrow—so that he will be able to tell the press and everyone else that poor Mr. Greenberg died of a heart attack. If it had happened in Culver City or in Westwood or in Hollywood, that would be something else. Not in Beverly Hills—and least of all north of Wilshire Boulevard. So today I will prove there was no murder, and tomorrow I will go to the funeral and the next day we will all have a picnic at my uncle's farm."

"That's very nice, but you're teasing me, aren't you?"

"No."

"Where were you this morning?"

"With a rabbi," he said.

"A rabbi? That's a Jewish priest, isn't it?" He burst out laughing, and she said plaintively, "Why must you laugh at me? I don't pretend to know all these things. You knew I was an old-fashioned girl when you married me. Now you're sorry you married me."

"If you are such an old-fashioned girl," he said, "then why do you allow me to carry the bundles into the house?"

"Because I try to learn the things you teach me," she said sweetly.

The lady at the Screen Actors Guild had that quality of faded beauty that is so abundant in Hollywood and so occasional in the rest of the country. She was in her late sixties, Masuto judged, but with the bone structure of a star and the practiced dignity of at least a bit-part player. He seemed to remember having seen her in this film or that, and he wished he could refer to one of them with any certainty and thereby win her wholehearted cooperation. But he knew that if he faked a memory of her playing opposite Mary Pickford she would be insulted, and if he made it Joan Crawford, she would inform him that she had never been an actress. Things turned out that way for him.

When he showed her his badge, she studied him curiously and challengingly. It was plain that she did not approve of Oriental policemen or trust in geographic accidents of birth: Irritated a little, she wondered what she could do for him.

"You do keep membership records from year to year?"

"Not for the public," she informed him.

"I am not the public. I am Detective Sergeant Masuto, of the Beverly Hills Police Force. I told you that. I showed you my badge."

"Have you a warrant?"

"No, I have no warrant. I don't want to pry into your records. I want one simple fact. I want the address of an actress who may or may not belong to the Guild."

"This is Hollywood, not Beverly Hills. I think I should call the police here—"

"My dear lady," Masuto said softly, "I do not get angry or provoked, but if you insist on interfering, you will end up by being quite uncomfortable. Now listen to me. Eleven years ago, a girl called Samantha may or may not have joined this organization. I understand that you can play a speaking roll once without joining, but then must join before the second job. Is that so?"

"Yes, and you might as well tell me her name."

"And yours, Miss?"

"Arthur."

"All right, Miss Arthur. Her name was Samantha."

"Samantha what?"

"I don't know. I have one name—Samantha."

"Then don't you think you ought to come back with the second name before you throw your weight around a poor, defenseless old lady?" she asked icily.

"I may or may not be able to find the second name. That is not your problem. I want every Samantha who joined the Guild eleven years ago, give or take a few months on either end. The name is not a common one and there can hardly be too many."

"Indeed!" said Miss Arthur.

"Indeed," Masuto smiled.

Whereupon Miss Arthur led him into another office where two girls sat, both of them younger even when their ages were added together, and where she figuratively washed her hands of Masuto.

"Who is she?" Masuto asked them. "I mean, who was she? The name sort of rings a bell."

"Della Arthur? And you didn't remember?" asked one.

"He didn't remember," said the other.

"She hates you. She'll cut your heart out. We'll let you out the back way, officer. We'll protect you."

"Are you married?"

"I'm married."

"Then we'll let her kill you. You know, all the Beverly Hills policemen are very handsome. Is that how they pick you?"

"I want—" Masuto began.

"We know," said one of them. "We heard. Enough of this light-hearted girlish talk. Only we don't file membership by year of admission. We file by name, and you don't have the family name."

"But there must be some annual bookkeeping."

"Oh, yes—yes. If she paid dues, we should have the receipts and the duplicate statements." The girl was dark haired and bright eyed, and she licked her lips when she looked at Masuto. "Why are they always married? Never mind. Come on, we'll go in the file room and study 1955 and we'll find a Samantha. Of course, you know that's a phony name," she said to Masuto.

She had led him into the next room, facing a whole wall of files, when he turned and looked at her curiously.

"Why do you say that, Miss—?"

"Just call me Jenny."

"OK, Jenny. Why?"

"Well, isn't it obvious?"

"Not to my inscrutable Oriental mind. I grew up in a Japanese community, let us say a little apart from your folk-ways."

"You know, Sergeant, you got a nice sense of humor. Cool, if you follow me." She had opened a file drawer and was riffling through it with practiced fingers as she spoke. "Suppose this Samantha is a kid of twenty or so in 1955. That makes her born in 1935, right?"

"Give or take a few years—yes."

"Middle of the depression—who's going to give a kid a nutty name like Samantha? Today's another matter, but around then, from what I hear, people weren't thinking about these stylish names."

"Good. Go on."

"I bet you a pretty her last name's a phony too."

"How's that?"

"You know—like Glendale or Frazer or Buckingham or Sanford, but no Kaminski or Levy or Jones or Richter—"

"You'd make an excellent cop," Masuto said admiringly.

"Nah. Half the names here are phonies. It's part of the profession."

"Do they also have to register their real names?"

"No rule about that. Some do. Most don't. If an actor takes a stage name, it becomes part of him. He usually can't live with two names. Hold on—here's a beginning. What do you know about that! Samantha Adams. Here's the address, on Sixth Street in Hollywood. That's a sorry block of bungalows turned rooming house a long time ago—so this kid was no millionaire."

Masuto copied down the name and address in his pad. There was no telephone number.

"No payment either," continued Jenny. "The large sum is for membership," she told Masuto, showing him the statement. "Almost two hundred with the dues, which is not hay by any means. You see, Sergeant, that's the initiation fee, entrance fee, lifetime. But it was never paid. Neither was the dues payment—that is, the first payment. Here's the follow-up statement and the second statement. That finishes the year. So this kid you're looking for never joined the Guild. She had one job, maybe two—but not three. I mean in the profession. Maybe she went back to slinging hash. That's another union. And she's the only one. No more Samantha's for 1955."

"You amaze me," Masuto nodded.

"You want me to amaze you some more, officer? I'm only doing it because you're the sexy type. I'll tell you something else about this kid. She never played anything real legitimate. Translated, that means adult theatre. She was never AEA."

"What's AEA?"

"Actors Equity. Legitimate theatre. Also, she was never AFTRA, which is TV and radio artists, and she never did the clubs—no stripping, no Las Vegas, not even the crumb joints. That's because she never claimed AGVA. So either she dumped it all—or else."

"How do you know all this?"

"No mystery. Look, we have this big overall membership fee of two hundred dollars. But there are also three other major theatrical unions, and if one had to duplicate the entrance fee for every membership, some of these kids would die first. So we scale it. If you're an Equity member, we give a credit of one hundred dollars. We also have a code of notation for the statements. So that's how I do it. And if your wife locks the door on you, give me a ring right here. Nine to five. You just ask for Jenny. One Samantha, one Jenny. I told you the last name would be a phony too. Samantha Adams—get that."

Out on Sunset Boulevard and walking toward his car, Masuto wondered vaguely how it would be to be single and to date someone like this Jenny. He had only dated a Caucasian girl once, and she had been shapely but stupid. It had not been a satisfactory evening at all. He was impatient at himself for allowing his thoughts to wander. It was wasteful and childish, and he gathered them together.

Sixth Street, east of Gower; it was an old, old Hollywood bungalow built of spit and slats, as they said, almost half a century before, with the sign out, "Furnished Rooms. Transients Accommodated." In the old manner—the way most California houses had been before air-conditioning—the windows were closed and the blinds were drawn against the hot noon-day sun. Masuto rang the bell, and a fat, frowzy woman of fifty or so, her feet in old slippers, her ample body in a bathrobe and her breath alcoholic, opened the door and said sourly. "I know—you're a cop."

"You're very perceptive."

"Nuts. You got it written all over you, and I ain't fooled by the Charlie Chan makeup. What do you want? I run a clean, if a lousy house. Only men. This ain't no Beverly Drive, so I don't want no hookers giving me heartache."

"I'm looking for a girl."

"Then you're looking through the wrong keyhole, Officer Chan. I only rent to men."

"That wasn't the case eleven years ago, I am sure."

"Good God Almighty, nothing was the case eleven years ago. I was a hootchie-kootchie dancer eleven years ago, believe it or not. Sure, I took in a lady now and then in those days. But what do I remember? I ain't no elephant, except in appearance."

"This girl's name was Samantha Adams."

"Samantha Adams. You don't say."

"Maybe eighteen, twenty years old. Blue eyes, blonde hair, good figure, maybe five feet six or seven inches tall—"

"Poor Officer Chan—what are you, an LA cop?"

"Beverly Hills," Masuto replied, taking out his billfold and showing her his badge.

"That accounts for it. Some day they give you a day off, wander along the Sunset Strip—you'll find maybe ten thousand babes to answer your description—no! No, wait a moment. Samantha Adams. That wasn't her real name. Some other name—no, I can't remember the other name for the life of me, but I remember her. I used to kid her about that Samantha business. Poor kid—poor, stupid kid."

"Why do you say that?" Masuto asked softly.

"Ah, she had no brains. You know, mister, for a dame this is the hardest, lousiest, dirtiest dark bunghole of a town in all these USA. Make it—you don't even exist out here unless you got a stainless steel ramrod up your you-know-where. This kid was soft—all the time soft and scared. Then one day she is going to lick the world and she goes off on a job at some studio—I think at World Wide, over in the Valley. Something happens. I don't know what—but here's a kid has the heart torn out of her. She has the curse after that, and we can't stop the bleeding, so I finally get a doctor and pay him. She comes out of it finally, but very weak and not good up on top. She's broke and a month behind. What the hell, I never threw a kid out on the street. That's why I stopped it with the dames. I know what it is to be one, and I ain't got the cabbage for an institution. So I don't even mention it to this Samantha kid, but one day she walks out. Leaves me her lousy suitcase and her few lousy clothes for payment—I should sell them. Can you imagine? Yes, sir, this world is one big joyride."

"You said your name is Mrs. Baker?"

"Dolly Baker, sonny."

"You never saw her again?"

"No. That was 'Goodby Samantha.' "

"And you can't remember her name—the other name?"

"It'll come to me."

"You wouldn't have a register or anything like that?"

"Buster," she smiled, "what do I look like, a sap? They can make their space ships without my poor widow's mite."

He grinned back at her. "Thanks, Mrs. Baker. You have great heart, and I think that when you reflect on it and realize that I bear no harm for this poor girl, you will remember. Here's my card. Will you call me when the name comes back to you?"

"Masao Masuto," she read from the card. "I like you, Buster. I'll call you, but if that poor kid is in something that stinks, find the lousy male bastard that put her there and go easy on her. Will you?"

"I'll try, Mrs. Baker."

"You're Leo, aren't you?" she asked, looking at him narrowly.

"How did you know?" He was impressed but not astounded, recalling that he had shown her the open wallet with badge and identity card.

"I'm sensitive to such things. I am Scorpio myself—very perceptive. That girl didn't steal anything. She did not hurt anyone. You take my word for that."

"It's eleven years later."

"People don't change—not the deep nut of them. You ought to know that, Officer Chan."

CHAPTER
THREE

MURPHY

ANDERSON

It was just 12:15, just past midday, when Detective Sergeant Masuto parked his car behind one of the new savings and loan office buildings on Wilshire Boulevard in Beverly Hills. Northeastern Films had the entire sixth floor, with at least one hundred thousand dollars worth of modern-Italian-Southern-California decor; but today the bright edge of wealth was muted by the haze of death. The men and women who worked in the offices of Northeastern were depressed by the fact that it was incumbent upon them to be depressed by the death of Al Greenberg.

The girl at the reception desk looked upon Masuto bleakly as he told her that he had an appointment with Mr. Anderson. She spoke into the phone and then she rose and led Masuto through a section of minor offices to the rear of the floor. This whole end of the floor was divided into three offices. According to the names on the door, the center office belonged to Al Greenberg, the one on the left to John D. Cotter, and the one on the right to Murphy Anderson.

Expressionless faces examined them as they walked through, and when they reached Anderson's office, the big, white-haired man opened the door himself, invited Masuto to be seated, and closed the door behind him. Masuto lowered himself into a straight-backed Italian import, and Anderson apologized for not having Cotter there with them.

"You don't know what this has done to us, Sergeant. Jack's been at the bank all morning, and that's only the beginning. I have been talking to five hundred people and trying to help Phoebe arrange the funeral proceedings at the same time." He looked at his watch. "As a matter of fact, I have a very important luncheon meeting at one. I imagine we can finish by then. I have been talking to your boss at the police station, and he agrees that there is absolutely no sense in pursuing the murder angle. We have no evidence of murder, no real suspicion of anyone, and a very definite knowledge of poor Al's illness. Jack Cotter is willing to forget what he heard. Do you agree?"

"It hardly matters whether I agree or not," Masuto said, spreading his hands slightly. "Mine is a negative search—simply to dispel any lingering doubts. I think the very fact that this was kept out of the papers helps your desire."

"Thank God for that. I don't mind telling you—but in confidence—that we are in the middle of the biggest move in the history of this business, the acquisition of the remaining library of World Wide Films—for eighteen million dollars. Jack Cotter finished signing the papers this morning. If this had broken as murder, the deal would have been postponed or killed completely."

"Then if we were fanciful," Masuto smiled, "we could say that the murderer attempted to frustrate your deal."

"Then why didn't she break the story to the press?"

Masuto shrugged. "Who knows? Could you tell me something, perhaps, about your company."

"To what point?"

"Again—who knows? But I am curious. If I am not mistaken, Mr. Greenberg began the company some fifteen years ago?"

"Closer to twelve years. He and I began together, and then we took Jack Cotter in. Al began to produce TV shows about fifteen years ago. He was one of the first. I was his lawyer, and he organized the company to produce and I went in with him. But I don't take any of the credit. I am a lawyer and a businessman, a good lawyer and a pretty good businessman, but I think I would make a lousy producer. Whatever North-eastern is, Al Greenberg is mainly responsible."

"How did Jack Cotter come into it?"

"Jack was a sort of Western star back in the late 'thirties. He made five feature films for Asterlux, and they went bankrupt in 1940—or almost bankrupt. They liquidated their assets and settled. They owed Jack a hundred thousand dollars in back wages, and as a settlement they gave him the American distribution rights to the five Westerns. Who ever knew then how TV would eat feature films! Back in 1957, Jack proposed to throw his five features into our operation in return for a piece of stock and a vice-presidency in the company. We needed the features and we took him in."

"Is Sidney Burke also in the firm?"

"Not exactly in it. He began with our publicity right from the beginning. He's good. At first he worked almost for nothing. Then he got some stock. He still does our publicity, but he has his own company."

"Would you mind telling me who the stockholders are?"

"Why?"

"Because it would be easier if you told me," Masuto said, "than if I had to track down the information. I could, you know."

"You still want to make something out of this, don't you?"

"No. What is there, is there, Mr. Anderson. If nothing is there—"

"OK. There are five stockholders—or were. Al held sixteen thousand shares. His wife, Phoebe, five thousand, a gift from him when they were married. Sidney has two thousand and Jack has four thousand. I own six thousand shares, which makes me the second largest stockholder."

"And Mr. Tulley—Mike Tulley?"

"He has no shares. Why should he? We hired him three years ago and we made him a TV star. But at this point our shares have a book value of almost three hundred dollars each. There's no market on them, but if there were, it would be enormous."

"And now what happens to Mr. and Mrs. Greenberg's shares?"

"Nothing happens to Phoebe's—unless she decides to sell. And I have advised her not to and I will continue to so advise her. But Al's personal stock, according to our initial agreement, goes back into the company treasury, and his estate is paid fifty percent of book value. Providing Jack and I refuse to purchase."

"How's that?"

"If any one of the three officers dies, the remaining two have the right to divide his stock and purchase it at twenty-five percent of book value. The remaining twenty-five percent is then paid by the company treasury. It's a peculiar arrangement, but perfectly legal and it protects the officers and major stockholders.

"And what do you and Mr. Cotter intend to do?"

"We'll buy the stock, of course. Are you thinking of that as a motive? But whose motive for Al's death, Sergeant? I am the only one who profits. I gain control, God help me. There's no reason for you to believe me, but I'd blow this business and ten like it to give Al a week of extra living."

"We were not to talk of murder, but simply to eliminate any possibility of it. Forgive me if I raise a rather shameful matter, Mr. Anderson, but do you remember an incident with a girl called Samantha? Eleven years ago."

Murphy Anderson stared at Masuto for a long moment. Then he swung on his heel and walked to the window. When he turned back, his face was cold and set.

"What the hell business is that of yours, Sergeant?"

"Last night, Mike Tulley asked me to come over. He told me about the incident. He was very frightened. I gathered that he is under the impression that one of you—one of your four men, or five if we include Greenberg—is married to Samantha."

"Let me tell you something about Al Greenberg, Sergeant. I never spoke of this until now. But Al never touched that kid. I'm not defending myself or Jack or Mike or Sidney. What we are, we are. But Al went into that dressing room, looked at the kid, had a few words with her and came out. He was the last. Don't worry—I remember, I goddamn well remember. Jack had disappeared, and when Sidney saw Al's face, he took off. Al said to me, 'If anything like this ever happens again on one of my sets, Murph, I will kill you and everyone else concerned with my own hands. And I'm not kidding. You were high in my esteem, and now you are low as a turd—you and that stinking shithead Sidney.' Maybe not those exact words, but that was the tune."

"Then if what you say is true," Masuto said slowly, "why are we all quietly thinking that Samantha murdered him?"

"Baloney. Why would she wait eleven years?"

"Then would you mind telling me the gist of your discussion with Mr. Cotter, concerning Samantha?"

"I would mind. It has no bearing here."

"Have you also spoken to Sidney Burke about it?"

"You know, I don't like those questions, Sergeant Masuto. Not one goddamn bit. Your job is to protect the citizens of this community, not to harass them. I am no stranger at City Hall—"

"You know well enough what my job is, Mr. Anderson. You are an officer of the court, so don't threaten me. I don't threaten you. This case is as sticky as flypaper, and my hands are full of it and I am trying to walk a tight rope at the same time. I ask you something, and you could blow your top and slug me, and what would that solve?"

"I don't blow my top. So if you got any questions, ask them and then get to hell out of here!"

"Do you believe your wife is Samantha?" Masuto asked flatly.

Anderson's face whitened and he clenched his fists. He took a step toward Masuto, and then his telephone rang. He picked it up, shouted into it, "I told you, no calls!" and slammed it back into its cradle. It rang again. He picked it up and listened. The white of his face became whiter.

"Oh, my God," he said. "My God—my God."

He put the telephone down and stared hopelessly at Masuto.

"What happened?" Masuto asked him.

"Mike Tulley has just been murdered. Shot. With his wife's gun."

There were cars all around the Tulley house. This one had not been kept quiet. There were newspapermen at the place and more still arriving. Over a dozen cars were crowded in and around the driveway.

Officer Frank Seaton supervised the half-dozen uniformed men who were trying to keep the newspaper people and the curious out of the house—and at the same time keep the traffic moving on Benedict Canyon Road. Inside the house, Detective Beckman was in charge. They were waiting for Masuto to arrive before they removed the body, and Beckman immediately led Masuto into the study. Murphy Anderson stayed in the living room. Anderson remained silent. Like so many big, fleshy men, a mood could age him. He had not spoken a word on the way over with Masuto, and he said nothing now as he slumped into a chair in the living room.

"Why?" asked Detective Beckman, nodding at him.

"He's the boss now," Masuto said. "I want him here. Something's going on inside him that I don't know about."

Beckman closed the door of the study behind them—the same room Masuto had been in the night before, except that now it was full of smoke from Dr. Sam Baxter's cigar. There were also the fingerprint man, the photographer and two men from the hospital, Beverly Hills being too small a community to boast its own police autopsy facilities. The mortal remains of Mike Tulley lay on the floor, covered by a thin rubber sheet, which Dr. Baxter callously threw back. Tulley's body was stripped to the waist. There were three small, ugly bullet holes in his chest.

"There you are, Masao," said Baxter. "Close range. Thirty-two lady's gun. Smith and Wesson automatic. Victim died of heart failure but not of a heart attack."

"Your sense of humor leaves something to be desired," Masuto said. "God help him."

"Macabre job, macabre humor. I don't get too many murders, Masao, but they mash themselves up in cars day in and day out. Half the human race is in a frenzied race to eliminate itself. Can we take him away?"

Masuto nodded, and the hospital attendants put the body on a stretcher and carried it out.

"What about them?" Beckman asked, motioning to fingerprints and photography.

"They should be finished now."

Reluctantly, the fingerprint man and the photographer allowed themselves to be ushered out of the room. Dr. Baxter dropped into a chair and relit his cigar. Detective Beckman seated himself on the built-in couch. Masuto remained standing, staring at the blood blot on the carpet. Tall, sliding aluminum doors at one side of the study opened onto planting and swimming pool—that heady badge of status that is almost obligatory in Beverly Hills. The contained vista was very beautiful, and Masuto thought he recognized the work of Hono Asaki, the landscape gardener who was very much in demand at the moment. Standing there, Masuto attempted to feel something of what the dead man had felt. It was not good to die in the face of such beauty—in youth and vigor. But then, it is not good to die, anywhere, anyplace.

Beckman rose, went to the table, and picked up a cardboard box. It contained the gun.

"You want to look at this, Masao?"

"Her gun?"

"Right."

"She admits it?"

"Right."

"Send it over to ballistics. Where is she?"

"Upstairs, lying down. She was hysterical. Doc gave her something to quiet her down."

"What did you give her?" Masuto asked Baxter.

"A placebo. Two aspirin. No shock, just lady hysterics. She quieted down almost immediately."

"You're a witch doctor," Beckman said.

"Aren't we all?"

"Do you want to see her now?" asked Beckman.

"Later. Tell me about it. It seems I make a practice of coming in after everyone else is seated."

"As long as you're on time for the next one. As far as we can put it together, this is it. According to the wife. She's the only witness. The lady who did the killing—"

"Lady?"

"So it would seem. I am giving you Mrs. Tulley's version, because it's the only version we got. This lady killer, who seems to be the coldest dish dish around this town, evidently parked her car down the road toward Lexington. One of our cops saw it there when he was making his rounds, but he didn't give it a second glance. It was a cream-colored car, he thinks, but it could be dull yellow, and it could be either a Pontiac, an Olds or a Buick, or maybe just something that looks like one of them. That's what you train a cop for, to be observant. Well, she walked up to the driveway, and either Tulley let her into the house himself or she came around here and in through the windows. They have a housekeeper, who was in the kitchen. They have a maid, who was upstairs. Maybe Tulley knew she was coming. Anyway from when the cop saw the car, we guess that this killer-type broad arrived here at about noon or thereabouts. Ten or fifteen minutes later, Mrs. Tulley comes down. She is dressed and on her way to make a lunch date at the Beverly Wilshire. The lunch date is a Susie Cohn, and we checked that out because she called here to see what was keeping Lenore. But Mrs. Tulley has to have a word with her husband before she leaves the house and she comes to the study, tries the door, finds it locked. 'Mike!' she calls out. 'Open up.' Then she hears a woman's voice, 'The mills of the gods, you—' "

At this point, Detective Beckman consulted his notebook.

"Yeah, this is it, 'The mills of the gods, you dirty louse!' Then Tulley yells, 'What are you talking like that for? Are you nuts? Put away that gun!' Then three shots, deliberate, one, two, three. Then the sound of Tulley's body hitting the floor. Then Mrs. Tulley begins to scream. The cook comes running. The maid comes running. There is Mrs. Tulley screaming and pounding on the door. They think they hear a car start—but it doesn't send any message to them. Then the maid gets the idea to run around to the big sliding windows. As she leaves the house, she sees Tulley's car swing out of the driveway to the right. It's parked on Benedict Canyon Road, where the killer picked up her own car and drove off, just as cool as a cucumber. Apparently, she knocked off Tulley and then walked through the sliding doors into the garden, like a lady should, got into Tulley's car and took off."

"Fingerprints on the gun?"

"Are you kidding?" Beckman said.

"What do you think?"

"What should I think? If Mrs. Tulley let him have it, how did she get around to the other side of a locked door in all of ten seconds, and who drove Tulley's car out and down almost to Lexington? They all seem to have heard the car start, and the maid saw it swing out of the driveway. Mrs. Tulley left the maid upstairs so that accounts for her. The cook is an old Mexican lady, and Doc had to give her the real thing, not a placebo. So what is left?"

"Speculation," Masuto said thoughtfully. "Fascinating speculation."

"You put the two broads together?" Beckman asked.

"At least the two deaths," Masuto replied. "The poor Chief wanted so desperately not to have a murder in Beverly Hills."

"Come in," Lenore Tulley said in reply to Masuto's knock. She was not in bed, but sitting by the window, fully dressed and smoking a cigarette. Unlike the rest of the house, Mrs. Tulley's bedroom was aggressively nonmodern, with a mahogany four-poster bed, a large hooked rug, dotted Swiss curtains, and two very fine and expensive early American chests. While Masuto's knowledge of furniture and decor was by no means encyclopedic or wholly discriminating, he was possessed of good taste and he recognized that while the room was odd, or at least at odds with the rest of the house, it was neither vulgar nor pretentious.

"My hair used to be brown," Lenore Tulley said evenly. "I graduated Smith, class of '56. I am not a bona fide California product, and the furniture in this room was in my room in Connecticut when I was a kid. I am frightened but not grief-stricken, Sergeant. Let me make that plain. It is an ugly thing—and very upsetting too—to have your husband murdered while you are forced to stand on the wrong side of a locked door and do nothing about it. Believe me, if it were possible, I would have saved my husband's life. I disliked him intensely, but I had no desire to see him murdered. If I do any weeping, it is only for myself. One never really recovers from a murder, does one?"

"That all depends," Masuto said, smiling slightly. "The victim never recovers, does he? The murderer sometimes recovers, I suppose. The innocent bystander—well—tell me, if you disliked Mike Tulley so, why did you remain married to him?"

She shrugged. "That's almost too complex to unravel. We separated twice. I am very wealthy—much more than he—but more recently. My father died last year, and I inherited a great deal. There's a community property law in this state. I was not in love with anyone else. I am neurotic as hell and I see an analyst five times a week, and in this rotten social blister called Los Angeles, there's a certain value in being married to a TV star. There's no other status out here. Also, Mike made divorce a rough thing—"

"Then generally speaking, his death benefits and liberates you," Masuto said softly, not knowing what reaction this would evoke from her.

But she only shrugged and nodded. "If you want to look at it that way. I suppose poor Mike made it a little easier for me. I don't know."

"And the murder—can you talk about it now?"

"Why not?"

"Dr. Baxter said you were hysterical."

"So I was upset. That idiot doctor of yours gave me a couple of aspirin. He partakes of a general Beverly Hills belief in the stupidity of women. I'm all right now."

"As I understand it, you were on your way out to make a luncheon date and you knocked at the door of the study. You were coming from upstairs?"

"That's right."

"From this room?"

"Yes."

"How long had you been here in this room?"

"About an hour—dressing, makeup. My maid, Binnie, was with me—not to help me dress. I can dress perfectly well by myself and I prefer to. But Binnie had a fight yesterday with some stupid kid she's dating, and she was crying on my shoulder."

"You left her in the room when you went out?"

"No, she followed me out on the landing and began to whine about what should she do."

"Giving you an absolutely perfect alibi," Masuto reflected.

"Well, don't hate me for that, Sergeant. No one will believe it. By tonight, everyone will have made up his or her mind that I killed poor Mike."

"I don't think so. Now, you knocked on the door. Did you hear the woman's voice immediately?"

"No, there was an interval of silence. I suppose you could count ten. Then that crazy voice."

"Crazy? Why crazy?"

"That's it. I don't know."

"But you said crazy voice. Why?"

"Because it was different, I suppose. A high, hysterical voice. It shook and trembled. I just never heard a voice like that before."

"Then it did not remind you of anyone you know?"

"Maybe. I am not sure."

"Look, Mrs. Tulley, either it did remind you or it did not. Which is it?"

"It reminded me. It reminded me of someone's voice."

"Who's?"

"I don't know."

"Dear lady, please. Be reasonable. If it reminded you of a voice, you must know who it reminded you of."

"I don't."

"All right. Was the voice mocking? Hateful?"

"Mocking, I would say."

"And your husband's voice?"

"Afraid. Oh, my God, he was so afraid—you know, I can't feel any real grief and yet it breaks my heart. He was so afraid." She began to cry and went over to one of the chests for a fresh handkerchief.

"Are you all right?" Masuto asked.

"Quite. Go on, please. I want to see the bitch who did this drawn and quartered. Why? What gave her the right? Because a man's a louse? If you go around killing every man who is a louse to some dame, then you'll end the male population, period! I hate her. Tulley—Tulley was just a permanent adolescent, an all-American boy who never grew up, just like every other all-American boy. Why did she kill him? He wasn't even a real, high-class louse. He was only a slob, a good-looking TV slob."

"What bitch?" Masuto asked. "Samantha?"

She studied him narrowly for a moment. "What do you know about Samantha?"

"A bit here. A bit there. What do you know about her?"

She cried a bit again, and then she dried her eyes and said, "I wish I was like you, Sergeant."

"How is that?"

"Japanese. Out of it. So I could stand back and look at it. You must get some kind of special kick out of looking at a sewer."

"I live in the same sewer," Masuto said. "Also, I'm a Nisei. Here I am and here I live. I would like to talk about Samantha."

"Oh, I just bet you would!"

"Will you?"

"You are damn right I will. Talk and anything else that will put a rope around that bitch's neck. Shall I tell you something, Mr. Detective? I had not seen my father for two years, but when he died it was the worst thing that ever happened to me until now. Maybe worse, because I loved him and I could never break down the wall between us. Do you know who I ran to the day he died?"

"Al Greenberg?"

"That's right, Al Greenberg. And that rotten bitch murdered Al Greenberg and now she murdered Mike."

"When did you find out about Samantha?"

"Last night. After you left. It was a stinking, dirty mess, just the way this whole thing is. I don't know how to tell it to you."

"Any way. Try. I'm not a human being. I'm a cop."

"He accused me of being Samantha, Sergeant. Can you imagine? He accused me of being Samantha."

"Well, that's not so strange. He was overwrought, terrified, filled with guilt. Did you know about Samantha at that point? When he accused you?"

"No. I did not. Furthermore, I made him understand that when he and his anthropoid buddies were having their gangshag, I was in Smith College in western Massachusetts. And then that fool—that poor fool had the nerve to ask me whether I could prove it."

"Then you knew what had happened to Samantha?"

"No. Not then. I'm mixing up the sequence last night—that's because I'm upset."

"I understand," Masuto said. "He accused you of being Samantha, but you did not know what he meant?"

"Exactly. I said to him, 'Mike, are you nuts?' Oh, I was no joy. I hate myself. But I did not know he was going to be killed. I said, 'Mike, I always knew you were a louse, but I always figured you for a louse with marbles. Do I have to tell you that I am your own miserable, everloving wife, Lenore? Smith College, class of '56. Have you really flipped? Haven't you looked at my yearbook? What kind of a nut are you? And who is this Samantha?' Then he wanted out of the whole thing, but I wouldn't let go. Then he told me. I think he enjoyed telling me."

"The dressing room, the part in a TV show, the arrangements that Sidney Burke made?"

"Right down the line. Oh, he was a daisy, my Mike—right down the line. Do you mind if I have a drink?"

"Go ahead."

"Will you join me?"

Masuto shook his head. Lenore Tulley went to a cedar chest, opened it and by that motion caused a small but well-equipped bar to rise out of its depths. She poured herself a straight vodka and threw it down her throat.

"You're sure you won't join me?" she asked Masuto again. "You know— you're a good-looking cop. How old are you?"

"Old enough not to drink in a lady's bedroom while I am on duty."

"How about that? Shouldn't you have a stenographer in here taking notes and all that?"

"No. You're not a suspect—"

Detective Sy Beckman knocked on the door, and then entered. "Masao," he said, "what about the news boys talking to Mrs. Tulley? Also the CBS and ABC and NBC trucks are outside. They all want Mrs. Tulley."

Masuto looked inquiringly at Lenore Tulley, who shook her head and said, "I have had it. They can drop dead, the lot of them. Los Angeles, farewell. They can get lost in the smog."

"You'll have to talk to them sooner or later," Beckman said.

"Then later."

"Tell them she is prostrated and unable to talk to anyone."

"No!" she exclaimed.

"Tell them that," Masuto said.

Beckman left, and Lenore Tulley said to Masuto, "You got a hell of a lot of nerve for a—"

"For a Jap?"

"Just don't push me around. I have had enough of being pushed around."

Masuto rose abruptly and started for the door.

"Where are you going?" she demanded.

"To look for whoever killed your husband, instead of pushing you around."

"Oh, stop being a horse's ass and sit down," she said. "I never met a male who didn't have all the engaging tactics of a frustrated six-year-old. You're married, right?"

"Right."

"I never met a decent man who wasn't. Only the slobs are *libres*."

"Libres?"

"That's what they call the cabs in Mexico. It means they're free for customers."

"Murphy Anderson is sitting down in your living room."

"Let him set. You keep testing, don't you?"

"That's what they pay me for, Mrs. Tulley—"

"Call me Lenore. You've moved into my bedroom." She poured herself another vodka and tossed it down, shivered, and said to Masuto, "What are you, anyway? I mean, Christian or Mormon or ancestor worship or what?"

"I am a Buddhist, Mrs. Tulley. You've been married six years. No children?"

"That is none of your damn business. Christ, maybe it is. I don't know what is your business. I was married to Mike. You know, he kept a little book of every dame he took to bed, one hundred and twenty-seven entries, names, places, dates and physical descriptions, just in case he should confuse them."

"He showed it to you?"

"No, my dear Detective Masuto. I got at it when he was away. Dirty curiosity. And you want me to have kids with that? Oh, no—thank God, that's one I missed." She stared at him then with awakened interest. "Good Lord, you still think that maybe I am Samantha, don't you?"

"No, you're not Samantha. But suppose we take four of your friends, Mrs. Tulley—Trude Burke, Phoebe Greenberg, Stacy Anderson and Arlene Cotter—"

"My friends?"

"You know them well, don't you?"

"What is well? Arlene Cotter is a bitch with the mouth of a snake. Stacy folds her hands across her belly and she drinks too much. She's contented Beverly Hills. Phoebe Greenberg—well, no one knows her. I don't even think Phoebe knows her. The day after she married Al, she became Great Lady of Beverly Hills. It's the only part she ever had and she decided she would play it better without any speaking lines. And Trude Burke is a little tramp."

"Oh? What do you mean when you call someone a tramp?"

She downed a third vodka and replied, "I mean I'm being a bitch. And if you don't know what a tramp is, my inscrutable Oriental, look it up in Mencken on slang."

"And which of the four is Samantha, Mrs. Tulley?"

"You must be kidding."

"Not at all. Will you answer a question truthfully—one question?"

"You're impugning me, and I no longer like you, Mr. Chan. I know damn well what you intend to ask me. You are going to say, 'My dear Mrs. Tulley, is one of them Samantha?' The answer is yes. One of them is Samantha. You're goddamn right one of them is!"

"Which one?"

Lenore Tulley shook her head. She was a little drunk and she was becoming thoughtful.

"Which one?"

"Fuzz," she answered with distaste. "What am I doing here in my own bedroom with an Oriental fuzz playing psychological games with me? Drop dead, Mr. Detective."

"You said you wanted to get your husband's killer."

"Did I? What could I have been thinking of? Killing Mike was a public service. She deserves a medal."

In the bedlam downstairs, Murphy Anderson sat like a lost child, hunched over in his chair, warding off the reporters and hiding from the TV cameras, which were still barred from the house.

Masuto watched him as Beckman said, "Do you want to talk to the maid, housekeeper?"

"No. Get their statements."

"There's no one you want to arrest?" Beckman asked hopefully.

"No—no one."

"Let me get out of here, would you?" Murphy Anderson asked.

"You don't want to talk to the widow?"

"No, I don't want to talk to the widow. I only want to get out of here."

"All right," Masuto nodded. "I think I have had enough of this place too. I'll drive you over to your office. Now remember, they will crawl all over you when you leave here. Just walk straight ahead with me. Say nothing."

"I'm a lawyer," Anderson growled.

"Of course you are. How stupid of me!"

Out in the sunshine, they pushed past reporters, the curious, and the TV people. A cop came alongside of Masuto and said softly, "They got a call downtown from a Mrs. Baker. She wants you should drop by and talk to her."

"All right. I'll get to it."

He got Murphy Anderson to his car and into it, and then they were worming their way through the traffic, down Benedict Canyon Drive to Sunset. Anderson lay back in his seat, his eyes closed.

"How stupid of me," Masuto repeated. "Forgetting that you are a lawyer and asking you whether you thought your wife was Samantha. A nasty question, and an invitation to give evidence against your wife."

"Evidence? What the hell, nothing I say to you means anything in a court!"

"And what does Tulley's death do to your company?"

"It's a blow. It's a shot in the belly. It means that the show is over. No more 'Lonesome Rider.' Well, we're insured—I mean Mike was insured in our favor."

"How much?"

"A quarter of a million dollars."

"That's a comfort, isn't it?"

"It's a comfort, as you say, but we're still in the red. We lose a lot more than a quarter of a million."

"Well, to a cop such numbers have no practical meaning. I do apologize for an inconsiderate question. But tell me, please, who do you think is Samantha?"

"Now that's nicely put, isn't it, Sergeant? Who do I think is Samantha? I can tell you who Samantha is—she's a little tramp who bit off more than she could chew. I'm sick of all this weeping over a stupid kid who invites disaster. But who is Samantha? The answer is no one. This whole Samantha kick is a phony."

"Then you don't think Samantha murdered Tulley?"

"I do not."

"And you don't think that one of your associates might be married to Samantha?"

"Nuts."

They were at Wilshire now. Masuto said that he would like to come up to the offices for just a moment. Anderson protested only a bit.

"The whole world has fallen in. There are only twelve hundred things for me to do, Sergeant. Why don't you give me a break for today."

"Murderers are always inconsiderate. But Detective Beckman tells me that Cotter is in the office, and I would like to have a word with him."

But it turned out that Cotter had been there and left.

"Did he say where he was going?" Anderson asked his secretary.

"I imagined he was going over to poor Mr. Tulley's home."

"When was that?"

"At least a half hour ago. I had two ham-on-ryes and two coffees sent up. They're inside. The coffee is still warm. I felt that perhaps you would not have time to eat."

"You felt right," Anderson replied, leading Masuto into his office.

The sandwiches were on a tray on his desk. "Actually, they are ham and cheese. The world caves in, but you go on eating—especially when you're a compulsive eater. That's my problem. You know, I'm becoming fond of you, Sergeant. That snotty Oriental manner is intriguing. How about I put you in a TV pilot? We got to have something to replace the 'Lonesome Rider,' who's plenty lonesome now, believe me. Ever thought of being an actor?"

"Who hasn't?" Masuto smiled. "It's the occupational day dream of Los Angeles. I have a cousin who works all the time. He's that heavy-set, sadistic General who always sits at a table eating, and says, 'Take American out, shoot him.' My wife's sister was in the Brando film."

"Have a sandwich."

"I am honored," Masuto said, taking the sandwich gratefully. He was starved. He bit into it and chewed thoughtfully and then said, "Didn't anyone like Tulley?"

"Everyone loved him. He received over a thousand letters a week—fans. They adored him. In Chicago, they tore off his pants."

"Just between you and me, Mr. Anderson—who do you think killed him?"

"Have some coffee."

"Of course," Masuto said, accepting the coffee, "that's the trouble with this case. Every one of you knows who the killer is. Maybe the candidate isn't the same in every case, but you all know. Only, there's one thing you apparently can't get into your respective skulls—that this killer is a homicidal maniac, and that he will kill again and again and again."

"That's your guess."

"No. That the way the symbols are arranged—but you don't believe in symbols anymore, and you don't see them. You are a people enlightened—"

The loudspeaker intercom on Anderson's desk crackled at that moment, and his secretary said, "I have a call for Detective Sergeant Masuto."

"Any name?" Masuto asked.

"Oh, yes. She said you would know her. Her name is Samantha."

Anderson reached for the phone, but Masuto gripped his arm and said quickly, "Do you have a private line in the office?"

"There, in the corner," pointing to a phone on an end table next to the couch.

"Get on it. Call the operator. Use my name, give her the main number, and trace us. Quick."

Then, as Anderson ran across the room to the other phone, Masuto lifted the one on the desk and said, "Hello. This is Sergeant Masuto."

"All right, Masuto—this is Samantha. Now listen carefully. I am not going to repeat." The voice was the precise, controlled theatrically trained voice of a professional.

"Now wait a minute. Let me get my pad."

"Come off it, Masuto. I know you're having the call traced right now. That will take you at least eleven minutes. I don't propose to give you more than five."

"You're optimistic if you think we can trace a call in eleven minutes. How do I know you're Samantha?"

"How? Because I know what went on in that lousy trailer room when that little louse, Sidney Burke, arranged for his gangshag."

"A good many ladies seem to know," Masuto said.

"No, no. Not at all. Let me give you the rundown, Sergeant. Max Green was in that room, and he's dead—"

"Who is Max Green?" Masuto interrupted.

"Interrupt me once more, mister, and I hang up. Now are you ready to listen?"

"Go ahead."

"Max Green was there, and he's dead. A rotten little creep called Fred Saxton was there, and he's dead. Al Greenberg was there and he's dead. Mike Tulley was there, and he's dead. Which leaves Jack Cotter, Murphy Anderson and Sidney Burke. Four down, three to go. You know, Sergeant, just to convince that heathen and doubting Oriental mind of yours, the gun that killed Mike Tulley was a 32-caliber Smith and Wesson. It was his wife's gun. I shot him three times in the chest. None of that has been on the air yet. Check me and see. As for the other three—tell them to expect me."

She hung up, and Masuto replaced the phone and said to Anderson, "Let it go, Mr. Anderson. She's off."

"Was it Samantha?" he asked eagerly.

"That's what she said."

"What else did she say?"

Almost word for word, Masuto repeated what the woman had said—all of it, leaving nothing out, and watching Murphy Anderson's face as he spoke. At the end, he said to Anderson, "Who is Fred Saxton and who is Mike Green?"

"Oh, my God," Anderson whispered.

"Who are they?"

"Fred Saxton was the production manager on the 'Lonesome Rider.' Max Green was the assistant producer."

"Isn't that sort of the same job?"

"Sort of."

"Then I presume they're both dead?"

"Yes, they're dead. We had changed the title from assistant producer to production manager and then we gave the job to Fred Saxton."

"How did they die, Mr. Anderson?"

"Max died a normal death. My God, this thing is insane enough without making it crazier. Max died of a heart attack, over a year ago."

"How old was he?"

"I don't know—forty-six, forty-seven."

"Then it wasn't so normal, was it?"

"Why? It's young, but people die of heart attacks in their forties. It happens."

"And how did Fred Saxton die?"

"One of these stupid accidents—" He broke off, rose suddenly, and went to a little bar in the room and poured himself a glass of brandy.

"You want a little brandy, Sergeant?"

"No. So maybe it was not an accident. What happened?"

Anderson drank the brandy, wincing and making faces. "His skull was crushed. On one of the sound stages we rent over at World Wide. A hundred-pound sandbag counterweight fell from the beam where it was rigged. He never knew what hit him. Died instantly. Terrible—just terrible."

"I thought everything was lead counterweights and electric winches today."

"This was an old stage. Those bags could have been up there for years—I don't know. But it could have been an accident too."

"I suppose so," Masuto admitted.

"Can I tell Jack and Sidney about what she said?"

"Why not? A few minutes ago, you refused to give an inch about our Samantha. Have you changed your mind?"

"I don't know," Anderson replied.

CHAPTER
FOUR

PEGGY GROTON

When Masuto entered City Hall on Santa Monica Boulevard, he was already aware of a glow of notoriety in which the city would alternately squirm and bask. Beverly Hills was hardly a place for violent murder. He sometimes thought of the place as a toy city, with a toy police force to guard people who dreamed away their lives, but those were very private thoughts and not proper to any bona fide policeman. Usually, he came and went unnoticed, but today reporters tried to buttonhole him, and curious ones, town bureaucrats and employees, begged to be let in on the facts.

His chief also begged. "What I want to know, Masao, is do the two deaths connect? Do we have some kind of a double killing on our hands?"

"Maybe a triple killing," Masuto said. "This is one with a taste for blood and death. This is a demon. But you don't believe in demons, do you?"

"I also do not buy any high-class Oriental philosophy at this moment. I also don't like a cop who gets on a connecting bug and goes off on the mass-killer kick. Just before you came in, it was on the wire that some dame goes off Mulholland Drive on the Valley side. You'll connect that up too."

"What dame?"

"I don't know. It's Hollywood anyway. Haven't we got enough trouble? Let the city worry about it."

"Who's up there?"

"I don't know, rescue service and city cops, I suppose. What's the difference?"

"Did the car burn?"

"How do I know if the car burned?"

"Chief, do me a favor," Masuto said, trying to control his excitement. "Believe me—something is happening, something is working out. Get them on the radiophone and tell them to hold everything until I get there. Not to touch the car. I don't mean they should not take the woman to the hospital—"

"The woman's dead, Saito."

"Of course—of course. Will you phone them?"

"They're city cops—all right, I'll phone. I had to go and hire a Japanese cop. But what about all this? Where are we? Was Al Greenberg murdered?"

"He was murdered."

"You're sure?"

"No one's ever sure about such a killing."

"And Tulley?"

"The same killer. That's a very strong opinion. More opinion is that the same civilized joker murdered a third man, one Fred Saxton, on the World Wide lot about seven weeks ago. Perhaps a fourth man—that waits to be seen. And nothing is going to wish it away."

* . *

Mulholland Drive was a high rib out of a sea of yellow smog. To Masuto, as always, the sight was unreal and hideous, and his eyes burned. He parked on the edge of a snarl of cars and people that had stopped traffic entirely, and only halfhearted efforts were being made to put the traffic through. As Masuto learned and as he had expected, there were no witnesses. The rescue car was there and two police cars and a sheriff's car and the crawling traffic. And eight motorcycles. The riders were between eighteen and twenty-four years old. They were all bearded and most of them were stripped to the waist. Motorcycle boots, black leather trousers and cigars. They sprawled by their bikes, surly, angry, frustrated. Masuto walked past them to the edge of the slope. The car was about a hundred and fifty yards below, not burnt but thoroughly smashed. Stretcher bearers were crawling carefully up the slope with the woman's body. She was strapped into the stretcher, her face covered, so apparently she was dead. Some cops were around the car.

Lieutenant Pete Bones of the Los Angeles police saw Masuto and called to him, "Howdy, Masao. I thought you had your own stiffs to bury."

"When death comes to town, he stays for a while, doesn't he?"

"That's nicely put. What are you doing up here?"

"Who are the Hell's Angels boys?" pointing to the motorcycle riders.

"They saw the car tumble from around the bend, across that little canyon there."

"Did they see it leave the road?"

Bones shook his head. "They saw one turn and then it come to rest against that rock—the way they tell it."

Masuto nodded thoughtfully, closed his eyes for a long moment, and then nodded again.

"Well, what?" Bones demanded. "It's a Mulholland Drive accident. The books are full of them. If a month went by without someone killing himself on this crazy road, I'd ask for my pension. You live in a crazy town, you get crazy deaths. Look at those bareass lunatics on their damn motor-cycles."

"They are more comprehensible and less terrifying than that car down there," Masuto said.

"Why? Furthermore, what does your boss mean, hold it? What should we hold?"

"I didn't want you to drag the car away."

"Without a crane? Furthermore—ah, the hell with it. You want to see the body?"

"Yes. Just to satisfy myself that her skull was caved in from behind—maybe back of the temple."

A cop in plain clothes pulled himself up on to the road, and Pete Bones said to him, "Kelly, this here is Masao Masuto from the Beverly force and he has got himself a sort of crystal ball. He says the lady's skull is bashed in from behind."

The man called Kelly gave Masuto a sharp glance and said hello suspiciously.

"Let's go have a look," he told them.

They walked over to where the ambulance man was eas-ing the stretcher into the ambulance.

"How did she die?" Bones asked him.

"Isn't it obvious, officer? You go over Mulholland in one of those tin cans and you die."

"I mean what happened to her physically? And don't be a wiseguy."

"She got banged up. Broken bones, shock, internal injuries, and heart failure."

"What about her skull?"

"Bad fracture."

"How bad?"

"Her skull was smashed in. In nontechnical language, she was struck a hard blow slightly behind her right temple—a very hard blow."

"From the accident?"

"How else?"

"We're asking you!" Kelly snarled. "Don't be such a goddamn wiseguy. How did it happen? Could it happen from the accident?"

"Please uncover her," Masuto asked.

"OK—OK. Don't get excited. You ask me could this skull injury happen from such an accident. Jesus Christ, just look over the edge at that car down there."

He was uncovering the body, when one of the motorcyclists walked over and demanded, "What have you got on us? Every goddamn thing happens in LA County, you got to pin it on us. We want to move on."

"Drop dead," Kelly said.

"Sure. That's the prerogative of fuzz. I answer you back, and you break a pair of brass knucks across my mouth—"

"What the hell is eating this creep?"

"Why don't you just simmer down—" Bones began, but then he and Masuto noticed that the boy's eyes were fixed on the face of the dead woman.

"You know her, buster?" Bones asked him.

"I know nothing. I don't even know my right name. I don't even know how I got here."

"Now just a minute, young feller," Masuto said. "This is not my own place. I'm here as a guest of these officers. But I think they will go along with me if I put my oar in." He glanced at Bones and Kelly who nodded slightly, and Masuto went on, "On the one hand—treat us as people, we treat you as people. I don't really care if you tour the country in a jock—until you break some law. I don't know of any law you broke. Be decent and you ride away from here in ten minutes, because I'll put myself on record for you. But if you make it hard for them, they'll make it hard for you. Is that all right?" he asked Kelly, who nodded without answering.

"What do you want?" the bearded boy asked.

"Who is she?"

"So I know her—so ten thousand guys knew her. She's an old stripper called Peggy Groton. I guess she's almost forty years old. Ran out of steam. She became a hooker, but what's the percentage for an old hooker in this town? You go down on the strip and bend a finger and the chickies come running. Who needs to pay? That's all I know about her. I caught her act, it was lousy. Then I been to parties where she performed and after that for a couple of bucks she would make it. She turns my stomach—lousy whore."

"Sure, she turns your stomach," Bones said.

"I'd like to turn your stomach," Kelly said. "I sure could turn your stomach."

"You said you'd let us go if I cooperated."

"Who the hell wants you?" Bones asked with disgust.

"Is she a user?" Masuto asked.

"How do I know?"

"She's a user," the ambulance man replied. "Or was. You always lose your tenses with these stiffs. Look." He raised her arm, pointed to a cluster of punctures. "She was a big one—user and loser. They all are—all alike."

"But you didn't know she had a habit?" Kelly said to the bearded kid.

"How should I know?"

"Let him go," Masuto said tiredly. "Let the lot of them go. They are unreal. They play a game with you. They irritate you. They take our eyes away from the target."

"Let them go. You tell me, I jump to it," Kelly scowled.

"Oh, hell, let them go," Bones said. "If Masao says they are clear of this, they're clear of it. Send them away. They make me itch and want to scratch just to look at them."

Kelly went to tell them to move on, and Bones said to Masao, "Enough?"

Masuto was looking at a drawn, tired, ravaged face that might once have been lovely. Once. Even in death, Peggy Groton was robbed of identity, of meaning. He shivered.

"Yes, you can take her away."

They bundled the stretcher unceremoniously into the ambulance and drove off. Then the motorcycles roared by, the riders leaving a string of Anglo-Saxon words behind them. One of the rescue men came up the slope with Peggy Groton's purse and handed it to Bones.

"Want to have a look?" Bones asked Masuto.

"There should be about five hundred dollars in there. There might also be the murderer's address and phone number. Maybe. Maybe not. You know, Pete, this monster we are contending with has made every error, every stupid play that a killer can make—and still we can't pin it or stop it."

"And you say there's half a grand in here—right here in the bag of a broken down hooker."

"Maybe. Maybe not."

"X-ray eyes," said Kelly. "You going to tell us she was murdered?"

"She was."

"How? Who?"

"I'll tell you how—"

Bones had meanwhile opened the purse, and now he was holding out a stack of twenty dollar bills.

"—probably with a lug wrench that the murderer lifted from a filling station. Then, I guess, he threw it down in the yucca there." Masuto bent, picked up a rock, and flung it down the slope. It landed a long way down, far beyond the car. "Somewhere around there—"

"And the money?"

"She was paid off, God help her."

"Six hundred dollars," Bones said.

"She was good," Masuto said thoughtfully.

"How do you know?"

"Names—addresses?"

Bones held up a worn address book. "Do you want to go through it?"

Masuto shrugged. "When you're through with it, I'd appreciate a list of the contents. You might send it up to City Hall."

"Don't you want to see it?"

Masuto shook his head.

"You mean because it's our murder?" Kelly demanded hotly.

"Who said it's murder?" Bones reminded him. "Ain't we got enough problems?"

"He says so. He says the name of the killer is in that book."

"No, I didn't say that at all," Masuto objected. "Still—"

He reached for the little book, riffled through it, saw nothing to catch his eye and then gave it back to Bones. He walked over to his car, and Bones called after him,

"Be in touch!"

"I will," Masuto promised.

* * *

The day was wearing through. Masao Masuto had that feeling—not extraordinary for a Buddhist—that the day was a repeat. It had all happened before. It had happened a thousand times before; perhaps nothing changed, perhaps a little changed. He was a stranger in a strange place. He drove east on Mulholland Drive to its connection with Laurel Canyon Boulevard, past the housing developments on top of the skinny ridge of hill. On the Valley side the smog was yellow and noxious; on the other side, on his right, the buttocks of the lower hills were gashed and sheared for the ninety-thousand-dollar homes, where you could sleep above the smog. It occurred to him idly, but with certainty, that he had once known another existence, lived and perished. This was his purgatory. He smiled rather sadly at the thought, remembered the face of Peggy Groton, hooker and onetime stripper, and then turned right onto Laurel Canyon Boulevard. His mind was open and receptive. When he reached Hollywood Boulevard he knew what to do, and he turned east and then south on La Brea.

The bungalow on Sixth Street was even more forlorn revisited than it had been on first sight. In itself—its form, shape, its single tired palm tree in the postage stamp front yard—in itself it was all the brief history, the tawdry illusion that was Hollywood. Just as its mistress was the past of Hollywood, the single long generation that had turned some bright-eyed young girl into this slatternly rooming-house keeper.

She must have been sitting by the window and waiting, for she opened the door, smiled slightly and said, "I knew you'd come back, Mr. Moto."

"How did you know?"

"Horoscopes and stuff. Anyway, I like you. I had dreams about you. That brought you back. What shall I call you? I can't keep on being a crumby racist and calling you Mr. Chan and Mr. Moto. It makes me ashamed of myself."

"Call me Masao."

"All right, Masao. Will you join me in a cup of tea?" She was quite serious. She was dressed now; her hair was combed; and Masuto liked her better than ever. He did not seek for reasons why. He allowed himself to like her because he liked her.

"I would be honored," he said, bowing slightly. "May I revert to poor politeness? I would find nothing more refreshing than a cup of tea."

She led him into her kitchen, and he was pleased by its cleanliness, by the fact of a modern refrigerator, a good electric stove, and a new vinyl floor. Obviously, the kitchen was all that she retained as her home. She brewed tea and sliced up a grocery store poundcake. But she did not offer him a drink of liquor or take one herself.

"I want you to know that I got an attitude toward cops," she said. "I don't like cops. I think that's a healthy attitude, but that's from my point of view."

"I understand. Why do you exclude me?"

"I don't know. Maybe because you don't seem to be a part of this lousy establishment. That's a nice word. When I was a kid, that word didn't exist for us. But it says something. Don't you agree?"

"It says something."

"And you figure you'll come back here and start talking to me and maybe jog my memory and I'll remember about Samantha."

"Possibly."

"What do you want her for, Masao? When they put a high-class educated Beverly Hills cop like you on something, and you keep asking questions, then it must be pretty big. Does it connect up with Mike Tulley's murder?"

He watched her without answering.

"It's been on the radio. Look, sonny, everyone knows, but how you work that poor kid into it is more than I can take. Is the tea all right?"

"Fine."

"No sugar?"

"No."

"You know, I read a lot," she said.

"That's a habit an actress gets into. To wait and wait, to be destroyed and frustrated endlessly—"

"How did you know I was an actress, Masao?"

"That's not such a brilliant guess in Hollywood, is it?"

"There are old bums in Hollywood who aren't actresses."

"You're not an old bum," he said sharply. "Don't lower yourself. Don't denigrate yourself."

"Then don't play games with me, Masao."

"You think I come here and taste your tea to play games with you? If you think that, then you are most mistaken."

She regarded him thoughtfully and silently for a while, and during that time, he sipped his tea and said nothing. Then she tasted her own tea, and asked him, "You're not a Christian, are you?"

"No. I am a Buddhist."

"That's different, isn't it?"

"Yes, quite different"

"How?"

He shook his head and smiled.

"That's no answer."

"How can I answer you?" he asked seriously.

"You can try."

Masuto held out his hand above the table, the fingers spread. "To you, Mrs. Dolly Baker," he said softly, "skin is something that separates a human hand, a human being from the rest of the universe. Is that so?"

She nodded.

"As I think, the skin connects me with the rest of the universe. Do you understand?"

For almost a full minute, she sat in silence; and then she said to him, "I told you before that I read a lot. You pick up odds and ends of things."

"What sort of thing?"

"Like the expression the British have for it. They call it a 'copper's nark.' That's good. It sounds like what it is. What do we call it? A fink? A stoolie?"

"I must know about Samantha. Human lives depend on that. Can you say that you will let anyone go to his death if you have the power to change it? Can you sit in judgement? Can you exercise the power of life and death?"

Tears welled into her eyes. Her cheeks became puffy. Suddenly her moment of competence was over and she became a fat, frightened old lady.

"You knew the name all the time," he said.

She nodded.

"Do you want to tell me."

"Her name was Gertrude Bestner, poor kid. God help her. God help her whatever she's into. She was such a loser—"

He walked into the Chief's office, and Kelly and Bones were there, the three of them angry; the Chief annoyed angry, Bones puzzled angry, and Kelly burning angry. Kelly did not like him; Kelly did not like the way he carried himself. Masuto could put himself in Kelly's place. Kelly would tolerate a Nisei, but there are limits to toleration. Kelly and Bones were in Beverly Hills now, and they did not like Beverly Hills or its pocket-size police force. That was understandable.

"You got explaining to do, Masao," the Chief said.

"We all have. That is a condition of mankind."

"Screw the philosophy," said Kelly. "We found the lug wrench."

"The what?"

Bones was the least angry of the three, the most intrigued, the most puzzled. "You remember, Masao, you said that she was murdered with a lug wrench. Then you tossed that rock down into the canyon. Well, we put everyone we had down there and combed out the place. We killed two rattlers—can you imagine?"

"I seen one on Mulholland a week ago," Kelly said. "The hell with that! I want to know how come he knew this broad was knocked over with a lug wrench."

"You got explaining to do, Masao," the Chief repeated seriously.

"I didn't know it," Masuto said. "I guessed."

Kelly threw a flat hand at him and said, "Sure, you guessed. First you guessed she was scragged. Then you guessed the lug wrench. Then you guessed the money in her purse. Balls! That's just too goddamn much guessing for me, and you know what I think about your guesses? I think they're phony as you are!"

"Wait a minute—hold on!" the Chief snapped. "You're in my house now, Kelly. Don't dirty my floors."

"To hell with whose house I'm in! I'm talking about murder—murder that took place in the City of Los Angeles. We got a corpus and we got a murder weapon, and we got enough blood and hair on the lug wrench to link them together. So don't tell me about spitting on the floor. Just tell me where your cop fits in."

Face white, the Chief rose up behind his desk and said very softly, in a voice that Masuto and every other cop on the force had learned to dread, "Just who the hell do you think you're talking to, Kelly! Let me tell you something. I try to be a good neighbor, but one more yap out of you that anyone here is trying to bunco you, and so help me God, I'll lock you up. Make trouble for me you may, but right now you're in Beverly Hills and just keep that in mind."

Kelly was as white as the Chief, and watching them, Masuto felt calm and detached. He himself had been forgotten; they were two men making a power play, and what they felt was their honor had been irritated, scraped bare. Now Bones stepped over to Kelly and took his arm and said, "Just work easy." And then he said to the Chief, "So Kelly's got a big temper and a big mouth. I been his partner six years, Chief. He's a good cop, I am, Masao is. I don't know what we're ripping at each other for."

"Forget it," the Chief growled. "What have you got to say for yourself, Masao?"

"Nothing explains intuition," Masuto said. "Shall I try to turn it into reason?"

"Try," the Chief said drily.

"Murder explodes, a sort of chain reaction. We make it too difficult to be a human being, and then something snaps and the person is no longer a person but a killer, and this thing keeps snapping and the killer kills. We are filled with horror, because we inhabit the same unreasonable world— and how long can we remain human? The killer has ceased to be human, and I fit myself into the killer's world. Now I will try to see with his eyes, feel with his nerves, and move as he moves. So everything becomes something else. A car goes over the shoulder on Mulholland Drive. I see it with the eyes of the killer and it becomes a part of the logic of the killer and his progress through our world—"

"But cars go over Mulholland," Bones objected. "It happens every day."

"Then I could be wrong. But what are the odds at this moment? At exactly this moment? I could be wrong, but the odds are that I am right."

"And the lug wrench?"

It was lying on a sheet of paper on the Chief's desk, a garage tool, three-quarters at one end and half an inch at the other, about a foot long and roughly straight.

"You can pick one up in a garage. The attendant turns his back and you're armed. How many things like that are lying around? It could have been a monkey wrench, but the odds are on this. And the money is no mystery either. She had to be paid off in advance."

"Then why didn't the killer take back his roll?"

"No time, maybe. The killer could hear the kids on their motorbikes. Or maybe the money didn't mean enough for the killer to try."

"Six yards and you toss it away like confetti!" Kelly snorted.

"Why was she killed?" the Chief asked.

"The payoff was one thing, but the killer couldn't take any chances."

"OK, Masao—who killed her?" the Chief asked.

"I don't know."

"Why don't you guess," Kelly said.

"Tomorrow I'll guess," Masuto told him.

"But you know," the Chief insisted.

"I don't know."

"Masao, if you're playing games with me—"

"I told you I don't know."

"But you tie this in with Greenberg and Tulley?"

"Both of them. They were both murdered by the same person." He hesitated, and the Chief caught it and said, "It was three, before the car went over."

"All right—you want me out on a limb, I'll go there. His name was Fred Saxton. He was 49 years old and he was production manager for Al Greenberg. He was murdered out at the Wide World studios seven weeks ago."

"I know the case," Bones said. "That was an accident. A counterweight came loose and hit him."

"It wasn't an accident," Masuto said.

"How the hell do you know?" Kelly demanded. "We don't have a police force in LA—we just got a bunch of bums, bums who sit around on their asses all day and do nothing. We don't bother investigating a case. No, sir. A guy gets his head broken with a sandbag, we don't give it a second thought. It never occurs to us that maybe someone scrags him. We just write it down as an accident. That's because we're stupid."

"Who's bugging you?" Bones demanded. "Every accident is an accident only until you know better."

"But this joker knows better than anyone."

"It happens."

"The hell it happens," Kelly said. "I'm not satisfied—not one bit. And speaking for myself, you haven't heard the end of this—not by a long shot."

He went to the desk and began to wrap the lug wrench in the piece of paper.

"Fingerprints?" Masuto asked innocently.

"Fingerprints? You been reading too much Fu Manchu."

He put the lug wrench in his pocket and stamped out. Bones stood looking after him hopelessly, and the Chief sat behind his desk, staring moodily at Masuto.

"Do me a favor, would you, Pete?" Masuto asked Bones.

Bones looked at the Chief, then at Masuto, and said, "You know, Masao, you could do me a favor. What do I do about this? A car goes over the shoulder on Mulholland Drive, and I got to come back to the boss with Kelly riding me and tell him how it's a murder, but we can't tell him who did the murder because you won't guess no more."

"Tomorrow."

"And suppose tomorrow you don't want to guess?"

"Masao," the Chief said, "is this the only way you can play it?"

"I have three of them. One is the killer. They all spin threads, like damned little spiders. Three killers, three motives, three possibilities. I think I could guess. Then I guess wrong, and I have done precisely what the killer desires. This killer is not smart—diabolical but not smart. Every mistake in the book. Blunder after blunder, but because we are dealing with a lunatic, even the blunders work."

"Bones, do him his goddamn favor," the Chief said. "And as for you, Masao—you haven't even filed a report."

"When do I write it? In my sleep?"

"What do you want, Masao?" Bones asked him.

"I want to find out what happened to a kid called Samantha Adams. That's her stage name. Her real name is Gertrude Bestner. She was born in 1936 or 1937, and her last known address was here in Los Angeles on Sixth near Gower. I'll give you all the facts and details. The last fix I have on her is 1955, a rooming house on Sixth, run then and now by Mrs. Dolly Baker. So you start with 1955 and bring it up to today or as far as it goes. Where is she? Dead or alive? Doing what? Where was she?"

"You don't want much, do you?"

"I want it tonight."

"You're nuts," Bones said.

"Well, then how soon? Shave the hours, and maybe you give a life to someone."

"Will you back him up, Chief?" Bones asked.

The Chief nodded.

"Tomorrow. Maybe," Bones said. "But only if she stayed in LA. If she took off, maybe a month, a year—or you can kiss your whole project goodby."

"Try?"

"I said I'd try."

"I want it the first moment you have it. I'll keep my band open in the car. The moment you have it, you can phone here, and the dispatcher will give it to me."

"All right. And what do we do with the Peggy Groton thing? Keep it open?"

"You damn well do. It's murder, isn't it?"

"That's what you say, Masao."

"Tomorrow night I'll buy you both a drink."

"Saki—and take me out for one of your Japanese meals."

"If I can fix it with my wife."

"I thought you Japanese—"

"I am a Nisei," Masuto explained.

CHAPTER
FIVE

PHOEBE

GREENBERG

On his way out, the girl at the dispatch desk called after him, "Masao!"

He came back, and she told him that there was a call for him. "A Mrs. Greenberg."

It took him a moment to relate it to a face and a person, and then he took the phone, and a low and pleasant voice said, "Sergeant Masuto, this is Mrs. Greenberg—Phoebe Greenberg. Rabbi Gitlin told me you spoke with him this morning."

"Oh, yes—yes, we had a talk."

"He was impressed with you."

"I was impressed with him," Masuto said.

"He said that you were a friend of my—of my husband."

"Yes, in a way."

"In any way—then I would like you to come to the funeral tomorrow. But that isn't what I called you about. I would like to speak to you, if I might."

"When?"

"Now. Is that possible?"

"In ten minutes—or less. I am leaving now."

But the Chief intercepted him and said, "What about it, Masao? You're way out on a limb and I'm with you."

"I told you, tomorrow."

"I sure as God hope so, Masao."

Even with the interruption, Masuto was at the Greenberg home in eight minutes, and now it was a little after four o'clock in the afternoon. The driveway was full and there were cars in front of the house; and in the living room, Murphy Anderson and his plump wife, Stacy, Jack Cotter alone, and Sidney Burke alone.

They would be off to the chapel later to pay their respects to the deceased. Now they were here to pay their respects to the living.

"Two chapels." Sidney Burke said pointedly. He resented the fact that they were on opposite sides of Beverly Hills, as if he could see no reason on earth why two people in dying should not have the thoughtfulness to be of the same faith.

"Where is Mrs. Greenberg?" Masuto asked.

They explained that she was in the viewing room with Rabbi Gitlin. "I suppose he's some comfort to her," Jack Cotter said, "but the last thing in the world I would have imagined is that Phoebe needed that kind of thing."

"Why?"

"Her relationship with Al—"

"Oh, why don't you shut up, Jack," Anderson interrupted.

"I don't like to be talked to like that," Cotter said coldly.

Stacy Anderson burst out, "Have you met Rabbi Gitlin, Sergeant Masuto? He's absolutely fascinating. He's—"

Rising, Murphy Anderson said, "I think we must go, Stacy, if we want to get to both chapels tonight."

"Poor Lenore," Stacy said, as if she only now remembered that Mike Tulley was dead. "What a dreadful thing she went through. Just imagine—to be trapped on one side of a door while your husband is being murdered by some dreadful woman on the other side of the door. It's perfectly dreadful. Dreadful." She enjoyed the word.

"Sergeant Masuto," Anderson said, "the three of us—Mr. Cotter, Mr. Burke and myself—would like to talk to you tonight. We feel that it's very important."

"Where?"

"My house. I'm on North Rodeo. Say about nine?"

"I'll be there," Masuto agreed.

The Japanese houseman came back into the room at that point and speaking in Japanese told Masuto that Mrs. Greenberg would like to see him.

"Why in hell doesn't he talk English?" Cotter growled.

"I am sorry," Masuto apologized. "He apparently forgot himself with me—there is a natural desire to use one's own language. He simply told me that Mrs. Greenberg would like to see me."

Masuto followed the houseman into the viewing room. Pale, deep circles under her eyes, Phoebe Greenberg greeted him with evident relief. Rabbi Gitlin, sprawled in a chair at one side of the room, nodded at him. Phoebe asked him whether he would have a drink. She had a drink in her hand. She wore a pale green at-home that was most becoming and gave her a sort of ethereal appearance.

"If you wonder why I don't wear black, Mr. Masuto," she said, "it is because my husband hated symbols as a substitute for reality. He bought me this dress himself. I have very few abilities and very few ways to pay tribute to him."

"You have the only ability that counts," Masuto answered.

"And what is that?"

"To see yourself as a human being."

"I don't really understand that," she said, frowning. "But I am glad that you came here. I was very troubled about what I should do, and Rabbi Gitlin suggested that I talk to you. He said that you would hear whatever I had to say with understanding."

"That's very kind of you," Masuto told the rabbi.

Gitlin rose and said, "Perhaps it would be best if I left you alone—both of you."

"No, no," Phoebe protested. "I want you to remain."

"All right." Gitlin sank back into the chair. Masuto remained standing and Phoebe Greenberg paced nervously as she spoke.

"I didn't want to bring this whole thing up. I wasn't going to. My husband was a very sick man, Mr. Masuto. I knew this, because his physician told me and also instructed me in what to do in an emergency. I can't talk very well about the relationship between my husband and me. We were only married three years, and his illness precluded any normal relationship. But I think I worshipped the ground he walked on. I never looked at another man after I married him, Mr. Masuto. Well, that's done, and I cannot weep or carry on. Some can, some can't. I was going to wash this whole wretched thing out of my mind until Mike was killed today. Tell me, do you think that the same person who murdered Mike Tulley killed my husband?"

"Let me answer that obliquely, Mrs. Greenberg. No one will ever know, unless there is some sort of a confession, whether or not your husband was murdered. But I do know this—that if he was murdered, it was the same person. And I can tell you that this same person coldbloodedly killed two others."

"Oh, no! Who?"

"Did you know a man called Fred Saxton?"

"Yes—yes, I knew Fred. He worked for Al—for my husband. But his death—it was one of those awful accidents."

"I don't think so, any more than the death of a woman called Peggy Groton, whose car went over the shoulder up on Mulholland Drive today, was an accident. There is very little doubt in my mind that both of these people were murdered."

"That's a pretty terrifying statement," Gitlin said. "What are you trying to tell us, Sergeant? That four murders were committed? Then what kind of horror is loose among us?"

"You're asking for a philosophical conclusion, rabbi. I am only a policeman."

"It's not fashionable to faint, is it?" Phoebe asked.

Masuto and the rabbi helped her to a chair. Very pale, she sat there and said, "When I was a little girl, my mother used to tell me about fainting and smelling salts and that sort of thing. It was very fashionable once, but I guess no one faints any more. You never hear about it. I don't even have smelling salts in the house, whatever they are." She took a deep breath and went on, "I am going to tell you about this, Mr. Masuto. It may be wrong and vile to speak about it, because it happened a long time ago. But I must tell you about it—I must."

Masuto waited. The rabbi glanced from Phoebe to Masuto, opened his mouth to say something, then clamped it shut.

"A terrible thing happened eleven years ago on a set where my husband was producing a TV segment. A man— well, it was Sidney Burke, because I will have to name names or this whole thing is meaningless. Sidney got some young kid actress to agree to have sex with some men on the set in return for a tiny part in the show. You have to be an actress yourself to know what these crazy kids will do for a part—any part. They all live with some kind of childish, pathetic dream that once they are seen, they will all instantaneously become Natalie Wood. So Sidney arranged this ghastly affair and—oh, it's so hard for me to speak about it."

"I know about it," Masuto said shortly.

"You do?" She was genuinely surprised.

"Who told you about this? Your husband?"

She nodded.

"What did he tell you was his role in the affair?"

She stared at Masuto for a long moment, and then she shook her head. "No. Oh, no. You are not going to tell me that he lied to me—"

"I didn't say he lied to you. I only asked you to tell me what he said was his role in the affair."

She turned desperately to Rabbi Gitlin, who said, "Tell him, Phoebe. Let's get this whole filthy business out into the open. There's no other way."

Then she said deliberately, "My husband did not lie to me, Mr. Masuto. He told me that the moment he found out what was happening, he put an end to it. He was sick and angry."

"I don't think he lied," Masuto said. "That's essentially the same thing that Murphy Anderson told me—that he came on it and put a stop to it."

"Thank you," she whispered.

"Still, it is very important that you tell me exactly what your husband told you about this affair—and anything else you ever heard about it."

"But if what my husband told me was true, why was he murdered? She must have known—"

"Who must have known, Mrs. Greenberg?"

"Samantha."

"Oh?"

"I said Samantha. Do you know who she is?" she cried.

"As much as anyone knows who she is."

"Then why—"

"That will not help," Masuto said. "You are piling up premises. You are trying to be logical. But most of the logic we live with is a lie, and most of our attempts to be logical are only attempts to evade the reality. So if we have a puzzle, stop trying to solve it. Don't cling to thoughts and notions. Let them pass through your mind and then dismiss them—or treat them all with equal indifference. Nothing that will ever happen or become known to you can change anything about your husband's relationship to you."

She turned to the rabbi pathetically. "Is that true?"

"Quite true," Gitlin said.

"But if you will answer my questions, *you* can help," Masuto told her.

"What questions?"

"As far as you know, who were the men involved in this incident eleven years ago?"

"Must I?"

"I know their names," Masuto said. "I am asking for corroboration, which is very important."

She took a deep breath and nodded. "Very well. You know about Mike Tulley. Poor Mike. He walked into all these things. He always had to prove that he was a man, and that bitch he was married to never let him believe he was a man for more than five minutes. Oh, I am sorry over poor, silly Mike. Then Jack Cotter." She made a face.

"How can you explain about Cotter? Jack is a Hollywood cowboy. Maybe the only time he was actually alive was when he put on his cowboy suit and his six-guns on the back lot. It's a special spongy kind of brain. They really think they are cowboys. The back lot is the universe. It's real. Do I make any sense?"

"You make sense," Masuto said. "And Murphy Anderson?"

"Murphy. I could never understand it about Murphy, but then I appear to understand very little about men. Sidney Burke, of course. What can one say about Sidney? Max Green—poor Max. He was such a fool—poor Max died of a heart attack a year ago, and then Freddy Saxton. Of course. That's why you asked me about him. And it wasn't an accident?"

"I am afraid not," Masuto said.

"What kind of a devil is she? Freddy has six children. Six kids. So he did something vile eleven years ago. Does that condemn him to death and his six kids—what does this all mean?"

Masuto turned to the rabbi, who shook his head. "I am past speculation on that point. I don't know what anything very much means—except that we store up horror. We prepay for it, so to speak, and then we are astonished when it happens."

"What can one say about Sidney Burke?" Masuto asked her.

"What? Really, what?" She sighed. "When I asked Al why he didn't break Sidney's back, he said a very peculiar thing—that you cannot make a moral judgement of a person who is utterly without morality. Anyway, Sidney is Hollywood—I mean the place is full of Sidneys. Sidney doesn't do evil—he is just completely unaware of any difference between good and evil. Sidney is the ultimate amoral. If you asked him about that wretched gangshag he set up eleven years ago, he might be nervous—but not ashamed. He was doing everyone a favor. He was doing Samantha a favor by getting her a job on TV. He was doing the boys a favor by getting them a free lay on the set. And he was being progressive. He was forwarding the whole industry in his own way. That's the way Sidney is. He comes in dressed in his black silk suit with his pointed shoes and his thirty-dollar white-on-white tab shirt, and he gives you that big grin of his and a big kiss, and he never really gets angry at anything you say to him and he's also thinking of some kind of favor he can do for you. That's because he wants so much to be liked—"

Her voice trailed away. Masuto was listening with astonishment. This was Phoebe Greenberg, who should have been a senseless blonde who never made it as an actress. He looked at the rabbi, who permitted himself a slight smile.

"I go home," Masuto said—"that is, sometimes I go home, and then when I do my wife says to me, tell me about today. What kind of a day was it?"

"It might surprise you," the rabbi said, "to find that her day is equally inscrutable."

"Perhaps. But we have been talking about this and that, Mrs. Greenberg. You didn't call me over here to chat. You called me here to tell me who is Samantha, didn't you?"

"What a notion!"

"But you did."

"I think you fancy yourself, Mr. Masuto, because you happen to be Japanese. It gives you a sort of racial crystal ball which you can bring out whenever the mood suits you."

"I think we both fancy ourselves," Masuto said flatly. "All people do. All people build their own aura, their own mask that separates them from the world. Perhaps mine is that of the inscrutable Oriental—I imagine the rabbi chose that word deliberately—and Rabbi Gitlin goes through life as a large, confused innocent, as much of a mask as my own Oriental magic kit. And you, Mrs. Greenberg—"

"And me?"

"You are the professional Hollywood dumb blonde. Do you mind me being a bit shaken by what is underneath?"

"And how do you know that I am a professional dumb blonde?" she asked coldly.

"A word here and a word there. I listen. So why don't we stop fencing. Who do you think is Samantha?"

"Shall I tell him?" she asked the rabbi.

"That's up to you, Phoebe."

"Very well. Samantha is Trude Burke, Sidney's wife."

The Japanese butler brought tea and tiny sandwiches, and he told Phoebe that there had been a call from the funeral chapel and that people were beginning to arrive, and that some relatives of Mr. Greenberg were arriving from the East and would go directly there, that his two sons were expected—his daughter was in Europe and could not be reached—and when would she be there?

"I should go now," she said, "but I must talk to Mr. Masuto. Please have some sandwiches, Mr. Masuto."

"I'll go there directly," said Rabbi Gitlin. "I can arrange for my wife to be there."

"The truth is, I am afraid to go there," she said.

"Well, that's natural, Phoebe. Take your time, but come. You must. Meanwhile, my wife and I will constitute ourselves a sort of semifamily committee. There are no other relatives here in Los Angeles, are there?"

"No, but Murph is the closest friend Al had, and he and Stacy will be there. I'll try to come within the hour."

Masuto, his mouth full of sandwich—eating with the feeling that this would be as close to dinner as circumstances might permit—motioned for the rabbi to wait.

"Please." He swallowed quickly.

"What is it, Sergeant?"

"Have you spoken about this, Mrs. Greenberg,—about your feeling that Trude Burke is Samantha—to anyone else?"

"No. Only to you and Rabbi Gitlin."

"Good. Now listen to me, Rabbi—you are not to mention this, not even in passing, not even as a nameless suspicion, not to Anderson or Cotter or Burke. And not to their wives—"

"But surely," Phoebe broke in, "you don't—"

"I damn well do, and I tell you, Rabbi, that one word about this can mean Mrs. Greenberg's death. No—one word about it *will* mean Mrs. Greenberg's death."

" 'Damn well,' " the Rabbi repeated. "Slang sits oddly with you, you know. Of course—just as you say."

He left them then, and Masuto stuffed another sandwich into his mouth, worked it down quickly, dialed the City Hall, got the Chief and said to him,

"I want two cops on motorcycles, one in front of the Greenberg place on North Canon and one in the mews behind it, and I want it covered all night."

"You know that means I got to put two men on overtime," the Chief pointed out.

"With all respect to my esteemed boss," Masuto said, "I am aware of his financial difficulties. My heart bleeds for the poverty of those who guard the wealthiest city in the world."

The Chief's "Go to hell!" was audible across the room. Masuto turned back to Phoebe to apologize, and she, in the midst of pouring tea, had stopped and was staring at him bleakly.

"What have I done!" she said.

"Oh? What have you done, Mrs. Greenberg?"

"You believe what I said about Trude."

"Don't you?" he asked.

"No. No. Of course not! Oh, what a precious Oriental dunce of a detective you are to believe me."

"Then why did you tell me what you told me?"

"Because I believed it. But I didn't believe it because it was true. I believed it because I detest her, and because Rosie Valero, who does my hair, told me that Trude's gorgeous strawberry blonde is a bottle job, and that they do her once a week, and they not only do her hair but her eye lashes and her eyebrows and her damned pubic tufts and whatever other hair she has on her body, and Rosie thinks she had some sort of nose job. And why should she go to that kind of trouble for a worm like Sidney unless she was pretending to be a horse of another color. And the thought of Al—of poor, fat, good Al, who was so kind to everyone and who never hurt a soul in his life—the thought of him being murdered by some rotten little slut, well, it was just more than I could stand, and so I told you. But I didn't believe it. I just had to tell you."

"But you told the Rabbi first?"

"Yes."

"And what did he say?"

"He said that he didn't put much stock in it and that he didn't think you would put much stock in it, so it couldn't do Trude any harm, but that I should go ahead and tell you and get myself a good, deep condition of guilt, which would act as some kind of a psychic purge, and then I would hate myself, and then I would feel better."

"He's a remarkable man," Masuto answered thoughtfully. "Yes, indeed. And now you hate yourself."

"I think I hate you, because you are stupid enough to believe me."

"How do you know that I believe you, Mrs. Greenberg?"

"Because you called for those cops to be around the house all night."

"To protect you from a killer. You know, there are a dozen holes in your story, but isn't one thing absolutely obvious?"

"What?"

"That Samantha would have to be diabolically clever, and that the only one of the lot of you clever enough to be her is you—yourself, Mrs. Greenberg."

"How dare you!"

"And that lovely hair of yours—isn't it what you call a bottle job?"

"Oh, what a miserable, wretched—oh no. No. You can't do this, because I am a woman all alone here. Insult me. Accuse me of the murder of my husband."

"Dear Mrs. Greenberg," he sighed. "Have I accused you of anything? I am afraid my deadpan humor is perfectly wretched. I will tell you flatly what you already know—that you are not Samantha and that you are a very clever, and more importantly, a reasonably wise woman. I admire you a great deal. But I think I know people enough to realize that you would weep if you had to kill a mouse."

She nodded silently.

"You know," he added, "Mr. Burke was the only one who knew Samantha before he got her into that dressing room. So he could hardly blunder into a marriage with her."

"I wonder," she said. "I've been beastly, haven't I? Please do have another cup of tea and some sandwiches."

CHAPTER
SIX

SIDNEY BURKE

Masuto was surprised to see that Sidney Burke was still in the living room, sitting in a corner silently and listening to one of the friends of the deceased. There were about a dozen people there. Burke was listening and waiting, and when he saw Masuto, he jumped to his feet and intercepted the detective—who already, simply because he was a Nisei—was the object of all the eyes in the room.

"Let's shake this place," he said softly to Masuto. "I got to talk to you."

"I thought you went to the chapel with the others," Masuto said.

"Changed my mind." They were outside now. "I don't have a car here, Sarge. Can we get in yours and drive a little and talk a little? I know a little place up on La Cienega and Sunset, where we can have a quiet corner and I'll buy you a hamburger."

"I'll buy my own hamburger," Masuto said.

"That's an honest cop for you," said Burke. "So I won't corrupt you with a hamburger. Buy your own and I will

remember it as the last untarnished hamburger in Hollywood. Can you spare me half an hour? And is the place OK
with you?"

"What do you call it?"

"The Quiet Cow."

They got into Masuto's car, and he called the station on
his phone and told the Chief that he was going to a place
called The Quiet Cow with Sidney Burke, and would the
Chief have the dispatcher call his wife and tell her he would
not be home for dinner.

"And I have a meeting with Cotter and Anderson and
Burke later at Anderson's house."

"Did you ask for it?" the Chief demanded sourly.

"Anderson asked for it."

They drove off, and Burke said, "Great cops have bigger
cops upon their backs to bite them, and bigger cops have
bigger cops and so ad infinitum."

"That's very good," Masuto admitted. "What can I do for
you, Mr. Burke?"

"It ain't original."

"I didn't think so."

"OK. So by now you know about Samantha."

"A little."

"You know more than a little," Burke said. "Everybody's
crapping in their pants because each and every one of them
thinks he is next on Samantha's little list."

"But you're not worried."

"Worried? Jesus God, would I be riding around with a
cop if I was not worried? Of course I am worried. It's the
goddamn power complex. Kill one; you know it can be
done. With the second, you are riding high; and with the
third, she is a lousy little tin god—"

"Who is?"

"Samantha Adams—who else."

"What do you mean—third?"

"Don't put me on, Sarge. You know about Fred Saxton."

"An accident, I am told."

"Then you are told wrong."

"Samantha?"

"Don't kid me, Sarge. Don't put me on. I'm no hero and I don't intend to live the rest of my life with loose bowels. I am tired of being nervous."

They were up on Sunset now, and as they approached the Strip the traffic stopped, and there was a sound like a thousand kids yelling. A half a dozen deputies came running by, carrying riot batons, and across the avenue, a stream of teenagers, shouting taunts and defiance, poured in among the cars.

"That's the way it is with those long-hair creeps," Burke said. "Never taught them any discipline or morality. That's the way kids are brought up today."

Masuto managed a turn into Larrabee and headed for Wilshire. "That's no place for a Beverly Hills cop," he said. "I know a little Danish place on Wilshire. Will you settle for that?"

"Anyway you say. I got no more appetite anyway, and you can't afford what I consider a place fit to eat in. Just so long as I put it to you."

"Go ahead," Masuto said.

"You're running this case? Correct me if I am wrong."

"I like to think so," Masuto said.

"All right. Now listen—today, only a few hours ago, maybe two o'clock, maybe two-fifteen, I am driving along Mulholland toward Laurel Canyon, and a little red MG zips by me from the opposite direction. I see a strawberry head and I do a double take, and maybe half a mile along, I say to myself, that's got to be Trude, my wife. But I am not sure, because when a hot car passes you on Mulholland, you are watching the road not the car, but it fits her car and her head. Maybe. Next thing I know, I see prowl cars and an ambulance and kids with motorbikes—those lousy creeps with the beards—and I know there's some kind of accident, but the sight of blood makes me ill. I throw up when I see a lot of blood. Not good. So I crawl past, and that's that, except that I do a second double take. I see you. First I see you and I don't think nothing about it, because where there's an accident, there should be cops. Period. Then I say to myself, this part of Mulholland is Los Angeles, so what is a Beverly Hills cop doing casing a job in Los Angeles, when he should be sitting with his head in his hands trying to figure out who knocked over Mike Tulley and Al Goldberg?"

"That's pretty good."

"Well, it's no Charlie Chan film, but I got cops and murder on my brain, and I get home and there's Trude's MG in the carport, and now I am a nervous type, so I feel the hood. It's hot. So I go into the house and Trude's doing her nails to go to the chapel tonight, and I say to her, 'What were you doing up on Mulholland Drive, baby? I thought you were a big girl and grown out of doing tricks with the MG?' So she says to me, 'Drop dead. I never went near Mulholland Drive.' "

In the little Danish restaurant, Masuto sipped coffee and munched pastry and regarded Sidney Burke with interest and a degree of wonder. Burke ate little. He tried to explain to Masuto his distaste for a restaurant that was low-priced.

"Regardless of the quality of the food?" Masuto had asked curiously.

"My drawing is four thousand dollars a week, Sarge,"

Burke said. "Apart from expenses. What I eat in a restaurant is expenses. I can't explain that to you. It is not simply a matter of screwing the government. I get kicks from that, but that ain't all. I got the biggest and best PR outfit on the Coast. I got a very important interest in Northeastern Films. I got other interests. So I don't eat in a place like this. I can't afford to. Suppose someone says, I seen Burke—see? No good."

"How about The Quiet Cow?"

"That's a hamburger joint where the hamburgers are three bucks."

"I can't afford three bucks for a hamburger."

"I wasn't going to bribe you," Burke said. "I was just going to tell them you're a cop. You don't think Joey Donsen who runs the place is such a shmuck he's going to charge a cop."

Now, however, Burke was trying to tell Masuto about his wife, and he kept saying that he had to be sincere. "I got to be sincere," he told Masuto, "otherwise I can't make you understand about this girl I'm married to. Not that I got anything against Trude—you understand—she's just a louse. But that doesn't mean that Sidney Burke is a schmuck. I knew she was a louse when I married her. This is a kid, I just had to look at her and I was off. I want to be sincere. I am not the kind of a guy who flips over a tomato. What was worth banging, I banged—"

"But just to come back to the problem that confronts us," Masuto said, "with due deference to your sincerity, how can you believe that your wife is Samantha? You knew Samantha. You brought her to the studio—"

"I knew Samantha? Listen, Sarge, in the past fifteen years, I knew maybe two, three hundred broads who are maybe enough like Samantha to be her sister. The blonde

American way of life, with the little round puss, the turned up nose, the blue eyes, and the shapely ass. You can pick out ten any morning at the counter at Schwab's. At Central Casting, they decorate the walls with them. You wave a contract out at Santa Monica Beach, and you got a thousand of them. What do I know about Samantha? I picked her up at the counter at the Beverly Wilshire, paid for her hamburgers, gave her a ride and a night of pleasure. I thought the kid was grateful. She wanted a job more than anything in the world, so I got her a job. The boys would have been nice to her if she had just said two words. What's to get excited about?"

"Did Anderson tell you about the phone call from her?"

"That's right."

"And you think your wife could be Samantha. Isn't that a little farfetched? That she married you for revenge?"

"Farfetched! Sarge, you been spoiled by Japanese girls. This tomato of mine had her revenge in the first thirty days, and I been married to her for two years. I married my first wife when I was twenty-three. We got divorced two years later. She had a lousy disposition, if you know what I mean, the cranky kind. But compared to Trude, she was an angel. Believe me, I am being sincere."

"Still, you must remember Samantha."

"Absolutely. Just take a good look at Trude. She weighs at least ten-fifteen pounds more than Samantha. Samantha was a skinny kid. Samantha had that kind of pale, yellow-white do-it-yourself blonde hair. She wore it like a kid, combed down straight. Trude's got a head of strawberry-blonde curls that just sit natural all over her head. It must cost her a hundred dollars a week—all over, every place on her body there's a hair, it's dyed. She had a nose job seven years ago, not for looks but for what they call a deviated septum. Would you believe me, she hasn't got one picture from before that nose job—not one."

"That's understandable," Masuto said.

"Understandable? Sarge, on the question of broads, I am maybe an expert—in a small way. Would I want to pin this on my own wife, if I did not have a position? I am trying to be absolutely sincere. It is not understandable. A dame like Trude, she lives by her pictures. She can't always be looking into a mirror, can she?"

"When did you first have a suspicion that your wife might be Samantha?"

"Seven weeks ago—when that sandbag killed Freddie Saxton. One of the grips on the set saw a girl beat it out— just got a glimpse of her, and that was right before he found out about Freddie. The cops over there in the Valley talked to him, but he couldn't describe the girl. He just saw her run past and out of the soundstage, and he caught a glimpse of her."

Masuto filled his cup with coffee again and began to consume another Danish pastry, reflecting on the fact that so much evil is mediocre beyond belief; so much vileness, the writhing of frustrated children trapped in the bodies of adults. Anyway, it was not his to judge. He even felt a little ashamed of himself when he said, "Naturally, Mr. Burke, you brought the grip a picture of your wife."

"That's my duty as a citizen, Sarge."

"Naturally. But the grip could make no identification."

"No."

"Did he remember the girl having red hair?"

"All he could remember was blonde. So what? You think Trude's some kind of idiot? She'd wear a wig."

"Does she have wigs?" Masuto asked.

"Sarge, wake up. You're running with the wrong crowd. There ain't a dame in this town doesn't have a closet full of wigs."

Leaving this statement unchallenged, Masuto asked about detective agencies. "Surely, you would have thought of that, Mr. Burke?"

"I did."

"Which agency?"

"Intermountain. They're up on—"

"I know where they are." Masuto nodded. "Who do you deal with there—Frank Gillespie?"

"No, his partner, Adam Meyerwitz. I been dealing with them for years and they can be trusted one hundred percent. So I put them on the job. I told Meyerwitz the whole story. I told him I wanted it quick."

"Just out of curiosity," Masuto said, "what do they charge for a job like that?"

"Six hundred dollars a day. They were on it five days."

Masuto whistled.

"Well, there you are," said Burke. "You don't see them making no heroes out of Beverly Hills cops, do you, Sarge? A private eye, that's something else. He's America's lover boy."

"And what did Intermountain give you for six hundred dollars a day?"

"Nothing. Not one stinking, lousy thing. They found out that Trude Steffenson, the name she had when I married her, was not the name she was born with. But they couldn't come up with the name she was born with. They found indications that she had come to Hollywood in 1952, but from where they don't know, and they can't put a finger on her before 1961. Can you imagine? Can you imagine being married to a broad who's a phony from the word go? When I think of the way that broad took me in—"

"Are they still on it?"

"Are you kidding? At six hundred dollars a day? Anyhow, she's a smartass broad and she felt something, and then she went to the Pinkertons and hired her own man and found out and she comes home and tells me that she'd ruin me forever in the industry if I ever try something like that again."

"Could she?"

"She could make plenty of trouble for me. That's gratitude, Sarge. I marry a broad like that, who's worth maybe a yard for a night to some jackass from Kansas, and I give her everything in the world, but everything, and what do I get?"

"You know when Mike Tulley was killed?"

"Today."

"I mean the time."

"About twelve-thirty," Burke replied.

"Did you ask your wife where she was at that time?"

"I did," Burke said.

"And what was her answer?"

"Drop dead."

"What?"

"I mean that was her answer, Sarge. That's what you asked me, isn't it? Isn't it?"

"I asked you that."

"So I told you. She says to me, 'Drop dead.' "

"Nothing else?"

"Nothing else. We don't have conversations these days. Does the butcher talk to the goose he picks out? So why should she talk to me?"

"You haven't tried to divorce her?"

"With what she's got on me?"

"Will she be at the chapel now?"

"Who knows? Murph invited her to his house tonight for the meeting or whatever he intends to do."

"He did?"

"That's right. He did."

"Suppose we drive over to the chapel now," Masuto said. "I don't think Mrs. Greenberg will be offended by my presence there."

The chapel was on Wilshire, about a mile toward downtown. Here Greenberg's body would lie through the night, and from here it would be taken for burial the following day. There would be a brief service at Mt. Ephriam Cemetery the following day, after which the actual burial would take place. Now, at the chapel, close friends and relatives were gathering. Anderson and Cotter would both be there. From there, they and their wives would go to Anderson's house.

As Masuto drove his car into the parking lot behind the chapel, Sidney Burke voiced his uncertainties. "It's not like I don't regard you as a gentleman, Sarge," he said, "but won't it look peculiar?"

"Because I am a cop or because I am a Nisei?"

"Well, you got to admit that the combination is peculiar."

"Yet curiously enough," Masuto said quietly, "I was a friend of Al Greenberg."

"You?"

"Myself," Masuto nodded. "So if you don't mind, I'll pay my respects."

"Mind? Why should I mind?" He led the way toward the chapel. "Mind. You talk like I'm running this show. I don't mind. I'm the last one in the world to mind."

They entered the chapel, where they were met by a man in tails with a professionally funereal countenance. He asked them which of the several rooms in use that evening they were concerned with, and when they specified Al Greenberg, he sighed just enough and guided them to the proper place. There were about fifty people in the room, a high-ceilinged room, decorated in a popular West Coast style known as dubious-Hollywood-Gothic. Masuto entered and stood silently just inside the doorway. Burke joined Anderson and Cotter, and then Cotter walked purposefully over to Masuto and said hoarsely, "You ought to know better than to come here. Is nothing sacred to a cop?"

"I am a Beverly Hills cop, Mr. Cotter," Masuto said without rancor.

"What is that supposed to mean? That there's nothing sacred in Beverly Hills?"

"It's my own poor sense of humor, Mr. Cotter. I know this is neither the time or the place. But I must ask you something."

"You're right when you say this is neither the time nor the place."

"But if you would give me a moment—"

"OK—OK—ask."

"Did Samantha get the bit part she was brought down there for? I mean, was she actually filmed?"

"Big thought!" Cotter said sarcastically. "You really got it pinned."

"Do you mind answering."

"No. Jesus God, man, do you think she was in any condition to act?"

"I wasn't there," Masuto smiled, "so I don't speculate on her condition. Just as I make no judgements about what happened there."

"You could go too far, buddy boy. And you still haven't explained by what process you horn in here tonight."

"I felt I had to talk to Mrs. Greenberg and persuade her to join us tonight," Masuto said patiently.

"She is joining us. So that's that."

"Still, I must explain my presence. She's seen me now. I must explain the misunderstanding."

Cotter shook his head and walked back to join Anderson and Burke. Phoebe Greenberg, who had seen Masuto now, came over to him and said, "Why did you come here, Sergeant? Has some new terrible thing happened?"

"No. But I must speak to you."

"I'll see you later at Murph Anderson's house. I can't talk here. My husband's family is here. They have no notion that there was anything unusual about his death."

"I must talk to you now. If you would only step out into the corridor with me. I won't take more than five minutes of your time."

"Very well." She sighed, and he held the door open for her and she walked through. Outside, he looked at her sharply, and then said, "No one will ask you whether you loved your husband. Did you?"

"I loved him very much," she said flatly. "He saved my life. He gave me back to life. He was one of the few good men I have ever known. He did everything for me, and I did very little for him. Does that answer your question, Mr. Masuto?"

"Yes. Will you do something for him now?"

"What can I do for him? He's dead."

"Help me to take his murderer."

"He was murdered?"

"Yes. I have no doubt about it."

"How?"

"I think the murderer held a cushion over his face. He had an attack and died."

"What do you want me to do?"

"I want you to be at World Wide Studios tomorrow at ten-thirty or so in the morning. Do you have anything filming now?"

"Yes, we have two pilots in work. But you don't understand. The funeral is tomorrow."

"I do understand. Then you have makeup people there. I don't want you to make any arrangements in advance. Just turn up and tell them to make you up immediately."

"Who? Mr. Masuto, you simply do not have the faintest notion of how a studio operates. I can't just walk on to a soundstage and tell the makeup people to go to work on me. You have a film in process. You have a production manager, a director, a cast—"

"I know all that," Masuto said impatiently. "Aren't you forgetting one thing?"

"What's that?"

"That you own Northeastern Films."

"I do not. The partners will buy my husband's shares."

"Next week, next month. At this moment, you are the widow of the president. No one will question anything you ask—just so long as you make it plain that you are the boss. Believe me."

"Even a crazy request like makeup—?"

"Yes. Any request."

"And what shall I make up as?" she asked hopelessly.

"A middle-aged woman. Dark wig. Glasses. Padding around your middle."

"And that will help catch the murderer?"

"Yes."

"You give me your word?"

"Yes—except that all plans have a point of failure. This is dangerous, very dangerous. I will protect you as much as one human being can protect another. But it will still be very dangerous."

"And if I refuse, Mr. Masuto?"

"Then it will be even more dangerous, because the killer will kill you. We will try to protect you, but for how long?"

"I will do it," she said matter-of-factly.

"Good. You get into costume. Do you know where Stage 6 is?"

"The stage where poor Freddie died?"

"That's right. At exactly 11:10, I will be outside of Stage 6. I will look for you. If you don't see me, walk on and then return. But under no circumstances must you enter Stage 6 without me."

"Suppose I don't see you at all?"

"Then go back to where your people are shooting and call the Beverly Hills police and find out what happened to me, or whether there is any message for you."

"All right."

"And tonight, not one word of this. Not to anyone. Not to Anderson and not to his wife. Not to the Rabbi. Do you understand me?"

"I understand you, Mr. Masuto."

"Good. You are a very brave woman. Will you tell Mr. Burke to go with the others. I am going to leave now."

She nodded and returned to the mourning room. Masuto left the chapel and walked around to the parking lot. He got into his car, started the motor and drove slowly past the chapel into Wilshire Boulevard. Out of the corner of his eye, he saw that a side door into the chapel was half open. Behind the door, only darkness, and then as he came close to it, the darkness was broken by a tiny tongue of light, almost like the flicker of a firefly. There must have been a silencer on the gun—or perhaps the slight whip of a twenty-two caliber pistol was absorbed into the sound of his own motor.

It was when he stopped his car out on Wilshire and looked at the small, neat hole in his windshield that he realized the gun was a twenty-two, probably one of those tiny, deadly little pistols that nestle so well in a lady's handbag.

He leaped out of the car and ran back into the chapel, stumbling and skinning his knuckles in the stygian blackness of the side door. He crouched there, licking at his hand and cursing himself for a fool. What had he expected to find? If the murderer had waited, he, Masuto, would now be dead. Nothing put down Masuto so completely as to discover a wide, foolish hole in his own intelligence.

CHAPTER
SEVEN

STACY
ANDERSON

Masuto took a liberty that his chief would certainly note and resent and called his wife on his car radiophone. The children were asleep, and she was reading a mystery novel by Rex Stout. She was rather nervous, and pleased that he had called her; and after telling him about the children, she suggested that it would be a nice thing some day to take a vacation and go to New York City.

"A very long and expensive trip."

"In this book, it is a very pleasant place. Perhaps you will stop being a policeman and earn a great deal of money."

"That's not likely," he said.

"Will I ever see you again?"

"I think it's possible," he said.

"Now you tease me."

"Never."

"You have no more use for me, your wife, but only for the beautiful blondes one sees in Hollywood."

"That's right."

"I know. I know. There was a picture of Mike Tulley's wife in the evening paper—in the *Times*. She is so beautiful."

"The *Times* is a morning paper."

"Don't we get it in the evening? Is she as good as she is beautiful?"

"Who?"

"Lenore Tulley."

"I am happy to speak to you, and I love you very much," he said.

"But you never tell me about the wonderful things that happen to you."

"I love you anyway," he said.

"Michael has a sore throat."

"Is it bad?"

"No. I gave him some aspirin. I am sure he'll be better tomorrow."

Then Masuto said his goodbys, put away the telephone, and fingered the tiny hole in his windshield. He felt better since speaking to his wife. He felt better able to face the rest of the night.

Murphy Anderson's house on Rodeo Drive was gigantic Beverly Hills-half-timber-Tudor. Stacy Anderson must have left the chapel soon after Masuto, since she was already home to open the door for him and usher him into the red leather, brass nail, Oriental rug interior and through the baronial hall into an immense sunken living room, which sported medieval banners from its cross-beams. In a fireplace large enough to drive a sport car through, two huge imitation logs glowed with light and warmth, and in one corner a suit of armor leaned moodily on its spear.

"I felt someone had to be here to welcome you, Inspector," Stacy Anderson said, "so I made my apologies and rushed home."

"Sergeant, Mrs. Anderson."

"Sergeant?"

"I mean, we don't have inspectors. We should, I often feel."

"You are humorous. I mean, for a Japanese. We never give Orientals any credit for a sense of humor, and I fear we make a dreadful mistake—don't you?"

"I really couldn't say, Mrs. Anderson. I have never been in the Orient."

"What a shame!"

Could she be as stupid as she appeared, Masuto wondered, as insensitive and gauche? Or was she putting him on? Was she possibly one of those extraordinary women who can move through life playing the role of the fool, and who wears a fool's mask to cover the intelligence? Now it was hard to say, and he rejected any quick judgements. Certainly, she was a beautiful and seductive woman, about thirty-one or thirty-two, round, just the slightest bit plump, pale blue eyes contrasting strangely with her black hair. For the chapel, she had put on a dress of black velvet—a stunning repeat for her glowing hair. Masuto reflected that in today's America, it is almost unthinkable that a blonde woman should dye her hair black. Blondness was big business, a passion, a semiracist ingredient of the mythology current in the land. Yet few women could adorn themselves with anything more beautiful than Stacy Anderson's hair. Why shouldn't she dye it black?

He became conscious of the fact that he was staring at her and pulled his gaze away. She was in no way disturbed.

Quite to the contrary, she was pleased at being the object of his admiration. Masuto had the very strong feeling that she would be pleased to be the object of any man's admiration, and he was in no position to draw conclusions. Why Murphy Anderson had married her was only too evident, and why she had married him was almost equally obvious.

"Isn't this a huge room?" she asked. "You know, Murph has two children from his first marriage and they spend their summers with us and they're absolutely divine youngsters, so when Murph and I decided to buy a place here in Beverly Hills, I felt we should have something that was both homey and big enough for the kids to romp around in. This seemed just to fill the bill perfectly, and there's a wonderful big pool and a tennis court out back. But do you know, Inspector—"

"Sergeant," Masuto said.

"Of course. Sergeant. You know, they always seem to be a little overawed by the house until they get the hang of it. That takes time, you know."

"I suppose so."

"Do you like my dress?"

"It's very attractive."

"Thank you, dear Inspector. I wonder whether you would suggest something I might serve. I thought of champagne, but this isn't that kind of a party, is it?"

"I'm afraid not."

"Then each to his own desire."

"You don't appear to be very upset by anything today," Masuto said quite deliberately.

"Upset? You mean by Al's death?"

"And Tulley's murder."

"My goodness, Inspector, when you're a Mike Tulley you have to expect it, don't you? I mean, we used to watch the Perry Mason program on TV every now and then, and you always know who is going to get it, because it's the kind of person you feel so nasty about you could kill him yourself, and once I said to Murph that if we were running one of those programs in our own set, why it would be Mike Tulley, naturally."

"Then you have no sympathy for Mike Tulley?"

"Goodness, I adored Mike. What has that got to do with him being a louse? If I had to eliminate every man who's a louse, I'd become a Vestal Virgin or something. Is that right? Vestal Virgin? You know, I dated Mike. When we were kid actors. Did you know that I was an actress, Inspector?"

It was thick, turgid. He was in a dream. She was playing with him or she was an idiot—or he was an idiot. The smile was fixed on her face, and her sharp, tiny white teeth reminded him of a cat's fangs. Every so often, she would touch her lips with the point of her tongue and leave them red and glistening—and then she would pass the back of a thumbnail across the velvet that covered her breasts.

"Oh, a very good actress indeed. Not that I ever really got a chance—don't you think I am a good actress, Inspector?" she asked archly.

"And weren't you moved by Mr. Greenberg's death?"

"Al was a sweetheart, but he was so sick, Inspector—so sick. You have no idea. Murph used to tell me that Al would sometimes stay up all night, he was so afraid of dying in his sleep. Well, that's one of the risks you take when you marry a popsie. Not that I haven't dated popsies, and there was one from Houston, Texas, who was worth a hundred million if he was worth a dime, but he could barely walk, and his doctor said he might live another ten years. Well, that's a long stretch for a girl to wait, Inspector. I know what you're thinking. You're thinking that Murph's a popsie, but that white hair of his puts you on. Murph was fifty last week, and I don't call that a popsie, not by a long shot. So Phoebe knew exactly what she was getting into, and who can cry over five million dollars—or whatever Al leaves Phoebe?"

At that moment, Masuto heard cars stopping outside, and Stacy rose and said wistfully, "Oh, there they are. And we were having such a wonderful chat, weren't we, Inspector?"

But in the first group were only Arlene Cotter and Trude Burke. The men had gone on to the other chapel where Mike Tulley's body lay, and when they returned with Lenore Tulley, it was almost ten o'clock. Then they waited for Phoebe Greenberg, who arrived a few minutes later.

But in the waiting time, Arlene Cotter and Trude Burke managed three drinks each. Arlene drank straight gin on the rocks, and Trude mixed brandy, sherry and ice. They sat in the enormous living room and grinned maliciously at Masuto. They begged him to take a drink.

"One little sip, Sarge," Arlene Cotter urged him. "I have never seen a Nipponese drunk."

"That's a real nasty thing to say," Stacy observed. As hostess, she forbore to actually drink, but instead nipped dainty sips from the sherry bottle. "You ought to apologize."

"Come to think of it," Trude observed, "you take a lot of garbage, don't you, Sarge?"

"All in a day's work," Masuto shrugged.

"What does it take to burn you?"

"I don't burn."

"Come on, Mr. Chan," Arlene said nastily, "everybody burns. It's not a question of susceptibility but of degree.

Even our dark, comfortable little hostess here burns—right through the pretty pool of sherry that keeps her lit all day."

"How can you!" Stacy exclaimed dramatically.

"Because she's a bitch," Trude said. "It's easy enough, Stacy, if you only got a talent for it. Why be a louse, when with a little thought and effort you can be a thoroughgoing bitch like dear Arlene?"

"That's a lovely speech," Arlene replied, going to the bar and refurbishing her drink. "I've often wondered why Sidney never put you into the office, but I suppose your talents for public relations lie in other directions."

"Touché!" Trude grinned. "Did you hear it on TV or read it in a book?"

"Will you please stop!" Stacy cried. "How do you think the Inspector feels? He's a guest in my house."

"Oh, climb down, Stacy," Arlene said. "You know, you give me a pain in the ass. That's crude—"

"Say that again," Trude agreed.

"—but there are times when crudity is obligatory," she went on, paying no attention to Trude. "In the first place, Mr. Chan is a sergeant, not an inspector. In the second place, he is not one bit bothered by anything we say here. He welcomes it, and he considers himself very clever to be sitting there and waiting for the proper moment to pounce on some stupid remark we make."

"Then why don't you shut up," Trude said.

"Because I got nothing to hide from him, but with you the case is a horse of another color," Arlene said.

"My dear lady," Trude said, patting the pink curls that covered her head, "you don't even talk coherently, and before I'd crawl out on any limb and cut it off behind me, I'd think twice. Maybe three times. Because little old darling

Arlene from New Orleans is maybe a little old sitting duck to Trude here."

"Stop it!" Stacy said again. Masuto felt that she was trying to weep with vexation and was equally frustrated by the fact that the tears would not come.

"Now she's insinuating that I don't come from New Orleans," Arlene said to Masuto, a trace of a southern accent suddenly appearing in her voice. "But if I were married to Sidney Burke, I would stop insinuating. Because wherever I come from, doll, my husband doesn't practice a little pimping on the side."

"Balls," Trude said.

"What did you say?"

"You heard me, lovey. Because if there is any kind of pimping ever invented, dreamed of, or even speculated upon, Jack Cotter has had his finger in it. Sidney Burke may be a crumb, but at least he weighs in at one fifty and not at a ninth of a ton like that ex-Lothario butterball of yours."

"That's a beauty," Arlene said grandly. "I won't argue it—not for a moment. The truth is that Jack weighs two thirty, and most of it is hard bone and muscle and he could still break Sidney in two."

Stacy began to giggle. She stood in front of the bar, holding a tiny shot glass half full of sherry in her hand and giggling uncontrollably.

"What's gotten into you?" Arlene demanded.

"Oh, the two of you—you're just like two little girls in finishing school. And then they begin boasting about how strong their daddies are—"

"What!" Arlene exclaimed.

"Finishing school!" Trude shouted.

"God save us!" Arlene cried.

"Say that again, lovey."

"Tell us more about finishing school."

"And your daddy, honeybunch."

"All the daddies that you used to boast about."

Masuto was watching them, but particularly watching Stacy. Her giggles stopped. She flung the shot glass at Arlene, missing her by a hair's breadth. Her body tensed. The softness left it. And under the black velvet dress, her body seemed to have the flowing strength of a giant cat, and her pale eyes flashed. Stacy thrust out one hand toward the two women, and spoke coldly and menacingly. "That's enough. I've had a bellyful of you two bitches! Now just shut up or I'll break your necks—both of you! And don't think I can't do it!"

Even Masuto recoiled from the supressed hate and violence of Stacy Anderson. Arlene Cotter and Trude Burke simply sat in their chairs and said nothing and stared at the rug.

And then the men arrived with Lenore Tulley, and shortly after that, Phoebe Greenberg arrived.

There was a corner arrangement in the living room of two big Lawson couches—both in red leather and brass studs—and four facing armchairs. Lenore Tulley and Phoebe Greenberg sat on one couch, and facing them, Sidney Burke, Arlene Cotter and Trude Burke. Sidney sat in the middle. Murphy Anderson had an armchair, and his wife, Stacy, hovered between the guests and the bar. Masuto was in another armchair and Cotter, self-appointed to begin the meeting, had wrapped himself over a cockfight chair and rocked gently as he faced the others. He was a big man, and while he ran to fat, Masuto agreed with Arlene that he could handle himself. He had that look about him. Masuto recalled him now in the old Westerns he had played, and thinking of those films, Masuto realized with a curious sense of hopelessness and resignation that like the others, he was a particular product of this thing called the United States, shaped by Westerns and other mythology; a strange, strange product of his time, a slant-eyed, dark-skinned, Zen-Buddhist–California-Yankee–a condition that made him shiver a bit. Still he responded to Cotter with some tinge of that ancient hero worship. Cotter was consciously playing a role now. The great Tudor room was the set, and as players, the circle of people he faced were both dramatic and interesting. Masuto had no doubt but that he had rehearsed an opening statement over and over, when he spoke, he said the line well.

"One of us," he told them, flatly and without emotion," is a murderer."

There was an explosion of silence, a reaction Masuto understood very well indeed. Not one of the women said a word. Sidney Burke smiled self-consciously. Murphy Anderson shook his head slightly.

The silence stretched. It reached its breaking point. And Jack Cotter savored his moment. Then Stacy Anderson said crisply, "Jack, don't be an ass. These people are my friends. They are not murderers."

And Masuto asked himself, "What will I tell my wife tomorrow then–that there are two women here I admire enormously?" Of course he realized that he often chose strange people to admire. A man of prudence depended upon his own understanding more than upon his wife's.

"One of us is a murderer," Cotter repeated. "What's the use of horsing around? When I said that poor Al was murdered, the doctors pooh-poohed the whole thing. Well, I say, let's face it. You knew damn well, when Murph asked us here, just what we had in mind."

"Did I know it too, Jack?" Phoebe inquired.

"Let's stop beating around the bush. In one way or another, we all knew it. Aside from Sergeant Masuto, there are eight of us here, and one of the eight is a killer. Seven came because they had a genuine desire to see the killer exposed. The killer came because if she didn't come, she would give herself away."

"She?" Stacy Anderson raised a brow.

"Come on, Stacy—enough."

"And what does that mean?"

"It means that you know as well as I do that we're dealing with a woman," Jack Cotter said. "Mr. Masuto will bear witness to that." He turned to Masuto and demanded, "Am I right, Sergeant?"

"That I will bear witness to your statement?"

"Exactly."

"But how can I, Mr. Cotter? Do you think I know who the killer is?" The others were watching him intently now, and Masuto allowed his narrowed eyes to scan their faces.

"I think you have a damn good notion who the killer is."

"Suppose we were to grant that," Masuto said. "Suppose we were to grant that, simply for the sake of argument—and understand that I will accept your contention on no other basis. Suppose we say that I have a damn good notion of who the murderer is? What could I do with a damn good notion, as you put it? It's not proof. It will not stand up in any court of law. And if I had any real proof, do you imagine that I would have come to a charade like this? I think that you and Mr. Anderson have read too many murder mysteries, sir."

"That's a hell of a note!" Cotter snapped. "I think you got one hell of a goddamn nerve, Mister—"

"Oh, hold on, hold on, Jack," Murphy Anderson said. "Just take it easy. I was dubious about this idea in the first place, and I agreed to go along and give it a try because you were so certain that it would bring some results. But the fact of the matter is that Detective Masuto is right. We have no proof, and we have no right to keep anyone here who desires to leave. All we have is about seven yards of insinuations."

"Is that so," said Sidney Burke, rising abruptly. "Well, as far as I am concerned, some of these suspicions and insinuations got to be busted wide up."

"Oh, Sidney, sit down and don't be such a cockamamie shmuck," Trude said.

"Like hell I will. I am going to say my piece."

"Well, there it is," Trude sighed, spreading her arms. "He is going to say his piece."

"And to you too," he snapped, turning on Trude.

"I'm all ears."

"God damn it, Sidney," Anderson said, "whatever you got to say—say it and let's not have a family squabble."

"Oh, Murph doll, you are dreaming if you think we won't have family squabbles tonight," Arlene said. "By the dozen—believe me."

"You weary me so, why don't you shut up!" Trude said.

"All right—all of you!" Cotter ordered. "Now say your piece, Sidney."

"OK. I don't have to go into the Samantha thing again. You know about that bitch. Now I am going to be sincere—fully sincere, and let the pieces fall where they may. I was driving on Mulholland today, and I passed Trude in her MG going in the other direction. I went on and came on the accident. You all know about the accident by now. A one-time stripper named Peggy Groton went over the shoulder and was killed. The Sarge was there. He's on this case, but he was there in LA—and I say the two cases connect. You don't have to be no genius for that. I spoke to you and Murph about it before," he said to Cotter, "and you agreed with me. The two cases got to connect."

"Not necessarily," Masuto said.

"Then what in hell were you doing up there on Mulholland Drive in Los Angeles?"

"I have friends in the LA Police Department," Masuto told them. "Pete Bones is the name of one of them. I had business with him. I found him up there at the accident."

"Well, what about that, Sidney?" Anderson asked seriously.

"What about it? Does it account for the fact that I passed Trude driving away from the scene of the accident?"

Now Trude was on her feet. "Do you know what that crumby little bastard is trying to do?" she cried. "I'll tell you what he's trying to do! He's trying to set me up for the gas chamber! He's trying to finger me as Samantha! Does that make a record or does it not? My own husband fingering me for murder!"

"Take it easy," Anderson said. "No one is fingering you for any murder."

"Murph, for Christ's sake, open your eyes and stop being a calm, objective lawyer!" his wife shouted. "It's bad enough to have to live in the same town as Sidney Burke. Now I got him under my own roof talking like the little pisspot he is!"

"Oh, that's fine language!" Anderson exclaimed. "That's real fine language."

"The hell with my language!" Stacy shouted. "Next thing, he'll open a cathouse in the maid's room."

"Sure, you're a dame!" Sidney yelled back at her. "Go ahead. Call me anything you like. I'm gentleman enough not to bat you one."

"Shut up—all of you!" Cotter roared. "You're all behaving like a bunch of delinquent kids. Now just shut up for one lousy cotton-picking moment!"

A sort of silence prevailed. Sidney took a turn away from the couch and stopped to lean against the bar. Trude sank back into the couch. Phoebe watched Masuto, who sat back in his chair, breathing softly and evenly, his face blank, composed, receptive. Murphy took out a handkerchief and wiped his face, and Stacy walked to the bar and poured herself a shot glass half full of sherry. She ignored Sidney, and Masuto considered it as fine a job of ignoring as he had ever seen. His respect for Stacy Anderson rose another notch, and he considered how it would be to spend an evening with her. Just an evening, he assured himself.

"Anyone want a drink?" she asked.

"Give me a sherry and dry vermouth on the rocks," Lenore said. "It's intermission. Do you know they sell liquor in the New York theatres now—between the acts?"

"Just like London," Arlene Cotter said.

"Then you've been to London, darling," Lenore said. "What a well-travelled, cultured little dear you are!"

"Enough of that," Cotter told her. "Let's cut out this back-biting and get to the center of things." He addressed himself to Trude. "Where were you today between twelve noon and twelve-thirty?"

Trude laughed. "You are a lulu, Jack. The ever-living end, aren't you?"

"I am going to repeat that question," Cotter said. "Where were you today between twelve and twelve-thirty?"

"Drop dead, lover boy."

"You refuse to answer?"

"Are you nuts?" Trude demanded. "I don't have to answer your stupid questions. Where do you come off putting your nose into my business? You want this Samantha of yours—go find her. But I don't have to answer any of your stupid questions." She turned to Masuto. "Do I?"

"Not if you don't want to," Masuto said.

"Well then, you ask her the question," Cotter told Masuto.

"She doesn't have to answer me either."

"What? You mean you can ask her questions, and she can tell you to go run around the block?"

"Exactly."

Cotter turned to Anderson. "Murph—is that so?"

"That's so. I don't know what the hell you expect to accomplish here tonight, Jack."

"You poor jerks really think I am Samantha?" Trude said.

"They think we're all Samantha," Stacy said.

"Stacy!" Anderson protested.

"It's true, isn't it?"

"I've had enough of this," Arlene Cotter said. "I am going home before I start thinking about this crew we married and throw up."

"Stick around, lovey," Trude said. "If you walk out, they'll pin it on you."

"What I can't understand," Jack Cotter said to Masuto, "is why, now that we're all here together, you don't start asking questions and rooting out the truth."

"Because there's no truth in that."

"Don't tell me that!"

"Mr. Cotter," Masuto said softly, "suppose I began to ask questions, as you suggest. No one has to answer.

"Then when they don't answer, you got guilt."

"Is she guilty then?" the detective asked, pointing to Trude. "Because if she is, then our search is over."

"I didn't say she was guilty."

"Don't even infer it," Trude said, smiling pleasantly. "Because, Jackie dear, we are not inside some silly novel but here in this room and surrounded with witnesses. That jackass, my husband, over there by the bar, has already practically called me a murderer. But he is my husband, and so long as he pulls down better than six figures a year, he remains my husband. But you, Jackie, you ain't my husband, and just make one lousy crack about me and I will sue you for defamation of character so hard you'll be knocking at the gates of the actors' old age home. I'll sue you for every nickle you got, so don't go pushing the Sarge to ask me questions."

"Can she do that?" Cotter demanded of Anderson.

"I'm afraid so."

"I never called you a murderer. That's for the record. I want everyone here a witness to that fact. I never called you a murderer."

"Just what did you think you would accomplish with all this?" Stacy asked him.

"You know what I think," Sidney Burke said suddenly. "I think the company should hire the best private eyes here on the coast. We get as many privates as we need, and we blow this thing wide open. That's my sincere position."

"I don't believe it," Stacy said with disgust.

"Sidney is Sidney," Phoebe said tiredly, speaking for the first time. "He's been around for fifteen years, and suddenly, big deal, you discover that he's a louse. How about you and Murph?" she asked Cotter. "Aren't you lice? Aren't you the worst pair of lice that ever drove a pair of convertible Cadillacs in Bevery Hills? And you, Stacy—dear old Stacy."

"I'm willing to forget what you just said," Anderson told her. "You've had too much stress."

"I think we have all had too much stress," Stacy Anderson agreed. "We have all talked too much and said too much—which perhaps was exactly what our dear Mr. Masuto wanted."

"Not at all," Masuto said.

"Then why have you come?"

"I was asked to come."

"And only that? And that's why you've been sitting there all evening like a superior cat waiting to select the proper mouse to eat?"

"That's a very poetic image, Mrs. Anderson, but I am not a psychological detective. I am only a policeman in plain clothes."

"Then just what do you propose?" Cotter demanded. "That Murph and Sidney and I just sit on our hands and patiently allow ourselves to be murdered?"

"What, only the three of you? Why not the women?" Masuto asked.

"And you're not putting us on?" Sidney complained. "Oh, no—no, you're not putting us on, not one bit. Three men in this outfit are scragged, and you ask why the men."

"How about Peggy Groton?" Masuto said.

"Who's Peggy Groton?"

"The dead are quickly forgotten, aren't they?"

"She's the dame on Mulholland Drive," Cotter said.

"Anyway," Anderson said, "it seems that we three men are the most likely sitting ducks. Don't you agree with that, Mr. Masuto?"

"Possibly."

"Look," Anderson continued, "I have been thinking about this all evening, and I see no reason why Jack's statement should be taken at face value."

"What statement?" Cotter demanded.

"That the murderer is here in this room. How do we know that this Samantha is here? She might have never come near any of us. She might be a maid in someone's home. She might be a typist or secretary at the office. She might work on the set. The point I am making is that she might be anywhere."

"Haven't you worked over that Samantha business sufficiently?" Phoebe Greenberg said.

Stacy Anderson then turned to Masuto and said, "My dear policeman, since you refuse to question us, may I question you?"

"By all means." Masuto smiled.

"Where is this Samantha that these three dirty old men can't unhook from?"

"I have no idea."

"Does she exist?"

"I don't know."

"Oh, you are a great crystal ball. Is the murderer in this room? Jack says yes, Murph says no. Well?"

"Yes."

"What do you mean, yes? You're breaking your track record."

"You asked me whether the murderer is in this room. I said yes. The murderer is in this room."

"Then why don't you arrest him?"

The whole place tightened now. Masuto could hear their breathing, the difference in quality, the softness of some, the rasping quality of others. Sidney and Arlene lit cigarettes. The thin threads of smoke curled among the group.

"It is very interesting," Masuto observed, "that when a man speaks of the killer he designates him as a woman, and when a woman speaks of the murderer, she designates him as a man. There should be a neutral designation in a society as complex as ours—wouldn't you say? Some criminologists hold that murder never occurs without the presence of homosexuality—"

"Who the hell needs philosophy?" Cotter snapped.

"I don't like this talk about faggots," Sidney said. "To me, a man is what he is. That's all. That's my sincere feeling. A man is what he is. That's the way you judge him."

"You were asked a question, Sergeant Masuto," Murphy Anderson said. "You said you knew who the murderer is. Then you were asked why you don't arrest the murderer."

"No. Not at all," said Masuto. "I was not asked whether I knew who the murderer is. I was asked whether the murderer is in this room. I answered in the affirmative."

"Then I am asking you. Who is the murderer?"

Masuto waited for a long moment before he replied. No one moved. Each and every one of them there in that room was completely self-conscious about not moving.

"There are two reasons why I don't answer that," Masuto said. "First, I am not certain, not totally certain. Three men and a woman have been murdered. The murderer has been a fool, but a lucky fool. But this is a monstrous crime, and there must be certainty before I make the accusation. Second, I must have proof. An arrest is meaningless without proof."

"And until you get this proof?" Cotter demanded. "Do we just wait and die?"

They were all beginning to relax—as if the accusation of any one of them there and then would have been more than they could take.

"No. I think the case is breaking."

"Just what do you mean by that?" Anderson asked.

"There was a witness to one of the murders," Masuto said. He had been holding it all evening and waiting to drop it. He dropped it now. He dropped it almost casually and watched them.

Nothing. They tightened as a group, and they watched him.

"Which murder?" Cotter asked finally.

"Fred Saxton—your production manager who was killed by a counterweight seven weeks ago. That would appear to be a nearly perfect murder, but like every nearly perfect act it faces too many imponderables. One of them was this woman."

"What woman?" Trude asked softly.

"Just an actress, a character actress, age fifty-one, not too much work, only now and then. She lives. She has a husband. She minds her own business."

"Who is she?" Stacy asked sharply.

"How does she come into this?" Anderson wanted to know.

"She was a witness, Mr. Anderson," Masuto said. "The day Fred Saxton was killed, she wandered over to Stage 6. No reason for it. There is never any reason for the imponderables. She had been standing by for hours waiting for her take, and she was bored. So she poked into Stage 6 out of idle curiosity, and she saw someone with a hand on the rope release. Then the counterweight fell and Saxton was dead. In the excitement that followed, she slipped away. But as the day wore on she became aware of all the details involved, and being a reasonably intelligent woman, she put two and two together and came up with murder. But being a timid woman, she did what a great many people would do. She decided to keep her mouth shut and not get involved."

"And when did she change her mind?" Phoebe asked coldly, staring at Masuto. Their eyes met.

"Today, of course," Masuto replied.

"Why?"

"Because she heard about Mike Tulley's murder, and she put two and two and two together, and she called the Los Angeles police. They put a call out for me and we talked. They agreed to let me do it my way, because the Beverly Hills need took preference."

"And what is your way?" Anderson asked.

"Very simple, very direct. She's working out at World Wide tomorrow—you do have a permanent lease on Stage 6?" he asked Anderson.

"Not permanent, but we have it for another ten days. There's nothing shooting there now. We wound up our work there after Freddie's death. We made an arrangement with Grapheonics to keep their tour costumes there."

"What is Grapheonics?" Masuto asked.

"They're an animated cartoon outfit. 'Captain Devildom,' 'Space Ace Ambrose,' 'Major Meridean,' 'Tentacle Horror,' 'Captain Sharkman'—they have a slew of things that the kids eat up. Four to five on prime kiddie time. They've been so successful that World Wide asked them to become a part of the tour."

"The tour?"

"The 'studio tour.' They have those motor buses, you know, little open things, and they take tourists all over the sets and sound stages and the back lot. It's been enormously successful—so much so that they incorporated into the tour the characters from Grapheonics—in costume, of course.

World Wide likes it and Grapheonics likes it, and we allow Grapheonics to keep their costumes on Stage 6—in the wardrobe there. It's convenient for them. Just a gesture on our part."

"That won't interfere with my plan," Masuto said. "I would like all of us to get together tomorrow on Stage 6 at about ten minutes to eleven in the morning. Then I'll bring her to Stage 6, and she'll pick out the murderer."

"Just like that," Anderson said coldly.

"It's very simple. Yes. Just like that."

"And your murderer will come there like a lamb to the slaughter?"

"What alternative does the murderer have, Mr. Anderson?"

"I don't buy it!" Sidney Burke declared shrilly. "I don't buy it. It's a lousy, stupid scheme and I don't want any part of it. I have tried to be sincere through this whole crumby business, but now I've had a bellyful!"

"Sidney," Trude said sweetly.

"Now you listen to me—" he began.

"Oh, no—no, you cockamamie idiot, you just listen to me. A moment ago, you were calling me a murderer. But let's lay it on the line. You're too stupid to be Samantha, even if you had enough guts to be a woman, which you haven't. So no one here is going to think you are the killer. We both go to World Wide tomorrow, and we wind this business up. Once and for all, because I don't intend to live with it another day."

"I second that," Jack Cotter said. "The Sergeant makes sense. Do you agree?" he asked his wife.

Arlene shrugged. "I'm just along for the ride."

"Al's funeral is tomorrow," Anderson reminded them. "I don't see how Phoebe is going to get there."

"Can't we leave Phoebe out of this?" Stacy asked. "I just can't cast her as some bloody, maniacal killer."

"Then suppose you leave me out, cookie," Lenore said. "My alibi is as good as hers." She looked around from face to face. "And just in case you forget, I have my own dead to bury."

"Darling," said Arlene, "that line goes so much better in the original with Bogart than second hand with you."

"Go to hell!"

Phoebe looked at Masuto, who nodded just the slightest bit, and then Phoebe said, "I'll come. The funeral's in the afternoon, and if poor Al won't rest easier, at least I'll shed a few tears less for knowing who did it and why."

"Sidney?" Murphy asked.

"All right. I'm in the middle of this. I'm trying to be sincere—so I'm the number one louse. I'll be there."

"I'll be with him," Trude said.

"If I'm not dead," Sidney said. "I got to live through the night. Remember that."

"My heart bleeds for you."

"I just bet."

"All right, Sergeant," Anderson said, running his fingers nervously through his thick white hair. "We're agreed, we'll be there, and God help all of us."

Masuto followed Phoebe home. The cop on duty outside of her house was alert, and before Masuto had taken three steps, there was a gun in his ribs, and a harsh voice inquired, "What's wrong with the path, buster?"

He had deliberately stepped over the low hedge by the driveway to move through the shrubs in front of the veranda. A moment later the cop recognized him and apologized, and Masuto said, "Never mind the apologies. You guard this place as if it were Fort Knox."

"I'll do that, Sarge."

Masuto rang the front doorbell, and Phoebe opened the door herself.

"Don't open doors!" he snapped. "You have servants."

"Don't order me around either, Mr. Masuto. I have had my fill of you. You're a liar."

"I am, you are—" He walked into the entranceway, and she closed the door behind him. "We're all liars. I lie for my work. That's not a matter of morality."

"But it is morality to set me up like a sheep for slaughter. Or is that in the line of good police work."

He stared at her for a long moment, and then he shook his head. "Oh, no—Mrs. Greenberg. You misjudge me. I am a happily married man, but I have met a few women in my life who make me wonder whether being happily married is enough. You are one of them. You are a fine and beautiful woman—"

She burst out laughing. "Dear man," she said.

"Did I say something stupid."

She began to cry now. He gave her his handkerchief. "It's clean," he said. "I haven't used it today. But what have I done to make you cry?"

She shook her head.

"I am not risking your life," he said definitely. "There will be studio policemen there, both armed—two good men that we can count on. Nothing will happen to you."

"I don't care."

"But you must care."

"There's really not one damned thing left to care about."

"There's the world to live in," he said. "To live in it and taste it and feel it—open your eyes to it."

"Don't preach to me."

He shook his head. She seemed to sway, and then he took her in his arms. Afterwards, he wondered whether the act was of specific volition or not. He only held her against him, tightly, for one long moment. He didn't kiss her, and when a moment later he loosed his arms and she stepped back away from him, he felt a sense of awful loss. He had not kissed her. The embrace was not an embrace. A wind of foolish memory blew away what had never been, and he stood there feeling bereft and stupid.

She handed him his handkerchief. It had lipstick on it. He knew he would throw it away. He had no desire to try to explain to his wife why it had lipstick on it.

"I am sorry, Mrs. Greenberg," he said.

"Would you try to call me Phoebe, just once. Or don't you like the name?"

"It's a beautiful name."

"Then please call me Phoebe."

"Very well. I am sorry, Phoebe."

"For what?"

"For embracing you."

"Would you just tell me why you should be sorry because you embraced me?"

"There are three reasons, Phoebe. One, I am a cop. Two, I am a Nisei. Three, I am married. Perhaps a fourth reason more important than any—that you are Al Greenberg's widow."

"Oh, don't be such a precious damned fool! I loved my husband. I think I would have died for him, if need be—but not as a husband, and he never expected me to love him as a husband. But that's beside the point. You didn't even make a pass at me. You don't want to, and I don't want you to, and I do wish that you would stop acting like something out of a Japanese print. You're a man—a strong man who is reasonably decent and who turns up on the one day of my life when I need a man desperately. If things were different—"

"But they are not different," Masuto said.

"No, they are not different, are they? What is your first name?"

"Masao."

"Very well. Then from here on until the end of this, you will call me Phoebe and I will call you Masao. Is that agreed? Openly. Right?"

"I will call you Phoebe, and you will call me Masao."

"As good friends should."

"As good friends should," he repeated.

Then he left. On his way home, he threw away the handkerchief, just as he had known that he would.

CHAPTER EIGHT

GERTRUDE BESTNER

When Masuto entered his home in Culver City, his wife was waiting, her face drawn. She was an anxious mother. The house and her family were her world and all the world that she wanted, and she stubbornly refused to be Americanized. There were times when Masuto took great pleasure in this, and usually her anxieties were flattering to his own strength. But he had his own anxieties now, and he listened with some irritation to her story of Michael, the eight-year-old son, and his sore throat. Apparently, the sore throat was worse.

"Did you go to the doctor?" he asked.

She looked at him reproachfully. They had one car and she did not drive. She was always promising to learn to drive.

"Then why didn't you call the doctor to come here?"

"That's ten dollars, Masao. If I call the doctor every time a kid has a sore throat, we'll soon be penniless."

"We are penniless, the way you watch every dollar!"

"Masao!"

She always knew when something happened inside of him. It was not the things that occurred outside of him that worried her, but the strange responses that sometimes overtook him. That was the way it was tonight. In bed she left a space between their bodies, and when he whispered to her, she pretended that she was asleep.

Sleep came hard to him. He would doze off and come awake again. He dreamed of being lost in strange places—jungles and cities and boundless plains—but in each and every place there was Beverly Hills. Yet finally, he fell fully asleep and slept until the alarm awakened him at seven in the morning.

This morning, he was more than solicitous of his wife, Kati. He went out of his way to help her with the smallest child and then he made the seven wonderful faces for Michael, who would spend the day in bed. He was almost ready to leave when the telephone rang. Kati answered it. Masuto was outside the kitchen door when she called him, "It's Pete Bones."

He came back and picked up the phone and said, "Masao, Pete. I'm on my way out."

"Well, just hold still for a moment. We got a make on Gertrude Bestner."

"Who?"

"Oh, no—no, I don't believe it. You only give us the life and death howl, and research works fifteen hours straight, and now you ask me, who is Gertrude Bestner."

"Wait—you mean Samantha Adams, nee Gertrude Bestner?"

"Exactly."

"You mean you've found her?"

"In a manner of speaking," Bones said. "All that's mortal. She's buried in the County Pauper's Reserve."

"Dead."

"Very dead, Masao."

"You know—funny thing, but I felt it. The poor kid was a loser."

"Maybe."

"When did she die?" Masuto asked.

"Nineteen fifty-six, age nineteen, pneumonia, Mt. Sinai Hospital, emergency case; picked her up in the street where she had fainted; malnutrition, semistarvation, pulmonary—she died seven hours after admission to the hospital. Her death certificate was signed by the ward resident, name of Harry Levine. Practices medicine in Brentwood. I have name, address and telephone. Do you want it?"

"No," said Masuto.

"Funny thing, Masao, when she was admitted she gave them the name of Samantha Adams—the way these kids cling to the dream that it's theirs to make big, real big. It wasn't until she died that they got her real name from the ID in her purse."

"Where did she come from?"

"Chicago—but no connection, no family, no nearest of kin, nothing. A kid dies and it's like she's never been. Jesus, there are times when you could take this job and shove it right up your ever-loving."

"It's not the job, it's just the way things are," Masuto said.

"I suppose so. Look, we got her effects from the morgue file. Not much. A purse, a few incidentals—you know what a kid keeps with her—and a little leather-bound day book with a few phone numbers and some diary entries."

"Have you checked the phone numbers?"

"Aside from agencies and the unions and that kind of thing, they're all discontinued. She's got the number of Sidney Burke's PR outfit, but I guess you expected that."

"I expected it," Masuto said. "Did you read everything?"

"Well, it wasn't no *War and Peace*. Sure, I read it all."

"Anything?"

"Well, it depends on what you want. I got it here in front of me. On December 25th, 1955, she wrote, 'This is Xmas. It's a lousy Xmas. That's all I can say. It's a lousy, lousy Xmas. I had no date on Xmas Eve, and I walked around and I walked up to the Strip and I almost began to cry for feeling sorry for myself. Then I walked over to Fairfax and I bought a fruit cake for thirty-five cents. That left me with eighteen cents, but I had to have something even for a lousy Xmas like this. So I went home and stuffed myself with the fruit cake. It wasn't much good. It wasn't anything like the fruit cakes Mrs. Walensky used to make in Chi. They were great fruitcakes. God, I wish I was a kid again. I don't. It was lousy to be a kid. But God, I wish I was a kid again. Today, I'm sitting here in my room waiting for Santa Claus. This is Samantha, Santa Claus. Wishing you a lousy merry Xmas—"

"That's enough," said Masuto.

"There's more. A million laughs."

"Go to hell."

"That's a fine way to thank a buddy. Do you know what I told the boss—I told him to bill Beverly Hills for the time spent. You can afford it. You can afford to pave your streets with two-bit pieces."

"I'll tell them that at City Hall."

"Do you want to look at this stuff?"

"No."

"At least be grateful."

"Thanks," said Masuto. He replaced the telephone and then stood there staring at it.

"Masao," his wife said.

Not moving, he stared at the telephone. Perhaps not hearing, because she asked him again,

"Masao, please, what happened? Did something terrible happen?"

"Yes."

"What?"

"A girl died. A little girl died."

"How awful! is it someone close to you? Who is it?"

"I don't know her. I never saw her."

"I don't understand."

"She died ten years ago, and they buried her in a pauper's grave. Her name was Samantha. That was her stage name. Her real name was Gertrude Bestner, and in the whole world today, maybe only Pete Bones and I speak that name aloud."

"Samantha. Pete Bones. What strange names the Anglos use!"

"Anglos?"

"You don't like the word?"

"I don't know. It's just a word. We're not Mexicans."

"Is it a word only for the Mexicans? What do we call them?"

"People. Just people. That's enough."

"You're in a strange mood," she said. "This case has changed you. When will it be over?"

"Today, I think."

"Oh, God—Masao—"

"I will be in no danger," he said impatiently. "Nothing will happen to me. We will have a good dinner tonight, and I will tell you all about it."

"And it will be over?"

"All over and done with. I promise you that, and then I can go back to being a Beverly Hills policeman."

"And tomorrow is your day off," she said with delight. "We can have a picnic."

"If Michael is well enough."

"And where will we go, Masao?"

"To San Fernando, I think, to Soko's place. He promised that he would have the Sashu Roses from Japan. They are new, quite small, almost a mustard color, and they have a very good, strong smell. I am tired of these new beautiful tea roses that have no scent. We will eat in his garden, and then I will bring home the rose bushes and plant them."

"Good. Good."

He kissed her and went out to the car. The windshield was blurred with the wet morning mist, and upon it, in big block letters, he traced out SAMANTHA. Then he wiped it away with the palm of his hand, and then got in the car and drove off.

CHAPTER NINE

FRANK

JEFFERSON

In the mood that gripped him this morning, Masuto was unable to face the freeway with its maniacal roar of seventy-mile-an-hour traffic, and he decided to take a few minutes longer on his journey to the Valley and World Wide Studios by going through Beverly Drive to Coldwater Canyon. He was glad that he did. This was one of those utterly improbable Los Angeles mornings when there is neither smog nor fog and the air is as sharp and as clean as crystal. When he passed over the rise of Coldwater, the Valley lay etched below him, so clean and clear that he imagined he could see San Fernando in the distance.

Almost, the Valley reminded him of the way it had been when he was just a kid, with its acres of orange grove and mango grove and avocado and pecan, its woods and stately avenues of eucalyptus and little brooks and Mexican and Japanese farmers, its tiny towns, its fiestas and roadside picnic places. Scattered around the Valley were relatives and friends. Masuto's father then had an old, old Model A Ford, and when it was loaded with venerable family and grinning children, it was always a great adventure to see whether it could puff and grind its way over wonderful Coldwater Canyon Road.

All that gone—and overnight. The proliferating hundred thousand dollar houses had turned Coldwater into a sort of street, and every inch of the Valley below was subdivided and covered with frantically built wooden houses. The orchards were gone and the ranches were gone. Thirty thousand dollars an acre was a price no farmer could resist, and most of the year its green wetness lay under a cover of yellow, noxious smog.

He pushed all this away from him, telling himself that he was only a cop and that too much halfbaked philosophy was notoriously bad for policemen. And then, when he reached Ventura Boulevard, he deliberately went on to the freeway and raced over the last few miles to World Wide Studios at seventy miles an hour, as any proper Southern Californian should.

It was not yet nine o'clock in the morning, but the vast sprawling studio was already awake and working: the stream of extras parking their cars in the great expanse of the employees' lot, the stars parking their Ferreris and Rollses and Thunderbirds in the few precious shaded spots; the little studio electrics shunting back and forth; the grips and carpenters and electricians walking from their cars to the stages where they would work this morning; the executives, the producers and directors, halting in little groups of emphatic importance; the office workers pouring into the cafeteria for the cup of coffee they missed at home; the writers dragging their feet, bowed in the inevitable gloom of their profession; the cowboys and badmen and Civil War soldiers and gowned and beribboned ladies giving that final and delightful sense of color to the gigantic dream-factory—all of it a never-ending wonder to Masuto.

He always watched and reacted; it was always new and exciting. He waved to the guards at the gate as he drove in, and he preempted one of the spaces marked off for security and then he walked over to the security cottage, where Frank Jefferson presided. Frank Jefferson was a grizzled man in his middle sixties, a onetime cop, onetime head of one of the largest private detective agencies on the West Coast, and now, at a better salary than he had ever earned, in charge of the private police force of forty uniformed and un-uniformed men who guarded World Wide Studios.

He sat back in his swivel chair now, his feet—in the low, embossed cowboy boots he affected—up on his desk, and regarded Masuto with interest and respect.

"Masao," he said, "you are not the model of a public servant. You got a mind in that noodle of yours. Come out here and I'll start you at twelve thousand. A year from now you'll head up my plainclothes division at eighteen thousand. What do you say?"

Masuto smiled and shook his head.

"All right, the hell with it. No cop really has brains, or what for would he be a cop? What can I do for you?"

"Got fifteen minutes?"

"I got the whole morning if you need it." He opened his intercom and said to the girl outside, "Bubby, hold any calls, and if you do it real nice, I'll give you a brand new set of black lace panties I got in my drawer."

He grinned at Masuto. "Lousy sense of humor, huh? But I got a good reputation. I stopped patting behinds five years ago, so I can say anything I want to. I'm an eccentric—just like you, Masao. For half a century I been a coarse old bastard, but now I'm an eccentric. How about that?"

"It's an improvement."

"Ah! Like hell it is! It's a case of gonadal decay. Now what can I do for the police force of Beverly Hills?"

Masuto told him. He told him the entire story, and Jefferson listened with interest and approval.

"Pretty good," he said when Masuto had finished. "Pretty damn good."

"You agree with me?"

"Well! That's the question, isn't it? As a cop, Masao, I am inclined to agree. As a member of the jury, I don't convict on what you got. It's a series of indications but not evidence. The curse of a cop is no different from the curse of the world—subjectivity. Like you, I liked Al Greenberg. He was direct, simple, and kind—and if that ain't unusual in this business, I don't know what is. It's too easy to get mad at the thought of some swine knocking him over that way. As for Mike Tulley—well, I'll tell you. With actors it's this way, you either like them or you don't. Same as with kids. You either like kids or you don't, and if you don't there's nothing a kid can do that's right. Myself, I like actors. I know what they are. They are vain, narcissistic, totally self-absorbed, selfish, self-pitying, self-indulgent, and maybe a few other things. They are also generous, outgoing, emotional and sometimes the best kind of people to have around. So maybe I'll cry a few tears over Mike Tulley—and you might too. So judgement is not to be trusted one hundred percent. I think you're right, but even if you are wrong, it's good odds that you'll smoke out the bastard responsible for all this. I don't like the thought of a murder at World Wide. I don't like the thought that a killer can operate in this studio with impunity. God knows, you got enough going in a studio to give any cop gray hair just in the ordinary run of things. I don't want any carte blanche for murder, and I like to keep my own house clean. Now what do you want from me?"

"Can you take a walk over to Stage 6?" Masuto asked.

"All right."

They walked across the studio grounds toward Stage 6. Jefferson wore a big, expensive, pearl-colored Stetson, a sport coat with gray checks, and he packed a forty-five caliber revolver in a shoulder holster. "Protective coloration," he had once told Masuto. "It makes me a part of the place." But he was consciously a character, a big man, well over six feet. He knew everyone and said hello to everyone.

"Always let them underestimate you, Masao," he said. "But you know that as well as I do."

State 6 was a large, cement-covered square block of a building. It completed a street of stages and processing houses, and then there was a big open space, bounded on three sides with stages and storerooms, but open on the fourth side to the thousand-acre stretch of sage and mesquite-covered hills that made up the vast back lot of World Wide Studios. Up in those hills was all that was necessary to the operation of a modern, contained studio: ranches, blockhouses, frontier forts, Indian villages, lakes, rivers, falls, sections of steamboats, an African village, a French town a medieval castle, a casbah, a New York street scene, a London Street scene, alpine peaks, cliffs—all of it linked by a winding, improbable road which was the basis for the studio tour.

"This square," said Jefferson, "is the first stop for the tour. You know, star's dressing room, sound stage—they go through Stage 11, over there. Then they snoop through the carpentry shop and the plaster shop. Neither shop does the real work anymore. We've moved the main effort over to West Studio, but we still do enough here to give it a feeling of validity. This tour gives me a headache, and I'll have to put on six or seven extra men, but it is still the most original piece of entertainment anyone has thought of for a long time. Well, like I said, all the tour cars stop here. There's the first one coming now."

He pointed down the studio street to where a gaily painted bus of sorts had appeared. An open bus, its seats stretched full across like the seats in a San Francisco cable car, with front, back and sides, were open except for a striped yellow and black awning. The awning was supported by six upright posts. The bus carried some twenty-four people. There was no question but that they were out-of-state sightseers. They wore sport shirts, carried cameras, and ran strongly to old folks and children; and they had the incredibly innocent, ready-to-believe look of people transported to some place as unlikely as the moon.

"The bus is a six-cylinder GM special job, geared very low," Jefferson said. "The best it can do is twenty miles an hour, but on that one-lane road, that's more than enough. There are hairpin turns up there on the mountain that you wouldn't want to joyride over. Well, enough of that. You want to bring your kids out here for the tour, I'll get them passes."

"That's good of you," Masuto said.

"It is, bubby. Even the studio executives pay. Now let's get down to cases. Here's Stage 6. What do you want me to do?"

"You understand, Frank, that I can't map out all that's going to happen. Maybe nothing will happen. Maybe our killer knows it's a bluff."

"Maybe."

"But the odds are that I was believed, and if I was believed, the killer is as cool as ice and will plan to take out the witness. The killer is insane, and therefore the plan will be somewhat insane. Now we cannot anticipate the plan, but we can lay down certain rules for the game. Phoebe Greenberg will be outside. By the way—where will she make up?"

"They got their makeup department on Stage 9. They're shooting two pilots, one on Stage 9 and the other on Stage 10, but they coordinate the makeup and do it all on Stage 9. The makeup girl there is Jesse Klein, a real bubby. Why don't we walk over and talk to her?"

"Good enough." They started over to Stage 9. "She comes over from Stage 9 to Stage 6. By then, I'll have the whole lot of them, with the exception of Phoebe, in Stage 6."

"If they show."

"They'll show. You can be sure of that. Now here's what I mean when I say that I can lay down certain rules for the game. I tell them that they must stay on stage—that under no condition is anyone to leave the stage until I return. Then I go outside and meet Phoebe. Then, when I have left, one of them will find some way to evade the others and get out of the soundstage."

"Won't the others miss him right off?"

"No. The place is too big—and they're all mavericks. They won't stay together no matter what I tell them. Leave it to our killer to work it out."

"This is a mighty iffy business, bubby," Jefferson said.

"Of course it is. But what other way can we play it? I must gamble that only one of them will come out—and that's our cookie. How many doors does the stage have?"

"The hanger doors are locked. On the side facing the

street, there are two doors, one at each corner. Then there's the alley, with a third door. That's the side alley. Back alley has two fire exits from the flying bridges and outside fire escapes."

"Is there anything about this studio that you don't know?" Masuto asked.

"Very little, bubby—very little. If they pay me thirty-five thousand a year to walk around here in a cowboy hat, there's got to be a reason why."

"All right. I come out of that door—the one nearest us." They were at Stage 9 now, and Masuto pointed across the big square to Stage 6. "So that's covered. I want a man in the street to cover the other street door. I want a man in the alley, and I want a man behind the building to cover the fire exits. That's three men. Got them?"

"They're yours. When?"

"I want them behind the building at 10:40. On the nose. I'll meet them there."

"You got it. What else?"

"I want them armed."

"They're armed. But I don't want any shooting, Masao. They're good men and they know how to use their hands and they carry billies. I got a clean record on this lot. We never had shooting, not in the eighteen years I been here, and I don't want any now."

"The killer will be armed."

"Then if a gun is pulled, it's up to them to get the drop. Don't worry about that. When your killer shows, they will control the situation. I told you they're good men."

"I just hope to God they are."

"And I want to do it quiet and quick, Masao, because the tours keep coming. A bus moves into this square every three minutes and another one moves out. Everything is timed, controlled and staged. We could put five thousand people through the tour on a busy day, so just think of how that could be loused up. I get paid to keep things from getting loused up. All right, we'll work it out. Let's go into makeup now."

The room was for extras, for bit players, for second leads and any others who didn't have their own dressing rooms or their own makeup people. It was crowded, noisy, and dominated by a tall, hawk-faced, efficient woman with dark eyes and grey hair. This was Jesse Klein, and when she spotted Jefferson, her dour hatchet face broke into a grin and she yelled, "Hey, cowboy! We got a part for you in this one."

"Not me, bubby. You don't make no actor out of me."

"Why don't you stop with that bubby-business, you big ape? How do you think it sounds to people, the way you go around, bubby this and bubby that? Anyway, we're busy here. You don't want to act, you want to tear down the profession—beat it."

He took her arm, introduced Masuto softly, and asked her to step outside with them.

"That sounds like a dirty invitation."

"Come on, come on—stop with the wisecracks already, bubby."

"You know," she said, going out with them, "you got 1930 slang, old Franko. The kids don't say wisecracks anymore. There are no more wiseacres. That has gone the way of 23 sakiddoo. Today you break them up or you're putting them on or you're bleeding on them or you're talking cockamamie or something. What do you want, anyway?"

"You know Phoebe Greenberg, bubby?"

"Sure I know her, poor kid. She inherited nothing but lousy. Then she married poor Al, and the whole world said she had it made. Everyone—Phoebe, you got it made. You got the world by the short hairs. And everybody tells Al he married an angel. Are you a religious man, John Wayne?"

"I'll tell you what," Jefferson said. "You stop calling me John Wayne, I stop calling you bubby. Is that a deal?"

"It's a deal."

"So I'm not religious, bubby."

"All right—you religious?" she asked Masuto.

"It's a foreign religion, so go right ahead."

"Then I'll tell you about God. You want to know what God does for kicks? He's got these angels roaming the world, trying to find someone's happy or got it made. Then one of 'em yells up to God, 'Hey God, here's Phoebe down here. She's got it made!' Then? You know what then? Then— wham!"

"Sounds reasonable," Jefferson said. "The point is this. Phoebe is coming in in maybe ten, fifteen minutes, and she wants to be made up. She'll tell you how she wants to be made up. You make her up. You ask no questions. You make her up."

"Just like that?"

"Just like that. She wants a costume, get it for her. Who's on wardrobe?"

"Bessie Kenning."

Jefferson took a pad from his pocket and scribbled a few words. "Give that to Bessie," he told Jesse Klein, handing her the slip of paper.

"You don't want to tell me any more?"

"I don't want you to ask any more, bubby," he said. "I'll meet you at the cafeteria at one o'clock and I'll buy you lunch and I'll buy you an ice cream soda for desert, and we'll set the whole place talking about me. Then, if you behave, I may tell you what kind of tricks we're up to."

"You're all heart," she said.

He walked down toward Stage 6 with Masuto. "Wait in the alley at the back," he said. "I'll have the three boys with you in ten minutes."

"Time's running out," Masuto said.

"Don't worry. They'll be there."

CHAPTER
TEN

CAPTAIN

SHARKMAN

Masuto was nervous. Time crowded him and caught up
with him, and the whole machine was running too
rapidly. He was a man who liked to think, who mis-
trusted quick conclusions, and now there was no time to
think. He spent ten minutes waiting in the back alley,
increasingly irritated as the minutes ticked by; and then
when the three studio policemen appeared in uniform, his
annoyance reached the bursting point.

"Why aren't you in plain clothes?" he demanded.

"Because nobody told us to get into plain clothes," one
of them explained. "If you want us to, we'll go back and
change."

Masuto's watch said ten-forty. "No, it's too late. We'll
make out." Masuto caught himself and calmed himself. In
any case, it was not their fault. They simply did as they were
told. Suddenly, he was almost physically sick with a wave of
mistrust of Frank Jefferson. But then he overcame that. It
was insane and pointless—and unless he controlled his

thoughts and rode hard on his suspicions the entire fabric he was weaving would collapse. The point was not to mistrust Frank Jefferson, but to recognize an area of stupidity—which was always obvious in another person. It was his own errors, his own misjudgements and stupidities that might destroy him and Phoebe, not another's.

He explained the situation in as few words as possible. "I want the killer," he said, "but above all, I want Mrs. Greenberg unharmed."

"Don't worry about that, Sergeant."

"Don't worry," Masuto said bitterly. "How the hell can I not worry when I am told that no guns are to be fired?"

"Unless we have to."

"What determines that?"

"Circumstances."

"I am armed," said Masuto. "If the killer has a gun, I'll use mine—that is, if the killer's gun threatens Mrs. Greenberg or myself. If the killer shows no gun, I won't use mine. Is that agreed?"

They nodded slowly.

"All right. I am going into the stage now. Remember—if possible I will come out of there into the street at nine minutes after eleven. I don't think so, but conceivably I could have a gun in my hand. Just take a long, hard look before you make any decision. That's nineteen minutes from now—right?"

"Right."

"Then take your posts and stay on them."

Then Masuto walked out of the back alley, turned right at the side alley, through the hard shadow into the burning white sunlight of the studio street. The candidates for murder were prompt, but perhaps that was to be expected. Trude Burke's MG was parked in front of the stage, and a grip was climbing in to return it to the parking lot. Sidney and Trude were standing at the door to Stage 6, and Sidney said cheerfully, "We're waiting, Sarge. I don't go in there without an escort."

At the same moment, a huge black Northeastern company limousine drew up to the soundstage, and the uniformed chauffeur opened the door for the five people inside: Murphy Anderson, Stacy Anderson, Jack Cotter, Arlene Cotter, and Lenore Tulley.

"We thought we'd come together," Anderson explained to Masuto. "We wanted to bring Phoebe, but she had already left when I called her home."

"There was a message from her at the gate," Masuto told them. "There was some mix-up at the cemetery. Evidently, they had some sort of title problem about the grave site. She had to buy seven square feet of additional land, and there was nothing to it but they must have a certified check. She went to the bank first, then to the cemetery, and then she'll be here. It doesn't matter."

"We'll hold it up, then?" Cotter asked. They were all tense and nervous.

"No—no, we don't need Mrs. Greenberg."

"How do you know?" Cotter demanded.

"For Christ's sake, Jack—don't be a damn fool!" Stacy said.

Sidney and Trude Burke stepped over to join them, and Murphy Anderson said, "Hello, Sidney."

"I'm putting that in the record," Sidney said. "A leper needs hellos. He files them away. Take it from me, Murph—don't be Mr. Goodguy. No percentage."

"I don't like that," Cotter said. "You're too damn quick with that tongue of yours, Sidney, and one day you're going to choke on it."

"For crying out loud—" Anderson began. Cotter snapped at him, "Who the hell is Masuto here to act as any kind of judge and jury? It's no worse to think of Phoebe as the killer than it is to think of Trude as the killer—"

"Oh, drop dead," Trude told him. "I never knew a cowboy player who wasn't an idiot—so why don't you stop trying to be a bigger shmuck than God made you! Let's get inside and get this lousy horror over with."

"I'm for that," Lenore Tulley said.

Masuto opened the door to the soundstage, and Sidney went through and opened the inside sounddoor. One by one, they entered—Masuto last. It was exactly one minute after eleven o'clock.

Inside the door, they stood in a tight group, allowing their eyes to become used to the dim light. Directly in front of them, a pile of cable lay like a tangle of enormous snakes in a jungle of arc lights and reflectors. There was a standing set of a modern kitchen, tiny and surrealist in the great inclosed space, and in the background one side of an ocean liner. Otherwise, only two high, half-drawn cycs and the shadowy spaces of roof, catwalks and far walls. Still, it was a dark forest—full of lairs and windfalls.

"Mrs. Greenberg left word that she would be here no later than eleven-five, and it's almost that now," Masuto said.

"If Phoebe's pegged for the killer," Stacy said, "then I am getting out of here right now."

"No one said she is pegged for the killer," her husband reminded her.

"I hate this stage. Let's get out of here."

"I just realized," Trude said.

"What?"

"He got his first one here. This is where Freddie Saxton was killed. Of course."

"Which is why we're here, bright eyes," Sidney said. "And it's no he. We got a dirty-minded broad doing all this scragging."

They were drifting apart now, just as Masuto had predicted, gathering courage as they realized that the soundstage was only a soundstage—no more, no less.

"Clean-minded Sidney," Trude said. "That's why I married you, my turtle dove, because you're so clean-minded and sincere."

"You married me for my money."

"Big discovery."

Masuto said loudly, "Look everyone—stay together and stay inside. For your own protection, stay together—and under no circumstances is anyone to leave the soundstage without permission from me—not until the witness arrives."

"Where is Phoebe?" Cotter demanded petulantly. He was over by one of the great cycs now, and he called out to Anderson, "Murph, this is ripped—did you know? They'll bill us for a new cyc—they come to about seven hundred dollars."

"The hell with it!" Anderson said, "Stop worrying about the goddamn cyc."

"Mr. Anderson," Masuto said, "I'm stepping to the door to see if Mrs. Greenberg arrived. I'll be back in a moment."

"Sure." Then Anderson called to Cotter, "Anyway, I think that cyc was torn before. Forget it."

Masuto stepped through the soundstage door into the street, blinking in the hot sunlight. The soundstage had been dim, cool and silent. Out here, a steam calliope was blaring circus music from the other side of the square. Busses with their brightly striped awnings of yellow and black were rolling in and out of the square, and under the guidance of young men and women in costume, crowds of tourists were being ushered through the carpentry shop and the plaster shop and the mocked-up Soundstage 11 to see all the wonders of how movies were made. There were kids eating icecream cones and popcorn and frankfurters, boys and girls holding hands, cowboys, Indians and gay Western ladies of the movie saloons. And through it all moved the grotesque lumbering figures who were America's cartoon heroes—Captain Devildom, with five wiggling tentacles and a ray gun; Major Meridean, dressed like a gladiator but with a rocket belt that could zip him anywhere in the world to right wrongs and defeat master criminals; Space Ace Ambrose in his gleaming space suit of red, white, and blue anodized aluminum, and other symbols of character and courage.

The calliope was screaming out a Sousa March as Masuto crossed the street, turning to face the soundstage. At the far end of the stage, the uniformed studio guard stepped out of the alley and lounged a few steps down the street, so that he could watch the door without appearing too obvious.

At the same moment, out of the corner of his eyes, Masuto saw Phoebe leave Stage 9 and start toward him. At least, he was certain that the stout, dark-haired woman—hair greying and wearing a cheap blue cotton dress that fell four inches below her knees—was Phoebe Greenberg. It had to be. Yet he wouldn't have believed that any makeup could be so perfect.

Then she met his eyes and they exchanged glances and he made a slight circle of approval with his middle finger and his thumb and she dropped one lid, and he knew that it was Phoebe. But in that time, for one part of a moment, for one part of a second, he made the error of negligence and sheer stupidity that he was destined to make. For one instant, he took his eyes off the soundstage door. When he glanced at it again, Captain Sharkman stood in the street in front of the stage.

Even in that instant, Masuto could not help thinking what a remarkable and impressive costume it was. It was mad, but then the world was mad and this was a dream factory out of which rolled, day in and day out, the phantasies, romances and nightmares of an entire nation. This was why a thousand generations had lived and died and fought and toiled— so that an apparition called Captain Sharkman could strut slowly toward him on the sun-soaked studio street. Captain Sharkman was six and a half feet tall. From the waist down, each leg was the separate body of a shark, an astonishing imitation of the pasty white skin of the fish itself. The torso was white and pale grey, and the arms were two ugly appendages that ended in sharkfins, and the head was a shark's head, ugly, expressionless, uptilted with the under-cut jaw open. Through that opening, Captain Sharkman had vision, but the mask was cleverly constructed and no eye-holes were apparent. And on either side of Captain Shark-man's head, a pair of moist red gills moved in slow rhythm. Two red, white and blue striped epaulets gave him his rank.

During the next few seconds, things happened very quickly. Masuto saw the studio guard staring at Captain Sharkman but making no move to stop him. "Look for a murderer," he had been told. But no one told him to look for Captain Sharkman. If a decision was difficult for Masuto to make, it was impossible for the guard. If the guard followed Captain Sharkman, the door would be left unguarded.

"And what do I do?" Masuto asked himself.

But there was nothing to do. Captain Sharkman shuffled up the street toward him. Phoebe walked across the square toward him. Masuto stood and waited, and a tour bus slowly moved across the top of the street toward the high mesquite hills on the back lot. The plan, prepared so carefully, had come to pieces.

Masuto made his decision. He let go of his plan and he let go of Phoebe. It was wrong, and he wanted her out of there, and as the bus crossed in front of her, he yelled, "Get on that bus!"

She had a mind and she had good reactions. Masuto watched with pleasure how specifically and quickly she reacted to his command, stepping onto the bus as if she had been waiting for it, standing on the running board and hanging onto one of the steel uprights that supported the awning. The passengers giggled with pleasure at her makeup and costume, and the driver-guide spoke into his microphone, "One of our Western ladies of small repute, friends, right out of a border saloon, yes, sir—one of the many surprises—"

Captain Sharkman broke into an entirely unexpected and most unlikely sprint, swinging onto the running board on the opposite side of the bus, hooking an arm-fin around the steel support. Masuto raced after him, caught the upright at the very end of the bus and hung on there as the bus rolled out of the square and onto the beginning of the mountain road, and still Masuto did not know for certain whether the murderer was on the bus here with him or back on Soundstage 6, chatting with the others and laughing quietly at Masuto's stupidity. Well, that's the way it was; you were brilliant and intuitive and you built a plan step by step and removed every wrinkle and considered that finally it was foolproof, and then the unexpected.

"An unexpected pleasure," the driver said into the microphone that curved toward him from under his rear view mirror. "Here we have Captain Sharkman himself. Well, that's something to talk about, isn't it? We are taking the hairpin climb up there to the Peak of Despondency, and you can see the Norman tower up there built for the great remake of 'The Conqueror'—and we have two studio guests, this little lady from the old West and Captain Sharkman. In case any of you have not had the pleasure of watching Captain Sharkman perform his great deeds on TV, I can tell you that he is one of the great cartoon stars of Grapheonics, and he does his part in righting wrong, preventing crime, and defending the American way of life. In his college days, Captain Sharkman was all-American—at the Naval Academy. Three years after his graduation he was in command of an atomic submarine, the ill-fated Finray that exploded off the coast of Africa in 1961. But by some miracle of electronics, instead of dying in that atomic blast, Captain Sharkman and his crew were transformed in a strange evolutionary process provoked by the atomic blast. They became sharkmen, and so were able to continue their lives and adventures in defense of the free world and the American way—"

As the spiel droned on, the driver was manipulating the hairpin turns of the studio road, climbing higher and higher, until Masuto could see below him the studio laid out, sound stages like small blocks, and beyond the studio the whole hazy vista of the San Fernando Valley.

"You will all recollect," the driver continued, "that unfortunate accident in which an atomic bomb was lost off the coast of Spain. Well, we like to think that Captain Sharkman and his crew of fearless underwater heroes were instrumental in recovering it, and in their dangerous under-water existence, this is only one of their many, many tasks. At the top of the climb, at the Peak of Despondency, there is a souvenir and refreshment counter where you can purchase a small replica of Captain Sharkman, either entirely assem-bled or in plastic pieces, one dollar—"

They had slowed almost to a stop to take one of the hairpin turns and Masuto shouted, "Phoebe, drop off!"

Again, she obeyed. She dropped off the bus onto the edge of the road. Masuto dropped off. It hung in the bal-ance, and then as the bus rounded the curve, Masuto saw that Captain Sharkman had also dropped off.

It had worked. Masuto faced the murderer. Phoebe ran a few steps, and then she was next to Masuto. "Behind me and down the road," he snapped at her. He had drawn his pistol, and as Captain Sharkman came toward them, Masuto pointed the gun and said, "Don't make me kill you."

A hundred yards up the road and fifty feet above them, the bus had stopped, the passengers staring at what was happening below. The driver yelled, "What goes on there, old buddy?"

The passengers giggled self-consciously.

Phoebe paused a few yards behind Masuto, and now Captain Sharkman leaped toward Masuto.

Masuto fired twice at Captain Sharkmen's legs. Either the costume deflected the bullets or Masuto missed, and then Captain Sharkman was upon him, and a blow of the big arm-fin knocked the gun out of Masuto's hand. As he attempted to lunge past Masuto, the detective caught him with a backhand karate chop, knocking him off balance. Sharkman, slipped, stumbled and then caught himself. The two of them dropped into karate position now, and Masuto realized that his right hand was bleeding from the blow with the fin. The fin was hard as steel and rough to simulate real sharkskin. It would only take a single karate chop with that rocklike fin to stop Masuto, to break a neck or an arm or a shoulder—and Captain Sharkman was determined to have the blow, to bring it in, to finish Masuto and get the girl. He was senseless now, mindless, and he rushed Masuto and screamed as he made his chop.

It missed. The audience in the bus shouted with excitement and howled with laughter.

Masuto's own cry came with the blow he launched. It was the explosive karate sound, and his hand chopped into Sharkman's neck and hit plastic and foam rubber. He hit again as Sharkman lumbered for his own position. Masuto was quicker, like a mongoose with a cobra, but Sharkman was almost invulnerable in his cacoon of plastic and foam rubber. Again and again, Sharkman swung his lethal fin, and again and again Masuto avoided it—only once not entirely, and it opened his left sleeve and took the surface skin off his left arm, shoulder to elbow.

It was then that Phoebe was able to dart in and pick up Masuto's gun, and as the crowd in the bus hooted and yelled and screamed, "Fake! Watch it, Sharkman—they got a gun!"

Phoebe cried to him, "Masao—here's your gun!"

Masuto got the gun, but Phoebe was not quick enough and a glancing blow from the fin sent her sprawling on the road. Masuto fired point-blank at Captain Sharkman's head. Sharkman wheeled around, and Masuto fired twice into the open mouth—and Sharkman staggered back, back from the edge of the road, fell and rolled down, down the slope, breaking mesquite and cactus and finally coming to a stop in the little drainage culvert that was the edge of the lower turn of the road.

Masuto helped Phoebe to her feet. She rubbed her shoulder.

"It's not broken, is it?"

"It feels like it's broken into twenty pieces. Oh—Masao, it hurts like hell."

"See if you can move your arm."

She moved her arm tentatively. "It hurts, but I can move it." She pulled off the black wig. "I look rotten as a brunette," she said.

"It beats me," Masuto said softly. "It just beats me."

A bus climbing the hill had stopped, and the tourists were crowding around Mr. Sharkman, and the tourists from the bus above were arguing with the driver, who was trying to keep them from pouring down the road.

Helping Phoebe, Masuto went down the road, and when the bus driver began his protest, Masuto said tiredly, "Damn it, I'm a cop. So why don't you see if you can back down the road and get Frank Jefferson and tell him there's been trouble here and he should get to hell up here."

"You can't back down that road."

"Then run down it by foot, damn you!"

Meanwhile, two people in the crowd around Captain Sharkman were easing off his headpiece.

"What are you doing?" Masuto demanded.

"I'm a doctor," a small man with glasses said. "This man is hurt. I don't know what you did to him with that gun you have in your hand—"

"Then help him," Masuto said without feeling.

Phoebe, next to him, was shivering. She pressed up against him as they removed the headpiece.

"Oh, my God, it's Jack Cotter!" Phoebe said.

"Didn't you know?"

A bullet had gone through his neck, but there was no blood on his face. It was a pasty white, puffy; he looked like a pudgy, harmless man with pale blue eyes. The doctor bent over him for a minute or so, and then turned to Masuto and said, "Well, he's dead."

Masuto shrugged.

"Well, who are you, mister?" the doctor demanded.

"I'm a cop," Masuto said, putting the gun away in his jacket pocket.

"And who is he?"

Phoebe began to cry, and Masuto put his arm around her.

"That arm of yours needs attention," the doctor said to Masuto. "That's a pretty bad scrape."

Still Masuto stared at Cotter, and then he said quietly to Phoebe, "Stop crying. There's no need to cry now."

"He was Al's friend."

"He was nobody's friend," Masuto said.

"There's a dead man there," the doctor said. "I'm asking you who he is?"

"He's Captain Sharkman," Masuto said, and then he pulled Phoebe out of the crowd and they began to walk down the road back to the studio.

The bus driver yelled after them, "Mister, if you're a cop, what am I supposed to do with this stiff?"

"Leave it alone," Masuto said.

But now Jefferson was on his way, his long black car with its spinning top light of bright red and its screaming siren careening up the mountain road and then pulling to a stop alongside of Phoebe and Masuto. There was a driver, Jefferson and two uniformed guards, and the two guards leaped out of the car and Jefferson put on his best John Wayne manner, looming over Masuto and demanding,

"What the hell kind of bad business is this, Masao. I tell you no shooting and you gun a man down."

Masuto glanced at his left arm, the blood welling out of the long, ugly scrape, and said that he was sorry.

"Was it your man?"

"That's right."

"Was your guess right?"

"It was right," Masuto said.

"Well, I'll be damned. You just never know, do you?"

"You never know," Masuto agreed.

"That arm looks ugly, bubby," Jefferson said. "Get it tended to. You know where the studio clinic is."

"I know."

"I'd ride you down, but we got things up here. Can you walk?"

"I can walk."

"It's not bleeding very much. Just an ooze."

"I'll walk and I'll survive."

"We stopped the tour for the time being," Jefferson said. "I guess we'll lose maybe two hours. You know what that costs the studio."

"My heart is breaking," Masuto said.

"I can just see that. Look, when you get that arm fixed up, come around to my office. I want a statement from you. Also, I got to call in the LA cops."

"I'll come around," Masuto said.

They got back in the car and drove up the road to where the bus was parked and where the crowd of tourists could not pull themselves away from Jack Cotter's body. Masuto and Phoebe were alone on the road now. They stood there for a moment, and then Phoebe said, "That arm does look awful."

"It looks worse than it is. It's not really bleeding, and unless you're going to dress one of those bad scrapes, the best thing is to leave it alone."

"But doesn't it hurt terribly?"

"It hurts."

"You're a strange man," she said.

He shrugged and pointed down the road. "It's a long walk," he said.

"They walked on in silence for a while, and then she said, "You knew right along that it was Jack Cotter?"

"Yes."

"I'm going to be sick," she announced suddenly.

"Try not to be."

"I can't try not to be. I can't control it."

He supported her by the side of the road as she heaved and cried out in pain.

"Easy, Phoebe—what is it?"

"My shoulder. It hurts so when I throw up. Oh, I am so miserable."

"Do you feel better now?"

"A little," she said. "I feel a little better."

They began to walk again, slowly, Phoebe hanging onto Masuto's right arm. Phoebe asked him, "When did you know it was Jack Cotter."

"The first night. In the viewing room at your house."

"No. How could you?"

"Because only he heard Samantha's voice. No one else. Every one took it for granted that it was a woman, but no one else heard the voice."

"Then whose voice did Lenore Tulley hear?"

"Jack Cotter's. Maybe he was a rotten actor, but how good do you have to be to talk in falsetto?"

She walked on for a while, and then she shook her head and said, "I don't understand, Masao. Why? Why did he kill Freddie Saxton? Why did he kill Mike Tulley? Why did he kill Al?"

"Why does a killer kill? He had a motive—he wanted Northeastern Films. He wanted to be it, the top man, the owner, the boss. But for that he only had to get rid of two men, Murphy Anderson and your husband. But that would point directly to him, wouldn't it? So he decided that Samantha would do it, and he killed Mike Tulley and Fred Saxton to establish the Samantha-revenge motive."

"But that's insane."

"He was insane."

"You mean he began this seven weeks ago, and that he then murdered Fred Saxton only to lay the basis for linking Samantha to the other killings?"

"That's right. As a matter of fact, I imagine he got the idea a year ago, when your assistant producer, Max Green, died of a heart attack."

"It doesn't seem possible."

"Murder never seems possible—and this kind of insane, grotesque murder is even less than possible. Only, it happens."

"And that poor woman, Peggy Groton, who died up on Mulholland Drive—did he kill her too?"

"Yes."

"But why?"

"Do you remember the phone call from Samantha—the one received in the office?"

"In the office? Oh, yes—yes, Murph told me about it."

"Well, Cotter could imitate a woman's voice to the extent of a few words through a locked door—but not a whole conversation over the telephone. That had to be a real woman, and any woman who became a part of his lunatic murder scheme was doomed. He couldn't allow Peggy Groton to live, not for an hour, not for a half hour. He had to kill her and kill her quickly."

"Poor Al," she said. "Poor Al. He never had an enemy. Can you imagine living in this place and not having an enemy? Do you know, Masao, if we walked down the street and a panhandler stopped him, he never said no. He was the industry touch. You were never in the industry, so you don't know what I mean, but no one ever asked Al and was turned down. And then that fool of a Jack Cotter, that strutting, ridiculous cowboy hero—there'll never be a day of my life when I won't think of him killing Al, and Al pleading for that medicine that held his life—"

"But we'll never know," Masuto said. "It's always possible that he didn't kill your husband. Mr. Greenberg could have had a heart attack and Cotter could have taken advantage of it."

"And we won't know, will we?"

"I'm afraid not."

"You know, I have a feeling that if you let go of me, I'd be hysterical."

"No, you'll be all right."

"Will you come and talk to the others? Do you suppose they're still there—on Stage 6?"

"Why not? It's less than an hour since I left them."

"Will you talk to them?"

"No," Masuto said.

"Why not? Do you despise us so?"

"I don't despise you."

"What do you call it, Masao?"

"I don't despise you. I don't judge you."

"And isn't that a typical statement for those you despise?"

"No."

"It's so easy for you. You live behind that damned Oriental mask of yours—"

Masuto felt himself freezing, closing up.

"I'm sorry," she said. "Dear Masao—I am so terribly sorry. I don't know why I said that."

"You said it because you felt it."

"Oh, Christ—no. No. Don't talk to me like that, Masao."

"I don't know of any other way to talk to you, Mrs. Greenberg."

"Sure. There it is. You've got that great big goddamn Japanese mask spread all over your face, and lump me and all that I am because I can never get past it, and what am I anyway but a skinny, washed-out Anglo-Saxon blonde bitch who was just hanging on to you and vomiting over the side of the road; and two days after my husband died, here I am trying to make a pass at you—so why don't you just spit in my face instead of going through this damned *Sayonara* politeness routine!"

He stopped and turned to face her. They were almost down at the square now, and he could see that it was filled with tourists from the stopped buses, and an ambulance was squeezing through to come up the road, and behind the ambulance there was a Los Angeles police car, and they would be up next to him in a minute or two and what does one say in a minute or two that can explain the whole world and the way it is?

"Phoebe," he cried, "Phoebe, what in hell are you doing to me? I'm a Japanese, and the hell with this Nisei business!

I am a cop. I take home one hundred and forty-two dollars each week, and they give me a car. I am married. I have three kids. In all her life my wife never set foot in a home like yours, but she has a sister who works in one as a maid. My wife never used a foul word or ever lifted her voice in anger against me or one of my kids. I am not a Jew or a Christian or a Mormon or anything else that would have any meaning for you, and I love you but I will get over it. So help me God, I will get over it. And that's it. The end of it. The finish of it. No more."

Then the ambulance reached them, and she knew what he said was true and would hold.

At the studio clinic, while Masuto's arm was being dressed and while his jacket was being mended by one of the wardrobe tailors, a stream of people passed by to check his credentials and to hear his side of the story. Studio executives, Los Angeles cops, the district attorney, sheriff's deputies.

Finally his own Chief listened to what he had to say and then told him, "Good enough, Masao. You can have the rest of the day off."

"The redheaded one, Trude Burke, you know what she would say to that?"

"What would she say, Masao?"

"You're all heart. That's what she would say."

"Don't rate me, Masao. It's the taxpayers' money."

"Sure, it's the taxpayers' money."

"Anyone else would drag you down to the office for a full statement. I'm willing to wait a couple of days."

"Like I said, you're all heart."

"Yeah. Can you drive or do you want a chauffeur?"

"I can drive."

The arm hurt a bit, but it did not interfere with his driving, but at home, when his wife, Kati, put her hand on his arm, he winced with pain—and then he had to tell her most of what had happened. As she listened, her eyes filled with tears at the thought of the danger he had faced.

She served him a very simple lunch of tea-rice and green tea, and then he went out to the garden to fuss with his roses.

She brought out her basket of mending and she sat quietly by the back door of the house, doing her sewing while he pruned branches, cut roses, loosened soil and sprayed just a bit here and there. There was still an hour before the children returned from school, and an hour like this, with Masao in the garden and herself sitting by quietly with her work, was almost better than anything else in the world.

THE CASE OF THE ONE-PENNY ORANGE

CHAPTER ONE

JACK BRIGGS

They say that a house that might sell for a hundred thousand dollars in Scarsdale, New York, would easily fetch a quarter of a million on a good street in Beverly Hills, and without such niceties as cellar and attic. The Spanish Colonial house that Jack Briggs had just purchased, which was situated on Camden Drive between Elevado and Lomitas, would hardly rate one hundred thousand, even in Scarsdale, The price to Briggs was two hundred ninety-five thousand, of which he had put down one hundred twenty thousand in cash.

Detective Sergeant Masao Masuto was aware of the sale price, just as he was aware of the fact that the former owner of the house, Cliff Emmett, had had in quick succession a divorce, a film that bombed, and a heart attack—while the purchaser, Jack Briggs, was one-third owner of the very successful X-rated *Open Mind*—"a totally new departure in the porno field," as one critic put it. The fact that Masuto carried with him a sort of Who's Who in Beverly Hills—in his mind and unprinted—was a source of constant amazement to his colleagues on the fourteen-man detective force of the Beverly Hills Police Department. As for Masuto, this was not a matter of great effort; as a Japanese—a Nisei, which means a native-born American whose parents were Japanese immigrants—and the only Japanese on the force, he took his job a little more seriously than might otherwise have been the case. He was essentially of a curious disposition—and as he once put it, Beverly Hills provoked him to endless curiosity.

As, for example, the fact that Jack Briggs' house had been broken into and ransacked—and nothing was taken. He was on his way to headquarters from his home in Culver City when the word came through on his band, and the boss told him that he could look in if he wished to but that it was not absolutely necessary, since Detective Sy Beckman was already on the scene. For Masuto, a ripped-off house with its contents intact was more intriguing than a simple run-of-the-mill robbery. He was already on Santa Monica Boulevard when he got the word, and a few minutes later he parked his aging Datsun in front of the Briggs home.

Masuto had rather liked Cliff Emmett, whom he had met once in connection with a simple robbery and who had gone down with his own bundle of trouble; perhaps because he worked in Beverly Hills, Masuto did not envy the rich, and now as he looked at the sprawling ochre-colored house with its red tile roof, he wondered what had become of Emmett. Quick rich and quick poor—there was a lot of it in Beverly Hills.

Beckman's car and a police car were parked in front of the house, the police car occupied by Officer Frank Seaton, who was scribbling in a pad, and who nodded at Masuto and informed him that Beckman was inside.

"Nothing to it, Masao." He shrugged. Officer Seaton was not curious.

Beckman opened the front door for Masuto. He was alone in the tiled foyer. "This one's kinky," he said. "I don't like them kinky." Beckman was an enormous man, six feet three, slope-shouldered, with a large nose and chin and heavy brows, and belligerently Jewish and ethnically conscious. He adored Masuto.

"Why kinky?"

"Where there's breaking and entering, I like something stolen. They claim nothing's missing."

"Who claims?"

"Jack Briggs and his wife, Ellen. Occupants and owners. One child, Bernie, in school. Mother died, day before yesterday."

"His mother?" Masuto asked.

"Her mother. Funeral this morning. They come back and find the kitchen door jimmied open—lousy amateur job—and the place ransacked."

"Where are they?"

Beckman turned his head and nodded, and Masuto followed him into the living room. A huge wooden door connected it with the foyer. Two steps down. A big room, brown Mexican tiles on the floor, beamed ceiling, large ornate chairs and couch. For all that he had lived his life in California, Masuto could never get used to the local notion of what was decorative and what was beautiful. Briggs, a large, fleshy man, overweight, balding, was sprawled in an armchair, sipping a tall glass of whiskey and soda. His wife—good features, brown hair, slender—was slowly straightening the rooms, putting back in place the contents of drawers and sideboard that had been dumped aimlessly on the floor. Both of them depressed, morose—understandable enough, Masuto decided, in two people who return from a funeral to find their home ransacked and disordered.

Beckman made the introductions. "Detective Sergeant Masuto—this is Mrs. Briggs."

"I am honored," Masuto said. "I saw you in *Major Barbara*. You were very good."

A faint hint of a smile. "In that wretched little barn on Las Palmas?"

"I love the theater—even in wretched little barns. I have seen many splendid actors in such places."

The smile became more than a hint, and Masuto experienced the qualm of uneasiness he always felt when he allowed himself to fall into a formal speech pattern. It was part put-on and part a necessity that rose out of a section of his being; he was two persons, he always would be.

She thanked him, and Jack Briggs climbed out of the chair in response to Beckman's curt introduction. His look said that he was dubious about Orientals—particularly on the police force.

"Detective Beckman tells me nothing was taken," Masuto said.

"Because there was nothing worth taking." He was not a pleasant man; his wife turned her back on him and returned to the disorder. "Every nickel I had went into buying this barn. I been a long time hungry, Lieutenant."

"Sergeant," Masuto said gently, nodding at a pair of silver candlesticks that lay on the floor.

"Plated. They're not worth carrying away." Suddenly, he exploded in anger. "You see this room? Every goddamn room in the house—like a motherfuckin' earthquake! And for what? You know what you can do with Beverly Hills,

Lieutenant—you can take it and shove it you-know-where!"

"May I look at the other rooms?"

He was back in the chair with his drink. "Be my guest." His wife folded down to the floor, cross-legged, and began to weep gently, a broken ashtray in her hands, her position as broken and forlorn as the cheap piece of crockery. As Masuto left the room, followed by Beckman, he felt a wave of compassion for the woman—yet objectively. Perhaps his greatest virtue as a policeman lay in the fact that he was always the outsider.

They went from room to room. Every room in the house had been searched, not with care or skill but wildly and stupidly, drawers emptied, contents flung around on the floor, pictures taken from the walls, some of them ripped from the walls, some of them torn from their frames. An image was reflected, the fury of barbarians, but then the world that Masuto inhabited was a world of barbarians. In the kitchen and pantry the destruction was even worse, dishes swept to the floor and shattered, flatware dumped from the trays, sugar and flour bins emptied.

"They sure as hell wanted to find something very bad," Beckman said.

The kitchen door had been jimmied as unprofessionally as the search had been conducted, probably, Masuto decided, by the simple process of inserting the curved end of a short crowbar and forcing the door open.

"These are no pros," said Beckman.

"Unless they wanted us to grant them amateur status."

Beckman picked up a watch that lay on the kitchen table. "Why did they leave this? It's worth fifty bucks."

"Five with a fence. They weren't looking for watches."

They returned to the living room. Jack Briggs still sat where they had left him; Ellen Briggs was staring at a framed photo of a woman. She held it for Masuto to see.

"You photograph well," Masuto said.

"My mother. Years ago. Poor woman." She placed the picture on a table. "One room done. I'm afraid to face the rest of the house."

"Your home was searched," Masuto said to Briggs. "Not neatly, but very thoroughly. What were they looking for?"

"You got me." Briggs shrugged.

"You must have some idea."

"None. Just none."

He turned to Mrs. Briggs. "Your mother's death—did you insert a death notice in the newspaper?"

"In the L.A. *Times*, yes."

"So they knew the time of the funeral and when the place would be empty. I mean, there was no mistake, Mrs. Briggs. They wanted this house."

The doorbell rang. "I'll get it," Beckman said. He returned a moment later with Sweeney, the fingerprint man. "Fingerprints," he explained to the Briggses. "This is Officer Sweeney."

"Where do you want me to start, Sergeant?" he asked Masuto.

"Forget it," Masuto replied.

Sweeney turned and left, and Briggs said, "That's a hell of a note. Don't you give a damn who did this?"

"People who do this kind of thing don't leave fingerprints, Mr. Briggs." He turned to Mrs. Briggs. "I don't understand—if you will forgive me, I have to ask questions. Why just the two of you? After a funeral . . ."

"I know." She nodded wanly. "I have no relatives. My mother was a refugee from Germany. I was the only relative who escaped—I was just a child. She had some friends in New York, but when we moved out here, two months ago—well, it was a small funeral. My son, my husband, and myself."

"Your son?"

"We dropped him off at school and then drove here. We had lunch first, so there was no reason for him to miss the afternoon session. Better in school than to sit here and try to grapple with death. He's only twelve years old."

"Of course. I understand."

"I thought of something," Briggs said. "Maybe they figured I'd have a print of the film here."

"*Open Mind*?"

Briggs grinned. "So you're a porny freak."

"I read the trades," Masuto said coldly. "Suppose you had a print here. What would it be worth?"

"You can't really protect a porny print," Briggs said. "Certainly not in the foreign market. If the mob got hold of it, they could turn it into a hundred grand—no sweat."

"They're going to pirate it sooner or later," Beckman said sourly.

"Later—later."

"A print would be this size," Masuto said, holding his hands eighteen inches apart. "Bigger than a breadbox. You don't look for that in small drawers or behind the backing of a wall painting."

"You tell me."

The telephone rang. Ellen Briggs answered. "Yes, he's here. It's for you," she said to Masuto. "A Captain Wainwright." She handed the phone to Masuto.

"Masao," the chief of detectives said, "are you finished there?"

"Just about."

"Then get your ass over to Gaycheck's on North Canon. The stamp place."

"What's up?"

"You'll tell me. He's just been murdered. In broad daylight. So help me God, I don't know what this town's coming to!"

CHAPTER
TWO

IVAN GAYCHECK

Masuto was the observer, not the observed. By sight or name he knew at least half a thousand people out of the population of Beverly Hills, yet even those who had met him before would forget, and then evince surprise at the fact that this tall, slender Nisei was a policeman in their city. He had been to Ivan Gaycheck's stamp emporium only once, when the place had been burglarized, and Gaycheck, ranting, had claimed the loss of twenty-two thousand dollars' worth of stamps, but he remembered the man well—short, stout, a background of no ascribable nationality, an accent impossible to pin down, pale blue eyes, and a reputation in the trade for being only slightly on the brighter side of shady.

Now, in death, his blue eyes were wide open, his puffy face set in an expression of aggrieved surprise. He lay in the back room of his store, between two display cases and in front of the safe where he kept the most valuable of his treasures. The safe was unopened; the display cases were unopened; but between his two open eyes, directly in the middle of his forehead, was the small, neat puncture of a .22-caliber bullet. He was covered with a rubber morgue sheet, and guarded, better in death than in life, by Officer Cutler. The two ambulance attendants were waiting for the detectives, and Gaycheck's assistant was in the bathroom, being sick.

Masuto bent over the body, turned back the sheet, and stared for a moment or two at Gaycheck's face.

"Twenty-two," Beckman said.

"Close. Those are powder burns."

"Twenty-two short," Beckman said. "One of those little-bitsy guns. Ladies' purse gun."

"That's a brilliant deduction," Masuto said sourly.

At that moment, Dr. Sam Baxter, the medical examiner, entered the back room, rubbing his hands cheerfully and demanding to know where the corpse was. His question remained unanswered. He grinned, took out his glasses and polished them, then knelt by the body.

"He's a damn freak," Beckman said.

"Dead. Instantaneous. Bullet in the brain. Twenty-two caliber, I think, but I can't be sure until I dig it out."

"We didn't know he was dead," Beckman said.

Ronald Haber, the dead man's assistant, a man of about thirty, usually pasty-faced and even pastier now, came out of the bathroom, looked at the body, and did a quick about-face. The sound of him puking came through the closed door.

"Any other wounds?" Masuto asked.

"One was enough." Baxter pulled off the sheet. "Clean as a whistle. Didn't even disturb the handkerchief in his coat pocket. The man's surprised. The lady smiled at him, put her little gun in his face, and poof!"

"Why a lady?"

"Little gun, little lady."

"Brilliant," Masuto agreed moodily. "You should be a cop. When did it happen, Sam?"

"What time is it now?"

"Just three."

The doctor patted Gaycheck's cheeks and bent one of his arms. "Two hours ago—give or take a few minutes."

"Can we take it away, or are we on permanent assignment here?" one of the ambulance attendants demanded. "You know, there might just be a live one waiting for the wagon."

"Empty his pockets first," Masuto told Beckman.

Beckman emptied Gaycheck's pockets, piling change, bills, wallet, and keys on the display case. The attendants covered the body, lifted it onto a stretcher, and rolled it out. The assistant came out of the bathroom and stood in front of the bathroom door, shaking. Dr. Baxter picked up his black bag and left with a cheerful goodbye. Sweeney then entered.

"You want prints?" he asked Masuto aggressively.

Masuto shrugged.

"You lift a guy's spirits, Masao. You sure as hell do. You make him feel nice and secure in his job."

"Oh, go ahead and dust the place." Masuto sighed.

"Thanks."

Masuto turned to Officer Cutler and asked him who had found the body and who had called him. Cutler pointed to Haber.

"That one."

"Who's outside?" Masuto asked.

"Jackson."

"He can take off. I want you outside until we lock up and seal off."

"Right."

"And you answer no questions. None. No crowds. If the media come, shunt them over to the captain. No one gets inside. Fill in the captain on what we know, which is nothing. Throw the latch on the door and lock it behind you, and knock if you want back in."

Officer Cutler nodded and left. Masuto turned to Haber. "How do you feel?"

"Better now—I think."

"Would you like to sit down?" There was a small desk and a chair in one corner of the back room.

"Funny, there isn't even a bloodstain," Haber said, staring at the carpet.

"No. The bullet remained in his brain or in the back of the skull. Then, whoever shot him caught his body and eased it down. Very cool." Masuto glanced at Beckman and smiled slightly.

"How do you know?" Beckman demanded.

"The way the body was. No one dies and falls that way—on his back, laid out. No way. No, indeed."

"So it wasn't a dame."

"A strong, cool woman—who knows? You found the body?" he asked Haber. The assistant nodded. "Tell me about it," Masuto said.

"I leave for lunch at twelve-thirty. One hour. Mr. Gaycheck leaves—I mean he would have left, he usually left when I returned. He always had a two o'clock sitting reserved at Scandia. He would return about three-thirty, but if he had an appointment with a customer maybe earlier. I shouldn't say customer. He always insisted on the word *client*. I guess it doesn't matter now."

"No, it doesn't. Did he have an appointment today?"

"I don't think so. You can look at his appointment book."

"Where is it?"

Haber pointed to the desk, and Beckman walked over and picked up a leather-bound log book. He opened it and showed it to Masuto. For this day, nothing except two scrawled letters—*P* and *M*. Masuto held out the book to Haber.

"Does that mean anything to you?"

"PM—afternoon, I guess."

"He knew it was the afternoon," Beckman said.

"Yes, I suppose so."

Masuto riffled through the pages of the log. Dates, names, prices—no other notation of PM.

"He said nothing to you about any appointment today? Expecting someone?"

Haber shook his head.

"You went to lunch—where?"

"At Junior's. I had a corned-beef sandwich . . ."

"All right. What time did you return?"

"One-thirty. Exactly."

"Exactly?" Masuto raised an eyebrow.

"I am a precise person."

"Go on."

"I went in. No one in front. I came back here, and . . ." He spread his hands. "That's it. I saw him on the floor, dead. I called the police. Then I called an ambulance."

"How did you know he was dead?" Beckman snapped.

Masuto shook his head, and Haber began to blubber that nothing like this had ever happened to him before.

"All right," Masuto said, not unkindly. "You called the police. What then?"

"I was in front. I couldn't stay there."

"No one else came into the shop before the police?"

He shook his head. "We don't have many customers—clients—off the street. Mostly by appointment. But what I don't understand is, why didn't anyone hear the shot?"

"A twenty-two don't make that much noise," said Beckman. "There was two doors between here and the street. But if he took him in here, it must have been somebody he knew."

Masuto stared at Haber, who was frowning.

"Well?" Masuto demanded.

"I guess so," Haber agreed.

"Who?" demanded Beckman.

Haber shook his head. Masuto motioned toward the cases. "Was anything taken—stolen—or sold, or removed?"

"I didn't look."

"Well, look now."

While Haber brooded over the display cases and Sweeney finished his fingerprint work, Masuto called Captain Wainwright at headquarters. Wainwright was upset. "Now just hear me, Masao," he said. "This is not East Los Angeles. When a store is ripped off in one of the streets north of Wilshire and the owner is shot, it means every damn one of them will be breathing down my neck, the chief, the city manager, the mayor, and maybe fifty prominent citizens—and this is not a place without prominent citizens. . . ."

Haber stood in front of Masuto, shaking his head. "Nothing," he said.

"It doesn't appear to be robbery," Masuto told Wainwright. "At least not yet. Just a clean, neat murder." He put down the phone. "How sure are you?" he asked Haber.

"I know the contents of the cases. Anyway, they're all locked."

"Where is the key?"

Haber pointed to the small pile of stuff from Gaycheck's pockets. Sweeney packed his stuff away, grinning at Masuto.

"Nice prints, very nice prints. Nothing like a print on glass. You don't have the murder weapon?" he asked Masuto hopefully.

Masuto shook his head. He was going through the contents of Gaycheck's pockets. "This key?" he asked Haber. Haber nodded.

"The trouble with you," Sweeney said, "is that you got no faith in Western technology."

"Opens all the cases?" Masuto asked.

"All of them."

"Technology," Sweeney repeated, and then left.

"That man," said Beckman, "gives me a pain in the ass. He draws down eighteen thousand a year, and I never known his goddamn fingerprints to give us anything."

"How valuable is the stuff in the cases?" Masuto asked Haber.

"All of it? I don't know—maybe twenty, twenty-five thousand dollars."

"That's very interesting," Beckman said. "When his place was ripped off last June, he claimed a loss of twenty-two grand—it was twenty-two, wasn't it, Masao?"

"It was. One case smashed and emptied." He looked at Haber thoughtfully.

"I had nothing to do with that."

"Now those," said Masuto, pointing to a set of American stamps in the glass case, "what are they worth?"

"That's a complete set of the Trans-Mississippi Exposition, 1898, mint—a very nice set."

"Mint?"

"That means they're uncanceled, never been used for postage. In U.S. stamps, we deal only in mint, except for the very first issues. This set, well, it's very nice. We could get almost two thousand for it."

"Are there fences for stamps?" Beckman demanded.

"Fences?"

"People who buy stolen stamps," Masuto explained.

Haber hesitated. "I suppose so."

"And what might they pay for such a set?"

"There's really no way to identify mint stamps. I suppose a thief could sell these to a dealer in some other city for at least seven or eight hundred dollars."

"Why some other city?"

"Because if they were stolen, we'd circulate the information here in L.A. and dealers would be looking for them."

"And you're absolutely sure there's nothing missing from the cases?"

"I'm sure."

"Do you have the combination for the safe?"

"No, sir."

"Who has it?"

"Mr. Gaycheck."

"Where? Where did he keep it?"

"In his head, when he was alive."

"He must have written it down somewhere," Masuto insisted.

"No."

"How long have you worked here, Mr. Haber?"

"Five years—since Mr. Gaycheck opened the store."

"And all the times he opened the safe in those five years, you never caught the combination?"

"No, sir."

"Bullshit!" said Beckman.

"No, sir . . ." Haber began to shake again. "Because Mr. Gaycheck was a very careful man. He never opened the safe without blocking the view with his body."

"What did he keep in the safe?" Masuto asked.

"Any cash over fifty dollars. Also some bearer bonds of his own—I don't know how much. And if we had a very valuable stamp, he would put it in the safe."

"Like what?" Beckman snapped.

"Well, last week we had a ten-cent black 1847 George Washington. It was in fine condition and any collector would pay three thousand for it. He put that in the safe."

"Is it in there now?"

"No. We took it on commission from Holmbey's, downtown. The sale didn't come through and I brought it back yesterday. Are you going to arrest me?"

"For what?"

"Well—Mr. Gaycheck was murdered."

"Did you murder him?" Masuto asked gently.

"Good God, no!" Haber burst out. "Murder him? I never fired a gun in my life. I wouldn't know how. I have a bad back, so I was never even inducted."

"Then we won't arrest you, Mr. Haber." Masuto smiled. "Did Gaycheck have a wife, children, relatives? Have you notified anyone?"

"No, sir. He wasn't married. No one. He would mention that, no relatives, no family."

"Friends?"

"None that I knew of. He would have lunch occasionally with some of the other dealers or with a client. That was business."

"How old was he?" Masuto asked, going through the wallet now. An American Express card, a BankAmericard, a two-by-three photograph, but no driver's license.

"I don't know," Haber answered slowly. "I never asked him."

"Did he drive a car?"

"No. He has a small condominium on Burton Way. He either walked or used a cab."

"There's one hundred and three dollars here in his wallet. I want you to count it."

Haber's hand shook as he counted the money.

"These keys. For the shop and the apartment?"

Haber nodded.

"This key?" It was a third door key.

"This is the shop key," Haber said. "I suppose one of the others is his apartment."

"And the third key?"

"I don't know."

"No safe-deposit key. Did he have a box?"

"I don't know. I don't think so."

"All right. Give your address and telephone number to Detective Beckman. Then you can go home. But for the time being, I don't want you to leave the county."

"What about the store?"

"The store will be sealed until we can have the safe opened and examine its contents. The rest is up to the legal department at City Hall. Detective Beckman will give you a number you can call for information."

While Beckman took down Haber's address and phone number and ushered him out of the store, Masuto studied the photograph he had found in Gaycheck's wallet. It was a picture, head and shoulders, of a young woman, no older than twenty-five, no younger than twenty. Straight blond hair, two buttons open on the blouse, good-looking, and not unlike any one of several hundred girls to be seen any day on the streets of West Hollywood. He was still staring at it when Beckman returned.

"Sy," Masuto said, "take the keys and the wallet and check them into the property department. I'm hanging on to this photo, so make a note of that. When you get back to the station, you can start to type out the report. I'll talk to the captain and I'll fill you in if there's anything."

After Beckman left, Masuto continued to study the portrait for a while. Then he wandered around the back room, stared at the stamps in the locked cases, and went through the two drawers in the small desk. There were two ledgers, a large general cash book, and a smaller book. The larger book contained day-to-day transactions, but nothing under twenty-five dollars, as Masuto noted. In the smaller book were names and a sort of code mark next to each name, no identification of stamps and no prices. Not surprising, Masuto decided, in a man who must have had many cash transactions and who would have used any means he could to avoid paying taxes. There was also a comprehensive international stamp catalog.

Masuto put the ledgers and the stamp catalog under his arm, made sure the outside door was latched to lock, closed it behind him, and walked over to where Officer Cutler stood next to his patrol car. There was still a small crowd of the curious on the sidewalk, a KNX mobile unit parked behind Cutler's car, and Hennessy of the Los Angeles *Times* and Bailey from the *Examiner*. Both reporters blocked Masuto's way, pleading for something more than they had.

"You're only two blocks from the station," Masuto said. "Get it from the P.R. there." Then he told Cutler to leave, and picked up his own car and drove to the station.

He sat in Wainwright's office, waiting for the captain, who was with the city manager and the mayor, and when Wainwright returned his scowl was even more deeply etched than usual.

"Murder," he said, "is all right in East Los Angeles, in West Los Angeles, in Hollywood, and in the Valley. Not in Beverly Hills. For a half hour I was lectured on the impropriety of murder in Beverly Hills."

Masuto nodded sympathetically.

"Well, goddamn it, Masao, what have you got?"

"An interesting day. A robbery where nothing was taken and a murder where nothing was taken."

"The hell with the robbery at the Briggs home! What about Gaycheck?"

"They are both of interest. A day is a contrivance."

"I am not interested in Oriental philosophy."

"That's a pity. Now about Gaycheck—he was shot at close range with a small twenty-two-caliber weapon."

"So Baxter informed me," Wainwright said. "Twenty-two short, from what they call a purse gun, probably a Smith and Wesson. The bullet went through the brain and lodged in the back of the skull. What else?"

"By someone he knew. No sign of a struggle, no sign of any resistance. Someone raised the gun to his head and pulled the trigger, then grabbed Gaycheck and eased him down to the carpet. That is why, purse gun or not, I'm not going to assume it was a woman. Gaycheck must have weighed at least a hundred sixty pounds. It would have to be an extraordinary woman—cool enough to deal with a corpse, strong enough to handle the body."

"What about the next of kin?"

"None. A man alone. Did we check his prints?"

"Nothing at the F.B.I. or L.A.P.D."

"Interpol?"

"I thought of that. We sent them a Telex a half hour ago. What about this man Haber?"

Masuto nodded thoughtfully. "He intrigues me. He over-performed, vomiting, hands shaking. He's an eloquent liar. There's a safe in back of the store, and he denies knowing the combination. I think he's lying. I also think he could make an excellent guess at the murderer. He may know why Gaycheck was killed. He put on a show of going to pieces at the sight of the corpse, yet he's cool enough to play his own game. He lives on Lapeer, in West Hollywood. I would put a man on him."

"What kind of a safe?"

"Stayfix."

"All right. We'll have them send a man down in the morning to open it. And I want this cleaned up, Masao—quickly and efficiently."

"By tomorrow, no doubt."

"Don't put me on, Masao. This is no casual street gun-ning. We got leads and we got connections."

"And we also have a very cool and very self-possessed killer."

"That's what you draw your pay for."

"Thank you."

The door to Wainwright's office opened, and a girl entered with a sheet of yellow paper, which she handed to him. "Telex, Captain, from Interpol."

He read it and then said to Masuto, "You never know."

"Gaycheck?"

"His name is Gaylord Schwartzman—captain in the SS, fourth in command at Buchenwald, wanted by West Germany, East Germany, Israel, and France, disappeared in 1944, reported at various times in residence in Brazil, Argentina, and Canada."

"But not in Beverly Hills."

"No, not in Beverly Hills."

CHAPTER
THREE

ISHIDO

Masao Masuto lived in Culver City, and for those unfamiliar with the geography of Los Angeles it may be said that while Culver City is only a few minutes by car from Beverly Hills, by property values and population it is a continent away. Masuto's small, two-bedroom cottage was on a street of small cottages, differing only in the lushness and perfection of the shrubbery in front and the garden in back; for when he was not a policeman, when he was off duty, Masuto's world was rather simple and contained. He had a daughter, Ana, aged seven, and a son, Uraga, aged nine, a wife, Kati, and a rose garden where he spent many pleasant and contemplative hours. The rose garden, surrounded on three sides by a wall of hibiscus, contained a world of forty-three different rose bushes, ranging from antique cabbage roses to ultrasophisticated, hybrid, scentless black and purple modern miracles of horticulture. Masuto knew each plant, its strengths, its weaknesses, its moment of bloom, and he was not beyond trusting that in their own way the plants knew him.

His wife, Kati, had been raised in the old-fashioned way. She was a small, lovely, timid woman, and although she had been born in California, she had led a sheltered life. She did not drive a car. Her ventures on foot to the supermarket and the few other places that demanded her personal attention were undertaken with trepidation. Her home was her world, and she lived there in constant anxiety about the strange and violent profession her husband pursued. It was a world she knew only from his reports of his work—carefully censored.

When he came into the house this evening, she greeted him with restraint, yet with the relief that was always evident. His bath was ready. He greeted his children, spoke a few appropriate words to them, bathed in steaming-hot water, then slipped into the kimono Kati had ready for him. Then he went into the tiny screened-off area that was his meditation room.

As a Zen Buddhist, he tried to find time for some meditation, regardless of how much his day pressed upon him, forty-five minutes if possible, and at least a few minutes if no more than that was available. He knew that five minutes of perfect meditation accomplished more than an hour of struggling with his mind, trying to tame an unwilling beast. Now he sat cross-legged for thirty minutes, then went to his wife.

They had tea, sitting on two cushions with a small, black enamel table between them. Masuto honored the pouring and drinking of tea in the old way, and Kati waited for him to speak about his day.

"A man was murdered," he said finally.

Kati shook her head in horror and sympathy. She never understood how this man, who was her husband, could live and work with murder.

"I don't judge, but he was a man who was responsible for the deaths of many innocent people. Death waited a long time before it welcomed him."

"Did he suffer?"

"Less than those whom he killed," Masuto replied.

"Then something else troubles you. You are troubled."

"Oh, yes." He smiled. "But you must not be troubled. It's a small matter and very puzzling. Postage stamps."

"Postage stamps?"

"About which I know absolutely nothing. Not the stamps one buys at the post office to mail a letter, but stamps that people collect with greed and passion."

"But Uraga has a stamp album, which you bought for him. He bothers everyone for the stamps on letters from Japan."

"Of course," Masuto remembered. "And you recall why I bought it."

"The packet of stamps that he received as a gift from my kinsman, Ishido. How simple. If you would know about stamps—then go to Ishido. They say that his stamp collection is worth many thousands of dollars."

"Not so simple," said Masuto. "I would have to humble myself, and that is something that does not come easily to me. Ishido despises my birth, my ancestors, and my occupation."

"No," Kati protested weakly.

"He is Samurai. My father was a gardener. He has never forgiven you for marrying me, and he has never forgiven me for being a policeman."

"That is in your mind, not in his. You forget that he has lived in California for the past thirty years. He is not bound by the old ways. I have heard him speak highly of you."

"And we have never been guests in his house. In all the years we have been married, we have not been guests in his house."

"And did you invite him here?"

"Who am I to invite Ishido to my home?"

She refrained from observing that, for a sensible man, he could be both stubborn and foolish; she simply said that not only Ishido was proud, then followed it with that very Japanese expression, "So sorry, dear husband."

Masuto was silent all through dinner. When he was silent, the children were silent. It was not the most pleasant dinner. When he had finished eating, he rose from the table, went to the telephone, and dialed a number. Kati listened.

He spoke in Japanese, and Kati smiled slightly. The servants in Ishido's home spoke little English.

"I would speak with Ishido Dono. My name is Masao Masuto."

A pause. He glanced at Kati, and she stopped smiling.

"A thousand apologies, Ishido Dono. I interrupt you at the worst of moments. . . . You are too kind. I am thoughtless, but this is a matter of my work and I need your assistance and your wisdom. . . . Of course. In one hour. A thousand thanks."

Masuto put down the phone and said to his wife, "I will thank you to make no comment on what I have just done."

"I love you very much," she said. Then he smiled, and the children began to chatter.

Bel Air, while a part of Los Angeles, is if anything even more self-contained and more packed with wealth than Beverly Hills. It has its own private police force, which is called the Bel Air Patrol, and it has in its few square miles more castles, keeps, and baronial halls than one would find in a hundred miles of the River Rhine. Ishido's home was

high on a hill, and as Masuto drove that night up the winding road that led to the place, he reflected as so often before
on the oddity that was America, where a samurai, once at
war with these people, could in the same lifetime dwell in
peace and luxury in their very midst, both welcome and
respected. "Well, it is as it is," he said to himself, which is a
very Zen comment.

The single-story house was Japanese in style, surrounded by a wall of hedge and brick, glowing through its
translucent walls. The doorbell was an ancient Chinese
gong, and Ishido himself, clad in a black silk kimono,
opened the door, a particular gesture of welcome. Masuto
felt abashed by his own stubborn pride.

Ishido was a small man of about sixty, slender, with a
round, moonlike face. "So pleased, so delighted," he said,
speaking in Japanese. "My kinsman honors my poor, humble home."

"No, the honor is mine," Masuto replied in Japanese,
conscious of his bad accent but not to be outdone. "I am
overcome. I do not know how to thank you for your gra-
ciousness."

"My home is yours. You have been too long a stranger."

Once inside, Ishido switched to English. He had a slight
British intonation and almost no accent. He ushered Masuto
into his living room, which was rather large, about thirty
feet by twenty. It was furnished—or better said unfur-
nished—in the Japanese manner, with four splendid painted
screens, cushions on the floor, low tables, a room for himself and his family. His study was in the Western manner;
but it was a mark of consideration to take Masuto in here.

"You have a problem," he said. "I am pleased. It has
brought you to me."

"I hesitate to burden you with it."

"Is it police work?"

"Yes."

"How fascinating! Tell me about it."

"A man was murdered today. I am afraid that murder is my major province. You know I am chief of homicide in Beverly Hills."

"No. I didn't know. Fascinating. Who was the victim?"

"His name was Ivan Gaycheck."

"Gaycheck? Really." Ishido's moon face remained expressionless.

"I see you know him."

"I know him, but without pleasure."

"Have you dealt with him?"

"Once. I found him rude and unpleasant. You know, Masao, his name is nondescript—Ivan Gaycheck. It means nothing, but it suggests a Slav or a Hungarian. He was a German."

"Indeed? How do you know that?"

Ishido smiled. "I am right?"

"Yes."

"His accent. I have an excellent ear for accents. Tell me, how did death find him?"

"Someone he knew well shot him in the forehead with a small twenty-two-caliber pistol."

"Ah." No judgment. Watching his kinsman, Masuto read nothing. Well, a man like Ishido was not to be read easily.

"Your conclusions are part of your police work?"

"Hardly a very brilliant part," Masuto said. "We have the bullet and there was no sign of a struggle. The shot was at close range."

"And since he dealt in stamps, you postulate that his death might be connected with stamps. And since I am a collector, you come to me."

"But with apologies. I come only for information."

"Nonsense, Masao—if you will forgive me. If a stamp is central to this murder, then every collector of consequence must be suspect. A collector is a unique type of personality. I have heard that you are a Buddhist?"

He appeared to have changed the subject aimlessly, but Masuto knew that a man like Ishido did nothing aimlessly or thoughtlessly. "I am Zen. The Soto School."

"Ah so. A Buddhist seeks for meaning, in his way. A collector, a true collector, also seeks for meaning, very narrowly, very fanatically, but there are no ethical boundaries to his religion. Do you understand?"

Masuto nodded. They sat cross-legged, a low, polished teakwood table between them. Now a young woman appeared with tea things. She wore a kimono and obi and she was very lovely, but Ishido did not introduce her and Masuto knew that his wife was long dead. She set down the tray, poured pale yellow tea, and disappeared. Politely, Masuto made no inquiry. They sipped the tea, and then Ishido said:

"Therefore, I must be suspect."

"No."

"Why not?"

"You are my kinsman."

"That is no reason. You must ask me whether, for a true collector, there is any stamp worth killing for. Of course, with such a man as Ivan Gaycheck, there could be a thousand motives. Was he connected with the SS? Surely you have inquired at Interpol?"

"Yes."

"Then any Jew who discovered his identity would feel justified in an act of revenge."

"I don't think so," Masuto answered slowly. "That kind of act of violence is not in their pattern."

"But patterns change—as witness Israel."

"Perhaps. But I have a simple mind. When a stamp dealer is murdered, I look for a stamp." Masuto sipped his tea. "Now I will ask you—is any stamp worth an act of murder?"

"Who is to say what will prompt an act of murder? A man is killed in the street for a few dollars. You know that I was a colonel in the Imperial Army—war is a gigantic killing. Who is to say? My own passion is porcelain. I have always dreamed of owning a Bactrian horse of the T'ang dynasty—not the pottery horse, but that almost mythical T'ang horse which is said to have been made of Ch'ai war, which they describe as being thin as paper, resonant as musical stone, and blue as the sky between the rain clouds. Does it exist? Rumor has it that there is one in Peking and another in the Imperial Palace in Japan—but that is only rumor. I have never spoken to anyone who actually saw such a horse. Would I kill for such a thing? But that would depend on so many circumstances. A man like Gaycheck—I might well kill him, but not for a stamp. I only collect Japanese stamps. Well..." Ishido paused, smiled, and sipped his tea. "Yes, one stamp. In the Dragon series. Two colors with an inverted center. But, you see, Masao—I already have it. So the question is academic."

Masuto did an unforgivable thing. "Might I see it?" he asked.

Ishido stared at him evenly, his face reflecting Masuto's own carefully controlled indifference. Then he nodded, rose, and went into another room. He returned with a small black album and opened it to reveal what Masuto considered a very ordinary stamp, the dragon in the center inverted.

"How much is it worth, if I may ask so improper a question?"

"You are a policeman," Ishido said, his simple statement exiling Masuto from his world. "I bought it in Hong Kong twelve years ago. The seller was unsavory. I paid a thousand British pounds. At today's inflated prices—well, over seventy-five thousand dollars."

Still, Masuto did not go. He would not be invited back to Ishido's house, so whatever questions he would ask must be asked now. Since he was a policeman and no more than a policeman, he would play the policeman's role.

"Is this the most valuable stamp that exists?"

"Hardly. The land of my birth lacks that honor, but one does not judge a country or a person by the worth of his stamps. There is a stamp called the One-Penny 1848 Mauritius. Today, in perfect condition, it might sell for one hundred and fifty thousand dollars. I do not know whether any other stamp is more valuable."

It was almost eleven o'clock when Masuto returned to his home in Culver City. Kati was waiting for him. "Was it pleasant?" she asked him. "Were you greeted well?"

"I was greeted well, yes. With great courtesy."

"Oh?"

"I must make you unhappy, dear Kati. I came as a kinsman, I left as a policeman."

"Oh, so sorry! Such a pity!"

"I asked improper questions. And as far as my manners were concerned—well, I am a policeman."

"Who has ever complained about your manners?"

"Dear Kati." He sighed and walked to the bookshelves, where he took down a volume of the Encyclopedia Americana—the fine set that he had bought for his children only a year ago and of which he was very proud. He riffled through the pages, and then handed the book to Kati. She liked to read to him. Not only did it relax him, it gave her a sense of participating in his thoughts. He pointed to a paragraph and asked her to read to him.

"Mauritius," she began.

"No, dear wife—so sorry, but Ishido pronounced the word differently. He pronounced it Moreeshius. I am sure his pronunciation was correct."

"Yes, yes. Moreeshius. 'A densely populated island in the Indian Ocean about 550 miles east of Madagascar, is an independent nation within the Commonwealth of Nations. Its capital, Port Louis, also administers smaller island dependencies: Rodrigues, 350 miles east, and scattered coral groups, 250 to 580 miles away.' " She paused. "The next paragraph is about population. Shall I read that?"

"No. And after that?"

"The land. Then the economy."

"Are stamps mentioned?" Masuto asked.

"No, nothing about stamps. The next section is entitled 'History.' Shall I read it to you?"

"Only if it mentions stamps."

"Nothing about stamps," Kati said sadly. "But very interesting. Did you know that Mauritius was the home of the dodo bird?"

"The dodo bird is extinct."

"You mean there are no dodo birds—anywhere?"

"I am afraid not."

"How sad! But why are you asking about stamps—if it is something you can speak of?"

"Because there is a postage stamp issued in 1848 in that place called Mauritius that is worth in the neighborhood of a hundred and fifty thousand dollars."

"A single postage stamp?"

"Yes, Kati."

"But why? How can a tiny postage stamp be worth so much money?"

"I suppose because it is very rare. I would give a great deal to know whether one exists in Beverly Hills."

CHAPTER
FOUR

RONALD HABER

The telephone burst in on Masuto's sleep like a fire engine gone berserk. As he reached out to pick it up, he saw that the luminous dial of his clock said 4:20. In the background, Kati made small sounds of despair. She could never grow used to the telephone in the middle of the night.

Wainwright was on the phone and he minced no words. "Masao, Haber is dead. Murdered."

"What? Where? When?" Masuto was still fuzzy with sleep.

"In his apartment on Lapeer. I'm there with the sheriff's men, and I want you to get your ass over here."

"Now?"

"Now."

"It's four-twenty in the morning."

"If these lousy deputies could get me out of bed at four in the morning, I can damn well get you out at four-twenty, so get your ass over here and stop yammering."

While Masuto dressed, Kati put the teakettle on to boil, but he was in no mood to wait. He gulped down a glass of milk to settle his sour stomach and then climbed into his car and drove through the night—or morning—for the strange gray thickness of dawn was already beginning. Once again, as so often before, he pondered the geographical insanity that called itself Los Angeles. There was a city of Los Angeles and there was a county of Los Angeles. The city of Los Angeles had its own police force. The county of Los Angeles had a sheriff, with a vast force of deputies. Within the city of Los Angeles were other cities, such as Beverly Hills, which had their own police forces, and also within the city of Los Angeles were unincorporated areas, which were policed by the sheriff's deputies—and while there was a courtesy interchange of the right of movement and information, it did not make for efficiency.

Lapeer Street, where Masuto was bound, was in West Hollywood, an unincorporated area policed by the sheriff's deputies. When he arrived, three sheriff's cars were parked in front of the building, a small, unimpressive apartment house. He showed his credentials to the deputy at the street door. It was five o'clock now, a glint of dawn in the sky, but the stairway was dark, lit by a single weak bulb. The commotion had awakened other tenants, who, many of them half dressed or in robes, were standing curiously in their half-open doorways.

Haber's apartment was a one-bedroom, drably furnished flat. Always, on entering such a place, Masuto relied on his first impression—here a sense of bleakness, indifference, lack of imagination, and a degree of despair; the habitation revealed more than the man, even though the place was in disarray, furniture overturned, a lamp smashed, drawers emptied and dumped on the floor. Three deputies, a fingerprint man, a county photographer, two morgue men, and Wainwright crowded the living room. The morgue men had their rubber sheet still folded, evidently waiting for Masuto to see the body.

It was not a pretty sight. Haber lay in a corner, as if he had been flung there.

"Beaten to death," Wainwright said to Masuto.

"Animals," said one of the deputies. "This place is lousy with animals."

"Can we take him away, Sergeant?" one of the morgue men asked Masuto. He nodded. They put Haber's body on a stretcher, covered it with the rubber sheet, and marched out. Masuto stood silently, his eyes wandering around the room.

"Well?" Wainwright demanded.

Masuto shrugged. "Violence is the disease of our times. The sickness is not restricted to West Hollywood."

"I'm not asking for your damn philosophy."

"He's dead."

"Great! Brilliant! How does it tie in? It's sure as hell a different M.O."

"Murderers are not required to be consistent."

"You give me a pain in the ass," Wainwright said. "I ask you to clean up one lousy killing and now we got two."

"This one's in West Hollywood—theirs." Masuto nodded at the deputies.

"That's sweet."

"You gave me until tomorrow. It's not tomorrow yet."

"Tomorrow's today," Wainwright said. "All right. I'm sorry. This happened at about three A.M., so I got no sleep at all. I'm edgy. For God's sake, Masao, what have we got here?"

"I don't know," Masuto said thoughtfully.

One of the deputies said to Masuto, "Captain Wainwright here tells me that Haber worked for the dealer who was shot in Beverly Hills yesterday. Do you have a connection?"

Masuto was prompted to assure the deputy that there was a connection between every living creature and every event on earth; but he thought better of it and simply shook his head.

"Hell, Sergeant, you're not telling me it's a coincidence? Because if you are . . ."

"It's not a coincidence."

"You just said . . ."

"You asked me whether I have a connection. I shook my head," Masuto interrupted, almost with irritation. He disliked deputies, not out of any specific behavior on their part but simply because he did not have a high opinion of their intelligence, and it irritated him that he should be disturbed by something that was almost a common affliction of mankind. "I did not say there was no connection. There is. But what the connection is, I don't know."

Grinning, the fingerprint man said, "I got some beauts, Sarge. You want to see them?"

"What?"

"The prints. I took a set of Haber's. I got a dozen that don't belong to him."

"No, thank you," Masuto muttered.

"He's a lover," the fingerprint man said to the deputy at the door. Hurt, he was on his way out.

"Didn't you know, Billy," said the deputy, "they got nothing but smartass cops in Beverly Hills. All class. It ain't no asshole, like this place."

The fingerprint man departed. Another deputy said to the deputy at the door, "Just keep your mouth shut and stop being a horse's ass." Then he went over to Masuto. "I'm sorry, Sergeant. But a night detail's lousy, and around this time everyone gets edgy. My name's Williams, and I'm on night Homicide. Any help you and Captain Wainwright can give us, we appreciate."

"Balls," the deputy at the door muttered.

Williams gave him a stony look. Wainwright said nothing. He was watching Masuto with interest. They had worked together for too long for him to question anything Masuto said or did.

"You questioned the neighbors?" Masuto asked Williams.

"All of them."

"They were all awake?"

"There was a hell of a fight and racket in here. One of them called us. A young girl, name of Cindy Lang."

"Just one? How many tenants in the place?"

"Four on this floor. Those were the ones who heard it."

"And only one called you?"

"That's the way it is, Sergeant."

"Did any of them see anything?"

"They claim no."

"They're lying," said another deputy.

"Maybe yes, maybe no," Williams said. "Nobody wants to get involved."

"Running feet? That could tell something. Two feet sound one way. Four feet sound different."

Williams turned to the deputy at the door, who shrugged and said, "I never asked them that."

"Well, goddamn it, ask them!" Williams snapped. The deputy left, and Williams said to Masuto, "They heard a car start."

"They always hear a car start."

"Did they hear anything else?"

"Like what?"

"Voices."

"Men's voices. Nothing very clear."

"Any of the tenants know Haber?"

"No. Or so they say. He was a loner." Williams looked around the apartment. "They must have searched the place first. After they killed him, they took off."

"What was on his person?"

"Keys and wallet. You want to see it?"

Masuto nodded. Williams took a brown envelope out of his pocket and handed it to Masuto. Wainwright dropped into a chair, sighed deeply, and half closed his eyes. The deputy who had been at the door returned.

"Well?" Williams demanded.

"Some say two feet, some say four feet, some say six feet—which means one person or two or three."

"I couldn't have never figured that out," Williams said.

"What did Cindy Lang say?" Masuto asked. He was going through the wallet: Master Charge, driver's license, insurance card, but no bills. Three keys.

"If he had bills, they took them," said Williams. "I don't think they were after money, but it's a habit with hoods. They didn't want his credit card."

"Who's Cindy Lang?" the deputy asked.

"You got a brain like a sieve," Williams said disgustedly. "She's the kid who called us. The blonde in apartment F."

"Oh."

"Well, what did she say?"

"She says she thinks there were three of them."

Masuto nodded. Wainwright was dozing now. The photographer gathered his stuff and left.

"What killed him?" Masuto asked Williams.

"Skull fracture, over the left temple."

"Brass knuckles?"

"That's what the doctor thinks."

"You mind if I look around?"

"Be my guest. But this place has been searched like an earthquake hit it."

"They didn't find what they were looking for," Masuto said. "So they decided to beat it out of Haber. Except that he didn't have it."

"What?"

"Who knows?"

"Then how the hell do you know he didn't have it?"

"They killed him."

"Maybe after they took it."

"Maybe." Masuto went into the bedroom. The search was thorough, bedclothes torn off the bed, mattress turned over, pictures ripped off the walls—and in the bathroom, bottles emptied, toothpaste tube slit open. He went to the closet. Haber had been in his shirt-sleeves at the time of the murder. His jacket hung in the closet. Masuto took the jacket and spread it out on the bed. Wainwright had finished his nap, and he and Williams were watching now. Masuto folded back the lining, and there, attached to it with two strips of Scotch tape, was a small plastic envelope containing a single stamp.

"I'll be damned," Williams whispered.

Wainwright said nothing.

"Goddamn it, Sergeant, how did you know where that was?"

"I didn't know. I tried to crawl into Haber's mind—a little."

"Is that what they were after? That stamp?"

Masuto took the stamp out of the envelope carefully and examined it. "No."

"Masao, how do you know?" Wainwright demanded.

"It's a ten-cent black 1847 George Washington, and it's worth about three thousand dollars. They weren't after this and they weren't after three thousand dollars, because if they were he would have given it to them."

"What are you, a stamp expert?" Williams snorted.

"I don't know a thing about stamps. Haber told me about this stamp yesterday. He invented some cock-and-bull story." He turned to Wainwright. "Either Haber knew the stamp was in Gaycheck's pocket and took it before he called us, or it was in the safe and he knew the combination of the safe and he was lying."

"How about him killing Gaycheck for the stamp, and then we let the sheriff worry about it."

"No way," said Masuto.

"Anything else here?"

Masuto shook his head, replaced the stamp in the plastic envelope, and gave it to Williams. "I guess it belongs to Gaycheck, and he's dead. What about it, Captain?"

"Hold it for evidence. Let's see what happens. Anyway, I'm hungry. Let's get some breakfast, Masao."

"All right. But I want to talk to Cindy Lang,"

Masuto called his wife first. It was almost seven o'clock, and she had not slept since the telephone awakened both of them. "Masao," she said, "you must have a night's sleep and you must rest and we don't even see you anymore."

He tried to soothe her.

"Masao, I was reading a book on Women's Liberation, and first I was provoked, but now I am not sure. Not at all."

He put down the phone and told Wainwright that his wife was reading books on Women's Lib. "I always felt I should have married a Japanese girl. Now you're shaking my dream," Wainwright said. "Let's find Cindy Lang."

They walked down the hall and knocked at the door of apartment F. It opened the width of the safety chain, and Masuto had the impression of straight blond hair and suspicious blue eyes.

"We're from the Beverly Hills police," he said. "This is Captain Wainwright. I'm Detective Sergeant Masuto."

"Well, this is not Beverly Hills. I talked to the local fuzz. I told them what I know, which is nothing. I don't even know Haber."

"If you could spare us a few minutes," Masuto said gently. He showed her his badge.

She thought about it for a moment or two. Then, "Okay—but I got to get to work. I'm due in at seven-thirty." She dropped the chain and opened the door, and they entered the apartment: one room, a studio bed still unmade, some bright prints on the wall, and a rag rug. Cindy Lang was in her twenties, a slight, pretty girl wearing blue jeans and a blouse—a girl little different, Masuto thought, from a hundred others he would see on the streets of West Hollywood—where blue jeans and loose yellow hair, dyed or real, were almost required uniform.

"You called the sheriff last night?" Masuto asked her.

"That's right. It sounded like they were killing someone, so I called the fuzz. Does that make me anything?"

"It makes you part of the human race. No one else called them."

"All right, so I'm part of the human race. Now can I go to work?"

"You told the deputy that three people ran past here. How did you know it was three?"

"It sounded like three."

"What sounds like three?"

"Three people. Why don't you do your thing, Sergeant, and I'll do mine. I'm a waitress, and it's a lousy job but it's mine and it's all I got. If I'm late, I get my ass burned."

"I think you saw them. I think you opened your door and saw them."

"I think I didn't."

"If you saw them," Masuto said kindly, "then you may be the only one who did. That would be very important."

"Sure. You want to know what's important? Cindy's important, because if I don't take care of her, there ain't nobody else going to. You know where you are? You're in West Hollywood—not in Beverly Hills. This place is lousy with kinky creeps. Who's going to call the cops if they decide to beat up on me?"

"We can arrange with the sheriff . . ." Wainwright began, but she interrupted.

"Don't sell me those lousy deputies. I was coming home the other night and one of them stops me and tries to shake me down for twenty bucks and tells me my car stinks of pot, and I never touched a stick for two months, and then he pulls me in on suspicion of being a hooker, and I got to get my girl friend out in the middle of the night to swear I don't solicit, so don't tell me about deputies. They stink." She held the door open. "Now I got to go to work."

"I like her," Masuto said as they walked down the stairs to the street.

"I'd like her more if she talked."

"She talked. She told us there were three of them. Where do you want to eat?"

"Ben Frank's—up the Strip."

Masuto had ordered eggs, hot cakes, and sausage. From behind his two boiled eggs, Wainwright regarded him gloomily and asked how he ate that way and remained thin.

"Genes, metabolism."

"I don't like this, Masao—I don't like this whole rotten business. We got two murders. That stinks."

"One is the sheriff's."

"Like hell it is! The newspapers and the goddamn TV will tell the world that a Beverly Hills stamp dealer and his assistant were murdered. They already got us harboring a war criminal. I swear I don't want to go back to my office, because the city manager will be there, and the mayor, who's got nothing else to do but nitpick the cops, and what have you got besides that smug Oriental look on your face?"

"Nothing." Masuto was hungry. He kept eating.

"Boiled eggs. Why the hell don't you level with me?"

"Because my guesses would only show me off as a smartass Oriental, as you like to put it, and last night I learned that I'm about as Oriental as Jimmy Carter, and anyway, fifty percent of the time I'm wrong."

"And fifty percent of the time you're right." Wainwright looked at his watch. "It's seven forty-five, and the guy from the safe company will be on North Canon at eight o'clock. I want to be there when he opens the safe."

"It's open," Masuto said between bites.

"What's open?"

"The safe."

"What! What in hell are you trying to tell me, Masao?"

"You were pushing me for brilliant Oriental guesses. I made one."

"You're guessing?"

"I'm guessing."

"You're telling me that someone opened the safe and cleaned it out?"

"Only the first part. I'm guessing that last night someone opened the safe. If you want another guess, I would guess that it was empty, that Haber opened it and cleaned out whatever was worth cleaning out before he called the police. The second guess is easy, because no one will ever be able to prove whether I'm right or wrong."

"Then why in hell didn't you tell me that and tell me to put a man on the store?"

"Because I didn't know until I found the stamp in Haber's jacket, and then it was too late."

Wainwright rose.

"Where are you going?" Masuto asked.

"To the store."

"You haven't finished your eggs."

"Take the eggs and stuff them." Wainwright tossed two dollars on the table and stalked out.

Masuto finished eating without haste. He was puzzling over the fact that there were three keys in Haber's pocket. He had simply presumed that one of them was the key to the store, but if that were the case—no, it couldn't be. He paid his check and drove back to the house on Lapeer. Williams was just leaving, getting into his car when Masuto pulled up.

"Could I see the keys again?" Masuto asked him.

"You had your breakfast. I been in that lousy hole for five hours."

"Please forgive me."

Williams handed him the keys. He separated the car key and tried one of the door keys in the outside door of the apartment, the door that would be opened by a responsive buzz. It fit.

"The other one is to the apartment upstairs?" he asked Williams.

"Right. Why didn't you ask me? I could have told you."

"I like to do things the hard way," Masuto said. "Thank you."

Then he drove to Beverly Hills, to the store on North Canon. There was a prowl car parked in front, and behind it, Sy Beckman's car. Officer Frank Seaton opened the door for him. The place was a shambles, the cases broken open, stamps scattered everywhere.

"I thought you patrolled these streets," Masuto said.

"For Christ's sake, Sergeant, don't lean on me. I took enough chickenshit from the captain. Anyway, those velvet drapes were drawn, and anyway I didn't come on duty until seven o'clock this morning."

Beckman came out of the back room. "One lousy morning, Masao. What in hell's been going on?"

"Haber's been beaten to death in his place in West Hollywood."

"So I'm told. The captain's burning. What's eating him?"

"This and that. Is he here?"

"He went back to the station. He says for you to get your ass over and there as soon as you turn up."

Masuto nodded and went into the back room, followed by Beckman and Seaton. "They had the key to the front door," Seaton said. "Maybe if they had jimmied it open, someone would have noticed it."

"I'll tell them," Beckman said sourly. "Where do you suppose they got the key, Masao?"

"From Haber." He was staring at the safe. It was not a very good safe to begin with, but it was no professional job that had opened it. Neither was it strictly amateur, but rather somewhere between the two. They had drilled holes around the dial, torn off the dial, then forced the door open.

"What was in it?" he asked Beckman.

"Nothing. They cleaned it out and dumped the stuff on the floor with everything else." He motioned to the broken cabinets, the emptied desk drawers, the litter of stamps and papers. "Nothing that means anything. It's one hell of a mess, isn't it? I only got here half an hour ago and I got to straighten out this mess. You'd better get over to the station, Masao."

When Masuto entered Wainwright's office, a small, hawk-faced man of about fifty was already there, facing Wainwright, who sat behind his desk and greeted the detective without pleasure.

"This is Mr. Zev Kolan, the Israeli consul general in Los Angeles." And to the hawk-faced man, "This is Detective Sergeant Masao Masuto. He's in charge of the case."

Masuto shook hands—a very strong grip for so small a man. "What can I do for you, sir?"

"Give me some proof that Ivan Gaycheck is actually Gaylord Schwartzman."

"I told him that we sent the prints to Interpol and they made the identification," said Wainwright.

"Yes," said Mr. Kolan. "I am sorry to trouble you, but this has happened before. The Interpol records of Nazi officials are not dependable. There was just too much confusion and chaos at the end of the war. We would very much like to lay hands on Captain Gaylord Schwartzman, preferably alive, but if it is so, then dead. My government would like to know for certain."

"I don't see what I can do for you," Wainwright said.

"I saw Schwartzman once."

"You saw him?"

"He killed me." Both policemen stared at him. He did not appear insane, Masuto thought—no indeed, very sane. Kolan said softly, "Eight of us were condemned to death at

Buchenwald. I was fifteen then. He commanded the firing squad. I was hit in the shoulder, low, under the bone. Then Schwartzman drew his pistol and administered the coup de grace." He pointed to a pale scar on his temple. "He was careless. I was thrown into an open mass grave that they dug outside the walls. Hours later, I regained consciousness. I crawled out of the grave and made my way to a farm. They sheltered me. Not all Germans were Nazis. But I think I would recognize Schwartzman—even today, so many years later, even dead."

For a while after he finished speaking, the two policemen were silent. Then Wainwright said, "If you would please wait outside for a few minutes, Mr. Kolan?"

Kolan nodded and left. Wainwright stared at his hands for a moment or two, then said to Masuto, softly and ominously, "I don't like to be played for a horse's ass, Masao. How did you know the safe had been opened?"

"I didn't know. I made an educated guess. There's a family named Briggs on Camden Drive . . ."

"I know about the Briggs case. Nothing was taken."

"Gaycheck on the same day. Nothing is taken. Then Haber—and from the look of it, nothing was taken except whatever bills he had in his wallet."

"Whoever murdered Gaycheck didn't take his money."

"Someone else. The robbery crew was moving systematically. First Briggs, then Haber. They took the key to the store from Haber. You saw the store."

"I saw it."

"I guessed. It wasn't a brilliant guess—just a guess."

"And can you guess who murdered Gaycheck?"

"I might. But that would be the wildest guess of all—with nothing to support it."

"And Haber?"

"I couldn't even guess," Masuto said. "Maybe later. What do you want to do about Kolan?"

"The body's at Cleary's Mortuary. Take him over there and let him have a look. It's the least we can do."

Driving to the mortuary, Masuto explained to Kolan that Beverly Hills was too small and too peaceful to have a police morgue.

"Peaceful?"

"Most of the time. So we have a contract arrangement with several funeral homes. It suffices."

"You're Japanese, aren't you, Sergeant?"

"Yes. Nisei. That means born in America of Japanese parents."

"Have you ever been to Israel?"

"On a policeman's pay?" Masuto laughed. "I'd like to go. Someday—who knows? But I've never even been to Japan."

"You'll find it interesting."

There was a funeral in progress at Cleary's, and a tall, skinny man in striped pants and a frock coat whispered them into a back room. In front of the coffin, in what he called their "holding room," he explained that there had been an autopsy and that they had been given no instructions for embalming. "It will be messy," he apologized.

"His face?" Kolan asked.

"Very nice—very nice indeed." Then he opened the coffin, and for a few minutes Kolan stared at the chalk-white face of what had once been Ivan Gaycheck, né Gaylord Schwartzman.

Then he turned away and nodded.

"Schwartzman?" Masuto asked.

"It's Schwartzman—yes. It's a face I will never forget. Do I sound regretful? But not for that man in the coffin, Sergeant. We Jews have a saying that one must have compassion—even for one's enemies. But for that man I have no compassion, God forgive me. I had hoped it would not be him, so that one day we might take him alive. But it is. After thirty-three years, a death so peaceful, so easy."

"I think no death is easy," Masuto said. "And thirty-three years—how long is that in God's time?"

"I don't know," Kolan said. "But it's over now, isn't it?"

"It's over."

CHAPTER
FIVE

JASON HOLMBEY

It is said that no one knows all of Los Angeles, and that perhaps is no more mysterious than the saying that no one knows all of Brooklyn, and when one adds to this the fact that within Los Angeles County there are over fifty separate cities, districts, neighborhoods, cities within cities, and that all of them dwell together in a sort of amiable confusion, one simply accepts this improbable puzzle without trying to understand it. Yet in the midst of this is a venerable and valid old-fashioned city, with narrow streets, old buildings, new buildings, skyscrapers—a tight urban cluster that is known all over Los Angeles as "downtown."

It is said in Los Angeles that many people live out their lives in such places as Beverly Hills, San Fernando, Santa Monica, and Glendale without ever going downtown, but that is probably an exaggeration. Masuto, who knew the city better than most, having been born there, was a frequent visitor to downtown, and since he was an observant person, he remembered Holmbey's Stamp Center quite well. It was a most unlikely building, a small, three-story red brick Georgian house, nestled in a dingy section of Fourth Street, covered with ivy, and looking for all the world like a refugee from Berkeley Square in London. It was also the home of one of the largest stamp dealers in the United States.

It was nine-thirty when Masuto parked his car in the red no-parking spaces in front of Holmbey's, put his police card in plain view, and walked into the place, which looked more like an old-fashioned country bank than a stamp dealer's. There were oak counters, elderly gentlemen with green visors, and a gaunt, spinsterish woman who regarded him suspiciously and asked what she might do for him.

"I am a police officer," said Masuto, showing his identification. "I would like to talk to the manager."

"There is no manager, as you put it. Holmbey's is run by Mr. Jason Holmbey III."

"Then I'll talk to Mr. Jason Holmbey III."

"Please be seated, Mr. . . . ?"

"Sergeant Masuto."

"Mr. Masuto, while I see whether Mr. Holmbey can see you. Do you have an appointment?"

"I'm afraid not."

"Then I am afraid your visit has been in vain. Mr. Holmbey does not see people except by appointment."

Masuto was slow to irritation, and even when it occurred, he refused to allow it to show. Now he said softly, "Tell Mr. Holmbey that either he will see me and talk with me, or I will come back with a warrant and bring him in as a material witness to a murder." All of which was very sketchy and conceivably impossible, but which nevertheless made the required impression on the very gaunt and spinsterish woman and sent her hurrying away. A few minutes later, a man in his middle thirties, dressed in a vested herringbone tweed suit, with a cheerful face and wire-rimmed glasses, emerged through a door behind the showcases, glanced around, located Masuto, shook hands with him, and cheerfully asked what he might do for him.

"Agatha is our watchdog. She is very imposing, don't you think? She was my father's secretary, and her mission now is to protect me."

"Only a few questions," Masuto replied.

"Then suppose we sit down in my office." He indicated the way, and Masuto followed him into an imposing, oak-paneled room. There were two large oil portraits on the walls, which Masuto imagined depicted Holmbey I and Holmbey II.

"Now . . . ?"

"Sergeant Masuto."

"Sergeant Masuto. What can I do for you? And you, on the other hand—you would not mind showing me your credentials?"

Masuto opened his wallet and showed his badge.

"Ah! But you are a Beverly Hills policeman. Aren't you rather far off base?"

"No, sir. In Los Angeles County, any police detective working on a case has reciprocal rights—even to the extent of making an arrest."

"But you are not here to make an arrest. At least, I hope not. Of course—it's the Ivan Gaycheck business. I read about it in this morning's *Times*."

"More or less."

"Am I a suspect?"

"No, indeed."

"Why not? I disliked the man intensely. He's a dealer, I am a dealer. So why not?"

Masuto spread his hands disarmingly and smiled. "This woman—I believe you called her Agatha—you said her mission is to protect you. From what?"

"My dear Sergeant Masuto. I am sure the world of postage stamps is alien to you, but it is very much a world, and in that world I am considered—I say this without boasting—one of a half-dozen leading authorities. Holmbey's is the third largest dealer in the United States, the largest west of the Mississippi, so you will understand that I am sought out by an endless flow of collectors and dealers, for purchase, for sale, for authentication, for identification. My provenance is usually accepted by any dealer or collector. If I were not protected, my life would be a nightmare."

"So. You are very young for all that," Masuto said with respect.

"I grew up with stamps. Quite natural for a Holmbey."

"Well, I am grateful for the time you are granting me."

"Not at all. I'm fascinated. Crime and stamps rarely mix. Ask and I will answer to the best of my ability."

"Thank you. There is a stamp called the One-Penny 1848 Mauritius. How much is it worth?"

"The One-Penny 1848 Orange, imperforate . . ."

"Imperforate?"

"The little holes, you know, perforations. Imperforate simply means cut with a scissors or a cutting machine. No perforations."

"I see."

"Canceled, five thousand dollars. Uncanceled, about twice that."

Masuto shook his head. "No. Surely you are mistaken."

"I am never mistaken—in stamps." Holmbey smiled.

"But I was told . . ."

"By an expert? How much?"

"One hundred and fifty thousand dollars."

"Good heavens! Who was the expert—if you don't mind telling me his name?"

"Mr. Odi Ishido."

"Ishido? I know Ishido. Lovely gentleman, quite a competent amateur collector. Rather good on Japanese stamps, but he doesn't know beans about the British colonies. You know, there is a Mauritius stamp that is the most valuable in existence. Not the Post-Paid One-Penny 1848, but the One Penny Post-Office 1847. I suppose that's what Ishido had in mind."

"Then there is a One-Penny Mauritian stamp of great value?"

"Oh, yes, indeed. There certainly is. The One-Penny Orange of 1847 is the most valuable postage stamp in the world."

"But what gives a tiny bit of paper such value?" Masuto asked.

"Ah! Good question. First of all, it's the collector who gives it such value. If he did not desire it with demonic ferocity, well then, what would its value be? Nothing. And why does he value it? Mainly because of its rarity. When he has it, he has something that no one else or almost no one else in the world has. Why does one pay seventy thousand dollars for a Rolls-Royce? To have what few others have. Now I do not denigrate the collector. He is the lifeblood of our business. But there it is. And secondly— well, a stamp accumulates a mythology, thieves who try to steal it, kings and oil barons who vie for it, murderers who kill for it."

"Murderers?"

"I thought that would interest you, Sergeant. There's a whole history of murders to gain possession of stamps, but I am afraid I don't have time to go into that today. Tell me—why does this One-Penny Mauritius interest you?

"I have my reasons. Could you tell me something about it?"

"Well, just off the top of my head without going to the books: orange, you know, color of the ink. Shows the head of the young Queen Victoria. Engraved on copper by J. Barnard—rather a skilled engraver for such an out-of-the-way place. He was a watchmaker. This was his first attempt at stamps. You know, Mauritius is a bit of an island in the Indian Ocean. Curiously, it was the first British colony to print its own stamps. It was engraved and printed in Port Louis, largest town in Mauritius, and when Barnard engraved it he made a bit of an error. Errors—they make stamps valuable, indeed they do. Instead of putting *post paid* in his engraving, Barnard put *post office* there. Corrected it the following year, but the deed was done. Imperforate, as I said. They had no perforating machine on the island then, so the stamp had to be cut by hand. And lo, it was born—the One-Penny Orange 1847 Mauritius."

"Do you have one that I could look at?" Masuto asked.

"Do I have one? My dear Sergeant, if I had one—if I had one—well, I wouldn't have it. There are only fourteen recorded copies of the One-Penny Orange in the whole world. I'd sell it to Clevendon down in Texas for a king's ransom."

"Clevendon?"

"A very wealthy Texan who is one of the great collectors."

"Tell me, Mr. Holmbey, how many of these stamps are there?"

"In the world?"

"Yes."

"Recorded—fourteen. Unrecorded—who knows? Every now and then, one of them turns up. I suppose that originally they printed several hundred at least. I would have to look that up. I do know that the original plate still exists. You know, it wasn't until May 6, 1840, that Great Britain printed its first stamps. With us, it was even later, and it was not until twenty years later that anyone ever dreamed of collecting stamps in an album. What a pity, so much was destroyed and discarded. But one happy thing did come about. It almost immediately became quite fashionable to paper walls, screens, candy boxes with canceled stamps, and this did save many valuable issues."

"May I ask you who owns the One-Penny Orange?"

"Ah, indeed you may. In the world—well, I can name eight collectors who have it. Undoubtedly, there are others I do not know about."

"And in the United States?"

"Two. The Weill brothers in New Orleans own a cover with two penny stamps on it."

"And if you had it, what would you charge for it?"

"That depends. The last time I looked at the price in *Gibbons*—that's the British catalog—well, it was some years ago. It might have been the 1972 catalog. They had it for twenty-two thousand pounds. What was the pound then—two-sixty? Something of the sort. Well, I might put it up at auction with a base price of sixty thousand."

"You said . . ." Masuto began.

"Ah, you want it simple. It is not simple. You see, it depends on the stamp. If the stamp is on an original cover—well, then the sky is the limit. I think only five exist."

"Cover?"

"Envelope, in your terms. But in those days, Sergeant Masuto, they had no envelopes. They folded a sheet of paper and sealed it with wax. That would be the cover. The 1847 Orange on the original cover—and proven authentic—well, I don't know. I could pick up the phone here, put in a call to Clevendon, tell him what I had, and tell him the price was four hundred thousand dollars. And by God I think he'd pay it. No—I wouldn't do that. We have three generations of reputation to uphold. Oh, I'd let Clevendon know all right, let a few others know as well, and then I'd take it to London and put it up at auction with a bidding bottom of one hundred thousand pounds. Who knows? It might fetch half a million or more. Anything is possible in today's inflated world."

"And if such an original cover were to exist and be stolen, what would be the prospects for the thieves?"

"On the black market? No legitimate dealer or collector would touch it, but there are one or two Middle Eastern collectors and one in France—I mention no names. Of course, the price would be considerably less."

"But if there were no report of the theft—if it simply surfaced?"

"Ah, then the sky's the limit."

"And would the thief try to sell it here?"

"I think not. Stolen here? Why sell it here? London would be a better market." He cocked his head and regarded Masuto impishly. "Ah, Detective Masuto, behind that Oriental mask of yours lies an interesting speculation. You are apparently quite ready to be convinced that somewhere, somehow, the unpleasant Mr. Gaycheck found a One-Penny Orange—a motive for his murder. And you are also speculating that perhaps I could have done this not entirely unwholesome deed."

Masuto smiled.

"But you have only to look at me. Surely I am not the type who murders?"

"Is there a type who murders?"

"You are a most unusual policeman—but of course you know that. Yes, I would imagine there is a type that is given to acts of violence. Unlike myself. I lead a sequestered life. By the way, how was the good Gaycheck sent to his reward?"

"You did not like him."

"I found him distasteful."

"He was shot in the middle of the forehead with a small pistol, probably an automatic, with a twenty-two-caliber short slug. Short as distinguished from the high-velocity bullet. He died instantly."

"As a reward for his good deeds. By the way, he perished my debtor."

"Oh?"

"He owes me eighteen hundred dollars for a stamp I gave him on consignment."

"A ten-cent black 1847 George Washington?"

"Sergeant, you amaze me. Yes."

"It's being held in the sheriff's station on San Vicente in West Hollywood—in the property office. As evidence. If you put your claim in there and show proof of ownership and indebtedness, you should be able to have it in a few days. I thought it was worth three thousand."

"Catalog price. A collector might pay close to that. I gave it to Gaycheck on consignment. He said he had a customer for it."

"Then you did do business with Gaycheck?"

"I do business with any stamp dealer whose credit is not subject to suspicion. In business, one does not make moral judgments."

"Was there any reason to make a moral judgment of Ivan Gaycheck?"

"Come, come, Sergeant. You know precisely what I mean. By the way, how comes my stamp to the West Hollywood sheriff? Gaycheck was murdered in Beverly Hills."

"The stamp was found in the possession of Ronald Haber." Masuto's face was impassive, his eyes fixed on Holmbey. "He lives in West Hollywood."

"Gaycheck's assistant. I don't understand."

"Haber was murdered a few hours ago."

"Good heavens!" Holmbey drew a deep breath. "Murdered. What the devil goes on? Is it open season for stamp dealers?"

"I imagine that the person who killed Haber was looking for something of great value—which Haber may or may not have provided."

"The One-Penny Orange?"

"Perhaps."

"I still don't understand. I don't want to sound egotistical, but if there were a One-Penny Orange in Los Angeles or indeed anywhere in America, missing or presented for sale, I would know about it."

"I'm sure you would."

"Then what on earth gives you this fixation on the One-Penny Orange? Do you have any evidence, any reason to believe it exists?"

"Perhaps."

"Hardly an expansive answer. Well, Sergeant—" He glanced at his watch. "I've given you a half hour of my time. I have not done away with either Haber or Gaycheck, but you are welcome to add me to your list of suspects if it pleases you. And if you do come across that One-Penny Orange, I should be delighted to know about it."

"Only one more question."

"Yes?"

"You must know most of the important collectors in this area. Are there any of the stature of this man you mentioned—Clevendon?"

"There is no one of Clevendon's stature as a collector—unfortunately."

"Perhaps. But I speak of people who could afford the price of such a stamp."

"Yes, a few. But I see no reason why I should supply their names."

"I can't force you to," Masuto admitted. "On the other hand, I think the D.A. could be persuaded to issue a warrant that would permit me to examine your books—more time-consuming for me, and, I am sure, much more unpleasant for you."

Holmbey's mood changed. His face hardened and his blue eyes closed to slits. He stared at Masuto without replying.

"There are other ways," Masuto said quietly. "There are dealers in Beverly Hills and Westwood who could supply the information. I am not threatening you."

"Very well," Holmbey said coldly. "There are only four of them, and you're quite right. Any legitimate dealer would know who they are, so in fact I violate no confidence. Frank Goldway in Palos Verdes, Jerome Clayton in Pasadena, Raymond Cohen in Bel Air, and Lucille Bettner in Beverly Hills."

Masuto jotted down the names. "Thank you," he said, rising. "You've been very generous with your time."

On his way back to Beverly Hills, Masuto pulled into a gas station to fill his depleted tank, and while waiting he telephoned his cousin, Alan Toyada, who was in the research department of Merrill, Lynch, Pierce, Fenner & Smith.

"Well, Masao," Toyada greeted him, "I see you're working again. Live in Beverly Hills and get scragged."

"I am not interested in your poor sense of humor. I want to know about Holmbey's—the stamp dealer in downtown L.A."

"Masao, you know I specialize in Japanese stocks. Anyway, Holmbey's is not listed. It's a family outfit."

"You have Dun and Bradstreet and other sources. I want to know their condition, their financial standing—or whatever you call it."

"All right. Drop around this afternoon and I'll have it for you."

"Please, Alan, I want it now."

"Now? I can't drop everything. . . ."

"You can. It won't take you five minutes. I'm in a phone booth in a gas station, but I'll call you back in ten minutes."

"Masao, I can't just . . ."

"The next time you want a traffic ticket fixed . . ."

"When did you ever fix a ticket for me? When?"

"I'll call you back in ten minutes." Then Masuto hung up, paid for the gas, and drove off. Back in Beverly Hills, he stopped at a pay phone and called Toyada again.

"Okay, Masao—I got what you want. To put it succinctly, their condition is lousy. They are up to their ears in debt, and they have a quarter-of-a-million bank loan callable in about thirty days. Unless they have resources not listed, it's questionable whether they can meet it. Maybe they can float another loan to cover, maybe not. One doesn't know. If you're going to lend them money, think twice."

"Thank you."

"Look, Masao, if you're on the pad and you got money to burn, come around and see me. Stay away from places like Holmbey's."

"Very funny. Goodbye."

CHAPTER
SIX

ELLEN BRIGGS

Driving to North Camden—north being north of the railroad tracks, the line through Beverly Hills that separates the middle class from the rich—Masuto recalled that he had not only seen Ellen Briggs play Major Barbara but he had also seen her play Hedda Gabler at the Huntington Hartford Theatre, which was quite different from the little shack on Las Palmas where she had performed in the Shaw play. The part was notably different as well, for while he had never cared for the Ibsen play as a dramatic work, he was always intrigued by the character of Hedda Gabler—the frustrated, hate-filled woman whose morality had disappeared under the pressure of her anger, who could kill and destroy without compassion or regret. He had always wondered whether there could be a great performance of the Hedda Gabler role without the actress sharing some part of the nature of Ibsen's character.

Well, he knew very little about actresses; but why hadn't Ellen Briggs mentioned the Hedda Gabler role? How could any actress resist saying, once he had complimented her on the Major Barbara role, "But did you see me as Hedda Gabler at the Huntington Hartford?"

Of course, there were the circumstances. Her mother's death, the funeral, and then the breaking into her house and the senseless chaos visited upon it. Perhaps the additional misery of the talented actress who does not make it. She was at least forty now, and Masuto had spent his life close enough to the entertainment industry to know that, with a few incredible exceptions, the actor who does not make it by forty will never make it.

It was half-past ten in the morning when Masuto parked his car in front of the Spanish Colonial house on Camden, and he had that strange feeling—not unusual when one is awake most of the night—that somewhere he had lost a day. Also, he had missed his regular early morning practice of meditation. Well, a day like today is not so different from a koan; he smiled a bit at the thought. He himself practiced in the Soto School of Zen, but in the Rinzai School one meditated upon a thing called a koan, a proposition that defies reason; and Masuto had always felt that murder, the destruction of one human being by another, defied both reason and civilization. It was certainly not an apt comparison, but it amused him.

When he rang the doorbell, Ellen Briggs opened the door for him, and the change in her appearance from the day before was so marked that he had to look twice to make sure it was the same woman. She wore old blue jeans that fit her slender figure tightly and a blue work shirt open at the neck, and her hair was drawn back and tied behind her head. She looked twenty years younger than the grief-stricken woman he had seen the day before, and the lack of makeup added to her attractiveness.

She stared at him blankly for a moment, then smiled. "Of course—Detective Masuto."

"Good morning, Mrs. Briggs. May I come in?"

"Please."

The living room was back in place and orderly. "I'm working in the kitchen now," she explained. "It's good for me to have all this to do. You know, I don't suppose the thieves were in the house for more than an hour, but it will be three days before I clear up the wreckage."

"It's always easier to destroy," Masuto agreed. "Actors will rehearse a play for weeks, and a critic will destroy it with a few words."

"I like that notion." She stared at him with interest. "You are a most unusual policeman."

"You don't have to stop what you were doing. I will be happy to sit in the kitchen, and I can talk to you while you work. I just have a few questions to ask you."

"Would you like a cup of tea?"

"I would."

She led him into the kitchen. "No, I shall not go on working. We will have tea together."

He watched her with interest as she put up the water to boil, prepared the teapot, and set out a plate of sliced pound cake. She moved easily and gracefully, and he found himself admiring her and liking her.

"You have no accent at all," he observed.

"Accent?"

"Foreign accent, I mean. You were born in Germany?"

"But I left there when I was three years old. So the fact that I have no accent is hardly remarkable."

"That was in 1940?"

"Yes—but how did you know I was forty years old?"

"Just a guess."

"Not a flattering guess, Sergeant Masuto."

"It has nothing to do with your appearance. I simply felt it was before the war began. Later it would have been almost impossible."

"Yes, I suppose so. Do you want lemon with your tea?"

He shook his head. "Your father was Jewish?"

"Half Jewish—but in Nazi Germany that was enough. My mother was not Jewish, but Hitler was not concerned with such niceties."

"When did your father die?"

"He died in Germany, in a concentration camp. Some friends helped my mother to escape in 1940, and we got to England, and then here after the war."

"That must have been a hard time for both of you."

She put two slices of cake on a plate and handed it to him, looking at him rather quizzically. "I was very young. It was harder for my mother. But these things are not pleasant for me to talk about, and I don't see what such matters have to do with my home being broken into."

"Perhaps a great deal. I'm not sure. Please forgive me. I am trying to get to the bottom of something. It's like a puzzle, and I am trying to fit the pieces together."

"You mean the house being broken into? I don't understand."

"Partly that. You see, Mrs. Briggs, two people were murdered during the past twenty-four hours. I am investigating these murders. I imagine you haven't seen the morning paper?"

"No, I haven't. But what can this possibly have to do with my house being robbed?"

"I'm not sure. I think there's a connection."

"What kind of connection?"

"If you will only bear with me a little—and allow me some personal questions. It's very important."

"All right. But I'm very confused and I'm beginning to be frightened again."

"There's no reason for you to be frightened, and if we can get to the bottom of this, it will only add to your safety and your son's safety. By the way, where is your son?"

"At school. Why my son? What has he got to do with this?"

"I'm not sure—yet."

"Why don't you tell me the truth? What are you after? What is happening?"

She was becoming very upset, her eyes wet with moisture now. Masuto realized that she was a very emotional woman; well, what good actress wasn't? He said gently, "I will tell you what I am after, but let me do it my way. If you will simply answer my questions."

"All right."

"Yesterday—what time was the funeral?"

"Nine o'clock in the morning."

"And you returned here at one?"

"Closer to two."

"As I remember you told me yesterday, you had lunch and then you dropped your son off at school?"

"Yes."

"You all had lunch together?"

"No, just my son and I. I dropped my husband off at his office on Wilshire. He had some pressing things to attend to."

"At what time?"

"I don't remember, really. What difference does it make?"

"Try to remember."

"I think about noontime."

"Then how did your husband get back here to the house?"

"After I dropped Bernie off, I picked up Jack at his office. It was about one-thirty, maybe a little later."

"Your son's name is Bernard?"

"No, it's Bernie. He was named after my father."

"I see. Tell me something about your father, Mrs. Briggs."

"Why? How can it have anything to do with this?"

"It might."

"What shall I tell you? I hardly remember my father."

"Was he wealthy?"

"I suppose so. At one time. He was a publisher. Not a very large publisher, but a very good one."

"And what happened to his wealth?"

"What happened to the wealth of any German in Hitler's time who was Jewish or half Jewish? They took everything he had, everything. When we escaped and got to England, we had nothing but the clothes on our backs. Nothing. My mother found work as a cook in a little restaurant. Then when we got to America, she became a servant, a live-in cook. She was only sixty-one when she died—so young but worn out." Her eyes filled with tears now.

"I'm so sorry."

"No, it's all right. My husband gets furious when I talk about the old times. He doesn't care for Jews, and once he heard me tell Bernie that I was Jewish, because after what my mother and father had been through, what else could I say, but he was in a rage with me. Why am I telling you all this?"

"Please, I want to hear about it. That's why you're talking to me."

She smiled through her tears. "I like you, Sergeant

Masuto. I'll tell you a story, and maybe you'll understand better how I feel. I was once up for a very decent part, which I did not get. Well, I wasn't right for it. But I was interviewed by the producer—his name was Deutschmaster. He was a Jew who had been a refugee and then had returned to Germany and become a very important producer. He's dead now. Well, I noticed in the pocket of his vest, inside his jacket, he had two small silver spoons, and I asked him why. Do you know what he told me—he told me that when he was a refugee in Europe, he discovered that money could be worthless, or perhaps he had none, but he had a sterling silver spoon and it bought him life for a week. So you see, the two silver spoons he carried were, as he explained to me, a sort of symbolic reminder. Do you know what I am trying to say?"

"I think so." Then Masuto was silent, staring at her until he realized that she was becoming uncomfortable under his direct gaze. "Forgive me. Does the name Gaylord Schwartzman mean anything to you?"

"No. Should it?"

"I don't know. What concentration camp did your father die in, do you know?"

"Buchenwald."

"And you say he was well-to-do once, but when your mother escaped she had nothing. But how could that be? I am not impugning anything you say, please believe me, but many others escaped and many of them brought small things with them—jewels, things of that sort."

"Whatever she had went to pay for our way out."

"You said that you arrived in England penniless and empty-handed. Empty-handed—do you mean that literally?"

"But you are asking me to remember something that happened when I was three years old."

"Try. Luggage. A large handbag. Some treasured things—things that would be important to her but worthless even to the Nazis."

"What kind of things?"

"Perhaps letters from your father—pictures, a few small mementos, things a woman would treasure."

She nodded slowly. "Yes, she had some things like that. There were some snapshots of herself and my father, some letters, a few other things, a lock of my baby hair."

"Do you still have these things?"

"Yes."

"Where are they?"

"In her room, but her room was so upset, like the other rooms. I haven't gotten to it yet. I worked on my son's room this morning. I felt that Mother's could wait—since she's gone."

"May I look in her room?"

Ellen Briggs stiffened now and faced Masuto squarely. "No, Sergeant. No. Not unless you tell me what you're after and why. I have been very patient with you, but no more. You are not here with a search warrant or by any official right, but only through my tolerance. And my tolerance has run out."

Masuto smiled. "Very well. I'll tell you.

"Yesterday, shortly before I came here, a man was murdered. He had lived for years in Beverly Hills under the name of Ivan Gaycheck. He was a stamp dealer, with a shop on North Canon Drive. His real name was Gaylord Schwartzman, and he was once a captain in the SS—at Buchenwald. He was shot through the head with a small pistol. But his store was not robbed then. Nothing was disturbed. Last night his assistant, a man by the name of Ronald Haber, was beaten to death in his apartment in

West Hollywood. His apartment was ransacked, as your house was. A few hours later, Gaycheck's store was ransacked."

Staring at him wide-eyed, she shook her head. "What has that to do with us?"

"I put together a scenario of sorts. I must, you know. Otherwise I would fumble around blindly. Gaycheck made a notation on his calendar—PM. Just the two letters. There is a stamp of enormous value. It was issued in 1847 on the island of Mauritius in the Indian Ocean. It is called the One-Penny Orange. Penny Mauritius, PM. I am guessing. Your house ransacked, nothing taken. Your father, dead in Buchenwald. Gaycheck—Schwartzman, and Buchenwald. Haber's apartment, your house, Gaycheck's store."

"I still don't understand you."

"Try, Mrs. Briggs. Put yourself in the place of your father—in the 1930s in Germany. He knows that sooner or later he will be arrested—unless he escapes. But if he escapes, his property will be forfeit. He plans an escape from Germany, some way to take something with him, so that he will not arrive at his destination as a pauper. But what should he take? Money? Where can he hide it if he is stopped and searched? Jewels? The same problem. The SS were not novices at searching, and your father was not the first one to think of this problem. Now tell me something— do you know what books your father's firm published?"

"Some of them. My mother loved books. She told me many stories about my father's publishing house."

"Did he ever publish any books that related to stamp collecting?"

Her face lit up with excitement. "Yes, he did! Of course! He published the German edition of *Gibbons* catalog."

"The British stamp catalog. Then he knew the value of

British colonial stamps, and he must have known dealers and collectors."

"I would suppose so."

"And he was a publisher, a well-read man. He would have known the stories of Edgar Allan Poe. Tell me, Mrs. Briggs, did you ever read *The Purloined Letter?*"

"I think so. Isn't that the story where a letter of great importance, instead of being hidden, is simply turned inside out and put in a letter holder with other letters?"

"Exactly. Now this is what I think your father did—and of course it is only a guess. But the pieces fit. I think that when your father realized what course he must take, he bought a stamp of great value, but not simply a stamp. An original cover."

"What on earth is an original cover?"

"I'm no stamp expert, but I have been informing myself today. An original cover means the stamp on the posted envelope. But I understand that in those times they did not put writing paper into an envelope. They wrote on a square sheet of paper and folded it to envelope size and sealed it. The envelope was the letter. Somewhere—perhaps we'll never know where—your father found and bought an original cover, very probably of the One-Penny 1847 Mauritius Orange. He then put it away, probably with some mementos that would excite no suspicion. He didn't try to hide it. He probably took the chance that no one who saw it would know what it was—thereby hiding it in the safest manner possible—by not hiding it at all."

"And if all this happened," she said in a whisper, "what would be the value of this—cover, as you call it?"

"Then, in 1939, I don't know. Certainly substantial. Today, I am told, it's worth over three hundred thousand dollars, perhaps more."

"Oh, my God—all those years of poverty. And if what you say is true, it was lost, just thrown away somewhere in Germany."

"I don't think so. You see, your father must have been arrested suddenly."

"He was."

"Certainly before he had an opportunity to explain to your mother what he had done. Or perhaps she was not to know. Perhaps it was to be his secret—and then it was too late to tell her. But I think she took the cover out of Germany with her."

"Oh, no. No. My mother worked as a servant."

"Because she never knew."

"What? What are you saying?"

"Understand me," Masuto said evenly. "I am building a premise. I don't know whether I am right or wrong. But I think that all these years that cover remained among your mother's possessions. Granted, she had very little—only a few mementos But I think that somewhere among her few possessions was this original cover. She may have kept it simply for sentimental reasons—or what is more likely is that your father told her that it was important to him, without ever telling her why."

"She did have a little packet of letters," Ellen remembered. "They were tied with a piece of ribbon. When I was a little girl she would look at them sometimes, but then she put them away and I don't think she looked at them for years."

"Where did she keep them?"

"I don't think I know. You see, we only moved into this house a week ago—it's such a splendid house. This is the first time Jack—my husband—made any money. I wanted her to have a few years of peace and happiness. . . ." She broke into tears, covering her face with her hands. "She wouldn't have! Oh, damn it, she wouldn't have. Jack hated her. She had no peace and no happiness. I wasn't even with her when she died."

"How did she die?"

"Oh, let me wash my face. I feel so rotten. All those years of wretched poverty, and there might have been a fortune under my nose. She could have lived like a human being. Please—please excuse me."

She fled into the bathroom behind the kitchen, leaving Masuto to sit there and stare at the half-eaten slice of cake on his plate and to wonder whether the edifice he had created was a total fiction. He liked her, respected her, and felt his heart go out to her—and pondered the strange fact that women like Ellen Briggs so often married men like Jack Briggs. Then she came back, her eyes reddened but dry.

"I'm all right now. I suppose you want to see Mother's room?"

"Yes. But I asked you before—and you don't have to answer if it's too painful—I asked you how your mother died."

"She died of a heart attack, Sergeant Masuto. Alone. I wasn't even there to be with her. Just three days ago. I had gone with Bernie to the school to register him. I left him there and came home. I went up to her room, and she was lying on her bed—dead."

"I am sorry," Masuto said. "I make you talk about things you don't want to talk about, and I force you to remember things you should not have to remember. I am so sorry."

She led the way up the stairs. All the bedrooms were off a central hallway. Her mother's was a corner room, bright and cheerful, with a wooden balcony. But it was still in total disorder, clothes on the floor, the drawers emptied and flung about senselessly, papers and letters scattered about. Ellen walked around, picking up envelopes and folded letters. Without a word, she handed them to Masuto. They were written in German and carried old stamps of the time of the Third Reich.

"These are the letters, Mrs. Briggs?"

She nodded. Masuto handed them back to her, then walked around the room—aimlessly, it appeared to Ellen, except that his dark eyes were restless and excited. Then he got down on his knees and reached under the bed. When he stood up, he had a piece of faded blue ribbon in his hand.

"Is this the ribbon that the letters were tied with?"

"Yes, I think so."

He stared at the ribbon until she was prompted to say, "What is it, Sergeant Masuto?"

"Don't you see? The ribbon was cut with a pair of scissors. Not with a knife, but with a pair of scissors."

"Well?"

He motioned at the room. "Do such people pick up scissors to cut a ribbon?" Suddenly he snapped the ribbon in his fingers. "See how easily it breaks." And even more abruptly, "Did you have the back door fixed?"

His tone of voice startled her. "Yes. The locksmith came early this morning. He not only fixed the lock, he put a bolt on the door."

Masuto looked at his watch. "It's twenty after eleven. What time does your son get out of school?"

"For lunch? Eleven forty-five. Why?"

"Come with me! We'll pick him up."

"But the school bus will bring him."

"I said we'll pick him up," Masuto snapped. "Now don't argue with me. Come."

In his car, she complained that he was arbitrary and rude.

"Not rude. I am never rude," Masuto protested. The accusation hurt him.

"You have no right to order me around like this."

"I have the right to keep a hurtful thing from happening to you and your son."

"What hurtful thing? What are you talking about?"

They were almost at the school now.

"Why doesn't your son have a hot lunch in school?" Masuto asked.

"You must know everything. You're the most inquisitive man I ever met."

"Yes, assuredly."

"He will have his lunch in school when I'm working. I'm not working now. I feel better when I prepare his lunch."

"I see." He pulled up next to the curb, with the school entrance plainly in sight. "It's just a few minutes. I'll wait here. Go to the door and bring him here when he comes out."

"But . . ."

"Please do as I say."

She got out of the car, turned to look at Masuto, swallowed whatever she had intended to say, and walked across to the school. Masuto snapped on his radiophone and called the dispatcher. "This is Masuto. I'm parked in front of Rogers' Primary School. I want the nearest patrol car on this street. Get him over here quickly, but slow as he goes down the street. I want him to park behind me, and then follow me when I pull away."

He got out of his car then, wondering, as he had so

often before, whether he was right in rarely carrying a gun. A time would surely come when he would regret that decision. He stood by his car, studying the area, the sun-drenched lawns, the empty walks. Not a soul was in sight. He told himself then, in that moment, that he had too much imagination for a good policeman.

A school bus pulled into the driveway next to the school; then a second one.

Then, down the street and parking next to the curb, facing his car, three men on motorcycles, wearing leather trousers, leather jackets, and helmets with sunproof visors; no faces were visible. This surprised him. Motorcycles were not a part of his calculations. Hadn't all the witnesses at Lapeer, where Haber had been murdered, spoken of the sound of a car starting? How could anyone confuse the sound of a car with the sound of three motorcycles?

Having parked the cycles and dismounted, they stood in a tight group; they watched Masuto, and they watched Ellen Briggs, who now stood in front of the school door. The door opened and the children began to come out. The three men in leather took a few steps and Masuto took a few steps. They watched him, and then they saw the patrol car pulled up behind Masuto's Datsun.

Masuto waved an arm, and the policeman got out of his car and came toward him. Ellen Briggs took her son's hand. Masuto never took his eyes from the cyclists.

The uniformed cop joined Masuto. "What's up, Sergeant?"

The three men moved back to their motorcycles, mounted, and roared away down the street. Masuto relaxed. Ellen Briggs and her son walked toward them. The boy, small, light-haired, was chattering to his mother.

"It's all right, Bailey," Masuto said to the policeman.

"I'm taking them over to their home, on Camden. Just follow me, and then park outside until I come out."

The policeman nodded and went back to his car. Masuto opened the door of his car for Ellen Briggs and her son. "Now, would you tell me . . ."

"I'm taking you home," Masuto said. "I'll talk to you there."

"You don't know how provoking this whole thing is."

"I do."

The boy whispered, "What is he, Mom? Is he some kind of cop? He's a Jap, isn't he?"

"Just be quiet."

Masuto parked in front of the house on Camden. "Wait here," he said to Ellen Briggs. The patrol car pulled up behind him. Masuto nodded at Officer Bailey, then walked down the driveway to the back of the house and looked at the kitchen door. He circled the house and came back.

"We'll go inside now," he said to Ellen.

"You are impossible," she said slowly.

"Just do as I say, please."

She and the boy walked with him to the door. She opened the door with her keys, and the boy went inside. Masuto touched her arm as she started to follow. "One moment, please, Mrs. Briggs." She turned to face him. "Do you trust me?"

"I would like to—if you would tell me what that charade at the school was all about."

"In time."

"Why must you be so damn mysterious?"

"Because I am in something with a dozen loose ends dangling, and I haven't put them together, and anything I say about it would only add to your worries. So would you please trust me."

She hesitated, thought about it for a moment or two, drew a deep breath, then sighed. "Very well."

"I don't want you to send your son back to school today. Keep him at home."

"But what shall I tell him?"

"Invent something. I want you to lock your doors. Stay in the house. The boy is not to go out to play."

"Not even in the backyard?"

"No, not even in the backyard."

"But I haven't done my shopping."

"Don't do any shopping today. Don't open the door for anyone."

"But this is ridiculous."

"No, it is not ridiculous. Will you do as I say?"

She stood there staring at Masuto. Then she nodded. "Very well."

"I'll try to come back this evening. I think it will be over by then—so it's only one afternoon."

"What shall I tell my husband?"

"What time will he be home?"

"Seven—perhaps later."

"Then you will simply tell him that I said what I said— for your safety and for the child's safety." She nodded unhappily. "Thank you."

He waited until she had gone inside and he had heard the door lock behind her. Then he walked back to where Officer Bailey sat in his patrol car.

"What the hell is this all about?" Bailey asked.

Masuto shrugged. "Can you come by here every half hour or so?"

"If it's all right with the chief."

"Tell him I asked for it—you or someone else."

"What am I looking for?"

"Motorcycles."

"The same three?"

"Maybe."

"You're really sure of yourself, aren't you?"

Again, Masuto shrugged. "Just keep your eyes open."

CHAPTER
SEVEN

ZEV KOLAN

It was twelve forty-five when Masuto returned to Beverly Hills police headquarters. He sent out for a sandwich and coffee, and then in the records room he picked up the last three days' Los Angeles *Times*. He chewed his ham and cheese without tasting it, while he read the death notice:

"Hilda Kramer, beloved wife of Wolf Bernie Kramer and mother of Ellen Kramer Briggs. Rest in peace."

Wainwright stopped by his desk. "What have you got, Masao?"

"A few pieces."

"Do you know who killed Gaycheck?"

"I think so."

"You wouldn't want to share that knowledge?"

"I could be wrong."

"You give me a pain in the ass—so help me God, you do, Masao."

"Being inscrutable is part of the ploy. Look, Captain, I think I know who murdered Gaycheck. I have no evidence, absolutely nothing. I also have a notion about Haber."

"Not the same party?"

"No, indeed. Hardly—but it's in motion. Maybe I can wrap it up by tomorrow, maybe never."

"That's cheerful."

"What I'm wondering," Masuto said, "is whether the L.A.P.D. would run an errand for us."

"Maybe. If we're nice to them. There have been times when they wanted errands on our turf. What do you have in mind?"

"I want to know about the gun—the little twenty-two-caliber job that killed Gaycheck. I think it was purchased in one of the gun stores downtown during the past week, maybe during the past three days. L.A.P.D. would know who carries that kind of merchandise. Ballistics is pretty certain it was an automatic, not a revolver, a purse gun, probably a fancy little toy with mother-of-pearl on the grip. I'm sure they don't sell many of those."

"Why downtown, Masao? This county is lousy with gun stores."

"Just a notion. Maybe they can track it down and get us a reading on who bought it."

"I'll give it a try."

As Wainwright turned away, Masuto said, "One other thing, Captain."

"Oh?"

"I want you to authorize two telephone calls." Detective Sy Beckman, sitting at the next desk, was listening and trying to look like he was not listening. "For Sy here," Masuto said, nodding at Beckman. "I want him to make the calls for me."

"I'm waiting," Wainwright said coldly. "Goddamn it, Masao . . ."

Masuto held up a hand and smiled.

"All right. Tell me."

"One to Germany. One to England."

"No."

"It's important."

"Use the Telex."

"It won't do. I need the telephone."

"No. That loudmouth will sit on the phone for an hour and I'll get a bill for three hundred dollars, and the city manager will burn my ass off."

"Don't blame me," said Beckman. "I don't even know what the hell you're talking about."

"Make the calls yourself," said the captain.

"I have other things to do. I want to clean this thing up and get out of it. I want to go home and sit in a hot bath for an hour and eat some civilized food and feed my roses."

"My heart bleeds for you. If you think I'm going to give Beckman a license to sit on the phone to Germany and England and bankrupt this department, you're crazy."

"If I enjoyed the expression, which I do not," Masuto said quietly, "I would say that my heart bleeds for you, Captain. You're only the chief of detectives in the wealthiest city in the world, and you're arguing about two telephone calls."

"Go to hell," said Wainwright, turning on his heel.

"The calls?"

"Make them, but so help me, Masao, I'd better know the reason why." And then he stalked away.

Beckman was staring at Masuto and grinning. "You do have a way with you, Masao." He readied his pencil and pad. "Who do I call?"

"First of all, there's a publisher in England, Gibbons— put that down, G-i-b-b-o-n-s. They publish the definitive British stamp catalog. Or maybe Gibbons is the name of the catalog, and someone else publishes it. I don't know, but you can call Holmbey's, the stamp dealer in downtown L.A., and get that information. Get through to Gibbons and find someone there who knows his business, and find out all you can about a stamp called the One-Penny 1847 Orange Mauritius."

"How do you spell Morashus?"

Masuto gave it to him. "But don't flounder around, Sy. I want specific information. I want to know whether there was an original cover—got that, original cover—floating around on the European continent in the late 1930s, and what happened to it. I suspect it disappeared. I want my suspicions confirmed."

"Come on, Masao. It don't make sense. How the hell would they know about one stamp in the 1930s?"

"They'd know, because this is maybe the most important stamp in the world."

"Okay." Beckman sighted. "I'll give it a try. Now what about the second call?"

"Get through to police headquarters in Bonn, West Germany. Maybe you want to pull in Guttman for that, you know, the cop on the night shift. He speaks German, or maybe they have someone over there who talks English."

"Guttman's asleep."

"Wake him up. No one worries about waking us up. Now I want to know this—whatever they have on Captain Gaylord Schwartzman of the SS. He was stationed at the concentration camp in Buchenwald, and after the war he disappeared. I want to know whether he ever had anything to do with a German publisher whose name was Wolf Bernie Kramer and who died in Buchenwald."

"Slow up," said Beckman, making notes on his yellow pad. "Spell 'Buchenwald.' "

"And that reminds me of something else," Masuto said. "When you talk to Gibbons, bring up the name of Kramer. He published the German edition of their catalog. Ask them specifically whether they can connect him in any way with the One-Penny Orange."

"I'm as confused as hell," said Beckman, "but I got it. What else?"

"I want to know two things—very important, if you can pin them down. I want to know how Kramer died in Buchenwald; and if it was by a firing squad, I want to know who commanded the firing squad. I also want to know whether they circulated Schwartzman's photo and where and whether it appeared . . ." Masuto broke off suddenly, lost in thought.

"Masao?"

"Look, there's a German magazine called *Der Spiegel* or something like that. It's a big news magazine, like *Time* in America. There's a good chance they have it on file down in the L.A. public library."

"Come on, Masao, I don't read German."

"Do we have a morgue shot of Gaycheck?"

"Front face and profile both. You know that."

"When you finish telephoning, take both shots downtown and spend the rest of the day with this magazine—if they got it. If they don't have it, we'll have to put the shots on the wire to Germany. But I think they have it."

"How far back?"

"Five years."

"Oh, Wainwright's going to love that."

"He'll love it. Now, is everything clear?"

"Clear as mud." He stared at Masuto. "Wait a minute. What am I looking for in this German magazine?"

"Gaycheck's face—thirty years younger."

"Sure. Nothing to it. You're a doozy, Masao."

"Well, we win some and we lose some. Keep in touch."

"Where will you be?"

"At the Israeli consulate, as soon as I find out where it is."

"And after that?"

"I'll find you, Sy. Either here or at the public library."

The office of the Israeli consul general was at 6380 Wilshire Boulevard, on that single avenue that is the pride of Los Angeles, and which citizens of the City of Angels compare to Fifth Avenue in New York, and perhaps not without modest reason. The consulate was on the seventeenth floor of an office building. Masuto showed his credentials to the receptionist, and a few minutes later he was shaking hands with Zev Kolan.

"I was reading about the case," Kolan said. "According to your chief of police, you have no leads. Am I one of your suspects, Sergeant Masuto?"

"Then what of our encounter at the funeral home?" Masuto asked, smiling.

"It would have been a useful defense—something to point suspicion elsewhere."

"There was a Zev Kolan who was a colonel of the Haganah in Israel's War of Liberation. Was that you?"

"I see you do your homework."

"Oh, no—no indeed. I've had no time for homework. But a few weeks ago I was reading David Ben-Gurion's memoirs. Only on my way over here I remembered your name."

"Ah. I wonder sometimes why the Japanese have so intense an interest in Israel. Will you have a cigar?" he asked, opening a box on his desk. "These are H. Upmanns—not from Cuba; I do not believe in breaking the laws of a country where you are a guest—but from Las Palmas in the Canary Islands. They are superb. I do believe there is no better cigar in the world. They are my only extravagance. Otherwise, I live a rather spartan existence."

"Thank you, but I don't smoke. Do you really feel that the Japanese have an extraordinary interest in Israel?"

"Yes—oh, yes. There are strange similarities between our two people. It would be a pleasure to talk about it sometime. But not now. You did not come here to discuss ethnic empathies."

"I'm afraid not. Why do you no longer call yourself colonel?"

"I have neither love nor admiration for the military life. Once, it was a necessity. Now I am too old."

"Ah so. Of course. May I ask a rather impolite question?"

Kolan clipped the end of a cigar and lit it. "Of course. You are a policeman. You must."

"Very well. Given the opportunity, would you have killed Gaylord Schwartzman?"

Kolan leaned back and regarded his cigar smoke thoughtfully. "The same question I ask myself. No, Sergeant, I don't think I would. Tell me, are you a Buddhist?"

"Yes. I practice Zen."

"Then, like myself, you are no stranger to death. Death is not terrible. It is the taking of life that is unspeakable and unforgivable. I would want to see Gaylord Schwartzman tried before a court in Jerusalem. I would want to see his guilt made public. His sentence is a matter of indifference to me. But I am sure you did not come here to ask me whether I killed Gaycheck any more than to discuss Israelis and Japanese."

"No. I came to talk about Buchenwald—if it doesn't distress you too much?"

"Whatever I can tell you. I have not treasured the memories, so they are somewhat vague."

"How long were you there?"

"About two years."

"I am interested in a German publisher who was sent to Buchenwald and who died there. His name was Wolf Bernie Kramer. Do you by any chance remember him?"

Kolan thought about it for a while, then shook his head. "I'm afraid not."

"Were many men executed in the manner you described—by a firing squad?"

"They preferred the gas chamber. The firing squad was special, a visible thing. To show—to make an example."

"Was Schwartzman always in command of the firing squad—during the time you were there?"

"I'm not sure. I have not been of much help, have I?"

The telephone rang. Kolan answered it. "For you," he said to Masuto, handing him the phone. "You can take it in the next room if you wish privacy."

"It's all right." Masuto took the phone. It was Beckman.

"Did it occur to you, Masao," he said, "that it is now nine o'clock in England?"

"I'm afraid not."

"Well, I lucked out. They have an answering service that was impressed with the fact that a Beverly Hills cop was calling London, and they put me through to one of the directors. He gave me the number of an old gentleman who has been with the firm for forty years—get that? Forty years. Feller by the name of Brisham, only you don't spell it that way. Anyway, I hit the jackpot. Are you listening?"

"I'm here," Masuto said.

"Well, stop being so goddamn silent. It seems there was a guy back in the thirties, name of Lord Skeffington, and it seems that lots of these British lords, they don't have the money for a pair of shoes. So this Skeffington inherits a stamp collection from his father, and what do you think is a part of it? Guess."

"The One-Penny Orange."

"Jackpot. The original cover. So he turns it over to Gibbons, they should be the agents and sell it for him, and they let the word out that they got it and it's up for grabs. It turns out they got a very good connection on the Continent, this same Wolf Kramer who publishes their catalog in German." Beckman paused to let it sink in.

"Go on," Masuto said.

"So Kramer comes up with a buyer, and the price is eight thousand pounds, and the pound was five dollars then, so that makes it forty thousand smackeroos, which ain't hay even back in those days."

"Who was the buyer?"

"That, my boy, is something they never found out. Kramer acted as the agent. But this old Brisham character, he tells me that it's his suspicion that Kramer himself was the buyer."

"What happened to the cover? Does he know?"

"Nobody knows. According to Brisham, it disappeared from the face of the earth. He claims that it could not have been sold or offered at auction anywhere without Gibbons knowing about it."

"Good. Sy, that's good—very good. Now get on the horn to Germany."

"Wait a moment—Masao, for Christ's sake, it's after ten P.M. in Germany."

"Police stations don't close."

"I didn't make one call. I made three calls. One to the answering service, one to the director, and one to Brisham. I asked for charges—one hundred and seventy-five bucks. Do you know what it's going to cost when I start tracking around Germany? Anyway . . ."

"Do it! Do you have Guttman there to translate?"

"He's on his way, sore as hell."

"Well, fill him in and get on with it."

He put down the phone and turned to Kolan, who was regarding him with interest.

"Forgive me for taking up so much of your time," Masuto said.

"I am fascinated."

"A few minutes more?"

"As long as you wish."

"I am told that Israeli Intelligence is just about the best in the world."

"Is it? Possibly, yet not good enough to tell us that the Yom Kippur War was coming. Perhaps it is estimable by comparison, since there is so little intelligence among any of the intelligence services. Intelligent human beings do not become spies, and it has become a rather loathsome profession. Perhaps we have more who are motivated by patriotism than other countries, perhaps because there is little else we can offer."

"And yet you were unable to find Schwartzman."

"That, Sergeant Masuto, is not the work of Israeli Intelligence. Do you know how many Schwartzmans there are still at large, still hidden among decent people? Hundreds." He watched Masuto thoughtfully through the smoke of his cigar, and Masuto, studying the hawklike face, the pale blue eyes, wondered how much he could ever know about such a man, regardless of how open and ingenuous his comments might be.

"You are trying to find out about Schwartzman in Germany," Kolan observed.

"Oh?"

"I could not help overhearing your conversation on the telephone."

"And you don't think I will discover anything worthwhile."

"Why do you say that?"

"Your manner."

"I am not prejudiced against the German police. They are handicapped because they want so desperately to forget."

"That isn't your handicap, Mr. Kolan."

"True. We want to remember. It is very important that we remember."

"I can understand that. I have only one more question, and then I will take up no more of your time."

"I assure you, my time is at your disposal."

"Do you collect stamps?"

"What an odd question! But of course—Schwartzman was a stamp dealer. A peculiar profession for a pathological madman to finish with. As a matter of fact, I do collect stamps—but only Israeli stamps."

"Thank you."

"Not at all. It has been a pleasure to know you, Sergeant Masuto. By the way, if my opinion is worth anything, I would guess that you will not find out who murdered Ivan Gaycheck."

Masuto smiled. "Oh I will certainly discover who killed him. But whether I can arrest the killer—well, who knows?" At the door to Kolan's office, he paused and said to the consul general, "You must not consider me slipshod in my methods because I did not ask you where you were between twelve and one o'clock yesterday."

"I would not think of you as being slipshod in your methods. Not at all. Do you want to know where I was between twelve and one o'clock yesterday?"

"I think not," said Masuto.

CHAPTER
EIGHT

JACK BRIGGS

AGAIN

Two o'clock. Masuto sat in his car, took out of his pocket the picture of the girl that he had found in Gaycheck's wallet, and brooded over it. Was it his own background that made him feel that fifty percent of the young women he saw in West Hollywood were identical with the girl in the photo? Or was it because a disproportionate number of young women with blue eyes and straight blond hair eventually make their way to Hollywood? On the other hand, wonders came out of a bottle, and there appeared to be an irresistible urge among such girls to look alike.

He put the picture back in his pocket and drove west on Wilshire Boulevard for about a mile to another high rise. There he scanned the directory, found the name of Jack Briggs listed under Pisces Productions, and wondered idly who was a Pisces, Jack Briggs or one of his partners—and how strange it was that so many Americans, bereft of any religion or faith, turned in such desperation to astrology. Pisces Productions was on the eleventh floor, and the reception room that Masuto entered proudly displayed blown-up stills from the current hit of Pisces, *Open Mind*. Trying not to appear too interested in nude women and oversized mammaries, Masuto asked the pretty girl at the reception desk whether Mr. Briggs was in.

"You're Mr. Kamino, the Japanese distributor, aren't you?" she said. "Mr. Briggs was not expecting you until later, but Mr. Maper is in. Mr. Briggs is still out to lunch, but he said that if you came early, I was to give you our presentation book of stills, because you can usually get a more thoughtful appraisal of the product from the stills than from the print. You do understand me? You do speak English?"

"Yes, I do speak English," Masuto said.

"Well, you certainly do. I think your English is marvelous. Absolutely marvelous. The way everybody in the world speaks English, and it just gives me an inferiority complex. I can't even say sukiyaki in Japanese, and you don't even have an accent."

"That's because I am not Mr. Kamino," Masuto explained. "When do you expect Mr. Briggs?"

"Then you're another Japanese distributor."

"No. So sorry. I'm a policeman."

"A Japanese policeman?" The outer door opened and she spread her hands. "There you are."

Masuto turned to see Briggs, who regarded him without pleasure. "You want to see me?" Briggs demanded.

"If you have a few minutes."

"I got an important meeting in ten minutes, Sergeant, and what happened yesterday is over, except for seventy-five bucks it cost me to have the door fixed."

"Then ten minutes, if you can spare it."

"Okay. Come on in."

He led the way into his office. He was a big man, heavy in the shoulders, his neck layered with fat—an odd match for the slender sensitivity of his wife. He liked to be with his work. The walls of his office were like double spreads from *Playboy* magazine. He dropped into the chair behind his desk and stared moodily at Masuto.

"It pisses me off," he said, "to be pushed around by a two-bit police force. If you clowns were doing your job my house wouldn't have been ripped off."

"No police force can prevent burglaries," Masuto said quietly. "We are not pushing you around, Mr. Briggs."

"Don't give me that crap. First you third-degree my wife, and now you're here. Who the hell are you to tell her she can't step out her front door?"

"I felt your wife and son were possibly in great danger."

"Horseshit. What danger?"

Masuto shrugged. "As you please. I only suggested it to her. But I am not only investigating a burglary. I am chief of homicide in what you characterize as our two-bit police force. I am investigating a murder."

"What murder?" It came out poorly. His surly aggressiveness had slipped away, and Masuto felt his simulated ignorance.

"Don't you read the papers?"

"I have been up to my ears all day."

"A stamp dealer in Beverly Hills was murdered yesterday—somewhere between twelve-thirty and one o'clock. I spoke to your wife about it. Didn't she tell you?"

"No."

"That's strange, Mr. Briggs."

"Why?"

"I told her that I felt there was a connection between the murder of Ivan Gaycheck and the break-in at your house. I'm amazed that she wouldn't mention it to you."

"She may have mentioned it. It slipped my mind."

"Ah so. Of course. She telephoned you today—or you telephoned her?"

"What difference does that make?"

"Just curiosity."

"I phoned her. Goddamn it, you come in here with these stupid accusations . . ."

"I make no accusations. Pardon me if that is the impression I give."

"Why don't you come out with what you're here for and let me get back to work."

"Did you know Ivan Gaycheck?"

"Who?"

"Ivan Gaycheck. The man who was murdered."

"No. I didn't know him. I never heard his name before."

"But your wife mentioned him."

"Look, mister—don't try to pull anything on me. If my wife mentioned his name, it slipped my mind."

Watching him keenly, Masuto said, "There is a Mauritius stamp called the One-Penny Orange. Does that mean anything to you?"

He was a few seconds slow. "What?"

"One-Penny Orange."

"What in hell are you talking about?"

"Then your wife did not mention that either?"

"Mention what?"

"The One-Penny Orange."

"Look, when I spoke to my wife, I was thinking of other things."

"The One-Penny Orange," Masuto said, rather didactically, "is a Mauritius postage stamp of great value. I have reason to believe that this stamp was in the possession of your mother-in-law, Mrs. Hilda Kramer. I also have reason to believe that it was stolen from her."

"You're out of your mind. My mother-in-law never had a pot to pee in."

"Nevertheless, I believe that she had this stamp in her possession for years—without knowing that she owned it."

"Play it any way you like." He looked at his watch. "My time is up, Masuto. I don't have to answer any questions. Furthermore, I don't intend to see you again. You got anything to say, you can say it to my lawyer."

"Why?"

"What in hell do you mean, why? Don't you understand English?"

"I mean that I haven't accused you of anything and I did not come here to arrest you for anything."

"I'm finished. That's all." He got up, walked around the desk, and opened the door. Masuto rose, walked to the door, then paused.

"Mr. Briggs?"

Briggs shook his head grimly.

"Mr. Briggs, wouldn't you, as a matter of plain curiosity, be interested to know what that particular One-Penny Orange is worth?"

Briggs stared at him without replying.

"Ah so—then I will tell you. It is worth over three hundred thousand dollars, and if you doubt my credibility you might call the Holmbey Stamp Center downtown and ask for Mr. Holmbey. I am sure he would be delighted to give you a price."

Blandly, innocently, Masuto's dark eyes met Briggs' pale blue eyes. He could almost feel Briggs' tension, the enormous effect he was making to control himself.

"Ah, so sorry," Masuto said sympathetically. "So much for so little. So very sorry." He smiled and walked out, feeling somewhat ashamed of playing a silly role, yet taking a non-Buddhist and bitter satisfaction in what he had just done.

He drove back to the station then, and on his way to his desk he poked his head into the room where Cora ran the various machines without which no modern police force can function.

"Greetings, Masao," Cora said. "Come in and let me try to tempt you."

"You always tempt me."

"And all I get is the inscrutable. What can I do for you?"

"Jack Briggs, B-r-i-g-g-s. Maybe the Jack stands for John on his birth certificate. From his accent, I'd guess he stems from Texas or maybe Oklahoma. He's in the porny trade, so maybe there's something there. Get a make on him if there is any from the F.B.I., and if there's nothing there, try the Texas State Police."

"The Texas Rangers."

"What?"

"That's what they call themselves—the Texas Rangers."

"Go on."

"Truth."

"Okay, Texas Rangers. But sit on it. Tell them it's critical, an emergency. I'll be at my desk—for a little while anyway."

Wainwright noticed Masuto coming into the squad room, and he stalked over to Masuto's desk and flung two slips of yellow paper down on the desktop. "Read them and weep," Wainwright snapped.

They were the charge slips for the telephone calls, one hundred seventy-five dollars to London, two hundred twelve to Germany.

"That's beautiful," said Wainwright. "That's just beautiful."

"What did Beckman get in Germany?"

"A big, fat nothing."

"Where is he now?"

"At the public library, where you instructed him to spend the afternoon sitting on his ass. It don't matter that the world goes on. Beckman spends the day in the library."

"We hit the jackpot on the London call."

"What jackpot? You know that forty years ago a German named Kramer maybe bought a very valuable stamp or maybe he didn't. That's one hell of a jackpot. Suppose you explain it to me, and suppose you tell me how I explain the call to Germany. We already knew who Gaycheck was. We got that on the Telex."

"You're upset," Masuto said gently.

"Sure I'm upset. We got two murders and we got nothing."

"Actually, one—because Haber belongs to the sheriff."

"Screw the lousy sheriff and his idiot deputies. We got two, because they're connected."

"I think we have three," Masuto said, even more gently.

"What!"

"If that's the way you look at it."

"What in hell do you mean? We got three murders? What am I, a joke? We got a murder and nobody tells me?"

"I'm telling you."

"All right, all right," he said, controlling himself and pulling a chair up next to Masuto's desk. "Suppose you tell me all about it, Masao. And make it good."

"The name of the victim is Hilda Kramer. She was the mother of Ellen Briggs. It was the Briggses' house on Camden that was burglarized yesterday."

"I know that. Hilda Kramer died of a heart attack."

"Apparently she had a bad heart and suffered a thrombosis. I think it was brought on in a struggle with someone who stole the One-Penny Orange from her."

"You're hipped on that One-Penny Orange. The break-in took place yesterday, two days after her death."

"I know."

"You got any evidence?"

"None."

"But you know who the killer is?"

"Yes."

"The same one who killed Gaycheck?" Wainwright asked sarcastically.

"No."

"Oh? Three murders and three killers."

"I'm afraid so."

"You know, Masao," Wainwright said slowly, "you leave me speechless. It's the first time, but you leave me speechless."

"So sorry."

"Okay. Look, Masao, I know you long enough and respect you enough to accept what you say—but it goes no further, not until you can bring me evidence and swear out a warrant and make an arrest. Not one word of this to the press or to anyone. Two murders in one day in Beverly Hills are enough. Three are impossible. Now who is the killer?"

Masuto shook his head. "Not now. Give me until nine tonight and I'll pin it down."

Whatever Wainwright might have said was interrupted by Masuto's telephone. He picked it up. It was Beckman, from the library.

"Masao, I've gone through the two years of *Der Spiegel* they keep on file. Nothing. No picture of Schwartzman or anyone who resembles him."

"Is two years all they have?"

"They have the eight years prior to that packed away in the basement. When I asked about it, they began to groan and whine."

"Let them groan and whine. I want you to get it out and go through it, every page."

"For God's sake, Masao, I'll be here until they close."

"I expect you will." He put down the phone and looked at Wainwright, who said:

"All right, Masao. Nine o'clock tonight. I'm going home and get a few hours of sleep. You might do the same."

"Thank you, but I'm not tired."

"Be patient and wait until I retire. You'll be the boss then."

Cora came over as Wainwright stalked away. "What was he whipping you about?"

"He didn't sleep last night. That makes him nervous. He wants me to be patient and wait until he retires."

"That'll be the day."

"What have you got for me?"

"From the F.B.I.—big zero. You get nothing from them unless you give them prints to put into their IBM machine. But the good old Texas Rangers came through."

"Did they!"

"Providing," Cora said, "that your Jack Briggs is the same as John Wesley Briggs. You didn't even tell me how old he is."

"The truth is, I didn't ask him. About fifty."

"Well, that fits. John Wesley Briggs, born in Dallas on the twelfth of March, nineteen twenty-six . . ."

"Twelfth of March. What is that called in that silly astrology thing?"

"It is not silly. Pisces. Don't knock what you don't know."

"Pisces Productions. Good. Go on."

"Three arrests before the age of twenty. One conviction—car stealing, suspended sentence on a juvenile plea."

"The others?"

"Both assaults. Charges dropped."

"Anything else?"

"One nice one that fits in with what you told me. In 1958, he was arrested for what the Rangers call publication of impermissible nudity. Isn't that cute? In other words, girlie magazines. That was before the lid was taken off pornography."

"No conviction?"

"No conviction. The magazine closed down and the D.A. dropped the charges. After that, Briggs seems to have left Texas. At least, the Rangers have nothing else on him. Rangers. Isn't that darling? Did I do all right?"

"You did beautifully," Masuto said.

"This darling Ranger I spoke to, he says that if you get him a set of prints, he'll work on it. Why don't you send me down there with the prints, Masao?"

"Because I want you where I can see your sweet face each morning."

"I'll just bet."

CHAPTER
NINE

CLEO

Accused of having a complex mind, Masuto would protest that his own manner of thinking and being was simple and direct. He was aware that he lived in perhaps the most complex society that the world had ever evolved; his problem was Always to find some simple and direct path through the complexity. He sat at his desk staring at the picture he had taken from Ivan Gaycheck's wallet the day before, the picture of a very pretty girl with straight blond hair. Putting together a jigsaw puzzle, there were only three pieces missing, and the picture of the girl was the only lead he had to one of the pieces, perhaps the key piece. Whereby he told himself that most very pretty girls came to Hollywood to become great stars and ended up waiting tables, selling clothes, turning to welfare, and in not a few cases practicing the world's oldest profession; but a fair number of them worked in film or television at least once, and in order to work in film or television, one had to join S.A.G., the Screen Actors Guild.

It was three thirty-five when he parked his car in front

of the Screen Actors Guild building on Sunset Boulevard in Hollywood. He went inside and showed his badge to a stout, unsmiling lady at the reception desk.

"What I would like," he said, "is to talk to someone who would know most of the membership by sight."

"Wouldn't we all!"

"What I mean is that I am looking for someone. I have her picture." He showed her the picture.

"Is she a member of the guild?"

"I don't know. That's what I'm trying to find out."

"Is she wanted for a crime?"

"She's not wanted for anything. I only want to talk to her, as part of an investigation."

The fat woman sighed. "I'll see what I can do. What's her name?"

"I don't know."

The fat woman stared at him in amazement. "Out of sight, Officer! You are a beauty. We only have thirty-three thousand members in this organization, and you want me to tell you who this lady is. Do you know that some of them never come in here at all? Some of them come in once? Do you know how many look enough like this kid to be her twin sister?" She was indignant and affronted, and her voice rose, decibel by decibel. The telephone operator at the opposite end of the long reception desk called out:

"Give him the Academy Book and let him look through it."

A third woman, who had been sitting in one of the chairs in the reception room, picked up a book as large as two telephone directories and carried it over to Masuto.

"Eighty-five percent of our members are unemployed," the fat woman told him. "They could be anywhere."

A fourth woman came out of the inside room, a big room where a dozen men and women sat at desks and typewriters. "He's cute," she observed. "Tall, dark, handsome—but there's no work for Orientals, no work for women, no work for anyone but cops."

"He's a cop," said the fat woman.

"You're putting me on."

"Why don't you let him go inside and show his picture around?" the telephone operator asked.

"Because it goes against my grain to cooperate with the fuzz."

The woman from inside took the picture from Masuto and stared at it. "I've seen this kid."

"Everyone's seen her," the fat woman said.

Still staring at the photo, she took Masuto by the hand and led him into the big room. "Show it," she said. "Maybe someone knows her."

The fourth desk drew a response. The thin, wistful girl who sat there in front of a computer nodded and said, "I've seen her."

"Do you know her name?" Masuto asked eagerly.

"I can't even remember where I've seen her. Wait a minute. Yes. Absolutely. I saw her at a party up in the hills. Freddy Wolchek brought her."

"You don't know her name?"

She shook her head.

"And where do I find this Freddy Wolchek?"

"Look, Officer, he's a nice guy. I don't want to send him any grief."

"I only want a lead to the girl."

"Okay—what time is it?"

"Almost four."

"If he's not working, he'll be at Schwab's. Sitting at the counter, I guess."

"What does he look like?"

"Big, heavy. He must be six-two. He has a reddish beard."

"And if he's working?"

"Who knows? Any one of the studios—I should be so lucky."

"Do you have an address for him?"

"Janey!" she called out. "Get Freddy Wolchek's address for me, would you?"

Schwab's, on Sunset Boulevard just east of Crescent Heights, was only a few minutes from the Screen Actors Guild. It was, as Masuto knew, not simply a drugstore but a sort of social center and gossip and information exchange for actors who were not working. Masuto paced the long lunch counter, spotted three bearded men, chose the largest, whose beard was tinged with red, and sat down next to him. The red beard was bent moodily over a cup of coffee.

"You're Freddy Wolchek?"

The red beard nodded without looking at him.

"Tracy Levitt, over at the Screen Actors Guild, said I might find you here."

Now the red beard looked at him.

"I'm Sergeant Masuto, Beverly Hills police."

"I'm clean," the red beard said. "I'm so clean I'm antiseptic. I don't even have the price of a joint. I'm Honest John. I never even been busted, never."

Masuto showed him the photo. "You know the girl?"

He stared at the photo and then nodded slowly, "That's Cleo. What has she done, knocked over a bank?"

"Does she knock over banks?"

"I wouldn't put it past her. She's bad medicine."

"Cleo what?"

"Damned if I know. She never told me."

"Tracy said you dated her. You brought her to a party."

"I didn't bring her. I picked her up there. That was a night. She is bad medicine, old buddy. She is a cokey. She is crazy—crazy."

"Where does she live?"

"Who knows?"

"Didn't you take her home?"

"She took me, old buddy. No, I didn't take her home. I lost her somewhere that night. Tell you what, though—I know where she works."

"Oh?"

"If you call it work. At least that's what she told me. I never checked it out. You know that little sort of beat-up shopping center in Topanga Canyon, maybe halfway between the Valley and the ocean?"

"I know the place," Masuto said.

"Well, there's a massage parlor there, it's called the Pink Flamingo. She massages. So she told me. I don't like to call any kid a hooker, because I've known some hookers, they were a damn sight nicer kids than a lot of Beverly Hills dames, but this Cleo . . ." He shook his head. "She is bad medicine."

Topanga Canyon is one of those strange anomalies that one finds in the vast spread of Los Angeles, a wild, beautiful, sparsely settled gash in the Santa Monica Mountains, cutting through from the San Fernando Valley to the Pacific. From Schwab's, Masuto drove over Laurel Canyon Pass into the San Fernando Valley, picking up the Ventura Freeway and driving west. It was still before five o'clock when he turned off the freeway and drove into Topanga Canyon, yet in spite of the fact that this was late spring, the daylight long and mellow, the canyon was already shadowed, the deep cleft gathering the ominous gloom of night hours before night would fall.

There were only three cars in the little shopping center when he pulled up in front of the Pink Flamingo and parked. He had never noticed the Pink Flamingo before, but it occurred to him that there was nothing very unusual about a massage parlor in Topanga Canyon, which had everything else from communes to sensitivity centers and nudist camps and TM temples.

He walked to the door, rang the bell, and waited. After a few moments the door was opened by a small Oriental man. "Massage?" He smiled. Masuto walked in without replying. The small man studied him. "You want nice massage?"

Masuto had thought he was Korean, but the accent was Japanese. "I want to see Cleo," Masuto said.

"Ah so. You know Cleo. She very nice. Very clever. Fourteen dollar, please."

They stood in a tiny, dimly lit entryway. Down a narrow hallway, Masuto could see the entrances to six cubicles, each with its own small drape. The sound of two women talking; a shrill laugh; some low groans, which might have indicated that a massage was proceeding satisfactorily.

"I'm not here for a massage," Masuto said sourly.

"No? No massage? No good then. No screwing here. I run clean, legal place."

"You run a pesthole, you miserable creature," Masuto said in Japanese. "I am a policeman. I want to see Cleo."

"No Cleo here!" His voice was shrill.

"You will speak in your native tongue! Do you take me for a fool?" Masuto snapped at him, still speaking Japanese. "Where is the girl I want? Either tell me or I'll break you in two, you wretched piece of offal."

"Inside—in the last booth."

Masuto strode down the hallway and flung back the curtain of the last booth. It was empty except for a massage table and a chair. Then he heard the sound of a door closing. As he turned back to the front, his way was blocked by a massively fat blond woman in a loose housecoat. She began to curse him.

"Lousy Jap pig! You lousy yellow mother . . ."

He pushed past her. The proprietor had disappeared. He ran to the door, flung it open, and dashed out. One of the three cars he had seen there, a red MG convertible, roared out of the parking lot and onto Topanga Boulevard, heading south. Masuto raced to his car, fumbled in his pocket for the key, cursing his stupidity, then got it started and swung around into Topanga. The red MG was already out of sight. He pushed his gas pedal down to the floor, got the Datsun up to fifty, managing somehow to hold the light car on the narrow, twisting road.

He turned on his radiophone and put out an A.P.B. call: "Red MG convertible. Driven by a girl. Name of Cleo. Blond hair, blue eyes, about twenty-five. Hold for questioning. I'm proceeding south on Topanga. She's about a mile ahead of me."

He was so intent on the road ahead that he heard the motorcycles before he saw them, and then they were on either side of him, two on his left and one on his right. Each rider carried a three-foot length of cycle chain clenched in gloved hands. He heard the chains crash against the body of the Datsun, and then his right-hand rear window was shattered. He bore down on his gas pedal, and still they were alongside him, systematically smashing his car to rubble. A chain end turned his windshield into a maze of cracks, the left-hand front window smashed—miraculously, none of the flying glass had cut him yet—blows thudded against the body of the car, again on his windshield, and he felt the glass shards on his face, heard the crazy drumming noise of the chains all over the car.

He did the only thing he could think of doing, instinctively. He stood on his brakes and turned his car violently to the left. The brakes screaming, the car almost turning over, he smashed into the metal guard rail, bracing himself with all his strength. The guard rail bent and bowed out over the precipice below, but it held, and at the same time the two motorcycles on his left crashed into his car, the first one striking the front of his motor, the rider flung like a thrown ball over the guard rail and down fifty feet into the rocky cleft of Topanga. The second motorcycle struck the back of the Datsun, and the rider was flung over the car and landed on the pavement.

The door on Masuto's left was bent out of shape and locked closed. He slid over the seat, pushing aside the broken glass, opened the right-hand door, and got out. Blood was running down onto his shirt, and as he touched his cheeks he realized that he had tiny glass cuts on his face and hands. In front of him, the second rider lay in a pool of blood on the pavement. No time to think or to know how badly he was hurt. The third motorcycle was roaring down on him. He leaped back and dodged the swung chain. The cyclist braked to a stop about fifty feet down the road, dismounted, and advanced on Masuto, swinging the chain. His face covered by his blue windmask and helmet, his body encased in black leather, he was a nightmare man-at-arms out of another world; and to increase the nightmare effect, two cars drove by, slowing without stopping.

A third car stopped. The driver got out just as the cyclist made his first pass at Masuto with the chain. Masuto dodged it. The driver got back in his car and drove away. The chain began to spin around the cyclist's head as he advanced on Masuto again. As much as Masuto could think of anything in two seconds, he considered the problem of a policeman who refused to carry a gun in America today and who was very confident of his skill in the martial arts. The cyclist struck and Masuto dodged, feeling the wind of the chain as it passed his face.

"Come on, you yellow bastard!" the cyclist shouted, spinning the chain and charging Masuto. The detective spun on his heel, bent, and kicked high and hard. He felt the chain touch his hair and then his foot connected with the cyclist's chest, and the man was off balance, swaying, and then Masuto kicked out again, almost in a pirouette, his toe in the cyclist's groin this time. The man fell to his knees, crying out in pain and clutching his groin, and Masuto drove his knee into the blue windmask. The man crumpled, and Masuto, his hands shaking, staggered to his car, got the cuffs he kept in the glove compartment, twisted the cyclist's hands behind him, and cuffed him. Then he went to the iron rail on the side of the road, bent over it, and vomited, conscious somewhere in some recess of his mind that three or four more cars had driven past without stopping while all this went on. He felt better after he had thrown up. The blood on his face had coagulated and he was not bleeding anymore. The cyclist he had handcuffed was still lying on his face in the road, groaning and whimpering. Masuto walked over to him and pulled off his helmet. He was a white man with long, sandy hair.

"Jesus, man," he whimpered, "you smashed my face. My nose is bleeding. I'll bleed to death."

"Not likely," said Masuto. He went to the second cyclist, who had been thrown over the car and flung onto the road, and now, for the first time since it began, a car stopped and the driver actually walked over to Masuto.

"I'm a policeman," Masuto said.

"I'm Doctor Marvin Goldberg. Are you hurt?"

Masuto pointed to the cyclist who lay motionless in a pool of blood. The doctor went over to him and felt his wrist.

"I think he's dead."

"There was another one," Masuto said. "He went over the rail and into the canyon." He went to the rail and the doctor followed him.

"There he is," Masuto said, pointing.

"I can't get down there. You'd better call Rescue."

"Could he be alive?"

"I don't know. It's fifty feet down and it's rock."

"I'll try my radiophone," Masuto said. "That one . . ." He pointed to the cyclist he had cuffed. "That one has a nose-bleed. I had to kick him in the face and in the testicles. You might have a look at him."

"I'll get my bag," the doctor said.

The radiophone was not working. Masuto stood there looking at the wreck of his car. "The phone's not working," he told the doctor. "They'll get here. They always do. How is he?"

"He'll be all right," the doctor said.

Masuto walked over to the cyclist, who was sitting up now, his hands clamped behind him.

"What's your name?"

"Tom Cleerey."

"All right, Cleerey. I'm putting you under arrest, and I'm going to read you your rights. You have the right to remain silent. I am arresting you for the attempted murder of Sergeant Masuto and for the murder of Ronald Haber. If you give up the right to remain silent, anything you say can and will be used against you in a court of law. You have the right to speak with an attorney . . ."

Other cars were stopping, now that it was over; a line began to back up on the canyon road, and the traffic halted in both directions. It was still daylight, but the shadows were long and deep on the macabre scene in the canyon. Masuto saw the flashing lights of the highway patrol, and a moment or two later two L.A.P.D. cops and a highway patrolman pushed through the gathering crowd.

"This one's dead, and there's another one down in the canyon," Masuto explained to them. "I'm Sergeant Masuto, Homocide, and I arrested that one—his name is Tom Cleerey—for the murder of Ronald Haber. That happened last night, over in West Hollywood."

"You're crazy!" Cleerey shouted.

"But what he tried to do to me with a bicycle chain— well, that happened here—so I don't know where it goes. I read him his rights. Dr. Goldberg here was witness to it."

"You called in on the red MG?" one of the L.A.P.D. cops asked.

"That's right."

"We got the girl. She's back in the black-and-white."

"That Haber thing was on Lapeer Street, wasn't it?" the other L.A.P.D. cop said. "Suppose we take them both over to San Vicente for starters."

"I'd like to ride with you," Masuto said. He nodded at his car. "It was a nice car, a really nice car."

CHAPTER
TEN

CLEO

CONTINUED

It was half-past seven when Masuto arrived at the sheriff's station on San Vicente Boulevard in West Hollywood, and Wainwright was waiting for him there.

"You look like hell," Wainwright said to him. "Why aren't you in the hospital or something?"

"I'm always amazed at the politeness of Caucasians."

"Screw politeness."

"I'm not in the hospital," Masuto said, "because I am all right. When we get back to the station I'll wash up and change my shirt."

"What about those cuts?"

"They stopped bleeding."

"Why don't you go home and rest?"

"I can accept anything from you but solicitude," Masuto said, smiling slightly. "I told you that I intend to put the pieces together tonight."

"Sure, you told me."

At that point Deputy Williams joined them. "The other two are dead," he told them, and said to Masuto, "I know

339

you made the collar and read Cleerey his rights, but wasn't that a hell of a way to go about it? You could have brought him back here."

"We don't want the credit," Wainwright said. "Goddamn it, what did you expect of Masao, with three demented thugs trying to kill him!" He turned on Masuto and said, "As for you, you give me one royal pain in the ass. Why in hell don't you carry a gun? If you had a gun . . ."

"I might be dead now," Masuto said amiably. "Look, Williams, drop the charge of attempted murder on me. You can make the charge for Haber's murder stick."

"How? Just tell me how. This Cleerey is screaming his head off, and we don't have one goddamn thing on him except that he resisted arrest and tried to kill you, which is something, but it don't clean the murder pad."

"Why don't we talk to Cleo," Masuto suggested.

"On her we got nothing, but nothing."

"We'll talk."

"She's not even a user."

"Cocaine."

"There's none on her and no tracks. So she sniffs. Go prove it. She's already called some shyster, and he'll have her out of here in ten minutes."

"Let's talk to her."

"You talk to her. We'll listen."

The three of them, Masuto, Williams, and Wainwright, went into the interrogation room, and then a matron brought Cleo there. It was the first time Masuto saw her. She was smaller and more slender than he had imagined, with a face of such wide-set blue-eyed innocence that she might well have played Saint Joan. The voice was something else, hoarse and low and cold.

"I got nothing to say," she told them. "You got nothing on me, and this ain't the end. Wait till my lawyer comes. We got a false arrest that will make me a bundle. That's it. I got nothing else to say."

"That's fair enough," said Masuto. "You don't have to say anything. Just listen, and I'll tell you a story."

"Bullshit."

"You met a man at a party," Masuto said. "His name was Ivan Gaycheck. He gave you cocaine. He wasn't a dealer, but he used it. . . ."

"I don't know any Ivan Gaycheck."

"You promised not to talk. Ivan Gaycheck was murdered. . . ."

"If you think you're going to hang Gaycheck's murder on me, you're crazy!"

"And after he was murdered, I went through his wallet, and found"—he took the photo out of his pocket—"this picture, which you gave him when you became his mistress."

Her lips tightened.

"Then, one night, he boasted. He boasted that he was going to get his hands on a stamp that was worth a fortune, and that he would sell it for an enormous profit. He even told you where the stamp was. He told you that it belonged to an old woman who did not even know that she possessed it. He probably promised you a share of his profits, but you were greedy, and you told Cleerey and his two associates about the stamp. Then you read an announcement in the Los Angeles *Times* that this woman, whose name was Hilda Kramer, had died and would be buried at such and such a time. You knew the house would be empty during the funeral, so you went there with your associates, broke in, and ransacked the place. But you did not find the stamp because the stamp was not there. And then Gaycheck was murdered."

"You lousy fuzz bastard! You think you're going to pin Gaycheck's murder on me. You're going to frame me, you bastard! You lousy Chink bastard!"

"Oh, no—no. You didn't murder Gaycheck. Neither did your associates murder him. I'm sure you thought about it, but you were too late. He was murdered while you were ransacking the Briggses' house on Camden Drive, so, you see, you have a perfect alibi."

Her face fell, as the anger washed out. She stared at him, confused now.

"But you did decide that Ronald Haber murdered Gaycheck," Masuto went on, "and that night, you and your three associates drove to Haber's apartment on Lapeer Street, and beat him and tortured him, and finally killed him."

"You're crazy!" she yelled.

"But you didn't find the stamp. Yet you were persevering. You then went to Gaycheck's shop and opened his safe. And still you didn't find the stamp. So it was all for nothing, and stupid and senseless—as senseless as the scheme to kidnap the Briggs child."

"Go to hell!"

Masuto rose, started to say something, then swallowed his words and began to pace back and forth across the interrogation room. Wainwright and Williams watched him keenly, but they said nothing.

"I don't judge you," Masuto said finally. "Who am I to judge anyone? It's true that you stood by and watched your friends beat Haber to death, but don't we all stand by and watch people suffer and die and never lift a finger? However, the law regards it differently. The law says that you are an accessory to a murder, and you will go to prison for the rest of your life. There's no way out of that. You can hire every lawyer in California—and there's still no way out for you."

The wide blue eyes were full of terror now. "You're lying. You haven't any proof. You're lying. You said Gaycheck gave me cocaine. He never gave me cocaine."

Masuto sat down, leaned across the table, and said gently, "I'm not lying, Cleo. I have proof. There's a girl who lives on the same floor as Haber lived on. When you left the place, she opened the door and she saw you. Do you understand? She saw you."

Recognition, memory. It mixed with the terror, and Masuto found his heart going out to her. She was defenseless now. The terror drove away her veneer of toughness. The blue eyes filled with moisture. "You bastard," she whispered. "Why don't you try to make it in this lousy place—as a dame! Try! Get yourself worked over until you're no better than a lousy lamb chop. I never killed nobody. It was Cleerey and Buck who wasted him. I begged them to stop. I pleaded with them to stop. Look at me! I weigh ninety-two pounds and you tell me I beat someone to death."

She put her head down on the table and began to sob. Masuto looked at Williams, who said, "Okay, I'll do what I can. I'll talk to the D.A. Are you sure this Cindy Lang over on Lapeer will testify? Are you sure she saw them?"

"Give her a break and she'll testify," Wainwright said. "Come on, Masao. We'll get you cleaned up."

Driving back to Beverly Hills, Wainwright asked Masuto how he felt.

"Good and decent. There's nothing I like better than to torture kids who have had the life beaten out of them."

"She's no kid. Don't let those blue eyes fool you."

"Then what is she, Captain? A monster of some sort? She never asked to be born into this hellhole that we call civilization. Where's her family? I don't see any hands stretched out to her."

"That's sentimental crap, Masao. She stood by and watched a man beaten to death."

"We all do, Captain. We all do."

"Look, I can live without your goddamn philosophy. We know who killed Haber. What about Gaycheck?"

"It's still a half hour before nine o'clock."

"And you're going to turn him up before nine?"

"I don't know," Masuto said tiredly. "We may never know who killed Gaycheck. It won't be the first unsolved murder, and it won't be the last."

"That's beautiful," Wainwright said.

At the station, Beckman was waiting, sitting on the edge of Masuto's desk, grinning.

"What the hell are you grinning about?" Wainwright asked sourly. "I ought to dock that four hundred dollars of telephoning from your salary, and then you two clowns would stop playing Scotland Yard."

"What's eating him, Masao?" Beckman asked as Wainwright marched into his office and slammed the door behind him. "And what did you run into? You look like you put your face into an electric fan."

"Small cuts and a lot of blood."

"I hear you cleared up the Haber thing. It sounds wild. What happened?"

"Got a clean shirt here, Sy?"

"I got more than that."

"Can you hold it until I wash up? Where's the shirt?"

"In my locker. Be my guest."

After he had washed up, rinsed his mouth, and gone over his face with a styptic pencil, Masuto felt better. He changed his shirt. His tie was patterned and the bloodstains hardly showed.

"That's better," Beckman said when he returned to the squad room. "You look almost human. What happened over at Topanga?"

"I had some trouble but then it turned out all right."

"I hear you totaled your Datsun."

"Is there anything on the lot I can use?"

"There's a loose patrol car. The chief said you could have it for a couple of days. Here's the keys." He tossed them over at Masuto.

"Thank you, Sy. What did you find at the library?"

"Just what the doctor ordered." He grinned again and took a folded sheet of paper out of his pocket. "Page twenty-two of *Der Spiegel*, September seventy-two—although what you want it for I can't figure out. We know Gaycheck was Schwartzman, and whatever his name was, we know he's dead." He spread out the sheet on the desk. "I tore it out—stealing public property. Who the hell's going to miss it anyway, five years old?" There, in the center of the page, was a five-by-seven portrait photo of a pudgy young man in the uniform of an SS officer.

"That's the name," Beckman said, pointing to the caption under the picture. "That's all I can read, but there it is. Gaylord Schwartzman. Anyway, I'd recognize him."

"Would you?"

"Masao, I spotted him before I read the name."

"Maybe. Do you have the morgue pictures?"

"Right here." Beckman took them out of his pocket and laid them next to the magazine photo. "Well, Masao—am I wrong?"

"No. He changed very little. Lost most of his hair, but otherwise . . ."

"No beard, no mustache, lives here in Beverly Hills, right here out in the open, and nobody recognizes him."

"Somebody did."

The telephone on Masuto's desk rang. It was Lieutenant Pete Bones from L.A.P.D. "Masao," he said, "I hear you had us running errands for you."

"I guess we did."

"You sound down. Not the usual Oriental confidence."

"I had a hard day."

"I hear you totaled that crummy Datsun you drive. Real cowboys and Indians out there at Topanga. They tell me the good guys won."

"You hear a lot down there."

"We keep our ears open. That's why we're so good. You want to know about that twenty-two that killed Gaycheck?"

"No, I don't want to hear about it," Masuto said sourly. "We just asked to keep you busy."

"Sarcasm, sarcasm."

"How do you know it's the gun that killed Gaycheck?"

"We don't know, because we haven't got the gun. You told us, and we consider you to be honorable."

"All right. What have you got?"

"That's the thanks I get. We had two men on this all day and we covered twenty-two gun stores, but what's that to you? You don't pay us taxes. You live up there with the swells in something that calls itself a city and doesn't even have a legitimate flophouse."

"Pete, I thank you. Now what have you got?"

"That's better. All right, over the past two weeks, only one store sold the kind of a purse gun you describe. Sam's Sporting Goods on San Pedro. Small automatic, five shots.

A little British gun made by Webley-Fosbery. Most of their makes fire six cartridges. This one shoots five. It has a light trigger action and it only shoots the twenty-two short. They stopped making them before World War Two. This one had a mother-of-pearl handle. Funny thing, the dealer asked the customer whether she wanted extra cartridges. She said no, all she wanted was the full magazine. She didn't know how to operate it. He showed her."

"She. A woman bought it?"

"That's right."

"Did you get a description?"

"We did. Here goes. Straight blond hair, down to her waist, blue eyes, very blue—the dealer remembered them specifically. Bluest eyes he ever saw. Beautiful pair of knockers, he couldn't stop raving about them. I'd say size thirty-six. Sweater, long skirt, the kind they drag around Hollywood—and an English accent."

"How old was she?"

"He says maybe twenty, twenty-five. Somewhere around there. Said she lived in the Hollywood Hills, with ripoffs all around her. She wanted the gun for protection."

"What did she sign on the register?"

"Angela Cartwright, 2240 Langley Drive. No such street in the Hollywood Hills. We checked it."

"Did you run the name through?"

"We did. No Angela Cartwright. You want to hear something else?"

"Let me guess."

"Go ahead, smartass. Guess."

"She wrote left-handed."

"How the hell did you know that? You're right. She signed the register with her left hand. It was like a little kid's scrawl.

"Wouldn't yours be if you wrote left-handed?"

"Now what the hell does that mean?"

"It means we'll never trace the handwriting. Pete, thanks. I'm very grateful."

"You want to leave it there, Masao?"

"For the time being."

He put down the phone and sat at his desk, staring into space. "Are you okay, Masao?" Beckman asked him.

"Sure. I'm all right, Sy."

"You're sure? You don't look all right."

"I'm okay."

"Anything else?"

"No, nothing else."

"Then it's okay with you if I push off now?"

"Okay," Masuto said.

"You don't want me to drive you? You look lousy."

"I can drive myself. Get out of here and go home and get some rest."

"Should I leave you the morgue pictures?"

"No, I don't need them."

Beckman picked up the photos. "Good night, Masao."

"Good night."

Masuto sat at his desk, his chin in his hands, staring into space. Wainwright stopped by on his way out. "Why don't you go home and go to bed," he said to Masuto.

"I will. All in good time."

"For Christ's sake, Masao, it's almost nine o'clock. You been up since four in the morning."

"I know."

"I was pretty nasty before. It's not you, Masao. It's my goddamn ulcers."

"I know."

"Don't think I don't know what you been through today. Don't think I don't respect it."

"Thank you."

"I mean that."

"I know."

"Well, good night."

"Good night, Captain."

After Wainwright had left, Masuto took out his notebook, found a number, and dialed it. "Mrs. Briggs?" he said.

"Yes. Who is this?"

"This is Sergeant Masuto. I'm calling to tell you that the danger is over. Permanently. Your son can come and go as he pleases."

"You're sure?"

"Yes, I'm quite sure."

"You've been very kind," she said. "I don't know how to thank you."

"There's no need to thank me. But you could help me."

"How?"

"I'd like to talk to you tonight."

"Of course. Why don't you come right over."

"I can't right now. It would be later, perhaps at eleven o'clock. Would that be too late?"

"Not at all. Please come whenever you are free. I never go to bed before midnight."

"Your husband won't object? I would want to talk to you privately."

"Sergeant Masuto, my husband is not here. He has left me."

"Left you?"

"We have separated. There will be a divorce. He packed his things this afternoon and moved into the Beverly

Wilshire Hotel. So you see, he cannot object to our talking privately."

"I'm so sorry."

"There is nothing for you to feel sorry about. It was a mutual decision. We both had reached a point of hatred that was unendurable. You must not think of me as a bereaved woman, except in terms of my grief over my mother's death. If it were not for that, I could say that I am a happier person than I have ever been during the past dozen years. I do not want to bore you with my past, but my marriage was not precisely made in heaven."

"I think I understand," Masuto said. "If you don't want me to come tonight . . ."

"But I do. I will wait for you. You can make it as late as you please."

CHAPTER ELEVEN

LUCILLE

BETTNER

till Masuto sat at his desk and stared into space. He had gone a whole day without meditation, without being quiet and trying to know who he was and where he was; and his weariness was due more to that than to lack of sleep. Then he opened a drawer of his desk and took out the two account books he had taken from Gaycheck's desk. He went through the small book, half hoping he would not find it. More than anything, he wanted to abandon it now, forget, go home and soak in a hot tub and listen to Kati's quiet talk, as she told him, detail for detail, what their children had done that day.

But it was there—Lucille Bettner—the same name that Holmbey had given him, with the address and the telephone number. He picked up the phone and dialed.

"Hello? Who is this?" The voice was soft, almost quavering, with just the faintest trace of an English accent.

"My name is Detective Sergeant Masao Masuto. I am chief of homicide at the Beverly Hills Police Department. I would very much appreciate it if you could spare me a few minutes of your time."

"But what on earth have I to do with homicide or the Beverly Hills Police Department? Are you sure you have the right person?"

"Your name is Lucille Bettner?"

"Yes."

"I am investigating the death of Ivan Gaycheck."

"Oh. I see."

"Could I come over now?"

"It's quite late."

"I realize that. But this is very important."

"Very well. Do you know how to find my house?"

"I think so."

"You will press the button at the gate. We have a television identification camera there, so you will have to provide some kind of identification. I am sorry to inconvenience you so, but that's the world we live in, isn't it?"

"I suppose so," Masuto agreed. "I'll be there shortly."

He went downstairs, got into the patrol car that Beckman had reserved for him, and drove north toward Sunset Boulevard. The night was cold and he felt chilled. He fumbled for the unfamiliar heating mechanism of the patrol car, failed to find it, and gave up. Vaguely, he remembered the Bettner estate, which could just be glimpsed from Sunset Boulevard. It was a great, half-timbered castle, built in the twenties, when Sunset Boulevard was a quiet carriage road and not the major traffic artery it is today. Then Sunset Boulevard was the treasured goal of the new rich, the film stars and directors and producers, and there they built their giant monuments to an era that is gone forever.

The Bettner house was set back from the road on a rise of ground, sheltered by a high hedge. Masuto turned off

Sunset into the driveway and found his way barred by an enormous iron gate. He got out of his car, pressed the button on the gatepost, then located the camera device. It was dark now, which meant that there was some kind of infrared device on the camera, and as Masuto displayed his badge to the camera eye, he reflected on this strange technological culture that had turned an entire nation into something that had never existed before.

"Okay," a man's voice said, coming from some hidden loudspeaker. "Get back in the car and drive up to the house."

Masuto followed the instructions obediently. The iron gate opened noiselessly, and he drove up the driveway to where a stone-pillared breezeway marked the entrance to the house. A dour gentleman dressed in black greeted him as he got out of the car.

"You can leave your car where it is, Officer. I'll take you to Mrs. Bettner."

The man in black led the way into the house, a huge, high-ceilinged foyer with straight-backed oak chairs set around it, purchased no doubt from some ancient British manor house, and then through an immense baronial living room, up a wide flight of stairs, down a hallway. The man in black knocked at a door.

"Mrs. Bettner?" He was almost shouting. "The policeman is here!"

"Well, bring him in, Alfred. Don't keep him standing in the hallway."

Alfred opened the door and Masuto entered.

"You can leave him here, Alfred. It's quite all right."

Alfred closed the door and Masuto looked around him. The combination bedroom and sitting room was cheerful and charming, done in pale pastel colors, very different from the room below. Mrs. Lucille Bettner sat in an armchair. She was a frail little woman, very old, certainly past eighty, Masuto decided, but her eyes were bright and alert, and her voice, though quavery, was aggressive and youthful.

"Oh, you are Japanese," she said. "How interesting! I didn't know that we had a Japanese on our police force. Los Angeles policemen are so young and handsome and unimaginative—it's quite discouraging, don't you think?"

"I am a Nisei, Mrs. Bettner."

"Still Japanese. Do you know, I spent seven months in Japan—but that was long, long ago, before that hideous war. I adore them. I have a Japanese acquaintance. A lovely gentleman whose name is Ishido. We have interests in common. Do you know him?"

"Yes, I do."

"Good. Now please sit down. Would you like something to drink?"

"No, ma'am," Masuto said as he seated himself. "But thank you."

"And you want to see me about that frightful Ivan Gaycheck affair. Actually, I knew him only slightly. We had a few business dealings—which I did not enjoy. I know that one doesn't speak ill of the dead, but I was not fond of Mr. Gaycheck. But I certainly didn't wish him dead—and one doesn't expect that sort of thing in Beverly Hills."

"No, ma'am, one doesn't."

"What is the world coming to!" She leaned toward him and smiled. "Do I have your name correctly—Sergeant Masuto?"

"Yes."

"Well, I suppose you want to ask me questions about my dealings with Mr. Gaycheck. Go right ahead."

"Thank you. You are a stamp collector, Mrs. Bettner?"

"My dear Sergeant Masuto, I am not simply a stamp

collector. I have one of the best collections in the United States. Possibly Clevendon's is better than mine, and I suppose that President Roosevelt's was rather unique, but it doesn't take much skill and effort to build a stamp collection when you have been president of the United States for more terms than one can count, and you must forgive me if I sound nasty, but I am a Republican and I was never an admirer of President Roosevelt. You see, my husband—I'm sure you have heard of him—well, he was an extraordinary man and he built an extraordinary studio and he left me more millions of dollars than you can shake a stick at; and in return I gave him my youth. I'm not sure it was a very good bargain. But there I was after he died, sixty-five years old, my family dead and gone back in England—and what does an old woman do? I was past my time of acting, and there are no parts for old women worth looking at, and my children are grown and gone. I was fit for nothing in particular, and through some whim I took up stamp collecting. Well, believe me, I found some purpose. You might sneer at this . . ."

"No, no," Masuto said hastily. "I would not dream of sneering at it."

"Be that as it may, Sergeant, it is something to be one of a very few. I love stamps and I know the field. I know more about stamps than anyone in Los Angeles, more than Ivan Gaycheck ever knew and more than that young wiseacre downtown, Mr. Jason Holmbey."

"I am sure you do." She had spoken in the loud tones of a person hard of hearing; Masuto now raised his voice. "Could you tell me when Gaycheck first spoke to you about the One-Penny Orange?"

She smiled and shook a finger at Masuto. "You are a sly one, aren't you? And you don't have to shout at me. My hearing is not of the best, but I can hear you quite well when you speak in a normal voice. So you know about the One-Penny Orange."

"Yes, I do."

"And when did he first mention it? I believe it was about a week ago. Yes, just a week ago."

"Did he have it then?"

"No. No, he did not. You see, he telephoned me and told me he was on the track of a One-Penny Orange on the original cover. I don't know how well versed you are in this, Sergeant Masuto, but a One-Penny Orange on the original cover is not unlike the paintings of Leonardo da Vinci—in one manner. We know how many there are and where they are. I have been trying to buy one for years, and Gaycheck knew this. He said he had a line on one and that he had every hope of obtaining it during the next few days. As a matter of fact, I made a good guess at which one it was—the cover that was sold in the 1930s and then disappeared from sight."

"You amaze me, Mrs. Bettner."

"Do I? Well, that's very nice. Thank you."

"That was a week ago?"

"Yes. He had the gall to ask me whether I was interested. He knew that I was. The gall of him!"

"And then?"

"He called me—let me see, was it three days ago? Yes."

"And he had the stamp."

"Yes. He called and told me that he had the stamp and was ready to do business. I told him that I wanted the provenance, that I would have no part of stolen goods. I am not one of those demented collectors who will buy stolen property and lock it away somewhere and gloat over it. My collection is public. I do articles for the *Collectors' Quarterly*."

"What did he say to that?" Masuto asked eagerly.

"He swore up and down that he had come by the cover honestly and that he had full legal title to it. But that means nothing with a man like Gaycheck. I told him that I wanted to see a bill of sale, and he said that was no problem, that he would have it for me."

"Did he mention the name of the seller?"

"No, he did not. Of course, he wouldn't—not until he made a deal with me."

"Did he set a price?"

"Well, first he insisted that I come down to his store and look at it. I suffer from arthritis, Sergeant Masuto, and it is very difficult for me to get around. I am not a recluse, but I leave my house only when I have to. I told Mr. Gaycheck that I would not dream of coming to his store until we had discussed the price."

"Then he did set a price?"

"A ridiculous price—three hundred thousand dollars."

"Is that really so ridiculous?"

"Not perhaps at auction. You see, Sergeant, at auction the owner would probably set a base price of one hundred thousand dollars. That is, the bidding would start only if there were an opening old of one hundred thousand. From there, the bidding might go to one hundred fifty thousand, two hundred, even four hundred thousand. Strange things happen at auctions. But in a straight deal between buyer and seller, three hundred thousand dollars is utterly exorbitant. I told him that, and he began to threaten me with sales to other collectors. I informed him that I was not impressed, and that he could call me again when he was ready to discuss reasonable terms."

"Why wouldn't he hold on to it and put it up at auction?" Masuto wanted to know.

"Ah. That is interesting, is it not, Sergeant. Why wouldn't he? I asked myself that. There could be only two reasons. One—that his provenance lacked substance and the stamp had been stolen."

"And you think that was the reason?"

"No. I think Gaycheck was convinced that he had legal title to the stamp."

"Are you sure?" Masuto pressed her. "This is very important for me to know. Are you sure that Gaycheck was convinced that he had legal title to the stamp?"

"Yes, I am. And I'll tell you why, Sergeant. You do not call a collector and anticipate the possession of a stamp to be stolen, and if you do have a stolen stamp, you don't try to deal with Lucille Bettner. You take it to Europe or the Middle East, where those oil kings will buy anything, stolen or not. And Gaycheck was ready to give me a bill of sale. There could be no deal without that."

"And does this thing you call provenance—I suppose it's a sort of pedigree—does this go with the bill of sale?"

"It certainly does. I would not touch such a stamp unless I knew who the previous owners were. If it turned out to be Skeffington's stamp, then I would want to know who had owned it between Skeffington and Gaycheck, and I would want proof that it had changed hands legally each time."

"And Gaycheck was willing to supply such proof?"

"So he said."

"I see. You said there were two reasons Gaycheck would be unwilling to put it up at auction. What is the other?"

"There is a great deal of publicity attendant to such an auction, Sergeant Masuto, especially if a One-Penny Orange is to go on the block. A man like Gaycheck is rather unsavory. His past might not bear scrutiny."

"And he never called back a third time?"

"No. He died yesterday."

Masuto rose. "You have been very kind and very patient."

"Not at all. This has been so pleasant."

"Only, there is one thing I don't understand."

"Yes, Sergeant?"

"You wanted the stamp so badly. Why did you take no steps to see whether it is still among Gaycheck's effects?"

"Because, Sergeant," she replied, smiling, "I am quite certain that Gaycheck was murdered for the stamp. So now it is a stolen stamp, and I have simply dismissed it from my mind."

"I see."

"Do you find my explanation adequate?"

"Quite adequate," Masuto said.

He was at the door when Mrs. Bettner said, "Sergeant?"

"Yes, Mrs. Bettner?"

"You know, the stamp will surface again. Such things always do. You have only to keep your eyes open, and then you will have your murderer."

"I'm afraid not."

"Why?"

"Because the murderer will probably do precisely as you suggest—take the stamp to Europe or the Middle East and sell it there."

"I suppose so. What a pity!"

"Thank you again, Mrs. Bettner." Then he left, closing the door behind him.

CHAPTER
TWELVE

ELLEN BRIGGS

AGAIN

I t was quarter to eleven when Ellen Briggs opened the
door for Masuto, and then she gave a startled exclama-
tion at the sight of his face. "You poor man! What have
they done to you?"

"It's nothing. I'll tell you about it. May I come in?"

"Please." She closed the door behind him and stared at
his face again. She had made no attempt to dress for his
coming. She still wore blue jeans and a work shirt, her
brown hair pulled back and tied behind her neck, her slender figure almost boylike, her dark eyes filled with compassion. "How awful! What happened to you?"

"You remember the three men on motorcycles outside of
the school?"

"Yes."

"I met up with them in Topanga Canyon."

"Oh, no."

"Now they'll never trouble you again."

"They robbed my house?"

"Yes."

"And you arrested them."

"Yes . . ."

"You don't want to talk about it, do you? I know that whatever happened must have been dreadful. I don't know how a man like you can be a policeman."

"How do you know what kind of man I am, Mrs. Briggs?"

"I know. Do you think you could call me Ellen? I feel I have known you such a long time. What is your first name?"

"Masao."

"Masao. That's a nice name. May I call you that?"

"If you wish."

"That's silly of me, isn't it? But I can't think of you as a policeman, only as a friend, and heaven knows, I have few enough friends. Please come inside. I'm in the kitchen again. Do you mind?"

"I don't mind, no."

He followed her into the kitchen and stood there rather awkwardly. "Do sit down, please," she said, "and don't pay any attention to me. You can't leap up every time I do." He nodded and sat down at the kitchen table. "You look so tired. Will you have some coffee? Or something to eat?"

"Do you know," he said, smiling for the first time, "I think I would. That is, if you don't mind. Suddenly I'm very hungry. I forgot my dinner entirely." Then he shook his head. "But no. That would be an imposition."

"It would not be an imposition. Do you know you have a very nice smile, but you ration it. Please. I'm a good cook."

"I don't want you to cook anything for me."

"What would you say to scrambled eggs, ham, brown rice, applesauce, butter, and toast? The rice is cooked. I only have to warm it. The whole thing won't take ten minutes."

"Right now it sounds like a banquet."

"Good. Do you want to smoke? Shall I bring you an ashtray?"

"I don't smoke, thank you." He watched her as she beat the eggs, sliced the ham, warmed the rice, and put the bread into the toaster. He felt that one can tell a great deal about a woman simply by watching her prepare a meal. Ellen Briggs was coordinated, alert, efficient. Her competence would flow over into anything she did, and whatever she did she would do well. Yet she had married Jack Briggs. Why? he wondered.

"What are you thinking, Detective?" she asked him.

"It would be impolite for me to reveal it."

"That's very Japanese." She grinned at him. "Tell me."

"All right. I was wondering how a woman like you came to marry Jack Briggs."

"You like women a great deal, Masao, but you don't know much about them."

"Why do you say that?"

"Because if you did, you would know that women like myself very often marry a Jack Briggs, and there's no way in the world they can explain why. It's called masochism."

"I know what it's called. That doesn't explain it."

"No, it doesn't." She piled his plate with eggs, ham, and brown rice. "Eat and don't think about such things. You know the story of the little boy who kept hitting his head against the wall. When they asked him why he did it, he explained that it felt so good when he stopped."

"Ah so." The food was delicious. Between mouthfuls, he asked her how her son was.

"He's asleep. I'm afraid I frightened him, keeping him locked up in the house all day. I haven't yet told him about his father."

She sat down opposite him at the kitchen table, putting her chin on her clasped hands and watching him, smiling slightly.

"You're very happy."

"Not very happy, no, Masao. I still have a knot of grief inside me for my mother. But without that—well, I am happier than I have been for a long, long time. I am free. Do you know what that means?"

"I think so."

"I have stopped hating Jack Briggs—well, almost. Hate is very corrosive. Doesn't it strike you as odd that I am talking to a detective whom I met only yesterday? But I refuse to think of you as a policeman. Are you married, Masao?"

"Yes."

"Happily?"

"As such things go, yes. My wife is a very simple and rather old-fashioned Japanese woman. She is very much in love with me."

"I can understand that. I think I am a little in love with you myself—just a very little, and nothing to trouble you or upset you."

Masuto put down his knife and fork and stared at her. She was wearing no makeup. Her fine deep brown eyes met his directly, and to his taste she was as beautiful a woman as he had ever known. Her nose was fine and straight, a slight flare at the nostrils, and her mouth was wide and expressive.

"It does trouble you. I'm sorry I said that."

"No. No, Ellen Briggs. It makes me feel warm and good— for the first time today. I thank you."

"Finish your food."

He ate the last scrap of food on his plate.

"Do you want more?" she asked him. "It's no trouble."

"No. This is fine. Thank you."

She took away his dish and refilled his coffee cup, and then again seated herself opposite him. "Please begin, Detective Masuto."

"Begin?"

"Your coming here tonight. You are my friend, I think, but you didn't come as a friend. You came as a policeman."

"I don't know."

"But you do know."

"Ah so." He nodded.

"When you say 'Ah so,' Masao, is it to remind people that you are Japanese?"

"It's a foolish habit." He sipped his coffee. "Ellen," he said, "when did you discover that your husband had sold the stamp?"

She was not surprised or perturbed at his question, and answered him directly and plainly. "The day after my mother died. The evening before the funeral."

"He told you?"

"Yes."

"How did he tell you? I mean, how much did he tell you or explain to you about the transaction?"

"Well, he told me that there was a stamp dealer in town who had been tracing this particular stamp, the One-Penny Orange, for years. Apparently a rare stamp is something like a famous painting. The dealers keep track of it as it is sold and resold, and I suppose they found some indication of my father buying it and then found out what had happened to our family. Anyway, this dealer finally traced it to my mother. He called Jack at the office, and they had lunch or something and discussed it. Of course, I'm telling you Jack's story. Jack said he would have to take the matter up with my mother, because if she had the stamp, even if she didn't know she had it, it belonged to her. Then Mother died, and since she was dead Jack felt that it was all right to take the stamp and sell it."

"To Ivan Gaycheck?"

"Yes, to Ivan Gaycheck."

"And how much did he say Gaycheck paid him for it?"

She rose and went to the counter where her purse lay. She brought it back to the table and opened it, saying as she did so, "He told me that Gaycheck paid him a thousand dollars in cash. Tax-free cash. He made a great point of that. He gave me half. He was cutting me in, as he put it." She took out of her purse five one-hundred-dollar bills and laid them on the table. "There it is—five hundred dollars for my mother's life."

"Why do you say that?"

She was silent for a while. Then she sighed and shook her head.

"But you don't believe your husband's story?" Masuto said.

"No, I don't."

"What do you think happened?"

"I think he went into my mother's room the day before— the day she died. I think he found the packet of letters and cut the ribbon, as you noticed. I think my mother found him going through the letters. They were very precious to her— the only thing of my father's that remained to her. I think she struggled with him, and in that struggle her heart gave way. Then Jack placed her body on the bed. She was dead. Who was to know how she died?"

"But all this is only conjecture, Ellen."

"I know."

"Why did you lie to me? Why didn't you tell me this when I saw you this morning?"

"To what end? As you say, it's only conjecture."

"Did you face your husband with your conjecture?"

"Yes, last night." She unbuttoned her cuff and pushed up her sleeve. Half of her arm was black and blue. "He uses his hands when he gets angry."

"Yet he agreed to the separation."

"Why shouldn't he have agreed, Masao?"

"Because he's a bastard and because we have community property in this state."

"I waived that. My mother had an insurance policy of five thousand dollars and I was the beneficiary. It's all I need and all I want. I signed a property waiver for my husband this afternoon. He will have the house and his money, and in return I get Bernie and his agreement not to contest the divorce."

"He'll give up his son?"

"Jack never loved anything. He couldn't. He's very happy to have the child out of his life."

"And what will you do, Ellen?"

"I'll go to England and get a divorce there or on the Continent. They still have theater in London, and where there's theater, I can work. I'm a good actress."

"I know that."

"And I won't be unhappy to leave. Beverly Hills is not for me. There's only one thing here that I regret leaving, and that's not for me in any case."

"And what's that, if I may ask?"

"Masao Masuto."

"You might find him a lot different than you imagine."

"No, I don't think so."

"But, Ellen, Gaycheck is dead. If your husband obtained and sold the stamp without legal right, it might still be recovered. It would belong to you."

She met his eyes directly and said, "But, Masao, you know and I know that the stamp will never be recovered. It is gone. Let that be the end of it."

"I told you that it was a stamp of great value. Do you remember? I said three hundred thousand dollars."

"I remember. I didn't believe you."

"I have been told that at auction it might well bring more."

"Truly? Or are you simply saying that?"

"I've never lied to you. I wouldn't."

"Then what do you suppose Gaycheck actually paid Jack for the stamp?"

"I could only guess. But since, given time, your husband would eventually discover its true value, I would guess that Gaycheck paid him at least fifty thousand dollars. Now, as I said, if you prove the transaction illegal, you can recover that money."

"You know that I can't, Masao." She smiled and reached across the table and placed her hand on his. Just a touch. Then she withdrew it. "Anyway, I am sure Jack made a mental inclusion of that in the settlement. Let him have it. Bernie is worth it." She looked at him—as tenderly, he thought, as any woman had ever looked at him.

"Poor Masao," she said gently. "What a quandary for an honorable man!"

"Perhaps less than you imagine. Did I tell you that I am a Zen Buddhist?"

"No. I don't know what that means."

"It's a very ancient thing in Japan, a way of life, a religion, a way of being—a way of watching and listening. But it precludes judgment. We don't judge."

"Ever?"

"Yes."

"Then how can you be a policeman?"

"With some agony, I suppose. It's my thing, as the kids say, my karma, my fate. It's the way I experience mankind. Others do it differently. But a policeman is not called upon to judge. He is given a set of rules and disciplines, and he obeys them."

"I see."

"Shall I tell you a story, Ellen?"

"If you wish. If it will keep you here. I dread your going away, because I know that when you do, I will never see you again."

"It's the story of a little girl, a child of great beauty and great sensitivity. A child who had to face the horrors of this life before any child should be called upon to do so."

"Has the child a name, Masao?"

"We'll call her Ellen."

"Yes, I imagined you would."

"When Ellen was very young, her father was taken away. Perhaps she remembered the incident, the brutality and savagery of it. Perhaps she knew it only from her mother telling her, and possibly she did not remember her father at all. But wisely or unwisely, her mother kept nothing from her. Her mother told her that her father had been taken to a place called Buchenwald, and that there he had been executed by a firing squad under the command of a man called Gaylord Schwartzman. Possibly Ellen's mother learned somehow that this Captain Schwartzman delivered the final killing shot himself. It was something he enjoyed doing."

Masuto paused, watching her. "You want me to continue?"

"Yes, Masao."

"I think it was less what happened to her father than what happened to her mother."

"Yes, Masao, you are probably right."

"The poverty, the indignity, the shame that her mother endured. When I look at the child, it seems to me that the mother must have been very beautiful once."

"But not when she died, Masao."

"I don't know when the child decided to become an actress, but the decision was inevitable."

"Why, Masao?" she asked him softly. "Why was the decision inevitable?"

"Because very early in life she prepared a role for herself."

"What role?"

"The role of one who brings justice, as she saw it, to an unjust world. The role of a debt collector—a debt owed to her mother and father. A very strange role for such a child."

"But a time must have come when the child became a woman. You know, Masao, you really don't understand women at all. You think you do, and I imagine you have loved many women in your own time and you respect them, but you don't understand them. I imagine that's the Japanese part of you."

"Perhaps you are right."

"Because when the child became a woman, she put aside childish things."

"If you say so."

"I don't say so. You are telling me a story. I simply adjust one of your characters."

"If you wish to," he said slowly, "you can continue the story."

"But that's impossible. It's your story. How could I possibly continue it?"

"Very well. Then I will go on. The child became a woman and the woman became an actress. She played many roles, but never abandoned the single, central role she had chosen for herself."

"She was very consistent."

"Oh, yes. I grant that. But she had a problem. While she had chosen her role, a part of the script was missing."

"What part, Masao?"

"Gaylord Schwartzman. You see, not only did she have no idea where he was or even whether he was alive or dead, but she had no notion of what he looked like."

"But, Masao, if this woman was as consistent as you say, she must have had a kind of faith."

"Yes, I suppose so. A kind of faith."

"And this faith would have assured her that Gaylord Schwartzman was alive. You see, Masao, if you make her a consistent character, then your story must be equally consistent."

"Yes," he agreed. "I see that I must make her an even more remarkable person than I had considered her to be."

"And what happened then?"

"Of course, it's not so strange."

"What is not so strange?"

"Each one has his karma. I must give her hers. She waited patiently, and then some years ago her patience was rewarded."

"How, Masao?"

"I'm not too sure of this part of the story, so I must guess. Her mother must have taught her to read German. Perhaps her mother was a subscriber to *Der Spiegel* . . ."

"*Der Spiegel?*"

"The German news magazine. Their *Time* magazine, so to speak."

"I see. Yes, go on."

"Or possibly she read the magazine herself. And then, one day, she was going through the September 1972 issue of *Der Spiegel* and there on page twenty-two she found a picture of Captain Gaylord Schwartzman."

"Bravo!" Ellen smiled and clapped her hands. "How precise you are, Masao, the date, the page—well, that is how a story should be told, precisely with all the facts. And what did your character do then?"

"She tore out the page and kept it with her. Oh, I imagine she looked at it until it fell to pieces, but the face of Captain Schwartzman was engraved on her memory. It no longer mattered whether she had the picture or not."

"But why? To what end?"

"Can't you guess?"

"I don't want to guess, Masao. I want to hear it from you. I want to hear your story."

"The answer is simple enough. Her faith told her that someday she would find Captain Schwartzman, and she had decided that when she did find him, she would kill him."

"But she couldn't have known she would find him."

"You yourself brought up the question of faith."

"I think your story would be more reasonable if you made it less than an obsession with her."

"If you wish."

"I keep reminding you that it is your story. What happened after she discovered the picture in . . ." She groped for the name.

"*Der Spiegel.*"

"*Der Spiegel,* yes."

"A great deal must have happened, but that is not directly pertinent to my story. The important fact—in terms of my story—is that five years later she moved to Beverly Hills, and then one day, possibly on the street, possibly through the window of his store, she saw Ivan Gaycheck—and she knew that she had found Captain Gaylord Schwartzman."

"And she recognized him, after so many years? That's not very plausible, is it, Masao?"

"I think it is. At least, I will make it that way for the sake of my story."

"Of course. It's your prerogative. I keep forgetting that it's your story."

"From that moment on she began to plan his death."

"His death? But, Masao, simply in terms of your story, and to be consistent, would you say that this character of yours began to plan an execution? Rather than a murder?"

"I didn't use the term *murder*."

"Sorry."

"She was a very clever woman, very cool, very determined. Did I say that she had brown eyes?"

"No, Masao, I don't think you did."

"But once, perhaps years ago, she played a role in the theater that called for blue eyes and blond hair. I said that her hair was brown, didn't I?"

"No, Masao."

"Well, theatrically, it is no problem. Blue contact lenses changed her eyes to blue, and a wig gave her blond hair. She had saved the wig and the lenses, so now they were available. Since she was very slender and had a boyish figure, she decided to give herself a large bust. A size-thirty-six brassiere, well padded, took care of that. She put on a long skirt and a sweater, and that way, carefully made up—

no problem for an actress—she became a very young and attractive woman with an English accent.

"But why, Masao? Why did your character go to all this trouble?"

"Because she was sensitive and bright and thoughtful— as very few killers are. For the most part, they are pathological. She was the exception."

"Are you sure of that?"

"Quite sure. You see, she realized that the great danger existed in the possibility that the purchase of a gun could be traced to her. She was determined that this would never happen."

"Yes. That would be very clever."

"Dressed in her disguise, she drove downtown to a store on San Pedro Avenue and bought a small twenty-two-caliber Webley-Fosbery automatic pistol. It was what they call—"

"Stop it, Masao!" she said suddenly. "Stop it! It's a silly game."

"You don't want to hear any more?"

"I do. Every bit of it. But not with this sophistry of your contriving a story."

"I think you're right."

"You are telling me how you think I killed Ivan Gaycheck. Go on."

"Very well. After you bought the gun, something happened that you didn't plan. Your husband found the stamp and sold it to Gaycheck. The day of the funeral, you dropped him off at his office. That was twelve o'clock. You had something to eat with your son, and then you dropped him at school. You drove to North Canon, parked, and walked over to Gaycheck's store. You knew that Haber left at twelve-thirty. Either he was gone, or you waited until he left. Then you went into the store. Possibly, you invented some story to make Gaycheck think you might be interested in the purchase of the One-Penny Orange. He would have had it in his safe. He opened the safe and took it out. He closed the safe and rose to face you. By then the gun was in your hand, and you shot him. You are a very strong woman, in spite of your slenderness—and very controlled. You straightened his body, to make it appear that someone of great strength had caught his body and lowered it to the ground. Then you put the One-Penny Orange in your purse, left the store, and drove home. That's it—all of it."

He was very tired now, tired and used up. He leaned back in his chair and watched her, wondering why, after he had spelled it out so carefully, he should still feel that to know this woman, to love her and receive her love in return, would be all that any man should ask of life.

Minute after minute passed, and she sat there and said nothing, only watching him. She had the slightest smile on her face.

"Masao . . ."

"Yes?"

"I am not shocked or frightened or bewildered. I knew what you were going to say when you telephoned me earlier. I knew why you were coming here."

"You did know?"

"Yes. Are you going to ask me whether what you spelled out is true?"

"No."

"Why?"

"Because I don't want you to lie to me."

"And you think I would?"

"Yes."

"Why?"

"Because in your mind, you are totally justified. You have no guilt, no remorse. You have been carrying a burden since you were a child, and now you have cast it off."

"You are so sure of yourself."

"I am a policeman. I know my job and I do it well."

"You are a brilliant and remarkable human being. Do you think there are many men like you? Yet you are willing to spend your life as a cop in this wretched town."

"I have my karma, you have yours."

"And what does that say and what does that signify? Oh, you make me so furious!"

"What else would you suggest?" he asked tiredly.

"What should I suggest, Masao? Oh, it's not that we have known each other twenty-four hours or so. Not that. I think I know you better than I have ever known a man before, and I want you desperately. To what end? We both know how utterly impossible it is."

"Yes, we both know that."

"So it's up to you. What will you do?"

"What can I do?" he asked her, suddenly terribly weary. "You have gotten rid of the pistol, the contact lenses, the wig—all the rest of it, and you are clever enough to have done it in such a way that they will never be found again. There were no witnesses. There is not one shred of evidence, and if I were to arrest you, the district attorney would throw me out of his office."

"You forget the One-Penny Orange."

"No, I don't forget the One-Penny Orange."

"You could have the house searched, if you are so sure of all your conjectures. If it's here, you would find it. And then you would have the evidence you need to arrest me."

"My dear Ellen, did I ever at any time since I first saw you, yesterday afternoon—did I ever underestimate you?"

"No, my dear, I don't think you did. But then, neither did I ever underestimate you."

"Your house has been disturbed enough. The One-Penny Orange isn't here."

"Then where is it?"

"In the mail, on its way to London, to some friend who will hold the letter until you arrive, or to general delivery—it doesn't matter. It's gone. Anyway, it's yours. It belongs to you."

"Thank you, Masao."

He almost lost his balance as he rose. "It's past midnight, and I'm very tired."

"Poor Masao."

"Ellen . . ." He cut off his words and shook his head. "No, I think we have both said enough."

"Masao?"

"Yes?"

"I must ask you something."

"All right."

"And you must tell me the truth. You must not lie to me. It's very important."

"I'll tell you the truth, if I can."

"If you had the evidence to support what you said here tonight—if you had it, Masao, would you arrest me?"

He didn't answer immediately. He stood there, his dark eyes half closed, his face a brooding mask. Then he said slowly, "Yes, I would."

"You would, yes. Somehow I'm glad you answered it that way."

"I must go now."

She walked with him to the front door, and there she said to him, "I won't see you again, ever, will I?"

"No."

"I'm leaving tomorrow."

"For Europe?"

"Yes. Bernie and I—we'll catch the noon plane for New York. From there to London. I suppose there are ways you can stop us."

"I won't stop you."

"Thank you, Masao.

She stood in front of him, looking up at him. She put her hands on his shoulders, tenderly, and then he took her in his arms and kissed her. He held her like that, fighting the feeling that he wanted never to let go, and then released her.

"Dear Masao," she whispered.

He opened the door, walked out, closed it behind him, got into the patrol car, and drove home to Culver City.

CHAPTER THIRTEEN

KATI

Kati must have been watching through a window for the arrival of his car, and when she saw the patrol car pull into the driveway she ran out, terror-stricken that this was news of what she had always feared. Her relief when she saw Masuto step out of the car was so great that she burst into sobs. He cradled her in his arms, calming her.

"It's all right, little Kati, it's all right." And then he said in Japanese, very softly, "My destiny is with you, beloved. You know that. I will always return when you wait for me."

She did not see his face until he had come through the kitchen door, and then she gasped in horror. "Oh, Masao, what did they do to you?"

"It is nothing. Only small flesh cuts. They don't even pain me."

"But how did it happen?"

"My car was smashed. I was cut by flying glass."

"How?"

"Dear Kati, I can't talk about it now. I am all right. There is only one thing I want, and I want it desperately."

"What is it, Masao?"

"A hot bath. As hot as you can draw it."

"But I have food waiting for you."

"I have eaten." He looked at her, her small, anxiety-filled face, her worried brown eyes, and then he gathered her in his arms and held her tightly. "Dear Kati," he whispered, "I am not much of a husband for you, am I? I fill your days with fear and doubting, and I give you so much pain."

"You are the best husband in the world. If I were to be reborn a thousand times, I would want no other husband than you."

"And I didn't even call you. I am a stupid and insensitive man. I don't deserve your love."

"You were occupied with your work, and that is as it should be. When I had worried sufficiently, I called Captain Wainwright. He told me that you were all right."

"Oh?"

"He said he will see you at eight o'clock in the morning."

"Ah so. Well, I will meditate a little, while you draw the bath."

He sat cross-legged, his body erect, his eyes half closed, trying to be without thought, to listen to the silence and to the darkness of the night. But it was no use, because on his mind's eye was printed the face of a woman who had murdered a man and who would go unpunished—and he himself, Masao Masuto, had concurred.

And then he asked himself, "Unpunished?" No one went unpunished, each made his own atonement, his own karma; and for two people, Masao Masuto and Ellen Briggs, the pain was established and it would never go away. He knew that.

Then he was able to meditate for a little while.

Barefoot, wrapped in a saffron-colored kimono, he went into the bathroom. The full tub was steaming. He let himself into it, wincing at first with the pain of the very hot water, and then relaxing as the heat seeped into his bones.

Kati came in, bearing a large, folded white towel, smiling with pleasure at the sight of him alive and well and relaxed in a steaming tub of hot water, such a fine, lean, long-legged, handsome man who did not realize that she was the luckiest woman on the face of the earth.

"I had the towel in the oven, Masao. It will stay hot. And I put a heating pad in the bed."

"You are very good to me."

"Little things. You must not thank me for little things."

"There are no little things in a gift of love," he said in Japanese.

She bowed formally, and in her flowered kimono, she was not of today but something out of an old Japanese print.

"I will sleep well," he said. "Don't wake me tomorrow. Unplug the phone. I intend to sleep for the next twelve hours."

"But if you are not there at eight o'clock, Captain Wainwright will call and be very angry."

"Tell him to go to hell," Masuto said.

"Masao! I would not dare say such a thing."

"Ah so. Then tell him that I am asleep and that you are afraid to awaken me."

"It would be untrue. I am never afraid of you."

"Then don't answer the phone, dear one," Masuto said, closing his eyes and relaxing into the heat of the bath.